Christine

Christine

OR

Woman's Trials & Triumphs

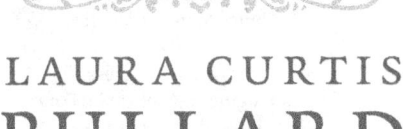

LAURA CURTIS
BULLARD

EDITED AND WITH
AN INTRODUCTION BY
DENISE M. KOHN

UNIVERSITY OF NEBRASKA PRESS
LINCOLN AND LONDON

Library of Congress
Cataloging-in-Publication Data
Bullard, Laura Curtis.
Christine, or, Woman's trials and triumphs /
Laura Curtis Bullard; edited and with
an introduction by Denise M. Kohn.
p. cm. — (Legacies of nineteenth-century
American women writers)
Includes bibliographical references.
ISBN 978-0-8032-1360-9 (pbk.: alk. paper)
1. Feminists—Fiction. 2. Women's rights—
Fiction. I. Kohn, Denise, 1963–
II. Title. III. Title: Christine.
IV. Title: Woman's trials and triumphs.
PS1199.B355C47 2010
813'.4—dc22   2010015349

Set in Quadraat by Kim Essman.
Designed by R. W. Boeche.

Contents

Acknowledgments

I am grateful to the many people who have been supportive of my work on Laura Curtis Bullard over the years. Sharon Harris and Karen Dandurand have provided invaluable feedback on the introduction, and without their support or patience it would not have been possible for *Christine* to be republished.

I want to thank Baldwin-Wallace College for the summer grant I received for this project, and Greensboro College, which also awarded me a summer grant for early research on Curtis Bullard. I am indebted to the Maine Women Writers Collection (MWWC) at the University of New England for giving me a summer fellowship, and most especially to Cally Gurley, director of the MWWC, for her inspiring enthusiasm and help, not only to me, but to all of those researching American women writers. Charlene Avallone kindly shared with me a paper she delivered at the 2005 Modern Language Association convention on *Christine*, *Isa*, and *Mary Lyndon*, which introduced me to the two latter novels. Elizabeth Stevens, a research librarian at the Bangor Public Library, and Earle G. Shettleworth of the Maine Historical Commission were extraordinarily generous in their help. As always, I am motivated by the example of Dorothy Baker, and this project would have been impossible without her encouragement. I also want to express my thanks to the editorial department of the University of Nebraska Press, and especially to Sara Springsteen, who was the project editor, and to Monica Phillips, who was the copyeditor for *Christine*.

I would also like to thank my parents, Dennis and Judy Kohn, and especially my mother, for her expertise as a librarian and her knowledge of New York City. Curtis Bullard dedicated *Christine* to her parents, who, she wrote, "have listened to these pages as I wrote and have at once been my audience and my critics." I, too, dedicate this book to my parents and also to my husband, Robert Shelton, who graciously acted as my audience and critic and, most of all, buoyed my belief that Curtis Bullard and her work should be placed back into history.

Introduction

> The only painful thought that filled her heart was the knowledge
> that she could do so little, and with *words of power* she endeavored
> to inspire her hearers with a desire to seek out and relieve the dis-
> tressed, as well as to press forward to claim the wider field which
> she pointed out as before them. —Laura Curtis Bullard, *Christine*
> (199; emphasis added)

When Laura Curtis Bullard wrote *Christine: Or Woman's Trials and Triumphs* she created one of antebellum America's most radical heroines: a woman's rights leader. Through the creation of
her unconventional title character, Curtis Bullard gave voice to
her own support for female suffrage, careers, and economic
independence, which was termed the "woman's rights" movement in the mid-nineteenth century and was considered scandalous, even sinful, by many Americans.[1] Curtis Bullard was
twenty-five when *Christine*, her second novel, was published in
1856, and she was the editor of a newspaper for women, the *Ladies' Visitor*. She continued her career after she was married and
became a mother, and in 1870 she succeeded Elizabeth Cady
Stanton and Susan B. Anthony as editor of the suffrage newspaper the *Revolution*, publishing essays about the social problems caused by women's inequality that she had earlier dra-
matized in *Christine*.

Christine is written in the tradition of the bildungsroman and
the reform novel of the nineteenth century. In an era when

women were considered to "unsex" themselves by public speaking, *Christine* sympathetically portrays a young woman who defies her family to join the lecture circuit for female suffrage and education. Curtis Bullard depicts her heroine's public career as a natural extension of women's charitable and reform work in the nineteenth century, thus asserting the "true womanhood" of woman's rights leaders at a time when they were reviled by many middle-class Americans.

While Curtis Bullard was editor of the *Revolution*, she was accused of adultery in the New York press, and the rumors resurfaced again as part of the notorious Beecher-Tilton trial. She spent her later years in less publicly prominent ways, writing essays, translating novels, and maintaining her friendships in the transatlantic literary world.

Although she had once been well known, Curtis Bullard and her work fell from history, and she was relegated to the level of footnote, if mentioned at all, in American literary and political histories. Until this edition, *Christine* had remained out of print since it was first published in 1856, and little biographical information had been known about Curtis Bullard.[2] Literary critic and cultural historian David S. Reynolds argues that "of all the oversights of literary and social historians of America, few are more heinous than the almost complete neglect of Laura Curtis Bullard" (*Beneath* 393). The goal of this edition is to introduce a new generation of readers to Curtis Bullard and her novel *Christine*.

Laura Jane Curtis: Novelist and Newspaper Editor
Laura Jane Curtis née Bullard was born in Freedom, Maine, on 21 November 1831.[3] She was the eldest of the five children of Lucy Winslow Curtis and Jeremiah Curtis, who believed in political engagement and entrepreneurship (Mosher 17).[4] The Curtises moved their young family to the northern Maine town of Calais, where Jeremiah Curtis helped to found the city's first

bank and the state's first railroad. He became a leader in the antislavery Liberty Party, losing campaigns for governor in 1841 and for Congress in 1847 on the Liberty ticket ("Jeremiah Curtis" 7; "Movement" 3; "National Intelligencer" 2). In 1850 the Curtis family lived in Bangor, where Jeremiah Curtis began the pharmaceutical business that eventually made him a millionaire.[5] Curtis Bullard's maternal grandmother, Charlotte Winslow, was a female physician known for her creation of a morphine-based tonic used to treat teething in children and aches and pains in adults. Although Mrs. Winslow's Soothing Syrup had been sold since 1835, Jeremiah Curtis patented the formula in 1852. Through a barrage of newspaper advertising, trading cards, and recipe booklets, he made his mother-in-law a household name (Holcombe 116).

By 1854 Jeremiah Curtis had moved the family pharmaceutical business to New York, which would become home to Curtis Bullard (Holcombe 116). In the same year, at the age of twenty-three, Curtis Bullard anonymously published her first novel, *Now-a-days!*, which drew upon her own knowledge of life in backwoods Maine. The novel's heroine, Esther Hastings, rejects a marriage proposal and must earn a living after the sudden death of her wealthy father. Esther, accustomed to a life of ease, leaves Bangor to work as a teacher in Aroostook County in northern Maine. Like the narrator in Caroline Kirkland's 1839 westering story, *A New Home—Who Will Follow?*, Esther learns about the manners and customs of frontier life as she is faced with different frameworks for domesticity. Although *Now-a-days!* has received little critical attention, it deserves to be read and studied within the traditions of the female bildungsroman, the pioneer novel, and regional realism.[6] The novel's rich detail of lumber camps and representations of dialects are evidence that as a young woman Curtis Bullard was familiar with the life and people of rural Maine.

After publishing *Now-a-days!*, Curtis Bullard founded and edited her own newspaper in New York, the *Ladies' Visitor, and*

Drawing Room Companion, which was published monthly from 1855 to 1861. The *Ladies' Visitor*, similar to many other popular newspapers of the day for women, published poetry, fiction, anecdotes, reviews, recipes, fashion news, and domestic advice. Curtis Bullard began her lifelong friendship with Louise Chandler Moulton, also a popular writer and novelist, who was a contributor to the *Ladies' Visitor*. The publisher of the newspaper was Curtis and Company, a part of the family's pharmaceutical business, and Mrs. Winslow's Soothing Syrup was one of the largest advertisers. The relationship between the family company and Curtis Bullard's work as a writer was mutually beneficial: Her paper helped support pharmacy sales to the target audience of women while Curtis and Company helped support her work as a writer and editor. Curtis Bullard's professional position as editor was important to her—the first page of each issue prominently names "Laura J. Curtis" or, after her marriage in 1859, "Laura Curtis Bullard" as "EDITOR." She also published her own short fiction in the paper, including the sensational story "My Husband's Mother," in which a couple gets divorced but later is reunited after the heroine visits her dying ex-husband, who soon recovers. Curtis Bullard's emphasis on sentimental reunion in the story's closure demonstrates the way that nineteenth-century women writers could address socially difficult themes such as divorce by using a narrative frame that was rhetorically sensitive to the values and plot expectations of middle-class readers.

The mid-1850s were an unusually active period for Curtis Bullard. In 1856, the same year she was editing her own newspaper and publishing her own short fiction, she also published *Christine*. Unlike her first novel, the title page to *Christine* included her name, "Laura J. Curtis," as author, a sign that she was building a reputation as a writer. She dedicated her second novel to her parents, "who have listened to these pages as I wrote, and have been at once my audience and my critics" (vi). Most antebellum women writers were careful to avoid appearances of asserting themselves or selling their work in the literary marketplace, let alone even suggesting that writing was both a career and a business. Curtis Bullard, however, unabashedly used the *Ladies' Visitor* to promote *Christine*. Several editions include large advertisements for the novel with the headline "Twenty Thousand Sold, and the rush still continues," along with excerpts from favorable reviews from newspapers around the country.[7] An excerpt from the *Cleveland Plain Dealer* praises *Christine* as "an admirable tale, differing from the generality of stories in that the author has marked out for herself an almost new path, and has acquitted her work with ability and excellence." The *Courier and Enquirer* calls Curtis Bullard "an artist, with her pen of more than uncommon power," especially praising her depiction of New England village life, while the *Montgomery Mail* reports that the novel has "created quite a sensation with those who keep up with the current of new novels." The *Baltimore Clipper* asserts that the "book is truly delightful; the author has marked out for herself a new field." The comments that Curtis Bullard chose to print were, of course, positive, but they are also consistent with other reviews that she did not include. *Peterson's Magazine* states that *Christine* "is so graphically told . . . that the reader, who has once begun the book, is reluctant to leave it till the end is finished" ("Reviews" 399). The influential *Knickerbocker* says the book is "well-written," with "characters finely drawn, and well sustained," even though the magazine carefully assures readers that "we do not quite agree with the author in her advocacy of Woman's Rights" ("New" 109). This praise from the mainstream press suggests Curtis Bullard's success in creating a novel with a heroine who is radical yet sympathetic to a middle-class readership.

Three years after she published *Christine*, Curtis Bullard married Enoch Bullard of Boston, an executive in the family's pharmaceutical business who later became president of the company.[8]

Enoch Bullard was twelve years her senior, and the marriage, at least by some accounts, may have been difficult at times. Louisa May Alcott, who was pleased to meet Curtis Bullard at a party in New York, wrote to her parents that she had heard that Enoch Bullard was a drunkard but an amiable gentleman who adored his wife but preferred to stay at home to drink privately, leaving her to her own set of friends (*Selected Letters* 214–17). Curtis Bullard "keeps his house for looks sake," Alcott reported.[9] Despite any marital problems, however, the couple was married for fifty-five years, until Enoch Bullard's death in 1904 at the age of eighty-four.

After her marriage, Curtis Bullard continued as editor of the *Ladies' Visitor*, but when she became pregnant at the age of thirty-one she left her position and the newspaper closed. For the next several years, Curtis Bullard devoted herself to her new role as a mother to her son, Harold Curtis Bullard.[10] During at least part of her marriage, she, her husband, and their son lived in the same large home in Brooklyn with her parents, with whom she enjoyed a close relationship throughout her life.[11] By the late 1860s she was immersed in reform groups and the growing women's club movement. She was one of the first members of Sorosis, a society for professional and literary women, which was founded in 1868 when the New York Press Club refused to admit women journalists to a dinner in honor of Charles Dickens (Merrill 157). When Stanton and Anthony founded the National Woman Suffrage Association (NWSA) in 1869, Curtis Bullard became the first corresponding secretary, along with Ida Greeley, daughter of Horace Greeley, the famous Republican leader and newspaper editor (Stanton and Gage 401). Curtis Bullard was also a NWSA delegate to the Woman's Industrial Congress in Berlin, an international convention that called for women's education and the rights of female workers. Other delegates included members of the reform elite such as Julia Ward Howe and Ernestine Rose, suggesting the contemporary fame of the representatives (Stanton and Gage 406; Hume 217–19). Anthony regularly published Curtis Bullard's travel narratives from London, Cologne, Lucerne, and Geneva in the *Revolution*, and she also read Curtis Bullard's letters and essays aloud at NWSA meetings.[12] In 1870, Curtis Bullard founded the Brooklyn Woman's Club with her friend Elizabeth Tilton, who was poetry editor of the *Revolution* ("Brooklyn" 3). Elizabeth was married to Theodore Tilton, the well-known editor of the liberal *New York Independent* and the protégé of Henry Ward Beecher.

The Revolution, *Woman's Rights, and Free Love*

In July 1870 Curtis Bullard became editor of the *Revolution*, the radical suffrage newspaper that Anthony and Stanton founded as the political organ for the NWSA. The paper, first published in January 1868 with Anthony as publisher and Stanton as editor, had faced many obstacles since its inception. Anthony and Stanton, who had campaigned with Republicans for abolition and universal suffrage, felt betrayed when the Republican Party decided that it would seek enfranchisement for African American men only. Stanton and Anthony defied the Republicans by campaigning for a constitutional amendment for universal suffrage, and at times they descended into racist rhetoric in their opposition to the Fifteenth Amendment (DuBois, *Reader* 92; Williams 425–26).

The motto of the *Revolution*, not to mention the name itself, expressed Stanton and Anthony's commitment to universal suffrage and their outrage with the Republicans: "Principles, Not Politics. Justice, Not Favors—Men Their Rights and Nothing More; Women Their Rights and Nothing Less." In this motto, Stanton and Anthony declared that the Republicans had abandoned the principle of universal suffrage in favor of political expediency in the belief that Americans were ready to enfranchise African American men but not women. Granting suffrage to women was simply justice, not a favor, the *Revolution* argued, and women were entitled to the same rights as men. In hope of financial support that never materialized, Anthony and Stanton allied their weekly paper with Democrat George Train, an outspoken racist, further angering Republicans, even though the Republicans had earlier arranged a joint speaking tour for Anthony and Train (Barry 173–87). Anthony incurred further criticism when she trained women as typesetters during the strike of a male typographical union (Barry 214–15). As a result, Greeley refused to run any notices for the *Revolution* in the *Tribune*, as did Wendell Phillips of the *Liberator* (Barry 186). Women's groups considered the *Revolution* so radical that they refused to share office space with it (I. Harper 360).

As publisher, Anthony had personally shouldered the financial responsibility of the *Revolution*, and by the spring of 1870 she could no longer ignore her mounting debt (Barry 223). Stanton refused to help Anthony by supporting the paper financially or by managing its daily operations. Anthony had hoped that editorial contributions from Harriet Beecher Stowe would sell more subscriptions, but Stowe asked that the name of the paper be changed to something less inflammatory, such as the *True Republic*, a suggestion Anthony refused (I. Harper 356–57; Anthony 225–26). After twenty-nine months of publishing the *Revolution*, Anthony assumed the paper's debt and sold the paper in May 1870 for one dollar. In a farewell editorial, Stanton introduced Curtis Bullard as the new editor, describing her as a "young, brave, brilliant, and beautiful" woman who brings to her work "rare culture, clear moral perceptions, enthusiasm, untiring industry and a liberality that comes from extensive travel, reading, and thought" (Stanton, "Who Shall" 328). Although Anthony anguished over giving up the paper, Stanton was relieved that Curtis Bullard had "generously assumed the care of the troublesome child" (Stanton, *Eighty Years* 182).

As the new mother of that "troublesome child," Curtis Bullard strove to make decisions to resolve some of the *Revolution*'s financial and political problems. Her experiences as a newspaper editor and as a member of a family involved in mass marketing likely gave her a stronger sense of the realities of the literary marketplace than Anthony and Stanton. In July 1870 Curtis Bullard published her first edition as editor in chief, with the Quaker abolitionist and financier Edwin A. Studwell as publisher. Her father became treasurer of the Revolution Association, a joint stock company formed to finance the paper, and trustees included two of her brothers, along with Stanton, Anthony, and Theodore Tilton ("Editorial Notes" 22). To increase revenue, the *Revolution* included more advertisements, including those from patent medicines, which Stanton and Anthony had rejected. Not surprisingly, many of those advertisements were for Curtis company products.

The members of the Revolution Association were also supporters of the newly founded Union Woman's Suffrage Society ("Editorial Notes" 22). In May 1870, the same month Anthony sold the *Revolution*, the NWSA changed its name to the Union Woman's Suffrage Society in hopes it could merge with the Boston-based American Woman Suffrage Association (AWSA) and heal the rivalry between the two groups (Anthony 239–40). The *Revolution* was to be the official organ of the new organization, and the Union officers must have seen Curtis Bullard as a figure who would be accepted by both sides. However, the AWSA, whose president was Beecher, rejected the proposed merger at its annual convention in 1871 because it objected to the Union's intent to combine arguments for suffrage with "the divorce question" ("A Woman's" 360). When the merger failed, the Union changed its name again to the NWSA.

The "divorce question" was a controversial social debate about liberalized divorce laws, women's inequality in marriage, and mothers' lack of custody rights. These concerns were often seen as part of the larger issue of "free love" that was wreaking havoc in the woman's rights movement in the 1870s. The term "free love" was a broad one, but in general, free-love advocates emphasized that mutual affection and happiness were the most important aspects of marriage or sexual relationships between men and women, not religious or legal bonds. Free-love advocates argued for an end to sexual double standards for men and women, as did most woman's rights leaders, but free-love advocates also argued against the institution of marriage (Curtis Bullard, "What" 104). By 1870 the national woman's rights movement was losing support over free love, which had scandalized middle-class America and many of the Christian social reformers whose interest in temperance and abolition had led them to the woman's movement. Stanton and Anthony shocked audiences by speaking openly about "legalized prostitution in marriage"—in other words, sex without mutual consent between a husband and wife. At a meeting in New York, Stanton announced that those "dabbling with the suffrage movement for women" should be aware that the movement supported "social equality, and next freedom, or in a word, free love" (DuBois, *Woman* 77–78). Although many suffrage supporters had been willing to discuss equality in marriage and liberalized divorce in smaller meetings, most tended to be more reticent at conventions. The public furor over free love made some activists question their support for suffrage and especially hurt the more radical NWSA and the *Revolution*.

The free-love debate puts into context one of Curtis Bullard's major changes to the *Revolution*: the motto. By 1870 when Curtis Bullard had become editor, the Fifteenth Amendment had been ratified and thus was a moot point. Free love, however, was not. Under Curtis Bullard, the *Revolution*'s new motto became "What therefore God hath joined together, let no man put asunder."[13] This verse from Matthew, frequently used in traditional wedding ceremonies, was printed directly below the words "The Revolution," which seems paradoxical. However, Curtis Bullard carefully selected her motto to quell the public's fear that woman's rights would be the end of the American family while at the same time defining "true marriage" as an egalitarian union.

Throughout *Christine*, Curtis Bullard's heroine argues that the Bible supports female equality and that those who disagree have simply failed in exegesis. As editor of the *Revolution*, Curtis Bullard took a similar stance, offering her own explication of the verse from Matthew. In an editorial about the new motto, she explains that a "true marriage" can never be ended by law ("Motto" 168). She pushes her argument even further, stating that the phrase "Whom God has joined together, let no man put asunder" also means that women should have an "equal place" with man "in the trades, in the colleges, in the lyceum, in the press, in literature, in science, in art, in government, in everything" ("Motto" 168). Using politically loaded terms, Curtis Bullard writes that women and men have been "systematically divorced" for too long in their work, but now woman can "enforce her marriage rights" to join man "in all the great ventures of human life" ("Motto" 168).

In the editorial "What Justifies Marriage?" Curtis Bullard critiques a social structure that means there is "no hope for two people shackled in the manacles of unhappy marriage, but a release by death," since the "fracture of the galling chain must be made at the expense of the reputation of one or both parties" (104). The editorial explicitly deconstructs the *Revolution*'s new motto, arguing, "Man has bound in wedlock many whom God hath not joined together. Indeed, it is difficult for a close observer not to come to the conclusion that marriage, as it now exists, is a curse to society and to the human race; it is a source, far more frequently, of misery than of happiness. What God intended for the crowning felicity of mankind has been distorted by the race into its crowning wretchedness" (104).

In this editorial, Curtis Bullard invites her readers to reinterpret the paper's motto in a radical way that echoes free-love philosophy. On the other hand, readers who were uncomfortable with free love could interpret the passage in a more moderate vein to mean that people should marry for love, not social or financial reasons. In this editorial, Curtis Bullard implicitly supports divorce but also carefully avoids using the word. Instead, she argues that people need to be more careful about choosing their spouses and calls for "a careful study" of the causes for success and failure in marriage.

The *Revolution*'s new motto is likely what prompted Anthony's friend and biographer Ida Husted Harper to mistakenly claim that Curtis Bullard turned the *Revolution* into a "literary and society journal," even though she praised Curtis Bullard as "much interested in reform work and possessed of literary ability" (I. Harper 361–63). Unfortunately, Harper's claim that Curtis Bullard changed the radical newspaper into a society and literary magazine has been asserted repeatedly throughout histories that mention the *Revolution*, relegating Curtis Bullard to footnotes that misrepresent her as the woman who abandoned the causes of the *Revolution*, if she is mentioned at all.[14] In reality the *Revolution* continued to champion woman's rights and, just as Anthony and Stanton had done, to publish fiction and poetry. Curtis Bullard's statement of purpose declares that the *Revolution* is "devoted to the welfare of Woman. . . . Called into existence to utter the cry of the ill-paid, of the unfriended, and of the disenfranchised, this journal is woman's voice speaking from woman's heart" ("Prospectus" 13).

After editing the *Revolution* for eighteen months, however, Curtis Bullard resigned.[15] In her last editorial on 12 October 1871, she expressed pride that as editor she called for women's social and civil equality with men—in other words, that she focused on issues of marriage and careers along with suffrage. However, she regretted that her "frequent and necessary absences from America render it impossible for me to do justice" to the paper ("Valedictory" 8). In closing, she adds the cryptic comment that "strange to say, after an experience of a year and a half in a reform movement, I have not lost faith in human nature" ("Valedictory" 8). Though Curtis Bullard had gone to Europe with her parents and eight-year-old son in December 1870, she was still working as editor and contributing articles. She may have felt obligated to accompany her aged parents on their travels and found that motherhood left her little time for editing a national weekly paper. The initial financial support for the paper may have waned; the financier Studwell was listed as publisher for only about three months, leaving the other members of the Revolution Association liable for the paper's annual production cost of $20,000, which could have been too costly despite their personal commitment to woman's rights ("Salutation" 360). These are all probable reasons why she gave up her position as editor, but her cryptic comment about retaining faith in human nature hints at another possible reason for her unexplained but "necessary" continued travel in Europe: to avoid malicious New York gossip.

In January 1871 Curtis Bullard was accused of adultery in the New York press. Three different papers, the *Brooklyn Daily Eagle*, *New York Democrat*, and *New York Globe*, published articles alleging an affair between Curtis Bullard and Tilton. On 24 January the morning *New York Democrat* announced—with salacious delight—a "queer story" that was "particularly active in commercial circles downtown" ("Tilton" 4). According to the rumor, Tilton had sailed from New York to meet "Mrs. Laura Curtis Bullard, the editress of the *Revolution*," who was in Europe (4). "There has been too much talk about these two of late, and it is now very much magnified," the paper states, rather ironically, since it is the paper that magnified the rumors (4). According to the paper, Tilton had not lived at his home for several months, and Mr. Bullard, who was near death, had run off to Texas. Although the *Democrat* warns that the account should "be taken with allowances," it also reassures readers that "we have assurances from unquestionably good authority" that it is "strictly true" (4). Later that day, the *New York Globe* repudiated the story. The *Globe* sent a reporter to the Tilton home, where Elizabeth Tilton, "with flashing eyes," denounced the story and said that her husband was not currently at home because he had just stepped out to conduct some business (4). The *Globe* also added that Mr. Bullard's trip to Texas was for business, and that, instead of being gravely ill and consumptive, he was "a stout, robust man, standing almost six feet in his stockings" (4). Two days later, the *Brooklyn Daily Eagle*, which claimed to have the largest circulation of any evening paper in America, reprinted the stories, including its own commentary under the headline "Tilton Traduced," with subheads such as "Poor Tilton" and the "Tilton Scandal." The *Eagle* characterized Tilton as a vain, though sincere, man whose downfall was a just reward for someone in the reform press who seemed to "worship no Deity but himself." Women at the *Revolution* office told the *Eagle* reporter that "some enemy of Tilton" was responsible for spreading the scandal (4). And even the *Eagle* said that the "true value" of the rumored elopement was "very little" (4).

The ramifications for Curtis Bullard and her family must have been difficult, if not devastating. Though she was an outspoken supporter of woman's rights, Curtis Bullard, like her heroine Christine, had striven to work within a framework of middle-class respectability. To argue for suffrage, egalitarian marriage, and better jobs for women may have been radical, but adultery was criminal. Such a charge would have cost Curtis Bullard the personal and public credibility she had worked so hard to earn as a writer and editor in the woman's rights movement. She was a public figure, but she was also a mother and the wife and daughter of business executives. Regardless of whether or not she was having an extramarital relationship with Tilton, these published accusations of adultery in 1871 could have ensured that she would lose custody rights to her son in the event of a divorce. Curtis Bullard and Tilton shared a close personal and professional friendship. They were both newspaper editors, active in the same woman's rights groups, and shared the same circle of friends in the reform movement. Theodore Tilton always denied the allegations of an affair with Curtis Bullard, even joking about them as if they were too ridiculous to take seriously. A month after the newspaper stories, in a letter to the suffrage leader Anna Dickinson, he said that his wife, Elizabeth, was busy "writing a sisterly letter to the lady with whom I was supposed to have run away to Europe" (qtd. in Fox 387). In a letter to Dickinson a year later, Curtis Bullard also implied that the rumors of her affair with Tilton were false. The two women enjoyed a strong friendship in 1872, and Curtis Bullard wrote to Dickinson that "nobody has made love to me—*nobody does*—I have a genius for friendships with men & women, but I am *not* one whom many men love. Sweet Anna I *love thee*" (qtd. in Gallman 112). The playful intensity of the correspondence between Dickinson and Curtis Bullard suggests a friendship that was both emotional and sensual, as were many female relationships in the nineteenth century (Gallman 112–15).

Curtis Bullard's relationships with Tilton and Dickinson demonstrate the nuanced complexities of interpreting heterosexual and same-sex relationships in the nineteenth century, especially amidst the free-love debates of the 1870s. Perhaps the greatest underlying truth of the stories about Curtis Bullard and Tilton in the New York press is that her reputation had become caught in the personal and professional battle between Tilton and Beecher.[16]

Several weeks before the newspaper stories, Henry Bowen, publisher of the *Independent*, had secured Beecher's support to fire Tilton as the paper's editor. Bowen had become incensed by Tilton's radical politics, especially his support for liberalized divorce, and he also told Beecher he was upset about a rumor that Tilton was having an affair with Curtis Bullard (Fox 146–49).[17] Beecher expressed his concern to Bowen about the rumors, which he had also heard. To further complicate matters, Tilton believed Beecher had seduced his wife, Elizabeth, and Bowen delivered Tilton's letter of accusation to Beecher, which demanded that Beecher resign from the pulpit (Applegate 401–2). A few days after Bowen spoke to Beecher about Curtis Bullard, a mutual friend angrily confronted Beecher and assured him that Curtis Bullard was innocent (*Theodore* 1:205). To Beecher's credit, he wrote Bowen a letter saying that he no longer believed the stories against Curtis Bullard (*Theodore* 1:67) However, Tilton still lost his position as editor and the rumors spread, culminating in the newspaper stories a few weeks later in January 1871.

The allegations of an affair with Tilton continued to haunt Curtis Bullard. In the spring of 1872 the woman's rights leader and free-love advocate Victoria Woodhull sent out anonymous blackmail letters to Curtis Bullard, Anthony, Lillie Devereux Blake, and several other suffrage leaders who opposed Woodhull's growing influence in the woman's rights movement (Kerr 75). Woodhull's free-love platform combined with her cheerful declarations of relationships with different men—later she would say that Tilton was her lover—and her divorce and second marriage had made her a notorious public figure. Woodhull mailed Curtis Bullard and the other women dummy copies of *Woodhull and Claflin's Weekly*, which included scurrilous stories of alleged sexual improprieties, and demanded $500 not to print them (Kerr 75). Tilton and Anthony insisted that Woodhull stop her threats, but some of the dummy copies were circulating.[18] Woodhull always maintained that she had never tried to blackmail anyone; however, she defended blackmail as women's "only method of righting themselves" in an essay in her newspaper (Farrell 120).

For Curtis Bullard, the blackmail threats seem rather belated since the accusations about her relationship with Tilton had been publicized in the New York press the year before and she had resigned as editor of the *Revolution*. Any recurrence of the scandal in Woodhull's paper, however, would have put Curtis Bullard and her family through another round of public humiliation. Blake, a writer and reform leader who had praised Curtis Bullard for changing the *Revolution*'s motto, was distraught that Woodhull might publish a false story claiming that she had been divorced (Blake 43; Farrell 127–29). Blake explained to her daughter that it did not matter that the story was untrue: "The truth never catches up with a lie! The lie runs too fast" (qtd. in Farrell 128–29). Blake's reaction to charges of divorce, which was legal even though it was not always considered respectable, puts into perspective the allegations of adultery against Curtis Bullard.

In November 1872 Woodhull published a story in her weekly newspaper that the married Beecher was having an affair with his parishioner and friend's wife, Elizabeth Tilton, including lurid allegations of "terrible orgies" in front of the Tilton children (Fox 157). In 1874 Tilton sued Beecher in civil court for adultery, and the trial splashed sensational stories of seduction and betrayal across the nation's newspapers, once again calling attention to the free-love debate that had set back the woman's suffrage movement. During the trial, part of the defense strategy was to show that Tilton was a hypocrite who had several affairs himself, and the story about an alleged affair with Curtis Bullard resurfaced again. At one point in the trial, the judge and defense lawyers discussed whether or not to state her full name in court, knowing that reading her name aloud would harm her reputation (*Theodore* 1:66–67). The judge determined that she could be referred to as "Mrs. B.," but later in the trial Curtis Bullard's name was mentioned without hesitation, and the rumors about her and Tilton were referred to as the "Bullard story" (*Theodore* 1:206–7, 2:51). During his testimony, Tilton was careful not to repeat Curtis Bullard's name when he denounced the New York press for making a "bold and vulgar allusion to a very honored lady in this city" when he sought to defend her—and himself—against the allegations of adultery (*Theodore* 1:512).

Stanton told her version of the beginnings of the Beecher scandal to the *Brooklyn Argus* in 1874; several days later her account was front-page national news (Fox 164). In the spring or fall of 1870, she, Anthony, Curtis Bullard, and the Tiltons had all been in Brooklyn together for the afternoon, which included a visit to the *Revolution*'s office, Stanton said (Fox 163). Stanton, Curtis Bullard, and Theodore went to the Curtis Bullard home, where they had dinner, while, through some sort of misunderstanding, Anthony and Elizabeth dined at the Tilton home, which greatly upset Elizabeth. Over dinner, Theodore told Stanton and Curtis Bullard the story of Elizabeth's "faithlessness," Stanton said, and later that night Elizabeth told a similar story to Anthony (Fox 163).

The charges and countercharges of the trial were intricate, but in the end Beecher was found innocent, and though his reputation was damaged he continued as a prominent minister and reformer. Elizabeth Tilton lived as a recluse in New York while Theodore Tilton, unable to secure a position as an editor, lived the rest of his life in relative poverty in France.

The trial, along with the blackmail attempts and the stories in the New York press, also took a toll on Curtis Bullard. To a certain extent, her career as a writer, editor, and activist in the woman's rights movement had become a casualty of the philosophical, political, and personal conflicts that were part of the movement itself. Her stance on free love, which acknowledged that it was wrong for spouses to be tied together in misery but at the same time recognized that divorce was not a viable solution for many women, tended to be more conservative than Stanton's, Tilton's, and certainly Woodhull's. Yet her loyalties in the movement were always aligned with Stanton and Anthony, not the more moderate AWSA of Lucy Stone and Beecher. Her public position as editor of the *Revolution* and her own editorials on marriage added to the titillation of the stories about her and Tilton in the New York press, as did Tilton's support of liberalized divorce in the *Independent*. In the conflict between Woodhull and the NWSA, Curtis Bullard was one of the women who became a target. And in the trial that defined the personal and professional lives of Tilton and Beecher, Curtis Bullard once again was caught in the battle.

After the Revolution

In the opening chapters of *Christine*, before the young heroine thinks about becoming a woman's rights leader, she hopes to be wealthy, educated, and have "a splendid house, where I would have all the great people, the writers, and all sorts of talented persons come, and I would help the poor authors, who struggle on and die sometimes in the midst of their struggles" (7). After she left the *Revolution*, Curtis Bullard devoted the rest of her life to fulfilling her young character's earliest dream, welcoming other transatlantic writers and reformers to her home. Contemporary accounts describe her as a woman of elegance and kindness, known for her "sparkle, sweetness, and graciousness" (Townsend 185). She maintained a lifelong friendship with Stanton, who was a frequent guest (Stanton, *Eighty* 388). Curtis Bullard introduced Emily Faithfull, the British reformer and publisher, to New York reform society, launching her on a speaking tour of America (Ratcliffe 43). Faithfull, who dedicated her novel *A Reed Shaken with the Wind* to Curtis Bullard, characterized her as an intellectual and socially brilliant woman whose evening gatherings rivaled those at the "noted houses in Paris and London" (Faithfull 5). When Oscar Wilde came to the United States in 1882 for a lecture tour, he, too, visited Curtis Bullard (Curtis Bullard, Letter). Other guests included the French novelist Alice Durand, whose pen name was Henri Greville, and Dora D'istria, a Romanian-Albanian writer and woman's rights advocate (Whiting 751; Stanton, *Eighty* 388). Along with Louise Chandler Moulton, Curtis Bullard supported the career of the blind British poet Phillip Bourke Marston (Moulton 173). Walt Whitman valued Curtis Bullard's praise and treasured a letter from her as a sign of his success (Reynolds, *Walt* 220, 528).

Curtis Bullard's wide-ranging, international friendships reflect the turn in her own literary career. She published several essays in Faithfull's *Victoria Magazine* and wrote an essay on Stanton in the book *Our Famous Women*. She translated three German novels, including *A Modern Midas* in 1884, which received a favorable notice in the *New York Times* and was popular enough to be reissued in 1900.[19] By the time she was in her sixties, her work as a writer seems to have ended, though she had not abandoned her old friends or the cause of woman's rights, making a donation for the support of the ailing Dickinson ("Little" 6). In 1904, after a long illness, Curtis Bullard's husband died at the age of eighty-four. In 1910, when she was seventy-eight, Curtis Bullard lived in Manhattan with her son.[20] She died at home on 19 January 1912 at the age of eighty-one and was buried in Mount Auburn Cemetery in Cambridge, Massachusetts, next to her husband and his parents.[21]

Although Curtis Bullard had once enjoyed a transatlantic reputation, her death was not remarked upon in any detail in the press. Her brief obituary in the *New York Times*, which is part of a long list of death notices, identifies her only as a widow and daughter and requests that no flowers be sent ("Laura Curtis Bullard" 13). Her identity as a writer, editor, and woman's rights activist fell out of the record of her life, foreshadowing the way that Curtis Bullard and her work would fall from political and literary history. The fact that Curtis Bullard was forgotten by subsequent generations is not unusual; indeed, it is paradigmatic. Nineteenth-century authors such as Lydia Maria

Child, Rose Terry Cooke, Rebecca Harding Davis, Fanny Fern, Harriet Jacobs, Elizabeth Stuart Phelps, and Catharine Maria Sedgwick were largely forgotten throughout most of the twentieth century but have now resumed a place of prominence in American literature. Curtis Bullard, too, deserves to be remembered for her work as a novelist, essayist, editor, and reform activist, but most of all for her novel *Christine: Or Woman's Trials and Triumphs*.

Curtis Bullard and Christine

In writing *Christine*, Curtis Bullard created one of antebellum America's most unconventional novels and heroines. The story seems destined to follow the plot of much of woman's fiction in the nineteenth century until the likable eponymous character chooses to become a woman's rights lecturer and writer. Although her family and friends are horrified, Christine's mentor, Mrs. Warner, assures her that she is destined for "a higher calling" than "woman's usual life" of marriage and motherhood: "God has taken you from that sphere. . . . Christine, it is yours to be the champion of your sex. The pioneer in the march of progress. You are to rouse the indifferent—to give voice to the suffering of your sex. This is God's will. . . . You are to speak in *words of power*" (157; emphasis added).

In writing *Christine*, Curtis Bullard not only created a novel that gives voice to a strong female character, she gave voice to her own belief that women's words and agency were powerful enough to change American society. In a period when women were considered too emotional, and thus unsuited for many public roles and politics, *Christine* asserts the liberal egalitarianism espoused by woman's rights leaders at the Seneca Falls Convention in 1848. While many other antebellum novels by women writers have outspoken female characters who counter a social structure designed to silence women, *Christine* asserts the right of the heroine and all women to a public voice—and to a vote, a career, and economic independence. The novel is one of the few of the antebellum period to have a woman's rights leader as a main character, especially as a sympathetic heroine.

When Curtis Bullard wrote *Christine* in 1856, woman's rights had already become its own cause separate from the temperance and abolitionist movements. In 1848 New York passed the Married Woman's Property Act, and later that year Lucretia Mott, Elizabeth Cady Stanton, and others presented the "Declaration of Sentiments" at Seneca Falls. In *Christine* Curtis Bullard represents the great opposition these women faced as lecturers during an era when most people thought that women should not speak in public to audiences of both men and women, let alone demand equality in education and politics. Woman's rights leaders were seen as violating traditional standards of true womanhood, making them unfeminine and thus unfit as wives and mothers. Since political and social equality would render women "unwomanly," many Americans feared that the so-called separate spheres of female and male duty would collapse, leading to the destruction of the family, the marketplace, and the government.

Curtis Bullard depicts one of the prevailing epithets hurled at woman's rights leaders in antebellum America when Christine's angry aunt warns her that she will "unsex" herself (163). This accusation of gender violation was common at midcentury; for example, the *Saturday Evening Post* declared that "the true dignity of womanhood can never be attained by woman's habitually unsexing herself" by lecturing on woman's rights ("Woman's Rights" 2). In gaining "political and pecuniary rights," the *Post* warned, woman may "lose the finer portion of her nature, and with it the love and reverence of man" ("Woman's Rights" 2). In 1852, an editorialist complained that the woman's rights convention in Syracuse illustrated the consequences of women leaving their "true sphere" (Stanton and Gage, *History* 853). The *Herald* pilloried the female delegates, describing them as "old maids, whose personal charms were never very attractive . . . some having so much of the virago in their disposition, that nature appears to have made a mistake in their gender—mannish women, like hens that crow; some of boundless vanity and egotism, who believe that they are superior in intellectual ability to 'all the world and the rest of mankind,' and delight to see their speeches and addresses in print" (Stanton and Gage, *History* 853). The following year the national woman's rights meeting in Brooklyn was dubbed the "mob convention" because the jeers from the hostile crowd made it impossible to hear the delegates. While Greeley's *Tribune* wrote favorably of the female speakers, the *Herald* described the convention as a "gathering of unsexed women—unsexed in mind all of them . . . publicly propounding the doctrine that they should be allowed to step outside of their appropriate sphere" (Stanton and Gage, *History* 556).

In such a cultural climate, most nineteenth-century women novelists, including Curtis Bullard, eschewed public speaking because they needed to strive for middle-class respectability to maintain their writing careers, which already made them vulnerable to charges of unfeminine egotism. Fanny Fern, a bestselling author and newspaper columnist, supported suffrage but declined requests to speak in public (Fern 369). Fern's subversive heroine in *Ruth Hall* (1854) considers many careers before becoming a writer, but she, too, never takes to the lectern. Harriet Beecher Stowe, the most famous writer in America, did not give public speeches during her European tours—she sat quietly on the stage as her remarks were read aloud by her husband (Hedrick 233–38). Louisa May Alcott, the creator of the intrepid Jo March, also avoided public speaking. When invited to speak to women at Vassar College and to members of Sorosis, Alcott, daughter of the orator Bronson Alcott, politely explained that she did not give public speeches, but in lieu of a lecture, she stood up, turned slowly around in a circle, and sat back down (Alcott, *Selected Letters* 207–8). Although Curtis Bullard was actively engaged in the woman's rights movement, she, too, did not like speaking on the stage and preferred to work as a conference participant, writer, and editor (Tilton, "Legend"). The refusal of these women, outspoken thinkers who maintained legions of devoted readers, to speak publicly illustrates the degree to which the fictional Christine moves beyond middle-class mores when she becomes not only a writer but also a woman's rights lecturer.

A few antebellum reform novels published before *Christine* included female lecturers as characters. In the short novel *The Lecturess* (1839) by Sarah Josepha Hale, the central character, Marian, gives up her work as a lecturer on woman's education when she marries. Later, she defies her husband by joining an abolitionist society and befriending another reform speaker, who is a clever and scheming woman.[22] Marian's husband leaves her, and on her deathbed Marian repents of her reform principles, declaring that it is a woman's job to make her husband happy and subvert her will to his. Hale's novel ultimately works as a lecture against female lecturers, supporting Hale's view that women should wield authority within their homes, a philosophy she promoted as the influential editor of *Godey's Lady's Book*.

Although Christine sometimes despairs that her work will never bear fruit, unlike Hale's heroine, she never repudiates her beliefs. Curtis Bullard, however, was careful that the radical nature of her novel did not cross into the notoriety generated by Caroline Chesebro's *Isa* (1852) and Mary Gove Nichols's *Mary Lyndon* (1855) and thus possibly alienate readers from the cause of woman's rights. Chesebro's main character, Isa, supports woman's rights primarily as a writer, not a lecturer, and she lives with her lover and coeditor, though the two are unmarried. Isa's rejection of marriage, not to mention her atheism, tended to validate many Americans' worst fears of woman's rights, and Chesebro herself seems ambivalent toward her character.[23]

In Nichols's autobiographical *Mary Lyndon*, the main character scandalized readers with her divorce and promise to leave her second husband if she no longer loves him. Although Mary speaks on woman's rights, her primary focus is health reform and the water cure.[24] In a subplot of *Christine*, Curtis Bullard sympathetically illustrates the problems women faced in divorce and in sexual relationships outside marriage, but Christine herself remains "respectable," ensuring that her arguments for equality are not overshadowed by scandal. Nearly two decades after the publication of *Christine*, the novel's influence can be seen in Alcott's nostalgic reform novel *Work: A Story of Experience* (1873). Alcott's spirited heroine, Christie, becomes a woman's rights speaker at the novel's end.[25] Ironically, Alcott's novel was serialized in Beecher's *Christian Union* in 1872–73, the year after Curtis Bullard resigned from the *Revolution*.

Christine is both a literary and political text, blending sensational tales of seduction, insanity, and abandonment from nineteenth-century popular culture with the philosophy of American liberal egalitarianism. Curtis Bullard writes with humor, irony, and drama, weaving her text with local color and literary and biblical allusions. The novel's pattern is dialogic, shifting between episodes of action and colloquies about woman's rights, employing psychological realism and political rhetoric. Curtis Bullard's goal was to represent the need for woman's rights to a middle-class audience of novel readers who may have shied away from reading the essays of writers such as Mary Wollstonecraft and Margaret Fuller or attending the lectures of speakers such as Lucy Stone or Susan B. Anthony.

Christine builds upon the tradition of the female bildungsroman, the novel of education and development, as the text dramatizes the ethical, emotional, and economic imperatives for female equality. Curtis Bullard tells the story of a young woman who leaves her rural home for an education and new life. Like the main character in a classic bildungsroman, she harbors an individualism and dreamy idealism that marks her as different from others. Christine embodies the traditions of the male bildungsroman, which focuses on the chronological development of the hero as he achieves independence, and the female bildungsroman, which emphasizes the heroine's interior quest and relation to community.[26] Since women's lives in the nineteenth century were measured by different markers than men's lives—familial connections and courtship rather than individualism and professional success—many popular female bildungsromane closed with marriage.

In Christine, Curtis Bullard melds the traditions of the male and female bildungsroman in the plot's structure. Christine's early failures on the family farm signify her inability to perform within community standards of practical, physical labor, especially female labor. She quickly proves herself inept at cleaning, cooking, and milking; even the simplest task of making beds proves to be difficult as she becomes engrossed in reading novels. Her passionate temper, lack of beauty, and love of reading are juxtaposed to the docile domesticity of her pretty sister, who is respected within the family and village. In the novel's humorous opening scene, Christine creates domestic chaos when she breaks the "household god," a china teapot, while reading a newspaper (6). She later is allowed to leave home and gain an education at the elite boarding school run by her widowed wealthy aunt, Julia Frothingham, whose cold elegance and autocratic power make her a negative example of female authority.

At midpoint in the novel, Christine seems to have fulfilled the plot arc of many nineteenth-century female bildungsromane: she leaves home, gains an education, and enjoys courtship. The novel should close, at this point, with references to wedding plans and the narrator's assurances of uninterrupted matrimonial bliss, even if those assurances are tinged with irony, à la Jane Austen and E.D.E.N. Southworth. Instead, Christine's true education begins when she takes to the public stage as a woman's rights lecturer, arguing for universal suffrage and economic opportunities for women. Curtis Bullard shifts the plot structure to align her novel more closely with the paradigm of the male quest for independence as Christine fully breaks from her community and sets out to make her way in the world, to live life on her own principles and establish her career.

One of the ways that Curtis Bullard makes Christine's arguments for female equality "respectable" is by presenting them as a logical extension of traditional American political thought. Christine argues:

Whatever a woman can do, and do well, we say let public opinion open the door for her to do, and let her be paid for her labor as much as a man would be, for the same amount. Let her try to do whatever she thinks she can do—if she fails, it will be no more than hundreds of men have done before her. And let her vote. She is under laws—let her have a voice in saying what they shall be. She is taxed—let her have the benefit of the principle which our fathers fought and bled to establish, no taxation without representation. (173–74)

And though Christine struggles to understand women who are different from her, she ultimately realizes that not all women share her temperament, and she is tolerant of those who disagree with her. Curtis Bullard presents the reader with a cast of female "types" offering different versions of "the trials and triumphs" of women. As a reform novel, Christine focuses on woman's rights, never mentioning temperance or abolition, the causes from which the woman's rights movement grew. While Christine refers to her support for "universal suffrage," a term that denoted support for voting rights for all people regardless of gender or race, the novel's focus is on female suffrage.

The novel's engagement with the rhetoric of "separate spheres" represents how this discourse of public versus private shaped middle-class women's experiences, and how woman's rights activists could reshape this traditional rhetorical stance for their own purposes. Feminist critics and historians have demonstrated that the demarcation between home and the marketplace was never a clear one, and Curtis Bullard's playful use of the word "sphere" suggests that it could also sometimes be more of a linguistic barrier than a literal one.[27] When Christine chooses to become a woman's rights lecturer, Mrs. Warner praises her for leaving the "sphere" of woman's "usual life" of marriage for a wider one (157). Instead of being "unsexed" by her choice, Christine is ennobled; she becomes the "champion of her sex," Mrs. Warner says, whereas marriage to a wealthy man would represent a "life of ease and self-indulgence" (157–58). Within this context, spheres are simply "usual," not natural or ordained, and Christine's rejection of convention is a moral choice that saves her from decadence. When Christine's friend Dr. Russell tells her of his "utter abhorrence to a woman stepping out of her sphere" into politics, Christine dismisses his objections as "sentimental nonsense" (331). Christine's response to Dr. Russell's use of the sphere mantra satirizes contemporary tropes of women as excessively emotional and sentimental; instead, in this case, it is the man of science who fails in logical reasoning.

Curtis Bullard also emphasizes the virtue of woman's rights leaders by portraying female social and political equality as a rational extension of women's culturally sanctioned benevolent work. By the 1850s, many women in the reform movement had become disillusioned with moral suasion and charity as means to change American society. Instead of focusing on traditional "female" methods of change, women activists began asserting the need for female suffrage and female leaders in benevolent institutions (Ginzberg 601–22). While the popular culture represented women in politics as power hungry and selfish, Christine is motivated by her desire to help others. In the quotation that is the epigraph to this introduction, Christine's oratory allows her to turn female benevolence into direct political action. Christine combines benevolence with rights as she inspires her audience with a "desire to seek out and relieve the distressed *as well as* to press forward to *claim* the wider field which she pointed out as before them" (199; emphasis added). As an individual, Christine can help a limited number of people, but her public "words of power" inspire her audience to help those in need, especially through the cause of social and political equality for women. Christine's lectures can reproduce her personal ideals within the public, persuading and influencing the many instead of only those within the sphere of her domestic circle.

Curtis Bullard's work to contextualize Christine's "unacceptable" profession and ideals within "acceptable" frameworks is central to the novel's argument that woman's rights are a logical part of American society. Christine's career is legitimized by the midcentury belief in American progress and the tradition of American Protestantism. By leaving the family farm, Christine finds financial success in a consumer economy that values her intellectual labor rather than her manual and reproductive labor. As a lecturer and writer who runs a home in the city for working women, Christine rejects the fashionable female education represented by her aunt's boarding school. The virulent critique of Christine's work by her father and aunt seem antithetical to the expanding economy of capitalism and a religious culture that linked the transcendental individual to social reform. Christine's own spiritual musings earn her the nickname "the preacher" from her classmates, and Mrs. Warner teaches her to see woman's rights as part of her Christian duty. The wife of a sea captain who is often absent, Mrs. Warner enjoys the right to speak plainly in the tradition of Yankee individualism. As the figurative "mother" of woman's rights in the novel, Mrs. Warner combines the domestic and the political—she sews constantly for her children and expounds the need for female equality. She tells Christine, "I have not lived entirely in vain. ... Your clear voice will ring out words of power that startle the sleepers. . . . People will call you blessed! They will reverence you as one who walks with God" (162). Like Stowe, Child, and Sedgwick, Curtis Bullard gives female characters the power to express moral and religious views that link them to the role of the minister in American society. In the character of Christine, however, Curtis Bullard reshapes and expands woman's role as a domestic minister into her heroine's work as a national lecturer. Christine, as her name suggests, carries out her Christian duty through her political activism.

Curtis Bullard underscores this link between religious and political authority when Mrs. Warner asks Christine when she will write essays. Christine replies: "Perhaps never. Essays are too often read by those who do not need them. Christ did not disdain to convey truth in parables. I will write in a form that will bring my words to all—the good who seek for the right and true, wherever it may be found, will hear me, and to the careless, who never seek for truth, I will whisper lessons so gently that they cannot offend, and yet, that may bear with them seeds which may spring up in the heart" (139). In her preference for parable, Christine rejects the essay, the genre most associated with the woman's rights movement. Although Christine does later write essays, this passage offers readers a deeper understanding of Curtis Bullard's motives in writing a woman's rights *novel* instead of a collection of essays. While the aesthetics of modernism tend to separate the literary and political, in the nineteenth century readers made no such distinctions. At the same time, however, a novel would attract readers who may have been hesitant or even opposed to reading an essay or treatise by a woman's rights leader. And though many nineteenth-century novels functioned as parables of social problems, *Christine* is unusual.

While the novel calls for social change by depicting the plight of those in need, Curtis Bullard pushes the novel's cultural work further by focusing primarily on the character of the female advocate. As the character of Christine gives voice to those who suffer, the text of *Christine* gives "womanhood" to the "unsexed." Curtis Bullard's portrayal of Christine represents woman's rights leaders as a new type of "true woman"—as active, independent, compassionate, and politically engaged individuals represented by Christine in the novel and leaders such as Mott, Stone, Anthony, and Stanton in nineteenth-century America. Even Christine's friend Dr. Russell, who disagrees with her ideas on suffrage, tells her, "You have proved yourself a *true woman*; misguided as I may think you in some respects, I honor your sincerity, your loftiness of purpose, and the work that you have done will live after you" (332–33; emphasis added). For nineteenth-century readers, Curtis Bullard wrote *Christine* to create emotional sympathy for female lecturers in order to foster political sympathy for woman's rights. For modern readers, *Christine* offers a deeper understanding of our cultural and literary past through its explicit discussions of marriage, motherhood, careers, and politics for women; indeed, the text of *Christine* examines issues that are still often at the core of political and social debate in America today.

Notes

1. I refer to her as Curtis Bullard on second reference because she published her novels *Now-a-days!* and *Christine* before her marriage under the name Laura J. Curtis and then later published essays and edited the *Revolution* under the name Laura Curtis Bullard.

2. For an earlier biographical study of Curtis Bullard, see "Legacy Profile" in *Legacy* 21.1 (2004): 74–82. Agger, Herndl, Leach, Reynolds, and Tracey discuss Curtis Bullard's work as a writer but also note the lack of biographical information. Agger includes a picture of a young woman in a riding hat with the caption "believed to be Laura J. Curtis Bullard, writer, editor, and advocate of woman's rights" (198). However, on the back of the original tintype, located at the Maine Historical Preservation Commission in Augusta, is handwritten "Bangor author/?Jane Appleton." I have been unable to find

any photos of Curtis Bullard or Appleton to verify the identity of the woman in the picture.

3. Laura Jane Curtis, Birth Record, Maine Department of Human Services, Vital Records/Statistics, Pre-1892 Delayed Returns, Microfilm, Roll 25.

4. 1850 U.S. Census, Penobscot County, Maine, Microform Roll 264.

5. 1850 U.S. Census, Penobscot County, Maine, Microform Roll 264. The census lists Jeremiah Curtis's occupation as "druggist."

6. *Now-a-days!* was published by T. L. Magagnos in 1854; University of Maine Press reprinted it in 1980 without critical or biographical material.

7. *Ladies' Visitor*, October 1860, 4. The quotations in this paragraph are from this advertisement for *Christine*, which was reprinted in other editions of the paper.

8. The couple was married in Brooklyn on 29 June 1859; see *New York Times*, 30 June 1859, 5. Enoch Bullard's family is not directly related to the more famous family of Eunice Bullard Beecher, wife of Henry Ward Beecher; see Bullard.

9. Alcott may have felt guilty about or doubted the veracity of this information, because part of this section of the letter was later crossed out, though it is still legible. See *Selected Letters* 217n8.

10. Harold Curtis Bullard was eighteen in 1880, according to the 1880 U.S. Census, which means he was born in 1862.

11. The 1880 U.S. Census shows Jeremiah and Lucy Curtis and Enoch, Laura, and Harold Bullard living at the same address in Brooklyn.

12. See "Workingwomen's" 8; "Weekly Meeting"; "Miss Anthony's"; and "Woman Suffrage Association."

13. Matt. 19:6.

14. For example, Dorr writes that Curtis Bullard turned the *Revolution* into a "genteel ladies' magazine" (225). Judith Harper writes that Curtis Bullard "planned a literary and social journal" (170). Barry writes that Curtis Bullard and Tilton turned the paper into a "literary and society journal" and that "the new editors refused to have anything to do with the old radicals" (223).

15. The new editor was Rev. William T. Clarke, and the paper shut down four months later.

16. While Goldsmith asserts that Tilton and Curtis Bullard were having an affair, Fox and Waller believe the allegations were not true. See Fox 387; Goldsmith 218; and Waller 120–21.

17. Bowen heard of the alleged Curtis Bullard–Tilton affair through a hysterical letter he received from Johanna Morse, Elizabeth Tilton's mother, who claimed that Tilton planned to leave Elizabeth and sail to Europe to meet Curtis Bullard (Applegate 401). Morse intensely disliked her son-in-law, and Applegate describes her as "crazy" (409). In her letter to Curtis Bullard on 13

January 1871, Elizabeth Tilton refers to a "cruel conspiracy made by my poor suffering mother" to "divorce" the Tiltons. Elizabeth also writes that the "slanders have been sown broadcast" and that Bowen has fired Theodore because of them (qtd. in Fox 345).

18. See also Barry 247–48; Farrell 127–29; Sachs 164–66; Theodore 1:157; Underhill 226.

19. Gypsy Friedl and Faithful unto Death were serialized in The Golden Age, a short-lived paper edited by Tilton. She translated a German edition of Modern Midas, written by the Hungarian novelist Maurus Jokai.

20. 1910 U.S. Census, Manhattan Ward 12, New York.

21. State of New York, Certificate and Record of Death, No. 2169, New York City Department of Records and Information Services, Municipal Archives.

22. Herndl calls Christine a "feminist revision" of the "anti-feminist" novel The Lecturess (64).

23. For a discussion of Isa, see Bardes and Gossett 64–67.

24. For a discussion of Mary Lyndon, see Myerson.

25. Other similarities are the character Philip, the heroines' early home lives, and the final scenes, in which Curtis Bullard's Christine commissions a painting and Alcott's Christie gazes at a commissioned painting.

26. See Buckley, who focuses on the male bildungsroman (16–27), and Abel, Hirsch, and Langland for a discussion of the female bildungsroman. Also see Fuderer and my essay "Reading Emma as a Lesson on 'Ladyhood': A Study in the Domestic Bildungsroman," Essays in Literature 22.1 (1995): 45–58.

27. See Davidson and Hatcher; Elbert.

Works Cited

Abel, Elizabeth, Marianne Hirsch, and Elizabeth Langland, eds. The Voyage In: Fictions of Female Development. Hanover: University Press of New England, 1983.

Agger, Lee. Women of Maine. Portland ME: Gannett, 1982.

Alcott, Louisa May. Selected Letters of Louisa May Alcott. Ed. Joel Myerson, Daniel Shealy, Madeleine B. Stern. Boston: Little, Brown, 1987.

———. Work: A Story of Experience. 1872. New York: Schocken, 1977.

Anthony, Katharine. Susan B. Anthony. Garden City: Doubleday, 1954.

Applegate, Debby. The Most Famous Man in America: The Biography of Henry Ward Beecher. New York: Three Leaves, 2006.

Bardes, Barbara A., and Suzanne Gossett. Declarations of Independence: Women and Political Power in Nineteenth-Century American Fiction. New Brunswick: Rutgers, 1990.

Barry, Kathleen. *Susan B. Anthony: Biography of a Singular Feminist*. New York: New York University Press, 1988.

Blake, Lillie Devereux. "The Divorce Question." Letter. *Revolution* 21 July 1870: 43.

"Brooklyn Women's Club." *Brooklyn Eagle* 7 Jan. 1870: 3.

Buckley, Jerome. *Season of Youth: The Bildungsroman from Dickens to Golding*. Cambridge: Harvard University Press, 1974.

Bullard, Edgar J. *The Other Bullards: A Genealogy*. Port Austin MI: n.p., 1928.

Curtis Bullard, Laura. *Christine: Or Woman's Trials and Triumphs*. New York: DeWitt and Davenport, 1856.

———. "Elizabeth Cady Stanton." *Our Famous Women*. Hartford: Worthington, 1884. 602–23.

———. Letter to Elizabeth Cady Stanton. 17 Nov. 1882. *Papers of Stanton and Anthony*. Microfilm reel 22, frame 745.

———. "Motto of This Journal." *Revolution* 15 Sept. 1870: 168.

———. "My Husband's Mother." *Ladies' Visitor, and Drawing Room Companion* Oct. 1856: 1.

———. *Now-a-days!* New York: Magagnos, 1854.

———. "Salutation from the Sea." *Revolution* 8 Dec. 1870: 360.

———. "Valedictory." *Revolution* 12 Oct. 1871: 8.

———. "What Justifies Marriage?" *Revolution* 18 Aug. 1870: 104.

Curtis Bullard, Laura, and Emma Herzong, trans. *A Modern Midas: A Romance*. By Maurus Jokai. New York: R. Worthington, 1884.

Davidson, Cathy, and Jessamyn Hatcher, eds. *No More Separate Spheres!* Durham: Duke University Press, 2002.

Dorr, Rhetta Childe. *Susan B. Anthony: The Woman Who Changed a Nation*. New York: AMS Press, 1970.

DuBois, Ellen. *The Elizabeth Cady Stanton–Susan B. Anthony Reader*. Boston: Northeastern University Press, 1992.

———. *Woman Suffrage and Women's Rights*. New York: New York University Press, 1998.

"Editorial Notes." *Independent* 26 May 1870: 22.

Elbert, Monika, ed. *Separate Spheres No More: Gender Convergence in American Literature, 1630–1930*. Tuscaloosa: University of Alabama, 2000.

Faithfull, Emily. *Three Visits to America*. Edinburgh: Douglas, 1884.

Farrell, Grace. *Lillie Devereux Blake: Retracing a Life Erased*. Amherst: University of Massachusetts Press, 2002.

Fern, Fanny. *Ruth Hall and Other Writings*. 1855. Ed. Joyce Warren. New Brunswick: Rutgers, 1986.

Fox, Richard Wrightman. *Trials of Intimacy: Love and Loss in the Beecher-Tilton Scandal*. Chicago: University of Chicago Press, 1999.

Fuderer, Laura Sue. *The Female Bildungsroman in English: An Annotated Bibliography of Criticism*. New York: MLA, 1990.

Gallman, J. Matthew. *America's Joan of Arc: The Life of Anna Elizabeth Dickinson*. Oxford: Oxford University Press, 2006.

Ginzberg, Lori. "'Moral Suasion Is Moral Balderdash': Women, Politics, and Social Activism in the 1850s." *Journal of American History* 73 (1986): 601–22.

Goldsmith, Barbara. *Other Powers: The Age of Suffrage, Spiritualism, and the Scandalous Victoria Woodhull*. New York: Knopf, 1998.

Harper, Ida Husted. *The Life and Work of Susan B. Anthony*. Indianapolis: Bowen-Merrill, 1899.

Harper, Judith E. *Susan B. Anthony: A Biographical Companion*. New York: ABL-CLIO, 1998.

Hedrick, Joan. *Harriet Beecher Stowe: A Life*. Oxford: Oxford University Press, 1994.

Herndl, Diane Price. *Invalid Women: Figuring Feminine Illness in American Fiction and Culture 1840–1940*. Chapel Hill: University of North Carolina Press, 1993.

Holcombe, Henry. *Patent Medicine Tax Stamps: A History of the Firms Using United States Private Die Proprietary Medicine Tax Stamps*. Lawrence MA: Quarterman, 1979.

Hume, R. W. "The Meeting of the Waters." *Woman's Advocate* 2.5 (1869): 217–19.

"Jeremiah Curtis." Obituary. *New York Daily Tribune* 25 Mar. 1883: 7.

Kerr, Andrea Moore. "White Woman's Rights, Black Men's Wrongs, Free Love, Blackmail, and the Formation of the American Suffrage Association." *One Woman, One Vote: Rediscovering the Woman Suffrage Movement*. Ed. Marjorie Sprull Wheeler. Troutdale OR: Newsage, 1995.

"Laura Curtis Bullard." Obituary. *New York Times* 20 Jan. 1912: 13.

Leach, William. *True Love and Perfect Union: The Feminist Reform of Sex and Society*. Middletown CT: Wesleyan University Press, 1989.

"A Little Fund." *Brooklyn Eagle* 27 Apr. 1891: 6.

Merrill, Margaret Manton. "Sorosis." *Cosmopolitan: A Monthly Illustrated Magazine* June 1893: 153–58.

"Miss Anthony's Suffrage Association." *New York Tribune* 4 Aug. 1869. *Papers of Stanton and Anthony*. Microfilm reel 13, frame 623.

Mosher, Elizabeth, ed. *Vital Records of Freedom, Waldo County, Maine, Prior to 1892*. Camden ME: Picton Press, 1991.

Moulton, Louise Chandler. "A Fullfilled Prediction." *Critic: Weekly Review of Literature and the Arts* 23 Apr. 1887: 173.

"Movement in Maine." *National Era* 4 Feb. 1847: 3.

Myerson, Joel. "Mary Gove Nichols' Mary Lyndon: A Forgotten Reform Novel." *American Literature* 58 (Dec. 1986): 523–40.

"National Intelligencer, New York Express, and Abolitionists." *National Era* 18 Nov. 1847: 2.

"New Publications." *Knickerbocker* July 1856: 109.

Papers of Elizabeth Cady Stanton and Susan B. Anthony. Ed. Patricia Holland and Ann D. Gordon. Microfilm. Wilmington: Scholarly Resources, 1991.

"Prospectus." *Revolution* 7 July 1870: 13.

Ratcliffe, Eric. *The Caxton of Her Age: The Career and Family Background of Emily Faithfull.* Upton-Upon Severn, UK: Images, 1993.

"Reviews." *Peterson's Magazine* May 1856: 399.

Reynolds, David S. *Beneath the American Renaissance: The Subversive Imagination in the Age of Emerson and Melville.* Cambridge MA: Harvard University Press, 1988.

———. *Walt Whitman's America: A Cultural Biography.* New York: Vintage, 1996.

Sachs, Emanie. *The Terrible Siren: Victoria Woodhull.* 1928. New York: Arno, 1978.

Stanton, Elizabeth Cady. *Eighty Years and More.* New York: T. Fisher Unwin, 1898.

———. "Who Shall Fill Our Places." *Revolution* 26 May 1870: 328.

Stanton, Elizabeth Cady, and Matilda Joslyn Gage, eds. *History of Woman Suffrage.* Vol. 2. Rochester: Charles Mann, 1881.

Theodore Tilton vs. Henry Ward Beecher. 2 vols. New York: McDivitt, Campbell, 1875.

Tilton, Theodore. "A Legend of Good Women." *The Golden Age* 1 July 1871: 6.

"Tilton Traduced." *Brooklyn Eagle* 26 Jan. 1871: 4.

Townsend, Virginia. "Summer Days in New York." *Arthur's Illustrated Home Magazine* Mar. 1874: 185.

Tracey, Karen. *Plots and Proposals: American Women's Fiction: 1850–90.* Urbana: University of Illinois Press, 2000.

Underhill, Lois Beachy. *The Woman Who Ran for President: The Many Lives of Victoria Woodhull.* New York: Bridge, 1995.

Waller, Altima. *Reverend Beecher and Mrs. Tilton: Sex and Class in Victorian America.* Amherst: University of Massachusetts Press, 1982.

"Weekly Meeting at the Bureau." *Revolution. Papers of Stanton and Anthony.* Microfilm reel 2, frame 45–46.

Whiting, Lillian. "Dora D'istria." *Chautauquan* Sept. 1895: 751.

Williams, Melissa S. "Feminism as an American Project: The Political Thought of Elizabeth Cady Stanton." *History of American Political Thought*. Ed. Bryan-Paul Frost and Jeffrey Sikkenga. Lanham MD: Lexington, 2003. 425–26.

"Woman's Rights Convention." *Saturday Evening Post* 2 Nov. 1850: 2.

"Woman Suffrage Association." *New York World* 4 Aug. 1869. *Papers of Stanton and Anthony*. Microfilm reel 13, frame 624.

"A Woman's View of the Two Societies." *Revolution* 8 Dec. 1870: 360.

"Workingwomen's Association." *New York Times* 6 May 1869: 8.

 Christine

CHAPTER ONE

The Farmhouse

The hands of the wooden clock pointed to half-past five. Mrs. Elliot bustled about her kitchen getting supper ready for the "men-folks," who were out haying. The table was already set, and the whole room presented a picture of neatness and comfort. The floor was uncarpeted, but very white, for Mrs. Elliot was one of the most notable of housewives. A turned-up bed, neatly curtained by a blue and white woven quilt, occupied one corner of the room; a pine table stood between the windows, and wooden chairs were set back stiffly against the wall at regular distances, looking as prim as if they were the old maids of their race. A pole hung a few inches below the ceiling, where some cup-towels, as white as the driven snow, were deposited. The fire-place was large; a tin baker stood before it, and the tea-kettle hung from the crane. On the mantel-piece were a cluster of tall iron candlesticks, and near by them the *Farmer's Almanac* hanging on a nail. This volume bore the marks of frequent usage, as well it might, for no day passed in which Farmer Elliot did not peruse its pages, although he had already more than once read its purely literary portions from the history of Farmer Thrifty, whose fences were always in good repair, to that of the unfortunate Thriftless, who, not only neglected these, but whose tools were always lost, or out of order, when wanted. The anecdotes, poetry, and conundrums in the appendix had also received their due share of attention. It was a book of general reference, containing, as it did, much useful information aside from that particularly referring to the weather, and its worth was enhanced by marginal notes in Mr. Elliot's upright handwriting, which served as chronological records of important events which had occurred on the farm, or in the household.

A large basket of work stood upon a small light-stand near a window, and close by it, on a low cricket, sat a young girl whose work had fallen from her lap to the floor, reading an old newspaper.

"Christine! Christine!" exclaimed her mother, suddenly pausing in one of her rapid journeys between the cellar and the kitchen, "Don't you see the tea-kettle is boiling? Get up and put the tea to steep."

Christine rose, went to the closet, and taking a china tea-pot from the shelf, poured some tea-leaves from the canister into it; then approaching the fire-place, she leaned awkwardly over the tin baker, and began to fill the tea-pot with hot water.

The tea-kettle slipped; a little hot water burnt Christine's fingers; she started aside; her dress caught on the baker and nearly overturned it, and in her confused attempt to set it upright again, the tea-pot slipped from her hand, fell against the tall andiron, and broke into several pieces. The pan, too, slipped out of the baker, and over went the nice cream biscuit into the ashes.

"Oh, dear!" exclaimed poor Christine, horrified, standing aghast at the ruin she had wrought, and "Goodness me!" screamed the shrill voice of her mother, as she sprang to the rescue.

"Christine Elliot! you are the most shiftless girl that ever was!" she exclaimed, as she snatched the biscuit from the hearth before they could be much injured. Then, for the first time, seeing the fragments of the tea-pot, she burst out into a fit of passion—

"Are you a fool? What possessed you to take that tea-pot, to steep the tea in? Get out of my sight! You were born to be the plague of my life. Don't open your lips to me, Miss—. To think of taking my best china tea-pot to set on the coals! Oh, you are the most provoking girl that ever was—"

But Christine heard no more. She had slipped out of the room into the garden.

Tears of shame and anger filled her eyes, as she threw herself at full length on the ground, burying her face in the grass, as she sobbed out, "I wish I was dead! Everybody hates me. I wish the grass grew over my grave!"

Her sister Bessie, who was picking currants for supper, looked at her compassionately. She did not appear surprised, for she had too often seen Christine in like fits of despondency and passion.

She allowed her to weep for a while; then, at last, sitting down by her sister, she threw her arms around her neck, and drawing her head into her lap, she bent over her and kissed her brow.

"What is the matter now?" she asked.

Christine, amid tears and sobs, told of her mishaps, concluding, "Mother is right. I am the plague of her life! Oh, why was I ever born? I am of no use to anybody in the world! What have I to live for?"

It was a strange sight. That young girl, in the morning of life, when all should have been bright in the present and full of promise for the future, longing to fling away the gift of existence; and her wild words and convulsive sobs illy harmonized with the quiet beauty of the scene. All else was peaceful there. The hot sun was sinking slowly in the west, and the clear, blue sky above, the soft, green grass beneath her, breathed the very spirit of tranquillity. The prolonged shrill sound of the grasshoppers, the hum of bees, the distant lowing of cattle, and the click of the scythe in the hay-field near, all seemed suited to the place, and detracted nothing from the beauty around.

The brown, unpainted farm-house, with its low roof and irregular windows, might perhaps in itself have been rather unsightly, but situated as it was, on an elevated table-land, surrounded by wooded hills on one side and sloping fields on the other, while far below, through thick foliage, gleamed the clear waters of a lake—it added all that was wanting to what had else been but a picture of still life. Its huge barn standing near the road, with its large barn-yard fenced in rather rudely by logs, betokened plenty; and a fine orchard opposite, its gnarled old trees loaded with fruit, said the same; hens and chickens clucked and chirped around; and a flock of geese, headed by a grey old gander, who, with the rest, was decked in a three-cornered yoke of wood, stalked along majestically, stretching their necks as if their decorations had been, instead of a mark of demerit, a token of distinction; nor are these the only geese in this world who glory in their shame.

The tall well-sweep and dripping bucket were not wanting in this rural picture, and taken altogether it would have been hard to find, even in New England, a more cheerful, comfortable farm-house and surroundings.

Meanwhile, Christine's sobs had grown fainter and fainter, as she lay half on the grass, half on her sister's bosom, and at last, like a grieved child, a long-drawn sigh alone escaped her at intervals.

Bessie had said nothing; she had only smoothed the disordered hair of her sister, and kissed her softly; but now, as she saw that the paroxysm of grief was over, she said aloud, as if in answer to her own thoughts, "Yes, something ought to be done. If you could only go away somewhere, my dear."

"Oh, if I only could!" exclaimed Christine, with a sudden burst of hope; then, checking herself, she bitterly added, "But what's the use of talking! I never shall. Here I must stay and drag out my life. Get up in the morning, scrub, wash dishes, churn, and do all sorts of drudgery, till night comes, and sleep only to go over the same thing the next day. Oh, it is not living, Bessie! I must have a change—I shall die—I shall grow crazy, or, what is worse, I shall grow wicked, as I do every day. I know it," she went on, with a fresh burst of sobs, "I feel impatient—I get angry—I don't try to please mother, or, if I do, my heart isn't in it, and I go wrong—and, if I do feel sorry, the very next time I'm tempted, I do the same thing; and so grow worse and worse—worse and worse!"

Tears streamed over Christine's face as she spoke—"What did God put me here for?" she exclaimed, and, as Bessie quickly interrupted her with, "Oh, Christine!" she went on—

"I know it's wicked, but oh, Bessie! I do have such thoughts. I ask myself what I am here for, where I do no good, and only grow bad; and I ask if it was a good God who placed me here. Then I say to myself, He knew that I couldn't grow better, and is it right for Him to punish me for it?"

"Oh, Christine!" again repeated Bessie, with a look of distress, "don't talk so! Don't think of such things!"

"But, I *must* think. Why, that isn't half so bad as I think sometimes. Sometimes, I don't know as there is a God—but not often, Bessie dear," she went on, as she saw the look of horror that crossed her sister's face, "Not often, Bessie; but, didn't such a thought ever flash through your mind, and a great many others like it?"

"Never—never!" repeated Bessie.

"Then I am different from everybody else," was Christine's inward exclamation. "Mother is right. I am odd, and I don't know but she's right when she says, I'm 'half cracked.' Am I crazy? Am I going to be?" and Christine tormented herself with a thousand fearful forebodings.

Bessie had again commenced her task of picking currants, and at last Christine began to help her, so that soon the bowl was heaped with the bright transparent fruit.

They were only just in time, for Mrs. Elliot came to the door that led into the garden.

"Girls!" she exclaimed, "ain't you most ready with them currants, or are you going to spend the rest of the day in the garden?"

She spoke angrily, for the broken tea-pot had given a sad shock to her temper; and her feelings may be sympathized with when we remember that this tea-pot had been for years a sort of household god, resting on the top shelf of the closet, as on an altar, to be worshipped by mother and children at a safe distance.

"Coming, mother," replied Bessie's clear voice, as they quickly obeyed the summons; while Mrs. Elliot took the tin horn from its place and blew a blast, shrill, loud and fierce, as if she had been the herald who summoned a beleaguered castle to sur-render. This having been accomplished, she made no further demonstrations of ill-temper, save in the quickened step with which she hastened from one room to another, in the prose-cution of her household duties.

Her summons was speedily answered; for a bevy of men, whose simple garb, consisting of pantaloons and shirt alone, gave full play to their muscular and sinewy forms, with bronzed faces and glowing cheeks, walked slowly up from the hay field, lifting their straw hats and wiping the perspiration from their heated brows as they came.

They entered the back porch, where water and towels were in readiness; the tin wash-basin, which served each in turn, glis-tened like silver, while the towel, which hung from a roller, was as white as it is in the nature of cloth to be.

The supper was smoking upon the table, and a few well-timed compliments to Mrs. Elliot on its excellence served to disperse the cloud which had gathered on her brow; and, though she could not avoid a reproachful glance at Christine when she passed her her cup of tea, yet on the whole she had recovered her usual good temper.

Little was said during the process of dispatching the meal, which was soon accomplished; and the whole party, headed by Farmer Elliot, started briskly for the field again, for a load of hay was to be deposited in the barn ere the day's work was done.

"I'll wash the dishes, girls," said Mrs. Elliot, "and you must go and get the cows and milk."

Christine heard and obeyed this command gladly, for she was always ready for a walk; and, snatching up her sun-bonnet, she was soon on her way, accompanied by Bessie.

They walked along some distance in silence. At last Christine spoke—

"I'd give all the world if I were rich."

"What if you were?" replied Bessie, replacing the bars which led into the pasture-field which they had just entered. "What would you do with it?"

"I would learn everything. Then I would have a splendid house, where I would have all the great people, the writers, and all sorts of talented persons come; and I would help the poor authors, who struggle on and die sometimes in the midst of their struggles, and yet," she went on thinking aloud, "perhaps, those very trials of theirs but make their talents known, as the oyster must die before the pearl is brought to light. I might, perhaps, keep the oyster alive but the pearl concealed. But, no, I'm talking nonsense; genius will come out, it can't be hidden; and, it is like a plant that in poor soil grows, indeed, and flourishes for a time—but, though it may blossom, doesn't live out half its days, because it's too delicate to thrive in cold, bleak places; but, when transplanted into a rich soil, grows more and more luxuriant and beautiful, because it is where God meant it to be.

How I should rejoice to do this transplanting. It would be almost equal to being *one of them*."

She paused and blushed deeply, for Bessie's laugh brought her back to earth.

"What a queer girl you are, Christine! I declare it is so funny to hear you talk. I don't half know what you mean, I'm sure. Now, if I was rich—" but her air castles were speedily dissipated by a vision of oxen and cows walking slowly towards the bars. One cow, Bessie's quick eye saw, was missing.

"Old Grizzle isn't here," she said, and leaving Christine to follow the main herd, she scampered off in pursuit of the straggler. She soon returned, driving Old Grizzle in triumph, and the whole herd were soon safely lodged in the barn-yard.

Then came the milking, where Bessie, as usual, quietly and successfully performed her task, while poor Christine, stool and pail in hand, vainly pursued the cows, who, taught by past experience, well knew that her hand was unskillful, and walked off as often as she approached them. When, at last, one was cornered, she was sure to take her seat on the wrong side, and, after getting fairly settled, the milk would not come, or, if she did obtain a little, it was followed by an impatient kick of the cow, who would again walk off, to be pursued by Christine as before; while all the while the rapid and musical flow of the milk in Bessie's pail, tantalized her poor sister.

"I shall never be good for anything," the girl would say to herself, and with bitter mortification she would submit to have her pail half filled from Bessie's, and see more than half the task performed by her brisk sister.

The milking was hardly over, when the heavily loaded hay-cart slowly entered the barn, and the fragrant load was speedily pitched off by brawny and powerful arms.

The day's work was over, and the men sauntered around, talking of the crops of this or that neighbor, or seated in the low rooms of the farm-house, discussed the merits of sheep, horses, and oxen.

Mrs. Elliot listened with interest to all such conversations, and occasionally took part in them; Bessie strayed off with James Cameron, a smart and handsome youth, who was assisting her father during the haying season, while Christine, tired of listening to what she felt no interest in, crept off to the second story, an unfinished chamber where boxes, chests, and all sorts of similar articles, were stored.

At one end of the room stood a loom, in which was a web of cloth yet unfinished; an old red chest stood near by which contained, together with a lot of old rubbish, several old-fashioned novels, some complete, but oftener wanting either one or two volumes.

Christine had read them again and again, but she never wearied of the woes of Julia de Roubigny, or of the heroic Thaddeus of Warsaw; she wept over these, shuddered with poor Emily in the mysterious Castle of Udolpho, and laughed and wondered in turn over the pages of Don Quixote.[1]

In these books she forgot herself, and too often forgot her tasks also, so that she was rudely recalled from the realms of imagination to the actual, which disgusted her more than ever. In fact, she lived almost entirely in a world of her own, and walked mechanically about, thinking of something far different from that on which she was engaged. The result was what might have been expected. Her kind-hearted but practical mother, at last, had her small stock of patience quite exhausted by Christine's continual drafts upon it; and, having on several occasions given her tasks to perform, and on her non-appearance after a sufficient length of time, discovered the culprit poring over a book, while the work was still undone, she had positively forbidden any more reading.

As well might she have forbidden the birds to fly or fish to swim.

She hid the books, but Christine seemed to have an instinctive knowledge where they were; and, though she did not read in her mother's presence, she snatched every opportunity to enjoy the forbidden pleasure.

Seated in the old loom, she would read for hours in the moonlight, or weave wild and fanciful visions there of her own.

A fabric of a far different kind from that which the shuttle of her good mother constructed there, it was, indeed; and, as that mother, in despair, had given up the task of making her child understand her operations in the loom, so would Christine have found it equally hopeless to have explained her web of mingled thoughts to her mother.

They could never understand each other. It was a marvel to each that the other could be interested in her chosen employments. "How you can read so much," her mother would say, "I can't see; and books, too, that you know by heart. But, then, you are so odd, I hadn't ought to be surprised at any of your freaks."

In her turn, Christine wondered at her mother's unfailing and unflagging interest in cleaning, washing, ironing, and baking; and, if her indolence annoyed her mother, Mrs. Elliot's untiring activity, in turn, wearied her.

Bessie was much like her mother. Very pretty, healthy, active, and cheerful, she was the light of the house.

She, no more than her mother, understood Christine's odd fancies, but she loved her sister sincerely, and pitied her extremely. Christine was grateful for her sympathy, though, had she been conscious that it was bestowed upon her on account of what she prized more than life, her gratitude might have been overpowered by astonishment and horror at that ill-judging sympathy, which, had it been possible, would have taken away from her, as an evil, the only thing which made life endurable to her.

Her father, a sturdy old farmer, would have had still less patience with her, had he understood her better. That she would never amount to much was his private opinion; further than that, except a sort of liking for her, he thought but little of her. He was proud of his sweet Bessie, as he was of having the best tilled farm in the vicinity, and her sprightly, winning ways were always a delight to him.

"It isn't natural," he would say to his wife, "to see a young one so still and quiet as Christine always was. Now Bessie was always as brisk and full of sport as a young kitten, and it's queer what ails Christine. If she does dance around a bit now and then, in a moment or two she's as sober as ever. I don't like to see an old head on young shoulders; but let her take her own course."

In about this way, he usually dismissed her from his thoughts, and thus, in a measure, alone, Christine's childhood had passed, and her youth was passing. Her eager, unsatisfied mind preyed upon her body; she grew thin and pale. She wanted something, she knew not what—conscious of a void that she knew not how to fill, she was always restless and unhappy. She had, at school, found comparative quiet; there her mind was employed, and she longed, oh, how ardently, to learn. That was now the one idea of her life, and she delved and worked over her school books, at times discouraged, indeed, and well-nigh despairing, yet never ready to give up the task she had set before her. She almost envied her blithe sister, Bessie, sometimes, as she saw her cheerful, happy, and contented in her home, and contrasted her own stormy, aspiring spirit with hers, but when she asked herself if she would be willing to exchange, "No, no," her whole soul would cry. "Better to struggle always, if the goal is never reached, than to pass on through life with calm indifference. Rather the hillside, bleak and cold though it may be, so that my course be upward, than the plain, bathed in sunshine, if I may never go beyond it."

CHAPTER TWO

The Village

Mrs. Elliot stood in an attitude of deep reflection, in the centre of the floor, broom in hand. She was looking intently on the bright row of milk-pans, which were resting on a bench outside of the door, for the purpose of drying in the warm sun; but she was not thinking of them.

The dash of the milk in the churn, for Bessie was churning in the back porch, suddenly recalled her from her reverie, and she hurried thither.

"Bessie," said she, "we're out of tea, and coffee, and sugar. What is going to be done?"

"Get some more, mother, I suppose," replied Bessie, wiping a drop of buttermilk from her cheek, which the refractory churn dash had thrown up.

"Yes, yes," said her mother, impatiently, "but how? The menfolks can't go; they're all too busy, and they can't stop to catch the horse and harness him. Besides the old horse is lame, and the colt is too frisky for women to drive."

"Well, then, mother, why can't Christine or I go?"

"Christine!" repeated Mrs. Elliot. "Why, you might as well send a baby. She'd set the basket down and run off after a flower, or she'd fall down herself. Something would be sure to happen to her, for something always is happening—" and she drew a long sigh.

"I'll go, then," said Bessie; "but I guess she'd better go, too. It's going to be pretty warm to-day, and, if I have to walk, I should like some help about carrying the bundles. The butter is coming," she said, giving a series of violent dashes up and down, and lifting off the cover from the tall churn. Sure enough there floated the butter, golden islands in a sea of buttermilk.

"What have we got to sell?" asked Bessie, as she heaped the rich golden mass into a tray, washing it, patting it skillfully, salting it, and moulding it, till, in round balls, it laid there, looking tempting enough for any epicure.

"Eggs and butter, I suppose," was her mother's reply.

"It's too warm to carry butter, mother; eggs to-day must do, and we have got plenty. So, if you'll fill a basket, I'll slip on a dress, and be ready in a jiffy. Where's Christine?" she asked, as she followed her mother to the dairy, where the new butter was speedily deposited, and Mrs. Elliot skimmed the rich, thick cream off the tops of the pans, and put it into a stone pot, to be ready for the next churning.

"I don't know, I'm sure. I sent her to make the beds, but I dare say she has got her nose stuck in a book, for she's been gone long enough to make forty beds."

"Oh well, I'll find her," said Bessie, and singing a merry song, she sprang up the unfinished stairway to the room where she supposed her sister to be.

There Christine stood, book in hand, by the side of a bed, whose quilts and pillows were heaped together on a chair.

"What are you doing, Chris?"

The girl started, threw down her book, and replied rather confusedly:

"Waiting for the beds to air."

Bessie laughed.

"Well, I guess they're aired enough now. Step round to the back side, and I'll help you make them, for I want you to go with me to the village. Now," said Bessie, after the task was finished, "put on your best dress, and we'll be off soon, before it gets any hotter."

Not many minutes had elapsed, when the two girls, basket in hand, sallied forth for the village, accompanied by their mother as far as the barn, which she entered, to search for eggs, to replace those which she had sent away, and the cackling of hens soon denoted that the invasion had taken place.

The girls walked on together, well satisfied with their attire, though a city belle would have laughed it to scorn. A simple calico dress, muslin cape, and straw bonnet, plainly trimmed, constituted the whole of their best attire, and, though cheap and plain, Bessie's clear complexion, sparkling eyes, and lithe and vigorous form, added grace to what she wore. She did, indeed, look very pretty, while, as for Christine, neither silks nor laces could have redeemed her from positive plainness. Rich dress would but have attracted attention to her large features, sallow cheeks, and gaunt form. She well knew that she was not beautiful, but as yet she did not regret it. She was passionately fond of the beauties of nature, and, as she walked along, the balmy air, the waving trees, smooth fields, and distant hills filled her with a wild delight. The sight of such beauty seemed to pervade her whole being, and thrilled to her very soul. At last she could no longer keep silence. She burst forth impetuously:

"Oh, Bessie, isn't it beautiful?"

"What, Christine?" was the chilling reply.

"Oh, everything," resumed Christine, too much excited to heed her sister's lack of sympathy. "Look all round. It is so glorious. Oh, Bessie, sometimes when I look on these beautiful scenes, I feel sure that, in some faint degree, I can understand the pleasure that God must feel in creating such glorious things;

and, Bessie, I'll tell you how I think God made us in His own image: He has given us a little of that power of creating. Now, painters must have such beautiful visions, and poets and all great men and women must see such lovely creations in their own minds, because we, every-day sort of people, you know, have the same thing, in a measure. I can't express it clearly, but you know, Bessie, what I mean."

"No, I'm sure I don't, Chris," cried her sister, with a gay laugh.

"We try and try," went on Christine, half aloud, "to bring out our ideas, but God hasn't given us quite power enough to do it here—we never can express fully what is so beautiful in our thoughts; but in Heaven, Bessie—in Heaven, it will be so joyful, because there we shall be able to do it *perfectly*. 'We shall be *satisfied* when we awake in His likeness.'"[2]

"If we ever get there," said Bessie, in a very solemn tone; for it was a part of her religion to speak solemnly, and Christine's method of talking of such things in her usual voice and manner, never seemed quite right to her.

"Do you know what spoils this earth, Bessie?"

"The fall of man, I suppose."

"Yes, I suppose that is the far back cause of it; but I was thinking of this dissatisfied spirit that we all have—this yearning after something beyond; it's that that spoils everything. It must be the fall, I think, for the animals don't have it. They are happy; but we all feel it. You feel *that*, don't you, Bessie, as if you were reaching, reaching forward continually for something. Don't you?" and she listened anxiously for the reply.

"I don't know what you mean," said Bessie. "Why, no; I'm pretty well contented."

"Well, then," suddenly exclaimed Christine, "I know what the reason is: it's because God has put you in the right place—that makes you satisfied. Why hasn't He put me there, too? Why hasn't He given me a work to do?"

"I am sure, Christine, you have work enough—more than you like to do."

"Oh, that isn't what I mean. You don't understand me—I wish somebody could. Shall I ever find anybody that will—somebody that will show me the right way?"

Bessie was silent for some time; she was weary of the conversation, and, merely saying, "If you could try to be a little more like other people, dear Chris, we should all be so glad," she relapsed again into silence.

"Now, we're just half-way to the village," said Bessie, as they climbed up a steep hill, and paused for a moment on its summit. "I'm pretty tired—ain't you?"

"Not very," said Christine, absently; then suddenly, as her eye rested on the basket of eggs, which Bessie had set down for a few minutes, she exclaimed, "I do believe I am the most selfish girl in the world. Here I've let you carry that heavy basket all the way!"

"Well, that's no matter," said Bessie; "you may help the rest of the way, and then it will be all right. Do you know how much eggs are a dozen?"

"No."

"Well, they were ninepence last time we sold any, and they ought to be as much as that now. Let me see—" and she went into a series of calculations, as they proceeded, while Christine answered "yes" and "no" at random, whenever appealed to; for she was engrossed again in her own reflections.

"Let's rest again," said Bessie, as they stood on the top of a hill, at whose foot lay the village.

Christine willingly consented, for she could have spent hours gazing at the landscape outspread before her.

Neat dwellings lay interspersed with broad fields, on one side, while the country, in its inequalities of hill and valley, dotted with an occasional farm-house, stretched far away on the other. All was silent, when suddenly a bell struck on their ears.

"It is only nine o'clock," said Bessie, for this was the bell of the academy—a tall building, whose spire gleamed through the trees which crowned a hill on the opposite side of a stream which flowed through the centre of the village.

"How I should like to go to the academy, this term—shouldn't you, Christine?" said Bessie.

"Oh, so much!" replied her sister.

"The girls say they have first-rate times," continued Bessie. "There are a great many scholars, and they have social parties at the houses where they board, and they are going to have an exhibition before long. I mean to go to that, anyway."

"How will you manage to?" asked Christine. "Father wouldn't go—and in the evening, so, I don't see how you could."

"Why," replied Bessie, blushing, "James Cameron is going to take me, and *you* are going, too."

"You are a dear, good, thoughtful sister," replied Christine, "I should really like it very much."

"Yes," said Bessie, "and they are going to have a play, a real play, *Pizarro*;—one of the girls told me all about it; she is going to be one of the actors in it.[3] Now, if we only went, we might have a part. I could do it as well as Kate McKenzie; but, we'll see it, anyhow—won't we, Chris, dear?"

"If we can," replied Christine, as they walked slowly down the hill and entered the main street of the village.

Amity was not a large place, but it boasted of two physicians, whose rival factions divided the town, a lawyer, and one or two merchants, whose stores contained almost every article that could be mentioned; ribbons and dress goods for the outer, as well as groceries for the supply of the inner man.[4] There were, also, some mills in the place, which gave their name to the village, for it was oftener called the Mills, than by any other title. Grist-mills, wool-carding, saw, and paper-mills, were scattered along the little stream which flowed through the village; there were, also, blacksmiths' and shoemakers' shops; nor was there wanting a hotel, whose creaking sign-board made known that here was the Traveller's Home.

True, the advent of a traveller was a rare occurrence, but there had been a time when it had been in flourishing circumstances; when it had been a stage tavern, its stable boasting of four horses, who replaced the four wearied ones daily at about noon, giving thereby opportunity for travellers to satisfy their hunger, and to Mrs. O'Reilly opportunity, likewise, to display her culinary skill; but these halcyon days were over. A relative of the proprietor of the stage line had established himself as an inn-keeper in the next village, some six miles distant; and, to Mrs. O'Reilly's great disgust, as well as to that of travellers also—as by this arrangement their dinner hour was somewhat retarded—the change of horses was effected there.

Mrs. O'Reilly, therefore, was compelled to rest on the laurels won in the past, but, with praiseworthy perseverance, she still kept public-house, though her great dining-room was now never used except in the winter, when it was sometimes called into requisition on the occasion of a ball. At such times, she was in her glory, and showed then what her powers might be, had she only been given a field for their exercise.

But, strange to say, in this thriving village, there was neither editor, meeting-house, or resident minister. Elder Wiggins, indeed, was "the stated supply" once in four weeks, and held forth in the Academy regularly every fourth Sabbath. Nearly all the village flocked to hear him on these occasions; yet they seemed content with this, and made no exertion to increase the frequency of his sermons.

Bessie and Christine had now entered Mr. Emerson's store, which was the principal one in Amity. It was a long, low, red building, which served also as post-office, for he was one of the chief dignitaries of the village, being, not only postmaster, but first selectman. He was a little, dapper man, and prided himself not a little on his good manners.

He bowed gracefully, as he imagined, at least, to the girls, as they approached the counter.

"Good morning, Misses Elliot," he said, giving his yard-stick, which he held in his hand, a flourish. "It is a luxuriant morning."

"Yes, very pleasant," replied Bessie, "but rather warm."

"Oh, excessively so, excessively so. I told Mrs. Emerson this morning, it would be. But, what can I do for you, this morning? Shall I show you some dress goods? I have some beautiful new styles for summer wear," and he began to throw piles of goods on the counter.

"Oh, no, Mr. Emerson," exclaimed Bessie, "I don't want to buy a dress; I won't trouble you to show them."

"No trouble—not the least, Bessie; as I often remark to Mrs. Emerson, it's my business to show my goods."

"But, really, Mr. Emerson, I have no time to examine them this morning. Have you any nice tea?"

"Oh, some of the very best. I carried some home to Mrs. Emerson, and she declared it was the best we had had for a long time."

"And would you like to buy some eggs?"

"Oh, yes, they come just in the right time. I was remarking this morning to Mrs. Emerson that we must try some fresh eggs; and nobody sends fresher eggs to market than Farmer Elliot."

While the bargain was being completed, Christine turned away, for she had too often heard the same allusions to Mrs. Emerson to be at all amused by their frequency; it rather excited her anger—for, if village gossip spoke truly, Mrs. Emerson, so far from being considered of importance by her husband, was in fact a mere cipher in her home; and, although her husband never sold a dress to a lady customer without asserting that Mrs. Emerson had, or was going to have, one precisely similar, it was considered rather a singular phenomenon, by the good ladies of Amity, that she never appeared in public dressed in any of these superabundant garments. It was, indeed, a pretty generally admitted fact that Mr. Emerson's smiles and graces of manner were reserved for the public alone.

The bargain was at last concluded, and the girls left the store, closely attended, as far as the door, by Mr. Emerson, who, amid a profusion of bows and smiles, bade them good morning.

"Now, Chris," said Bessie, "where shall we go to take dinner?"

The doctor's large, white house stood invitingly near, but Bessie declared her intention of dining with Mrs. O'Reilly; not because her house was an inn, for that was hardly remembered by the villagers, but, if the truth must be known, because Mrs. O'Reilly always could tell all the news; and Bessie, though a good-hearted girl in the main, was, in this respect, unlike the generality of her sex, in being the least bit in the world fond of gossip.

So she walked through the little garden, and entered, without knocking, Mrs. O'Reilly's kitchen. All was spotlessly clean there for the good lady was her own housemaid, and prided herself no little on her household skill.

There sat the mistress of the house herself, in a low rocking-chair, for her work was "done up" long since, and she was busily engaged in sewing.

She was a tall and rather stout woman, who, in her younger days, had made some pretensions to beauty. Even now, the widow bestowed a good deal of care on her personal appearance. Her thick, black hair was always neatly arranged, her dress always smart, and her eyes retained all their old sparkle and fire.

She greeted her visitors with great cordiality, and bustled about to take their bonnets and capes, which, having been accomplished, she threw open her parlor, and insisted on their walking in. It was not a large room, but it was as neat as the kitchen; for Mrs. O'Reilly was a sworn enemy to dirt in all its forms, and it was a boast of hers that any one might go from the top to the bottom of her house, on a voyage of discovery, and be unable to bring off even a tea-spoonful of dirt as a trophy. This room rejoiced in a carpet, which was the product of the widow's own loom; its wool had been sheared from her sheep, then spun, dyed, and woven into the fabric by her own hand. Stiff, green paper curtains shielded the windows, and rustled at every passing breeze.

The fireplace was filled with branches of evergreens, and tall, dried grasses, in tall vases, stood in the corner of the room. Two or three glass lamps served as mantel-ornaments, and a lounge, which was a specimen of Mrs. O'Reilly's powers in the upholstery line, and which did her credit, also; several cane-seat chairs, a table, and a looking-glass, the latter tastefully trimmed with green leaves, composed the furniture of the apartment.

Mrs. O'Reilly glanced at all around with no little pride, for her parlor was, in her opinion, extremely well-furnished; and, having seated herself and her guests to her satisfaction, she began to talk with great volubility.

Christine sat near the table, upon which laid one or two books, and she was soon too much engrossed in the contents of one, to heed the conversation going on. She was so entirely absorbed that she did not reply to one or two remarks which Mrs. O'Reilly addressed to her.

"Well, let her read," said her hostess, good-naturedly; "but, she beats all the gals I ever see for likin' books. How different folks is! Now, I couldn't be hired to sit down and read a book clean through to wunst, and she wouldn't like no better fun. Well, as I was sayin'," she went on, "it makes me as mad as a parched pea to hear Emerson, my dear and my darling his wife, before folks, when I know how ugly he is behind the curtain. She's too meek and quiet. If I only had him a week or two, I'd bring him into the traces. I'd make him stan' round; at any rate, we'd have a fight, and see who cum out best. I only wish I had him to manage a little while."

"I wish you had," replied Bessie, laughing; for she had an indistinct remembrance of having heard that, even in the lifetime of Mr. O'Reilly, his wife had held the reins of government.

"He's no more fit to be selectman than I be," said the widow, her broad, red face growing redder as she spoke, "and, if I could vote, I'd do my best to get him out of office. Did you hear how mean he served me about the post-office? You know I had been post-mistress always, after my poor, dear husband died, and never dreampt of being turned out. I don't believe there was a soul in the village that ever dreampt of it either, till that old skin-flint of an Emerson managed to get me out, and himself in. I wouldn't have cared so much for the money it brought in, for, thank goodness! I ain't beholden to post-offices for my livin'," continued the widow, drawing up her tall figure to its full height; "but, if you'll believe it, the mean, contemptible puppy actually had the impudence to say that the reason I mustn't keep it was because I peeked into the letters."

Her voice had gradually risen while she was speaking, and her eyes flashed fire. "What do you think of that?" she exclaimed.

"I shouldn't care," replied Bessie, soothingly. "Everybody at the Mills knows you," and, therefore, everybody believed Mr. Emerson, was her *mental* addition, which she wisely kept to herself. Ah, those little friendly *asides!*

But, of course, Mrs. O'Reilly would be the only one startled were they made public; or if *some* flat conversations, all propriety and made up of honeyed words, might suddenly be well-seasoned with the spice of truth, and it may be a little wickedness, could the unspoken thoughts that have flitted through the minds of each at once find utterance, of course, they are few in number. Talleyrand was a monster, indeed, to say that the use of language is to conceal one's thoughts![5] Of course, that principle, in everyday life, is rarely acted upon! Oh, no! The frank expression of our thoughts to each other, is the general rule, and any occasional departure from this, the exception.

"Care for old Emerson? Not the snap of my finger. He isn't worth talking about," replied Mrs. O'Reilly.

"Have you heard anything about the exhibition lately?" asked Bessie, quite willing to change the subject of conversation.

"Heard? I guess I have. It's nothing but exhibition from morning till night. I think it's perfectly ridiculous, too! It's shameful for people to encourage sech things. To think of actin' a play. I don't so much wonder at the young folks, for they can't be expected to have good judgment; but, when I see sech folks as Dr. Lewis, and Square Mercer, and the Preceptor, all in fur it, I must say I'm perfectly astonished. There's queer goin's on, I can tell ye; rehearsals and rehearsals!"

"But when is it to come off?"

"To-morrow night."

"Shan't you go?" asked Bessie.

"Oh, I may: I haven't quite made up my mind," was the reply; "but now it's getting towards dinner-time, and I must go out and see to it."

"Let me help you," said Bessie, and leaving Christine to her book, they were soon busily engaged together, Bessie setting the table handily, and talking as fast as ever of all the topics of interest at the Mills.

Suddenly, a carriage drove up to the door, and a lady alighted from it.

"Oh! Mrs. O'Reilly," exclaimed Bessie, who had been looking out of the window, "here is a stranger—a lady!"

"Oh, a traveller," replied that lady, in a very unconcerned tone, as if it was an every-day occurrence, though, in fact, she was as much surprised as Bessie.

She hastened to the door, and ushered the newcomer into the parlor, examining her, with one steady glance, from head to foot, and taking in her whole wardrobe at once.

A lady, every tone of her sweet, low voice, every gesture of her small, white hand, proclaimed her to be, and though her simple travelling costume, to Mrs. O'Reilly's unpractised eyes, did not appear suited to her position, yet she treated her, almost involuntarily, with great respect.

"Will you have your trunk taken to your room, ma'am?" asked the landlady.

"No. I imagine I am quite near my journey's end, and I do not wish any unnecessary delay."

This she said half to herself; then turning to Mrs. O'Reilly again, she asked: "Can you tell me, my good woman, the direction to Mr. John Elliot's house, and the distance there?"

"So you're goin' there, be you?" was the widow's truly Yankee reply.

The lady simply bowed in return.

"Well, now, if that haint queer! Why his gals is here this very day, and they are a goin' home right after dinner. Here's one on um," and she led the abashed Christine, who had dropped her book, and been gazing admiringly at the stranger, abruptly forward.

The lady said nothing, but gazed at the blushing, shrinking girl searchingly. Christine felt, to her very heart, that cold, keen penetrating glance, as if her whole system were laid bare before it.

"Her sister is in t'other room," continued Mrs. O'Reilly, and calling, "Bessie! Bessie!" she hastened to bring her forward also.

"So this is one of my nieces!" said the stranger, as the landlady disappeared, as if thinking aloud. "Perhaps you may have heard your father speak of your aunt Frothingham?"

"Oh, often! dear aunt!" Christine was on the point of crying out, enthusiastically, for though but little had ever been said of her, yet that little had been of a nature to make her aunt Frothingham an object of peculiar interest to Christine, and her father's beautiful sister had figured largely in her day-dreams.

She had hardly hoped ever to see her, yet how she had longed for it. She had been so confident that her aunt Julia would understand and love her that she had felt almost an insane desire to meet her. Now her wish was granted, and yet, like so many things ardently longed for, it brought with it only keen disappointment.

The chill that crept over her, as those bright, cold eyes surveyed her, effectually prevented her from making herself ridiculous by yielding to her first impulse, to spring to her aunt, wind her arms around her neck, and tell her how she had longed for this meeting. She knew, instinctively, that such an outburst would be most distasteful to the lady before her; that so far from understanding her, her aunt saw in her only an awkward, homely, country girl, with whose higher nature she could never feel the least sympathy, and whose wild imaginings would seem to her only a fit subject for ridicule. Christine's mind was a sealed book, and her aunt did not possess the power to open it. All these, and many similar thoughts, rushed through the girl's mind, as she stood silently and awkwardly before her newly found relative.

Mrs. Frothingham was, perhaps, equally disappointed, and, perhaps, did not relish the idea of an introduction to another niece of the same sort, for, as Mrs. O'Reilly reappeared, followed by Bessie, she said, rather impatiently turning from the glass, where she had been arranging her thick, clustering curls, "Pray, my good woman, is it not dinner-time? I am very hungry"; and, rather against her will, Mrs. O'Reilly, with unsatisfied curiosity, was forced to go back to the kitchen, leaving Bessie, smiling and blushing, to undergo the same scrutiny to which Christine had been subjected.

Evidently, Bessie made a more favorable impression, for Mrs. Frothingham stepped forward, and offered her hand kindly, saying, "Bessie, I am your aunt Julia."

In a moment, Bessie's arms were flung around her, and warm kisses were showered on her cheek.

"That will do, child—that will do!" exclaimed the lady, half surprised, half pleased, as she unwound the girl's clinging arms, and escaped from her embrace.

"Then it seems you have heard of me. Your sister, here, did not appear to know who I was, when I announced myself."

"Oh, father and mother often speak of you, dear auntie, and they will be so glad to see you. It is only two miles from here," Bessie went on, eagerly; "can't you go right on without waiting for anything?"

"Oh no, child, no! Don't starve me in your delight; after dinner, we will go as soon as possible. But now tell me, how is your father? Is he well?"

Bessie replied to these, and numerous inquiries, first drawing a chair close to her aunt, and taking her small and jewelled hand admiringly in her own.

Christine, silent and stiff, sat at a little distance, looking down if, by chance, Mrs. Frothingham's glance rested on her, though, whenever she felt that she was unnoticed, her eyes were fixed on her aunt's face.

She was certainly a very handsome woman. Her jet black hair curled naturally, and was arranged with much taste, so as to display the fine shape of her head, and not to hide the small, white ear. Her features were regular, her complexion dark, but clear, and her mouth, though rather too large, was redeemed from plainness by her white and well-shaped teeth, which she displayed frequently in her smiles. Her eyes were large and bright, and her whole countenance was animated and brilliant; but, notwithstanding her beauty, which was undeniable, for her figure was well-developed and symmetrical; and the little foot, in its brown gaiter, which peeped out from the folds of her dark dress, might almost have rivalled that celebrated one of Cinderella's; yet Christine felt that there was something wanting.

It was not grace, for every movement of her aunt was full of it; in short, her manner was one of her greatest charms. There was a sort of indolent repose, a quiet elegance, that pervaded her whole person, which seemed to leave nothing to be desired to add to her loveliness. Nor, could there have been any fault found with her face or figure; yet Christine saw, at once, that hers was the beauty of the outward alone, that soul was wanting there.

Intellect she might possess, but not heart; and, as we turn, disappointed, from a lovely flower on which Nature has bestowed every gift, but fragrance, so did Christine, with a sigh, end her protracted survey of the lovely woman before her.

She thought of all that she had heard of her aunt's history. She imagined her as she was, a young and artless country girl, who, in her simple beauty, had captivated the heart of the dashing man of the world, who had withstood the charms and graces of myriad belles.

She thought of her, placed by her husband, young, and all unused to the conventionalities of society, in the midst of his own circle, among his own high-bred and aristocratic family, who did not disguise their contempt of, and dislike to, his young wife.

Christine had heard that such had been her aunt's lot, and she had imagined her desolate, unhappy, and unappreciated. She had sympathized with her in her loneliness, and had longed to see her and cheer her in this, and the greater sorrow that had since come upon her, the death of her husband, leaving her alone, unshielded by him, without money and without friends; since, as Christine had imagined, her pride, lest her unhappiness should be discovered by the kind but ill-judging sympathy of her own relatives, had prevented her keeping up much knowledge of them; and his friends, no doubt, remained estranged from her.

But this romantic picture had no existence in reality. True, she had been at first regarded with contemptuous dislike by the family into which she had married; but Julia Frothingham was not so easily to be trampled upon. She had been a simple wild-flower, indeed, but, transplanted into the hot-bed of fashion, soon blossomed into more brilliant beauty than ever.

She knew that she was beautiful, and saw, also, that beauty was power; and, ere long, with well-disguised delight, as a leader of fashion, she saw her mother-in-law and sisters following, where she led the way. She was triumphant; what did she care that they hated her in their hearts?

So she queened it, to her heart's content, till her husband's death; then it was to be the turn of her relations to triumph, for they were wealthy, and she was poor, and must be dependent upon them. But, no, to their horror and disgust she determined to open a boarding-school, and had persevered. Her success here, also, had been wonderful. She had a large and flourishing school, admittance to which was eagerly sought for, since it had become, under her politic management, so fashionable that it was considered almost an essential requisite to a fashionable education to have *finished* at Mrs. Frothingham's.

Engrossed in her world, she had hardly bestowed a thought on her country brother, who alone was left of a once large family. But, of late, the thought of him had frequently obtruded itself upon her. He had always been her favorite brother. He had, in her childhood, been her constant playmate; in her girlhood, her unfailing friend. To him, she had confided all her hopes and fears before her marriage, and, in her widowhood, he had promptly, and with hearty warmth, offered her a home. He was still, to her, the brave and manly youth that she had seen him last, and all the affection of which she was capable, she lavished upon him.

So it had happened that she had yielded to the yearning that turned her steps to the old homestead, where her own childhood and youth had passed.

In the meantime, dinner was announced by Mrs. O'Reilly; and Bessie had, with no little pride, made known to the good woman that Mrs. Frothingham was her aunt; upon which that lady was at once besieged by questions, and overwhelmed with exclamations of wonder by the hostess, who had known Julia Elliot when she was a child.

Mrs. Frothingham's freezing dignity of manner affected her questioner no more than the wind that tossed her hair; and, finding that there was no other refuge than flight, Julia gladly availed herself of this, as soon as dinner was over; and, hardly had she gone from one door, accompanied by her nieces, than Mrs. O'Reilly was seen issuing from the other, tying her bonnet strings as she went; hurrying to impart to the neighbors the information that Julia Elliot had come to Amity—to wonder why she had never been before, since her marriage, and why she came now—together with any number of other equally important matters. In fact, ere two hours had passed, the history of Julia Frothingham, from her childhood up to the present time, had been canvassed by nearly everybody in town.

The ride to the homestead was rather a silent one. Christine would not, for the world, have intruded upon the reverie into which her aunt had fallen; and, fearful that Bessie would do so, she entered into a whispered conversation with her.

She imagined that she understood the feelings with which Julia again passed over the spots so familiar to her childhood, and so endeared to her by pleasant associations. She attributed to Julia all the crowding thoughts that filled her own dreamy mind, as she placed herself in imagination in her position, and felt for her acute anguish that the recollection of the lost lover of her youth must cause her.

Christine might have spared herself all this.

Mrs. Frothingham would have laughed her own right merry, silvery, and slightly sarcastic laugh, had she known what was passing in her niece's mind, and Christine would have been horrified had she known how little place the thoughts she had imagined held in her aunt's reverie.

It is well that we cannot see all that is passing in the breasts of each other. If we are sometimes misunderstood now, we should be as little known were our hidden feelings laid bare to general inspection.

Then, as now, the practical and poetical could never fully appreciate the qualities peculiar to each other, and if the wise arrangement, by which now each instinctively keeps those sentiments, which he feels would be distasteful to the other, in the background, should be annulled, many, who now imagine themselves friends, might be parted forever.

Then, as now, those who are congenial would be drawn together, but not as now would those whom slight bonds hold remain united.

A sudden turn in the road brought the low, brown farmhouse into view. Familiarity with the scene never destroyed the charm of the quiet landscape to Christine, and she would have been surprised had she realized that the plainness of the house made more of an impression on her aunt than the beauty of its situation.

They were greeted, on their arrival, with great cordiality. Mrs. Elliot ushered her sister-in-law into the *fore-room*, where the stiffly arranged furniture, and a certain something in the air, gave one an uncomfortable feeling, similar to that experienced by a mariner landing on an uninhabited island. In truth, that fore-room was almost an unknown land. Opened only on great occasions, for all practical purposes, it might as well have been dropped off from the house. When quite a young child, Christine had felt almost afraid of it, and, if obliged to pass through it, had always gone with suspended breath and quickened step, and now that the feeling of awe was lost, it was still a desolate and uninviting place to her.

Mrs. Frothingham had laid aside her bonnet and shawl in the little bedroom, which she knew, in old times, was the spare room, and now she anxiously asked for John.

Mrs. Elliot instantly seized the tin horn, and blew the accustomed summons, and ere long the sturdy form of the farmer was seen coming up the hill.

"He is coming!" said his wife, looking out of the window, and at the words the tide of worldliness, for a moment, flowed back from the submerged heart of the woman of fashion, as she sprang to meet her darling and only brother.

But her beaming smile, which, for a moment, supplied all that was wanting to her perfect beauty, died out, as the actual, rough-looking farmer took the place of the imaginary young and handsome brother, whom she had half expected to see. She had forgotten the lapse of years, and that time, which had touched her so lightly, united with hard labor, had made him prematurely old and grey.

He knew her instantly, but with him the time of romance, if it had ever existed, had long since passed, and his welcome, though cordial, was not what she had pictured it. It chilled her, and instantly she was the polished woman of the world again.

She smiled at herself for the solitary bit of romance that had yet lingered about her. It had been the one oasis in her desert heart, and now that had lost its freshness, and ere long would be entirely buried by the sands of time. Her eyes were opened, and she saw him as he was, sturdy, honest, and practical, rough, but none the less worthy of respect, well suited to his home, plain and simple as it was; and that home seemed less homelike every moment to her. Its low ceilings and small windows, its absence of draperies, its utter simplicity, made it seem dreary indeed, and she yawned at the bare idea of spending any length of time in such a place with no other society than that of her brother's family and those similar to it.

She answered with frankness John's inquiries as to her situation, and gave him the credit of being sincere in his expressions of pleasure that it was so prosperous. He, in turn, made known to her his purchases of land, explained to her what wood lots and pasture lands he had added to the old farm, and with no little exultation told her of his last year's harvests, and his prospects for the present. To all this, and to the troubles incident to farming, the weevil, the potato rot, the rust, and many others, she listened with polite attention, for this called into play one of the qualities which she had cultivated in society, the art of appearing interested in what was quite indifferent to her.

She only thought that John had grown very narrow-minded, but philosophically saying to herself, "We all change," she dismissed the subject from her mind.

At supper-time, she was secretly disgusted at being seated at table without a napkin, and with a two-pronged steel fork; but these were minor troubles compared with having around the same board the laborers of the farm; not only the sons of neighboring farmers, but really low and ignorant fellows, who plunged their own knives into the butter, their own teaspoons into the sugar, and helped themselves to any, or all, of the viands placed there, in the same primitive fashion. There was a natural dignity and propriety of manner about her brother and some of his laborers which would have prevented any of the grosser violations of etiquette, and it was all the more astonishing to Mrs. Frothingham that he could bear the want of it in others with such equanimity.

"I cannot stay here long," was her conclusion, "but, I will repay to John in part, now that it is in my power, his kindness to me."

So, after supper was over, sitting with John in the twilight, as she had done so many times when they were children, she began:

"You have two fine daughters, John."

He looked at her somewhat surprised, to see if she was sincere. The composure of her features was unruffled.

"Well, as to that," he replied, "they're well enough. Anybody can see which is the smartest; so, of course, it isn't worth while for me to try to hide it."

"Which?" asked his sister.

"Why, Bessie, of course."

"She is very pretty, and Christine is hopelessly plain," replied Julia, musingly: then, after a pause, she added, "They ought to be well-educated. You know what I mean, John. Something more is required, in these times, than when we were young; and, of course, they have no opportunity here. Now, if you are willing, I will take both of them to educate."

"Thank you, Julia; you mean well," replied Mr. Elliot, "but, still it would be all nonsense. They are a plain farmer's daughters; and, if they should go with you, and get their heads full of all sorts of notions, that may do very well for some girls, it would only disgust them with home and our plain way of living, just as it has you, Julia. They may go to school here—they may learn as much as they need; for women don't need to learn much to be good wives and mothers, and that will do for them."

"I don't agree with you, John," returned his sister.

"Of course not," interrupted Mr. Elliot; "I don't expect you to; but, my mind's made up. Besides, they don't want to go."

"Will you leave it to them?" asked Mrs. Frothingham, whom a little opposition only rendered more urgent to gain her cause.

Mr. Elliot glanced out of the window; there was his pretty Bessie coming towards the house, while James Cameron walked by her side, bearing two pails of milk foaming from the cows.

"Yes, ask Bessie," said the shrewd old man, pretty confident what her decision would be.

"Bessie, come here!" and the maiden obeyed the summons. As she stood there, her long, flaxen hair a little dishevelled by the night air, but only displaying more fully its golden abundance, her transparent complexion, bright, blue eyes, and mouth, dimpling into smiles, made her altogether, as her father thought, nor was he alone in his opinion, the prettiest girl in the country. Christine had followed her; and a more striking contrast could hardly have been found, than she presented.

Her form lacked the roundness that gave to Bessie's fresh and youthful figure its charm. Her dark, gleaming eyes, the only redeeming feature in her face, were deep-set, and thus gave a hollow expression to her countenance. Her sallow complexion never deepened into a tinge of color; and there was a sad, eager expression on her whole face, when it settled into quiet, that was far from pleasing. She slipped into a chair, near the door, to feast her eyes on the beauty of her aunt's countenance, which pleased her as any beauty did.

"Bessie," said her father, "your aunt says she'll take you to her school, and educate you; but, I tell her that it isn't worth while, to unfit you girls for your true position in life; that you had rather stay to home with your father and mother, to help them along, now that they are going down the hill of life, and never leave them, without it's to go to homes of your own. Now, wan't I right?"

"Stop, Bessie," said her aunt, as she was about to reply. "Had you not rather leave home for awhile, to be educated—to learn how to live—to have your mind expanded and cultivated—than to go on in a quiet, humdrum way all your life? It would not be deserting your father or mother, or neglecting your duty to them—it would only be performing a duty to yourself, that of cultivation."

"Fiddle-stick!" exclaimed the farmer. "Walk in, James!" to the young man who stood in the door. "Bessie, my child, decide."

"Decide for yourself!" interposed Mrs. Frothingham.

Bessie was about to speak, when suddenly her glance rested on Christine, who, with parted lips, eager eyes, and hands convulsively clasped together, was looking at her with an intensity of anxiety that went to her sister's heart.

"Father, I do not want to go, but, do let Christine. Do let her, dear father," she continued, leaning her cheek, caressingly, against his brow, and smoothing his thin locks with her soft hand. "Aunt Julia, I should never learn much. I don't like it, to tell the truth, but Christine loves books, oh, so dearly! Let her go!"

"Certainly," said Mrs. Frothingham, coldly, "if you consent, John."

"I will see," he replied; and, in an agony of hope and fear, for in no other way can Christine's state of mind be described, she passed a wakeful night, for to-morrow would be a crisis in her fate.

CHAPTER THREE

The Exhibition

The workmen had long before finished their breakfasts and gone to the hay-field, when Mrs. Frothingham entered the kitchen, which also served as dining-room; for Mrs. Elliot, well knowing that her usual breakfast hour would seem unreasonably early to her guest, had allowed her to sleep quietly on, and now had prepared a second meal.

Christine had been out to gather strawberries for her aunt, and their rich scarlet hue contrasted well with the snowy table-cloth. The nicest of cream biscuit smoked there, and there, too, was the sweetest of butter; coffee that had exhausted Mrs. Elliot's skill, and many other dainties—in fact, everything that could tempt a delicate appetite.

Mrs. Frothingham was dressed in a white muslin wrapper, which, confined at the waist, flowed back, displaying a skirt elegantly embroidered; her little foot was encased in the prettiest of toilet slippers, and her hair was half-hidden, half-revealed under a light breakfast-cap; on no occasion did she neglect her toilet, and now, as ever, she looked the very impersonation of delicacy and refinement, and about as much in place in that lowly kitchen as a tiara of pearls would have done on her good sister-in-law's slightly disordered tresses.

Christine undertook the task of serving her aunt, but often forgot to discharge her duties, so absorbed was she in admiration of her beautiful relative.

Mrs. Frothingham was not slow to perceive the impression her beauty had produced on her niece, nor was she insensible to this unintentional flattery. It somewhat softened her feelings towards the girl, and made the idea of taking her home with her, rather more palatable.

"Well, Christine," she said, "are you going back with me?"

Her tone was kind, and, with less embarrassment than usual, the girl replied, "I don't know, but I hope so."

Her voice was sweet and clear, and this pleased her aunt's fastidious taste.

"I may make something of her yet," she thought. "At any rate, she shall go."

"Miranda," she said, turning to her sister-in-law, who stood near, "are you not willing to let me take Christine under my charge for awhile?"

"Well, yes," replied Mrs. Elliot, "as I was telling John last night, she isn't good for much to home, for she never was handy at anything; but she's a pretty good girl after all," she went on, for once in her life, observing the tears that rushed to her daughter's eyes, "and if she could be qualified for a teacher, she might do well. So John and I concluded that if you would let her pay for her tuition after awhile, by teaching in your school, she might go; otherwise she can't, for John says he won't be beholden to anybody, if it is his sister, though we're both jist as much obliged to you."

"Very well," replied Mrs. Frothingham, "that need be no objection. If she proves capable, I shall be only too glad of her services as teacher. So we will consider it settled. She is to go."

Christine's eyes flashed with wild delight; she sprang to the door, for she could no longer control herself, and flying up stairs to her sanctuary, the unfinished chamber, she exclaimed, "I am going! I am going!" as if the old room, which had witnessed her sorrow and loneliness so often in the past, had been a living thing, and could sympathize now with her in her present happiness.

So delighted was she that she had, in this far greater pleasure, quite forgotten that which was in store for her on that very evening—the exhibition at the Academy. She was reminded of it, ere long, by Bessie, who came to tell her how glad she was that her sister's long cherished desire to go to school was to be gratified, and to talk over, also, the evening's entertainment.

A play neither had ever seen. Christine, indeed, had read all of Shakespeare's, which she had borrowed of the doctor. She had laughed and wept, by turns, as she had pored over those wonderful volumes; but though she knew that they were sometimes acted, she had but a vague idea of the manner in which it was done.

"Everything comes together, don't it, Bessie, dear?" said Christine. "I should have thought it was enough to go to the exhibition, and yet I am going with Aunt Julia, too. It is almost too much. I can hardly believe that I really am going."

Bessie replied kindly, and though, in her heart, she feared that her sister's pleasure would not be so great as she anticipated, she forbore to damp her joy by any of her own forebodings.

The day passed swiftly away, and at the appointed hour, James Cameron drove up to the door with his wagon, ready for its load.

Mrs. Frothingham had accepted their invitation to accompany them, and with Bessie and James occupied the only seat, while Christine sat behind on a cricket. All were in the best possible spirits, and merry laughter filled the air, as they drove slowly down the road to the Mills.

The Academy was brightly lighted, and crowds of villagers were already on their way thither, as our party alighted from the wagon, leaving James to tie his horse to the fence, at a little distance, where a great many other horses, attached to all manner of vehicles, were already fastened.

The entrance of Mrs. Frothingham created quite a sensation, but the whispered remarks on her dress and appearance were interrupted by a twitch of the green baize curtain, which hung down, concealing the stage from view.

It rose slowly, and displayed a wide platform which had been built over the dais where the preceptor usually sat; the walls and sides that bounded this were tastefully draped with cambric, which the imagination of the audience was expected to invest with the various scenery appropriate to the different occasions.

There was breathless silence in the assembly, and all gazed fixedly on the fair young daughter of the lawyer, who, in the person of Elvira, lay, in a graceful attitude, on a couch. Very pretty she looked in her white dress, the color coming and going in her cheek, as she felt, rather than saw, the gaze of so large an assembly. Valverde's entrance, a tall and not particularly graceful youth, however, somewhat relieved her, and though she forgot to rise at the proper time, and her voice, at first, was quite inaudible, in a few moments she so far recovered herself as to speak distinctly, though it was evident that she was thinking more of saying her part correctly than of putting any emotion into her words.

Valverde amply made up for any deficiencies in this line. He shouted his part at the top of his voice, and his exclamation, "Hear me, Elvira!" was given in a tone, and with an attitude, as if he had been addressing an army about to give battle.

It was evident that he had made what, in theatrical parlance, would be called "a decided hit"; and not even Pizarro, on his entrance, dressed in the brilliant uniform of Squire Mercer, which had seen service in the general muster field, where that worthy soldier had distinguished himself as one of the *aids*, could entirely overshadow the glory of the fortunate Valverde.

Pizarro's voice was equally loud as that of his secretary, and, like him, he so roared out every remark he made that ere long he became quite hoarse from his exertions. He paced up and down on the stage, as if he had been walking on a wager against time; he swung his arms and rattled his sword to such a degree that the audience were fairly electrified. So fierce was he that Christine actually trembled when the captive Orozembo was dragged in; and, though she admired, she half wondered at his boldness in braving the tyrant to his face.

Cora, Rolla, and Alonzo, each had their full share of admiration; in fact, never did a company play to a more indulgent or *appreciative* (which means the same thing) audience. Each of the players had his circle of friends and admirers present; and, if Cora did occasionally forget her speech, Alonzo was so obliging as to reply to what she *ought* to have said, and there was no unnecessary delay.

The play had been condensed by the actors, partly from the lack of performers to enact subordinate parts; for, though there had been a great supply of volunteers for Alonzo, Pizarro, and Rolla, there had been an equal scarcity of soldiers and other subordinates, and the transitions from one scene to another were, therefore, necessarily abrupt; but the scenes which were given were so powerfully rendered that they certainly overbalanced any minor defects.

Cora's anguish, indeed, was quite overpowering. She had forgotten, it is true, all that she ought to have said, and would have been placed in an awkward position, had it not suddenly occurred to her to faint away, a phase in her agony for which her fellow-performers were as unprepared as the audience; and their consequent perturbation was certainly the most natural part of the play, and caused that scene, also, to be universally admired.

Rolla's death struggles were truly frightful to behold. Many such death scenes would have exhausted him in reality. He rolled over and over—he groaned deep, unearthly groans—he

waved his arms wildly—and, in short, prolonged his dying ag-
onies to a most unmerciful length of time. It was evident that
he felt that this was his final appearance, and he was resolved
to make the most of his last gasp.

He did at last subside into comparative quiet; but it is uncertain whether he had decided to die even then, for before he had
time to commence another convulsion, the curtain fell.

So ended the great exhibition, which had served for food
for conversation for weeks previous, and did so for weeks to
come.

After the first burst of admiration was over came the reaction, as is usual in all such cases of rapturous delight. Mothers rejoiced that their daughters had not been engaged in such
a public affair, and poor Cora and Elvira were universally pronounced bold. It was discovered that nearly every lady in the village had, all the while, considered it highly improper, and would
on no account have allowed her daughter to take part in it. It
was also stated that the majority of the young men attending
the academy could not have been induced to have made such
fools of themselves as to have personated Rolla and Pizarro.
On the other hand, statements were made by the actors which
went to prove quite the contrary; and so great was the excitement that the exhibition on which the preceptor had counted
so much to increase the popularity of his school, bid fair to
have an entirely different effect. He received letters from the
trustees, requesting explanations.

He explained, reasoned, persuaded, and was at last only too
glad to have the subject dropped entirely, with the assurance
that as it was the first, so it should be the last exhibition of the
sort, under his administration, at least.

Of all these civil troubles, Farmer Elliot's family knew but
little. They were too far removed from the village to enter with
great zest into the topics of the day; and, just now, too, in addition to the duties of the farm, Christine was going away.

She had never been a personage of so much importance before, nor was she destined to remain so long.

Her wardrobe was very speedily got in order, and, with her aunt, she started on her first journey. How much she enjoyed her sail in the steamboat. How delightful it was to pass down the beautiful river, looking at the scenery in quiet, left to her own thoughts—for Mrs. Frothingham sat by, reading a new book. Christine wondered at her calmness, for she herself was in a rapturous state of excitement. All was so new to her, and all was to be so delightful in her new situation, that she felt perfectly happy.

The change from the steamboat to the cars at last, which was necessary to be made, aroused her aunt; and they were soon whirling along towards her new home.[6]

If she had enjoyed the quiet gliding of the steamboat, the rapid, exhilarating motion of the cars suited still better her eager and restless mood. It seemed to her almost as if she was flying, like Sinbad, on the roc's back, as she caught now a glimpse of rocks—now of smooth fields—and again of pleasant villages—in her rapid course.[7]

"We are near our journey's end, Christine," said her aunt. "I am glad enough. It is so terribly tedious to travel—a day actually seems as long as a week."

Christine made no reply, for she could not sympathize at all with the remark. To her, it seemed one of the greatest pleasures imaginable, to be able to go over the world when and where she chose.

CHAPTER FOUR

Woodland Vale

It was at the close of a pleasant day that Christine and her aunt reached Woodland Vale, where was situated Mrs. Frothingham's school.[8] It was not a large town, and she seemed to be well known as a personage of distinction, by the crowd of loiterers around the depot. They made way for her respectfully, as she entered her carriage, leaving her servant to attend to her baggage. It was a plain but elegant vehicle, displaying, as did everything else about its owner, her good taste.

A short ride brought them to the Seminary, a large, stone building, surrounded by extensive grounds, tastefully laid out, while tall trees were scattered around, singly or in small clumps, giving an air of naturalness to the grounds, which would else have seemed too artificial.

Mrs. Frothingham was met at the door by the housekeeper, a tall and stately personage, who greeted her mistress with great respect, and looked at the plainly dressed Christine with no little surprise.

"This is my niece, Miss Christine Elliot, Mrs. Rogers," said Mrs. Frothingham. "Have you a room in readiness for her?"

"I will have one in a few moments, ma'am," replied Mrs. Rogers, ushering Christine into a small but elegantly furnished apartment, called the reception-room.

Christine had never seen anything so beautiful, yet all was plain, though rich, there. Her foot sank into the soft carpet, whose deep, rich colors harmonized well with the heavy green curtains which shaded the bay-windows, where soft lace drapery also fell. A small marble table stood in the centre of the room, directly under a chandelier, and a large mirror, opposite the door, reflected the quaint-looking chairs, with their straight and carved backs, so perfectly that, at first, Christine took it to be the entrance into another apartment, and had been startled to perceive a stranger girl there.

"Oh, how beautiful it is!" was her thought, as she contrasted all around her with her own plainly furnished home, and it seemed to her that, in so lovely a spot, it would be impossible to be otherwise than happy.

She had yet to learn that happiness is wholly unaffected by externals.

She had sunk back on a luxurious lounge, half closing her eyes, and giving herself up to a sort of passive enjoyment, when Mrs. Rogers reappeared.

"I will show you your chamber, Miss," she said; and Christine followed her through a tessellated hall, whose lofty walls and her own echoing footsteps reminded her of palaces of which she had read. Up a winding stairway she followed her guide through another hall to a chamber, whose door stood open. She entered it and was again alone.

"Can this be mine?" was her delighted thought, as she glanced at the furniture of pale blue and gilt, the pretty chairs, the low bedstead, the bright carpet, and best of all, a small bookcase containing a few books.

The chamber was, indeed, very prettily, though simply, furnished, but to Christine's inexperienced eyes it was magnificent indeed.

From the window she gazed with new delight, for it commanded a fine view of the grounds around the building, and the sunset clouds of crimson and gold, in all their gorgeous and ever-changing beauty, were outspread before her.

She had stood there for a long while, all unconscious of the lapse of time, when a light rap was heard at her door, and her aunt entered. She was dressed in a bright blue silk; she wore also a delicate lace stomacher, and undersleeves of the same rich material.[9] Her whole attire was tasteful and becoming in the extreme, and if she had been in doubt as to her taste, Christine's glance of admiration might have satisfied a more exacting artist.

"What, Christine! your dress not yet changed?" she said, in a tone of surprise.

"I forgot, dear aunt," was Christine's timid reply. "It was so beautiful here that I did not realize how late it was."

"I dislike dilatoriness exceedingly," was Mrs. Frothingham's answer. "The tea-bell will soon ring, so pray proceed at once to change your dress."

Fortunately Christine was not detained by doubts as to which dress she should put on. She had but one best dress, her pink calico, which she quietly assumed, and in a few moments she was ready to accompany her aunt, who had been waiting for her to complete her toilet.

She glanced at her niece, and, merely saying, "We will soon remedy all that," led the way to another apartment, a large drawing-room.

Here, too, was everything that a luxurious taste could desire. Over all the elegant trifles there, Christine cast one hurried glance and hastened to gaze at the paintings with which the walls were hung.

"Oh, how lovely!" she exclaimed, pausing before a landscape, whose quiet beauty reminded her most forcibly of her own home. But before the next, Mariana, she held her breath with an emotion, half pleasure, half pain.[10] That beautiful, hopeless face—weary with hope deferred! Its expression went to her heart. She knew, even before its name was given, the history of that lovely woman. She had felt too keenly the unrest and eager longing depicted there, not to sympathize deeply with this in another, and gazing there, she forgot that it was but a painting, and tears rushed to her eyes.

She was recalled from her reverie by a sweet and plaintive melody. Mrs. Frothingham had seated herself at the piano, and touched its keys with a master hand. The music, the painting on which she had gazed so long, the stillness of the hour combined, had raised Christine to the highest pitch of excitement. She could bear it no longer, but flung herself on a couch, while tears that she could not restrain, and whose cause she would have been unable to tell, flowed fast over her cheeks. She wept on noiselessly, with a blissful sense of relief, when suddenly the tea-bell rang, and her aunt called to her to come into the dining-room. Ashamed of her tear-stained face, she obeyed.

"Bless me! What have we here!" exclaimed Mrs. Frothingham, in a tone of annoyance, as she glanced at the girl in the bright light. "For mercy's sake, what are you crying about? Are you home-sick?"

"No."

"Then, what in the name of common sense is the matter?"

"I don't know," murmured Christine.

"Nonsensical! You must know. What was it that made you cry? Speak—I must be told."

Her tone was imperative, and Christine replied, simply, "I think it was your music, Aunt Julia."

Mrs. Frothingham shrugged her shoulders. "More nonsensical still," was her impatient reply.

She said nothing more till they were about leaving the table, then she suddenly turned to her niece, and went on—

"Christine, there is nothing that I dislike more than affectation, and the affectation of sentimentality is certainly one of the most disgusting phases of that odious trait. I see a tendency to that in you, and must insist on your correcting it at once. Let me see no more of it."

"Indeed, Aunt Julia," began the girl, with eyes again swimming with tears; but Mrs. Frothingham interrupted her—

"There is no occasion for any display of your temper. That I certainly shall not permit. Control yourself at once, or retire to your room."

Christine was accustomed to self-control. She repressed the sobs that were ready to burst forth; and with a mingled feeling of sadness and awe, gazed on her aunt.

Was it possible that her sweet lips could syllable such cold, stern words? Could she, so delicate and beautiful, be harsh?

"It must be because I am so unprepossessing," was her thought. "Nobody can love me—nobody can understand me."

With deep humility, Christine returned to the parlor, and with a sad feeling of loneliness, she sat there once more, reserved and silent.

Mrs. Frothingham flung herself on a couch with a book in her hand; but, though she appeared to be reading, she was intently studying Christine's face. She prided herself on her penetration in reading character, but this time she was at fault. Sulky she pronounced her, as she gazed on the sad face and downcast eyes of the girl before her, and, with a vague feeling of dislike, she turned again to her book.

"Why was I so foolish as to plague myself with her?" she asked herself: "An ignorant, silly, ill-tempered, and awkward girl. Well, I have done it, and must make the best of it," was her mental reply.

"Christine, what are you in such a brown study about?" she said, aloud.

"Nothing," replied Christine, timidly, for she had seen enough of telling her real thoughts; nothing should tempt her to do that again.

"Pshaw!" said Mrs. Frothingham. "I detest equivocation—but, I might have known better than to ask such a question. I see you have not quite recovered your temper. I hope a night's sleep will restore you to your usual sweetness, at least."

"We shall have a good deal to do to-morrow," she resumed, after a silence which Christine did not venture to break. "You must go to town and get some dresses, to make you presentable before school commences. The vacation is now nearly over, and you have no time to spare. I should advise you now to retire; Mrs. Rogers may conduct you again to your room, or do you think that you remember where it is?"

"I can find it, I think," replied Christine, rising and approaching the door. She hesitated, turned back, and stopped again.

"What now?" said Mrs. Frothingham, coldly.

"Please forgive me!" exclaimed Christine, impetuously. "I am so sorry to have offended you."

"You can best prove your sorrow by avoiding a repetition of your offence," replied Mrs. Frothingham. "Certainly, I forgive you. Good-night."

"Good-night," said Christine, as, with eyes dim with tears, and heart swelling with sorrow at this cold reception of her advances, she sought her chamber. By turns angry with herself and again with her aunt, she lay weeping on her couch. She had imagined that, placed in a different position, she should be better understood, and, therefore, happier; but now she felt confident that this had been a delusive hope. She must still repress the expression of her thoughts, still go on wearily and unhappily, perhaps, her life long. Her heart rebelled at this, and, as of old, she angrily asked, "Why was I made so unlovely? So different from Bessie—from all the world? I will not try to improve," she bitterly thought. "God made me hateful, and as he has made me, so let me remain. It is no fault of mine."

With such, and still wilder and more bitter thoughts, she fell asleep.

She awoke the next morning with an indistinct recollection of some painful event which had happened to her, and as she dressed herself, and recalled her yesterday's experience, she resolved on a line of conduct for the future.

"I will treat my aunt respectfully, but with coldness equal to her own. I will trouble her with no expressions of love, or, in fact, of any other emotion. I will do as poor Bessie used to advise me, *appear* at least like other people; but, thank heaven, my thoughts are my own. So that I keep them to myself she has no right to interfere."

Quietly Christine bade her aunt good morning, and forced herself to reply, with outward politeness, to the remarks addressed to her.

Mrs. Frothingham contrasted the calm exterior of her niece with the stormy outbursts of the previous night, and congratulated herself on the improvement visible in her. "I can mould her as I choose," she said to herself, little dreaming that on the night before she had been as the softened steel, easily to be moulded, and that now this calm manner betokened only a return to such hardness that she would more easily break than bend.

Breakfast over, they prepared for a visit to the city.

Mrs. Frothingham, before starting, charged Christine not to exhibit any of her half-savage delight and astonishment at what she might see. A flash of the eye was all her reply, as they left the house.

No fashionable lady could have shown more indifference than did Christine, as they entered shop after shop making the various purchases. She allowed her aunt to decide what she would buy without a word, and followed her mechanically from counter to counter. The knowledge that all these articles were bought for her did not soften her in the least towards her aunt.

"It is her own selfish pride that prompts it," she said to herself; "why should I be grateful for it? Besides," she added, bitterly, "to be grateful is to be sentimental, which I must avoid."

They next went to a dressmaker, who held a long consultation with Mrs. Frothingham, and proceeded to fit Christine, who stood as passive as ever. At last, all was done, and they returned to Woodland Vale.

"I hope you are satisfied with your wardrobe," said Mrs. Frothingham.

"It is very handsome," replied Christine, "and I am much obliged to you."

The tone was as cold as Julia's, but the words were proper, and Mrs. Frothingham was satisfied. She was more than that, she was pleased, for Christine was growing quiet and lady-like.

CHAPTER FIVE

School-Life

It was the morning on which the term commenced. For several days past, one or two pupils, from a long distance, had arrived at the seminary and now a whole bevy of girls, from sixteen to eighteen years of age, assembled at Mrs. Frothingham's.

With what stately grace she welcomed them; it was more like the reception of a queen than an interview between teacher and pupil. Many a fair girl envied her the graceful inclination of the head, and the quiet elegance of her manners, and not even the haughtiest scion of a haughty family ventured to assume any airs in her presence.

All was decorous and quiet in the house, for noise of any kind was as sedulously guarded against as if it had been a crime. Mrs. Rogers was, in her way, as good a manager as Mrs. Frothingham herself, whose manners she aped so far as a naturally high and fierce temper could allow her to do so. She ruled with a rod of iron over the domestics, and in this department Mrs. Frothingham never interfered, satisfied, so that all went well, she never checked the exercise of her authority.

Mrs. Frothingham, herself, taught nothing.

She had a full corps of teachers, whom, as well as her pupils, it was her province to oversee—and she discharged her duties admirably. Nothing escaped her eye, and nothing could prevent her setting right whatever was amiss. She was never severe, yet nothing was dreaded more than a summons to her private parlor.

What transpired in that room was never made public, and the mystery that shrouded it made it more dreaded than any publicity could have done.

Mrs. Frothingham's *soirées*, which occurred once a fortnight, were also a peculiar feature of her establishment. They were attended by all the *élite* in the town, and by them alone, so that a card of invitation was as eagerly sought by a lady of doubtful position, who was making that desperate struggle to get into "the first society," as is a raft by a drowning man. The girls of the higher classes were always present on these occasions, unless some misdemeanor had caused them to forfeit their right of appearing there and no one knew better than did Mrs. Frothingham how to make a party pass off well.

Her pupils were allowed to mingle freely with the opposite sex on these occasions, but her Argus eye was upon them, and as assiduously as their own mothers could have done, did she watch the progress of a flirtation, ready to check it at any time, did it degenerate into regular love-making, or did it seem not just an eligible match.[11]

Matches were not frequent at Mrs. Frothingham's, and the few which had been kindled there had been entirely satisfactory to the friends on both sides, and though it of course increased her cares, she preferred keeping up her soirées as they were one great secret of her popularity.

"Any one can tell Mrs. Frothingham's graduates," said the mothers, "their manners are so perfect when they enter society. They do not appear like novices, but as if they had been accustomed to it their whole lives."

And why should they not? For *society* they were fitted. To shine in the circles of fashion was the end and aim of their education and ambition. For that end, they jabbered French, sang Italian, played the piano, harp, or guitar, and danced every imaginable figure.

By degrees, Christine began to be accustomed to the novel ways of her aunt's household. She had actually arrived at the point of acquitting herself with credit at the table, where, at first, she had betrayed utter ignorance of the use of finger-bowls and nut-pickers, and had also been quite forgetful that napkins were intended for use, not ornament.

In these matters, she had been drilled before the arrival of the pupils, and had now only to be glanced at by her aunt's vigilant eye, to remember and put in practice all that was required of her.

In school, too, there was the most rigorous attention paid to propriety of manner. A careless or awkward attitude was more severely reprimanded than a failure in a lesson, and here poor Christine found herself most frequently at fault. Engrossed in her studies she would bend over her book, till, too weary to remain in that position, she would lean back carelessly to rest herself, forgetting that there was such a thing as grace, till reminded, by the sharp voice of Miss Blanchette, that "Miss Elliot was forgetting herself."

She began soon to take dancing lessons, and here her awkwardness was more than ever conspicuous.

Monsieur Chapparel shrugged his shoulders when he glanced at her standing stiffly before him.

"*Mon Dieu!*" he exclaimed, when he saw her graceless attempt to take the first steps; and her consciousness that she was not only awkward, but that thirty pairs of eyes were fixed upon her, and that she was an object of ridicule to those same thirty owners of visual organs, only increased her embarrassment and stupidity. She was at last given up by the Professor, with an impatient charge to practice in her own apartment, and sitting down at one end of the long hall, she looked on with a mingled feeling of envy and disgust at the dancers there.

She was extremely unhappy, for painfully sensitive to ridicule, which she was too proud to show, she hated herself and all around her. "Better that I had remained in my own home," she thought, "than to come here to be despised."

Tears rushed to her eyes, for she felt that she was unnoticed, and might allow them to fall. She held her handkerchief to her eyes and wept quietly, and, as she supposed, unobserved. At length she ceased to weep, and glanced again at the gay girls who were circling round and round the room, to the delight of their teacher.

A couple came close by Christine, and one exclaimed, "Let me stop! I must tie my slipper-lacing; it is broken. Take some other partner!" and she sank on the bench where Christine was sitting.

"Ah, Miss Elliot," she said, "you are resting, too, I perceive."

"I have not been dancing," was Christine's reply.

"Not dancing! You don't like it, perhaps."

"I don't know anything about it," answered Christine. "This is my first lesson, and if I can judge anything from that, I detest it and the sound of a violin even."

Her companion threw back a cloud of flaxen curls that had fallen over her face as she bent over to fasten her lacing, which, after all, was not broken, and laughed a right merry laugh.

"Ah, Miss Elliot," she said, "it won't be long before you tell me that there is nothing in the world so delightful as dancing. Look now, at Terese Vaughan waltzing with Monsieur Chapparel—is she not lovely? How graceful she is!"

"But I am so stupid," sighed Christine, "I shall never learn. I feel so awkward hopping and standing on one foot, and drawing up the other, and all that sort of thing. I can never do it before such a host."

"Oh, I know all about that," replied the girl. "I have been through it all, and, if you wouldn't be offended, I think I could help you to take the steps in your own room."

"Will you, indeed? How kind!" exclaimed Christine.

"I will come after tea, to-night, shall I?"

"Yes, if you will."

"And now, before I go, for that sweet polka is altogether too fascinating to be resisted, and I must go and find a partner to dance with, let me introduce myself to you. You haven't an idea who I am, I know, now have you?"

"No," replied Christine, simply.

Her companion laughed.

"'I have not that honor,' you should have said, Miss Elliot, but I'll excuse you. In fact, this whole interview has been far from being according to rule. I should have said, 'Miss Elliot?' in an inquiring tone, on which you should have graciously inclined your head. I should then have said, 'Miss Annie Murray,' on which you should have taken my offered hand, and assured Miss Murray of the pleasure it gave you to make her acquaintance, &c., &c. Then we should have talked of the weather, the dancers, &c.; but, alas, we cannot remedy the past. Goodbye," and with a smile and wave of the hand, Annie Murray had joined the dancers.

Christine watched her slight figure, as she whirled around the room, with no little interest. She was extremely graceful, and was by no means the least attractive in the room. There were others there far handsomer, but there was a certain something about Annie that involuntarily attracted and fixed one's attention. Not one of her features, in itself, was beautiful, but she was generally allowed by all to be very pretty, nevertheless. Her complexion was, indeed, uncommonly clear, her eyes bright, her smile sweet and frank, and her manners easy, graceful, and entirely unaffected.

This freedom from affectation might have been her chief charm, for it could not be claimed for many of Mrs. Frothingham's pupils, who displayed every variety, from that of listless languor, to hauteur and coldness.

The polka was over, and Annie chatted gaily with many of her schoolmates. She did not again approach Christine until the close of the lesson, when, as she passed her, on her way to her room, she said, with her bright smile, "After tea, in your room. Remember!"

After tea, her light rap was heard, and she entered Christine's chamber.

"Are you ready, mademoiselle?" she said, gravely throwing herself into an easy-chair. "If so, proceed."

Christine hesitated.

"Proceed!" repeated Annie, with an impatient tap of her foot, and her pupil obeyed. It was done but very awkwardly. Her teacher could hardly repress a smile. "Very well!" she said. "Again!"—and, somewhat encouraged by her fancied success, this time Christine really did better.

"Bravo!" cried Annie, keeping her pupil unmercifully going over and over the steps, until she really had learned them perfectly.

"That will do, my dear Miss Christine," she said, at last. "Who knows but that you will be one day a celebrated danseuse. If so, pray remember your old teacher, Annie Murray. I shall expect a large reward for my services, particularly as I mean to keep on with my lessons, that is, till I get tired of teaching. And, now, I'll just look over your possessions as my pay for the first lesson. I shall take my pay as I go, you see."

Christine laughed and took her seat, watching Annie as she opened the closet and examined her dresses, commenting on them as she did so. "Very good taste displayed in your wardrobe, Miss Elliot, but allow me to say that you needn't feel very much complimented, for I haven't an idea that you selected it; and now for your bureau," she said, approaching it and opening a drawer.

"Oh, fie! fie! Does this belong to a young lady?" she said, imitating Miss Blanchette's voice exactly. "It is a perfect chaos—brushes, laces, books, pens, paper, slippers, &c., &c. Miss Elliot will please remedy this, before my next call. And now, just tell me something about yourself," she said, resuming her natural voice and manner, "for, do you know, I like you, and am determined that you shall like me in return."

"I have nothing to tell," replied Christine, "except that I have always lived at home, in the country, till my aunt brought me here to be educated."

"Well, that is too provoking," returned Annie. "Here I had made up my mind to listen to an extremely interesting story, for somehow I imagined that there was something marvellous and mysterious about you. But, it can't be helped, and you are not to blame, I suppose, for it; so I will keep on liking you, and still give you dancing lessons."

Christine said nothing.

"Why don't you ask me my history, now?" said Annie, turning to her companion.

"I didn't think of it," was the reply.

"In other words, you didn't care. That's flattering, to be sure. Nevertheless, you shall hear it. I am the only daughter of a wealthy gentleman in New York, where I was born and bred; and, as I am a city product, I know the country only by reputation. That there is such a place, I devoutly believe, as I believe in Russia. I have never seen it, though; for I don't call sailing past country-seats and villages on our way to the springs, or visiting fashionable sea-side resorts, going into the country, though ma does. No, I've been to springs and watering-places, and such affairs, but, as to the country, as I told you, I display faith of the purest sort, that without sight. I have an idea that it is very charming to live in the country, is it not?"

"It is beautiful," replied Christine, "but I was glad to leave it. Everybody likes change, I think," she added, musingly, while her deep eyes assumed that abstracted, earnest gaze so common to them, for she was thinking how she had longed for change, and how little happiness it had brought her.

Annie Murray sat looking intently at Christine; she evidently puzzled and amused her.

"Miss Elliot, you are getting tired of my agreeable company," she said, at last. "But, no, the truth is, you had forgotten that you were enjoying that pleasure. Never mind—no apologies; though, in fact, I don't believe you thought of making any. I shall certainly do myself the honor of calling again, for I don't doubt you will be happy to see me, though you haven't said so. Adieu, Miss Elliot, adieu," and, with a graceful curtsey, and "don't forget that chaotic drawer," Annie Murray left her happier than she had been for many a day. She felt that in her she had really gained a friend; and it was a very pleasant thought.

CHAPTER SIX

Tried and Sentenced

A year had passed, and rapidly to Christine, who plunged into her studies with a zeal and earnestness that bid fair to place her in the front rank of the pupils, and to outstrip all competitors, notwithstanding her former disadvantages. She had, for a long time, continued the private dancing lessons, under Annie Murray's tuition; and her teacher's cheerful, merry ways, and constant kindness, had quite won her heart. Aside from Annie, she had not made many friends, for she was reserved and made no advances, and her quiet, retiring manners did not attract many towards her.

But, Annie she really loved. She was never weary of performing tasks for her, such as the writing of exercises, doing of sums, and the like, for Annie was far from being a good scholar.

It was late in the evening, but Christine still bent over her books, quite engrossed in the solution of a mathematical problem. Suddenly, the sound of the hall clock striking ten aroused her; and, hastily putting aside her books, she prepared to obey the bell, which rung out its quick peals, the signal for retiring.

There was a slight tap at the door, and softly it opened, admitting the slight figure of Annie Murray, in her night-dress, alone.

Christine looked at her in surprise, and exclaimed, "For mercy's sake, why are you here? You are breaking the rules, and you know how particular Mrs. Frothingham is, in enforcing them."

"Don't speak so loud, Christine," whispered Annie, in reply. "Nobody will ever find it out, and I want so much to finish reading this charming book. My room-mate is so disagreeable she won't let the light burn for the fifteen minutes that we are allowed after ten, and so I slipped in here, seeing the light under the door. Now you will just let me stay here these few minutes, won't you?" she added, coaxingly.

"Yes," said Christine, rather unwillingly, and Annie seated herself at once, and read with avidity. Fifteen minutes flew by rapidly, and the step of the teacher, whose duty it was to see that all the lights were extinguished, was heard.

"Annie, Annie!" cried Christine, "Miss Durand is coming." And in an instant all was dark. The teacher passed by down the long hall, and returned again slowly; then the sound of her footsteps ceased.

"Now, Annie, good-night," said Christine, in a tone of great relief. "You can slip into your room, and nobody will be any the wiser."

But Annie only lighted the gas again, laid a mat against the doorsill, that the glare need not shine through into the hall, and seated herself again near the table.

"Annie Murray, are you crazy? Do put that light out instantly," exclaimed Christine, in low but determined tones.

"Oh, Miss Durand is safe in bed by this time, and I have only a few pages to read. I am dying to know how this book ends. Do let me sit here a few minutes. It will do you no harm, and I should think you might grant this little favor to one you pretend to love."

Christine hesitated, but made no reply, and Annie, taking her silence as consent, read on.

Christine fell into an uneasy slumber, and still Annie sat there reading.

Suddenly Christine was awakened by a stir in the apartment, and opening her eyes with a start, she saw Miss Durand standing in the door, and heard her stern voice, "What does this mean, Miss Elliot?"

Christine glanced round the room; no Annie was in sight; the light burned brightly, a chair was overset, and a book lay on the floor near the bed. At a glance she saw it all—that she would be considered the culprit, and with a deep sigh, she sank back upon the pillow from which she had started up on her first waking.

Miss Durand stepped forward and picked up the book, then tossed it from her with a look of disgust—

"One of Paul de Kock's execrable novels," she said.[12] "I understand it perfectly. You have not deceived me with your pretended sleep, and natural start and waking—excellent piece of acting as it was. I did at first think it possible that you forgot to turn off your gas, but this reveals the whole. I shall report you to Mrs. Frothingham immediately on her rising in the morning."

"Oh, Miss Durand have mercy! Do not, oh do not, I am innocent, indeed I am," began Christine, in the most supplicating tones, and wringing her hands in anguish.

The teacher looked at her with cool contempt. "I shall do my duty, Miss Elliot," she replied. "Rise and put out your light now," she added; and as Christine obeyed she lifted the book from the floor again, and saying, "I will take this valuable volume with me, and think perhaps now you may be trusted to retire again," left the room.

The instant the door closed after her, Christine felt herself encircled by soft arms, and Annie's sweet voice whispered,

"Heavens! how horribly I have been frightened. Every moment I expected those Argus eyes of Miss Durand would spy me out behind the curtain, and I trembled so lest you should say something that might lead to my discovery. I didn't believe you would betray me intentionally, Chris dear, but taken so by surprise as you were, I was terribly frightened lest some unguarded word should slip out. But you have saved me, best, dearest of friends!"

Christine withdrew herself from Annie's embrace and exclaimed, "Could you then stay in your hiding-place, and hear me charged with your fault, yet make no effort to shield me. Annie Murray, I would not have believed it of you. I did not know where you were; but to think that you were in this room, and saw and heard it all without one word to save me—Oh Annie, Annie! and I thought you were my friend!"

Annie's only reply was a flood of tears.

Christine's heart softened at the reality of the girl's distress.

"Poor child," she said, gently. "Do not take what I have said too much to heart—I was hasty—I know how it was. You were so stupefied, so taken by surprise, you could not speak. You were not yourself; but to-morrow you will confess it all."

"Oh, Christine, I cannot! Hate me, despise me, as I despise myself, but I cannot do it. It would kill me. The very idea of meeting Mrs. Frothingham's stern eye nearly drives me frantic; and worse than that, the disgrace. I am no favorite of hers. You have no idea how long my mother tried to get me here; and, now, if I should be sent home, and I dare say Mrs. Frothingham would be only too glad of the excuse, my mother would never forgive me.

"Oh, Christine, you do not know what you ask of me. Betray me if you will. I cannot prevent it; but no, I do not, I cannot believe that you will ruin your poor Annie. You can save me. She is your aunt, and you will receive nothing more than a reprimand, while I should be disgraced for ever. Oh, Christine, you will not betray me."

Her voice was full of agony, choked with sobs, and ever and anon she paused to try to keep back the tears which she could not restrain—the scalding drops fell on Christine's hand, which she clung to convulsively, as if to lose her hold of that was to lose all hope.

Christine could bear it no longer. Annie had been kind to her, and she blamed herself for her own want of firmness, to which she attributed the whole misfortune.

"Annie," said she, "I promise you I will not betray you."

Then, as Annie, began to shower caresses and thanks upon her, she pushed her gently away, saying, "I cannot bear that. Go, now, and leave me to my fate."

"I do not blame you, Christine," replied Annie, humbly; "I despise myself for my weakness; but you, so bold, so brave, cannot know how dreadfully I suffer."

"Go," was Christine's only reply, and in a moment she was alone.

Alone with her tormenting thoughts and self-reproaches; weary of the long night hours, tossing restlessly on her couch, yet dreading the morning, when she must face her aunt. Imagining the interview, by turns shrinking from the idea of it, or longing to have it over; or falling into an uneasy sleep, to wake, with a start, from dreadful dreams, only to realize that more dreadful things were in store for her in reality. For she built no false hopes on the bond of relationship between her judge and herself, and, at last, worn out by her feverish tossings on her bed, she rose, dressed herself, and paced up and down her room, holding her aching head tightly in her clasped hands, or pressing her throbbing brows on the window-pane, as she looked for the first grey beams of daybreak.

Morning came at last, and now that it had come, Christine thought that she would even pass through another night like the last, rather than to meet her aunt, as she must soon do. As the hours passed on, she felt like him of old in the iron shroud, which slowly, surely compressed its walls around him; so was time narrowing around her every instant bringing nearer the crisis in her fate. Each passing step thrilled through her every nerve, and sent a cold shudder over her frame.

At last there was a rap at the door, and a servant entered with her breakfast. She could not taste it, but allowed it to remain untouched where the waiter had placed it. A half-hour passed, and now came a summons to go to Mrs. Frothingham's apartment.

She followed mechanically, and was ushered into a darkened room, where, for the first few minutes, she could distinguish nothing. The door closed behind her, and she stood silently there, whether alone or not, she hardly knew. As her eyes grew more accustomed to the light, she saw her aunt, dressed in dark, heavy robes, sitting at the further end of the apartment.

Obeying her first impulse, she sprang forward, threw herself at her aunt's feet, and, without being able to speak, burst into a flood of tears.

Mrs. Frothingham waited till the violence of Christine's grief had subsided, till her tears were spent, and only a suppressed sob escaped her at intervals; then she spoke:

"I am ready to hear your confession."

Rapidly the whole scene of the past night flitted through the girl's mind. What could she say truthfully, without betraying Annie? Nothing—and with a choking voice, she exclaimed: "What shall I say?"

"Say!" repeated Mrs. Frothingham. "Tell the truth, girl. Where you got this execrable book. Tell me the whole story, immediately."

"The book is not mine," replied Christine.

"Who lent it to you?" asked Mrs. Frothingham.

"Nobody. It was not lent to me," sobbed Christine, checking herself suddenly, and bursting into tears.

"What do you mean, girl?" asked Mrs. Frothingham, sternly. "Do you think I am to sit here and cross-question you in this manner? Go on at once: tell me what you have done. Miss Durand

has told me her side of the story, let me hear yours, and, remember, no lies! If you do not wish to inculpate the one who
furnished you the book, you need not now—that is not now
the point. Confess at once your fault, tell me what excuses you
have to offer, and begin."

"I have nothing to confess, no excuses to make," sighed
Christine.

"Nothing to confess!" repeated Mrs. Frothingham, in a voice
of indignation. "Did you not read this book last night after the
hours, when we allow no lights to burn, thus breaking the rules,
and, when discovered, endeavor to feign sleep?"

"No, ma'am," sobbed Christine.

"What!" ejaculated her teacher, "you dare to deny it all: What
explanations have you to offer, then, of the appearances so
much against you?"

"None!" replied Christine.

Mrs. Frothingham's eyes flashed; her lip curled, as she gazed
on the prostrate form of the girl, who, unable to endure her gaze,
buried her face in her hands, then rising, she touched her contemptuously with her foot, and exclaimed, "Begone!"

Stung to the quick by this treatment, Christine clung convulsively to her aunt's robe, which swept by her, exclaiming,
"Oh, Aunt Julia, do not so utterly despise me! I confess I have
done wrong!"

The words, indistinctly uttered as they were, amidst sobs
and tears, at once arrested Mrs. Frothingham's attention. She
paused, and asked quickly, "Are you ready, then, to admit your
falsehood, to make full and free confession? Do so, if you would
be forgiven."

"Oh, would to Heaven that I could! but I cannot. I cannot,"
exclaimed the poor girl; and, thinking this hesitation arising
only from her want of courage to avow her fault, and disgusted
more and more with her half-confession, Mrs. Frothingham
sternly shook off the grasp with which the girl still clung to her

robe, as if she had been a venomous reptile, and, in her sternest voice, bade her "Go!"

"Go!" she repeated, as Christine slowly arose from the floor. "Your fault I could have forgiven. I did not look for gratitude from you, and you have not disappointed me in slyly setting an example of insubordination; but to select such a book as this for a companion, and worse than all, to lie to hide your fault, to persist in your falsehood, even when promised forgiveness, this shows a depth of depravity I had not looked for in one so young. And you are my brother's child. I blush to own that a drop of my blood flows in your polluted veins. Never dare again to call me 'aunt,' wretch that you are! Begone! Do not stand there shedding crocodile tears, you only increase my disgust. I can endure the sight of you no longer!"

She waved her hand with a gesture of disdain, but the girl did not move.

"Am I, then, to be sent home, in disgrace?" she asked, her pale lips quivering, and her pale hands clasped so convulsively that the fingers seemed buried in the flesh itself.

"No," replied Mrs. Frothingham. "You are to stay here in disgrace"; and, as she observed the sudden gleam of joy that sparkled in Christine's eyes, she added, "but understand what it is to remain here thus. It is only because it is a still greater punishment that I design for you than banishment could be. You, who have forfeited all claims to mercy; you, whose sin is so aggravated that it demands aggravated punishment, remain then, but as a Pariah, an outcast, with us, but not of us. Reflect well on what this is to be. Shunned, despised, degraded, as the liar, persisting in his falsehood, deserves to be."

With these words, she again waved her to the door—and, half-stupefied by the violence of her emotions, Christine staggered out of the apartment. Her eyes were swollen and aching from her long fit of weeping, her lips pale and quivering, her whole countenance haggard, and wearing an expression of the deepest suffering. A servant stood near the door, who assisted her to her chamber, for she could hardly support herself. Everything whirled about her; darkness gathered before her eyes, and just as she reached the threshold of her chamber, she fell heavily to the floor. The servants placed her on her bed, and applied restoratives; her aunt did not enter her room. Her punishment had begun. A Pariah she was, indeed. The strictest orders were given that no young lady should speak to her—no teacher address her, except in her recitations—and no servant, unless in the performance of her necessary duties.

Thus days passed; and Christine's last hope, that Annie, seeing her desolate condition, might confess her fault, or release her from her promise to keep the secret, died out within her.

Alas! the very severity of Christine's punishment, ignorant as she was of what had passed in the interview between aunt and niece, on which poor Christine had built her hopes of Annie's relenting, was, in reality, the greatest obstacle to her confession.

"If she is so unmerciful to her own niece, what would be my fate?" she said to herself; and so shut her eyes to the reproachful glances which Christine cast upon her, and endeavored to forget her own guilt.

CHAPTER SEVEN

Expiation

Cut off thus from all intercourse with those around her, looked upon with scornful, wondering, or pitying eyes, as the case might be—for her guilt was only vaguely guessed at, as it was Mrs. Frothingham's policy to keep secret the faults committed at her school—Christine had nothing left her but to toil on in her studies; and into these she threw her whole soul. In these she forgot, for a while, her own sorrows, and this she was glad to do, for she knew that she was growing bitter and sour towards all around her.

It was hard to hear the merry laugh and cheerful conversations of her schoolmates, and to know that she could not join them, and harder still to see those merry sounds hushed as she passed by, while the group would gaze at her with awe and wonder; to overhear sometimes, too, as she did, the various surmises as to her fault, a dreadful one, all agreed, that could deserve so severe a punishment.

The consciousness of her innocence did not support her under these trials. It seemed to her that it made them all the harder to bear. She could hope nothing for the future from Annie, and gradually she submitted to her fate with a passive endurance that was almost despair.

She had been poring over her books one evening, till her head and her very brain seemed to ache; and, leaning back in her chair, she thought of her old home, and longed, oh, how earnestly! for the sisterly love of her sweet Bessie; she who had never understood her, and yet who loved her so sincerely; she would never have doubted her, would never have believed her guilty, no matter how aggravated might be the apparent proof against her.

Gradually more peaceful thoughts stole over her. Her eyes closed, and again she was in the wide fields and shady woods so familiar to her; again she laid her head on the soft, green grass, and felt the light breeze lift the hair from her fevered brow. Bessie was by her side; she laid her cool, soft hand on her head, her fragrant breath floated over her cheek, her sweet lips were pressed to her own. She started up; it had been so real she could hardly think it a dream.

She looked around bewildered, where was she? No wide-spread hay-fields met her gaze; nothing but the four walls of her cell, as she bitterly called it.

She sighed a deep heavy sigh; was she dreaming, or was it in reality re-echoed? She looked quickly behind her—there stood the slight figure of Annie Murray. A fierce flash lighted Christine's pale face as she looked on the girl.

"Did you lay your hand on me? Did you dare to kiss me?" she exclaimed, angrily.

"Forgive me, Christine," was the poor girl's reply, as she crouched on a low stool near her chair.

Christine did not speak for many minutes. All that she had suffered came up before her, and when she lifted her bowed head to meet the fixed gaze of Annie, she said, bitterly—

"Are you not satisfied with your work that you must come again to break the rules, and then, in your own peculiarly skillful way, slip out, leaving me to bear the penalty of your fault?"

"Oh, Christine, do not speak so harshly," sobbed Annie. "Indeed, I have suffered too. I could bear it no longer, to see you innocent, and a close prisoner, shunned and despised, while I, the guilty one, was still treated with kindness. Oh, you have not suffered more intensely than I."

Joy sparkled in Christine's hollow eyes at these words.

"Annie, you have felt for me then. You were not so heartless after all, and you have come to tell me that you will absolve me from my promise?"

Her tone was painful in the depth of her imploring earnestness. Annie sat silent, weeping bitterly.

"Speak, Annie," Christine hurriedly went on. "Tell me, are you ready now? Shall I send a servant, and call my aunt here at once to hear it all?"

She rose, as she spoke, and approached the door, but Annie sprang forward and clutched eagerly at her dress.

"Stop, stop!" she cried. "Are you mad? Remember your promise!"

The light faded out from Christine's joyful face; she leaned heavily against a chair; the hopes that for an instant she had indulged, made it doubly bitter to sink back into the calm of despair. She roused herself. She would make one more effort—

"Annie," she said, "it is not for the fault that you committed that I am so severely punished; it is because I will not tell a lie, and admit that I am guilty. So, you see, you would not be severely blamed if you would confess. Do, for my sake, for your own, summon up courage, and tell the truth, or permit me to do so."

"Oh, no, no!" sobbed Annie, wildly, catching Christine's hand, "you will not tell; you promised, you promised! And every day has made it worse. If she would forgive the first crime, she would never pardon my allowing you to suffer for me. Oh, I never could bear it! You will not tell, good Christine," she went on, trembling in every limb. "Say, just once, that you will not!"

"I am not a liar," replied Christine, coldly, "and I have already given you my word. But if you knew what I endure—" she began.

Annie interrupted her, "I do know," she cried; "but you do not know one half of my agony. I am so frightened lest it should come out. I tremble at words that I imagine may have some clue to our mystery. I dream horrid dreams, and wake in a fright; then I am so fearful that I shall talk in my sleep of what I dream of continually. Your pale face, too, and weary look, haunt me every moment, I cannot escape them. In my gayest moments I think of you, alone and unhappy, and worse than all is the feeling I have towards myself. I know how selfish and mean I am, and what a hypocrite I am; every kind word makes me feel so guilty that I loathe myself. Christine, you cannot suffer worse than this."

"I pity you, Annie, indeed I do," said Christine, for she could not cherish anger against the poor, trembling culprit before her. "No," she said, "I would not exchange my situation for yours."

"But is there nothing we can do?" said Annie, breaking the silence that ensued. "Tell me once more what Mrs. Frothingham said."

Christine repeated what had passed at the interview. Every word that had been uttered was engraved on her memory in ineffaceable lines; the hot blood rushed to her cheek as she recalled her aunt's bitter words, and she mentally resolved never to deserve them.

She paused at last, and Annie went on—

"If you had only owned it, she would have forgiven all."

"Yes," replied Christine, mechanically.

"Well, why not?" resumed Annie, persuasively. "Why not tell her you did it?"

A glance of indignation shot from Christine's deep eyes.

"How dare you propose such a thing to me? Do you hope to degrade me to your own level? I have heard enough. If you came here only to insult me, now that you have accomplished your purpose, you had better retire."

Annie still sat in her low seat, glancing timidly at Christine who paced up and down the room in her fierce anger, waiting for her outburst of passion to subside. When at last she ceased her hurried walk, Annie rose.

"Forgive me, Christine," she said, humbly, "I do not blame you for hating me. Nobody ever can love me again!"

She took Christine's hand, pressed it to her lips, and in an instant was gone.

Christine was alone. She felt no longer angry. The humility of her friend had touched her, and she pitied her. She thought of the change that had come over that fair, young face within the few past months; the fresh, full cheek had grown thin and pale; the eyes, once so full of animation, were now heavy and listless, and that mouth, once wreathed with smiles, now wore only a wearied and troubled expression.

"Poor child! I was harsh to her!" she murmured, and her heart smote her. The offence was not thought of now; only the suffering which it was evident had embittered Annie Murray's young life as well as her own.

"I wish I had been more gentle with her, poor thing!" sighed Christine; and, as she walked up and down her chamber, she resolved to do all in her power to show Annie, when next they met, that she did not cherish unkind feelings towards her. She would smile pleasantly when she caught her eye, she would whisper, "Dear Annie," when she met her in the passages. "A bruised reed he shall not break."[13] These words haunted her continually. "Where have I seen these?" she asked herself. She thought of various authors. At last, half aloud, she exclaimed, "I have it—the Bible!" and, for the first time, since her exile, she took up the Bible, and was soon absorbed in its glorious poetry.

CHAPTER EIGHT

The Parvenu's Daughter

"What a blessed institution a holiday is, girls!" exclaimed a fresh-looking young girl, entering the small parlor in Mrs. Frothingham's house, which was known as the Young Ladies' Reception Room, and which was fitted up in excellent taste.

It looked very cheerful now, for the sun shone in brightly, adding even fresher tints to the rainbow-hued carpet, and lending a warmer glow to the faces of the young girls, who were assembled in the apartment. It had a very home-like and comfortable look, with its piano strewn with music, its table heaped with books and pamphlets, and the groups of girls, some sitting in a cluster, talking earnestly, and others lying on sofas, while one or two were seated near a table, work-baskets by their sides, engaged in some pretty piece of fancy-work. A few young ladies had books in their hands, but they did not seem to engross their attention so much as the gay chat of the merry group who sat in the centre of the room.

A pretty sight it was, those happy, careless girls, types, as they were, of almost every style of beauty—representatives of nearly every State in the Union. There were fresh, energetic, and blooming New England girls; frank, dashing maidens from the West;

dark-eyed and stately Southern exotics; sallow West Indian and sprightly French girls; and mingled with them slender, delicate, and stylish girls, city bred, and a class by themselves.

"Saturday is the finest day in the week," continued the newcomer, who had seated herself on the piano-stool, and touched now and then a note, as if playing an accompaniment to her own words.

"I should like Saturday better," yawned a tall and rather showy-looking girl on the sofa, "if it didn't come so near to Sunday, but that is almost enough to spoil it. The idea of going to church twice a day, to hear drowsy old Father Merrit drawl out his monotonous sermon, is enough to give any one the horrors."

"To be sure, Agnes, that is not very delightful," replied the first speaker; "but then you ought to do as I do; just go off in a day-dream of your own, and never mind what the old gentleman says. I just hear a hollow murmur like this," she said, taking a large shell from the mantel, and holding it to Agnes's ear, "and that doesn't disturb me; it helps me on. So it does the good wardens I know—they sit there as calm and composed as you please, and yet I'd wager any money they couldn't tell ten words of the parson's sermon, if they were obliged to do it, to save their lives."

"Well, Sallie," exclaimed Agnes, "don't talk any more about Sundays. 'Sufficient unto the day is the evil thereof.'[14] I believe you have disarranged my hair, with your shell," she added, rising languidly from the sofa, and proceeding to the mirror to replace the falling lock.

Sallie ran her fingers lightly over the keys of the piano, and then dashed off into a spirited polka. One or two of the girls, inspired by the music, sprang up, and were soon circling round the room. In the very midst of a bar, Miss Sallie stopped.

"Why don't you go on?" exclaimed the dancers, suddenly brought to a halt.

"I was thinking of home," she replied. "How Uncle Jake does flourish on that polka—don't he Ag? Oh, what wouldn't I give to see home, pa and ma, mammy and all the people. How many weeks is it before the examination?"

"Three months," replied a chorus of voices.

"Then we graduate, Agnes," went on Sallie, "and then for home. Don't you all long for the day to come?"

"I'm sure I do," said a fair-haired, blue-eyed girl, who had been circling round in the polka. "I do so long to come out. To go to balls and to the opera, for ma is so strict, she won't even let me enter the parlors when we have company now; but this winter I shall not be a school-girl—hateful words—any longer. I shall have finished! One of Mrs. Frothingham's graduates!"

"I suppose, Miss Rowena, that will be enough to ensure your success in society," said a tall and not particularly pretty girl, who had not before taken any part in the conversation.

"Allow me to inform you, Miss Helen Harper," said the girl, replying more to the tone than to the words spoken, "that the Howards have always been leaders in society. Ours is an old family. We can date back to some earl or duke, I forget just which, in England, as the founder."

"Well, what of that? My grandfather was an honest blacksmith, and I am prouder of that than if he had been some degenerate lord."

"I wouldn't tell of it," sneered Rowena, "if I did spring from such low beginnings."

Helen glanced around the room; she read in the faces of each and all that she had lost caste by this declaration. She laughed heartily.

"I verily believe," she said, "if I had declared that I had inherited the leprosy from my worthy grandfather, you wouldn't look more horrified. Now isn't this nonsensical pride? Are we to be judged by our ancestors, instead of by our own actions and merits? If so, I am glad I haven't Rowena's long line of sinners to answer for. My grandfather was a sturdy, honest, pious old Puritan, but a blacksmith, and a very good one, so I have a solid foundation to rest on, an iron one, at least. Which is better, that, or the broad back of the old Dutchman that you are so proud of, Miss Weisenbaum? I *won't* hurry you to reply," continued Helen; "I have something to attend to in my room, and will relieve you aristocratic young ladies of my plebeian presence."

"Rowena!" exclaimed several girls at once, in accents of horror, as the door closed after Helen. "Did you know that her grandfather was a blacksmith, or is she only in fun?"

"I didn't know anything about that, but I did know what I never intended to tell about her."

"What is it? What is it?" exclaimed several, in a breath.

Rowena hesitated.

"Do tell us," she was again urged.

"Her father was a retail grocer—"

"Heavens!" "You don't say so!" "Is it possible?" interrupted her auditors.

"And her mother," pursued Rowena, "was a shop-girl."

This capped the climax.

"How came she here?" asked Annie Murray, who had been a silent but attentive listener.

"To tell the truth," replied the descendant of the Howards, "my mother introduced her."

"Your mother!" exclaimed Annie, in surprise. "How happened it?"

"Why, you see, they moved up town, into an elegant house, in Fifth Avenue, and had it furnished without regard to expense, for Mrs. Harper was resolved to get into society. She moved heaven and earth to do it; and, to do her justice, she is a splendid-appearing woman. She made out to get into the first society; for, the truth is, in these degenerate days," said Rowena, with a sigh, "that wealth, judiciously expended, will do almost anything. Mother called on her, and liked her very much; but I never saw her so shocked as she was when she found out that she had made the acquaintance of a quondam shop-girl. At first she resolved to drop her, but finally she did not. She said, what is very true; though these parvenu people rarely ever take a firm place in society, yet their children do; so, for the children's sake, she tolerated Mrs. Harper, and obliged her by introducing Helen here. Helen seems to be more like her father, and don't have, nor ever will, one half the elegance of her shopgirl mother. So that's the way she got in here," concluded Rowena; and, in truth, this was the result of a long, and diplomatic course of policy between the high-born and poor, and the plebeian and wealthy families.

Mr. Harper knew little of his ambitious wife's struggles to gain a position for her children and herself among the fashionables of New York. He allowed her to take her own course, and she had bent all the energies of her active mind to this one end, and, after many struggles, and not a few humiliations, saw herself, at length, at the summit which she had so ardently longed to attain. It was a triumph which she alone enjoyed, for her husband, she knew, could not understand her desire or rejoice in its fulfillment; and her only daughter, Helen, inherited all her father's lack of false pride as to their antecedents, gloried in their prosperity as the result of her father's labor and talents, and despised even the word society, from having heard it so much talked of.

But she should go to Mrs. Frothingham's—that would change all her notions—so the mother thought, and upon this she acted; what the result was may be judged from the previous conversation.

Annie Murray broke the silence that ensued, after the brief sketch of the family history of the Harpers was concluded, by saying, "We laugh and sneer at these parvenu people a great deal, but, after all, they are to be pitied. Think of that proud Mrs. Harper, now, having to submit, as she did, to Mrs. Fitz Gerald's insults without resenting them, for fear she should not receive an invitation to that select soirée of Mrs. Fitz's at the close of the season."

"Did she get the invitation?" asked one or two eager voices.

"Yes," replied Annie, "but they say it cost Mrs. Harper that elegant diamond bracelet of hers, for Mrs. Fitz admired it, and that was enough."

"But it's Mrs. Harper's turn now," interrupted Rowena. "Mother used to tell Mrs. Fitz (she's ma's cousin, you see, and they are just like sisters), to let Mrs. Harper alone; that she was one of the kind that was sure to take the front rank in society sooner or later, one of the pushing kind, you know, and that she would be sure to retaliate whenever she got in power. Well, Mr. Fitz Gerald's business got involved, and, if you will believe it, through Mrs. Harper's influence in some way, Mr. Harper had him completely in his power, and Mrs. Fitz had to go to Mrs. Harper—actually humble herself, to beg her to save them from ruin. Wasn't that a triumph for the parvenu? Dear me, it's such a pity that society isn't here as it is in England, each class kept entirely and distinctly by itself. It don't make the lower orders any happier, this continual struggle of theirs to rise above their level, and I'm sure it's very annoying to people born in the upper classes to have les nouveaux riches continually intruding upon them."

"What, not through with society yet?" exclaimed the clear voice of Helen Harper, as she re-entered the room. "For my part, I'm tired of it! I had rather be shut up like that poor Miss Elliot, than to hear such a constant din of first families and upper classes. It's worse than the patter of the rain; and, by the way, girls," she said, "have any of you found out what that poor thing has done that's so dreadful? Annie Murray," she continued, "you used to be with her considerably before her disgrace, haven't you any idea what she was guilty of?"

Annie trembled, and turned pale, as Helen's searching eyes rested on her, but she replied—

"I! How should I know? Mrs. Frothingham keeps her own secrets. But, Christine is a good girl, and I don't believe she has done anything to deserve such close confinement."

"Neither do I," returned Helen, emphatically. "It's my opinion that she's suffering unjustly," and, again, her keen glance rested on Annie. She changed color and turned away, unable to bear that piercing gaze, which seemed to read her secret.

"La, Helen, what is it to you what the girl has done?" asked Rowena. "It's likely that Mrs. Frothingham knows what she is about; and, I can assure you that she wouldn't thank any of us for expressing our opinions on the subject. You know she always makes a mystery of every such thing."

"Yes, it is decidedly mysterious," replied Helen, slowly, and she mentally added, "I verily believe Annie Murray knows more than she chooses to tell. I will find out what it is. Annie," said she, aloud, "if you will come to my room, I'll teach you that new crotchet pattern you were wishing to learn."

"No, thank you, Helen," was the reply, "I don't care about trying it to-day; some other time will do as well."

"Aha! you don't care about being alone with me," was Helen's mental rejoinder to these words. "Very well," was her audible answer, and she turned away; while Annie joined a group who were listening, with profound attention, to Agnes Delancy's account of a fancy ball at New Orleans, her dress, and that of many others; not to be outdone, Rowena took up the subject of dress, in her turn, and described the wedding-dress of her elder sister, and that of her six bridesmaids, with other equally interesting particulars, to all of which her listeners paid distinguished attention, with the exception of Helen, who, tired of "corsages, berthes, and tulle,"[15] and who could not enter, with any interest, into the discussion of the merits of Valenciennes, Brussels, and point laces, withdrew again into her own room, after she had made some sarcastic remarks, which were, in her presence, received with contemptuous tossings of the head alone; but, no sooner had she gone, than she was universally declared to be low in her tastes, betraying in everything her ignoble origin.

"Low blood will show itself," was Rowena's concluding remark, and again she returned to the charge, running over the various kinds of laces, with their relative prices, as glibly as if she had served an apprenticeship at selling them.

CHAPTER NINE

The Confession

On her way to her room, Helen glanced in at the half-open door of Christine's apartment. Her pitying eye rested on the thin, sharp features of the girl, who sat there, leaning wearily back in her chair, pressing her hand to her head, apparently unconscious of all around her.

"This solitary imprisonment is a cruel punishment, no matter what she has done," thought Helen, "and I will find out what her offence is, at any rate."

But, for several days, she could get no opportunity to speak to Annie, who sedulously avoided her; and this studied avoidance only the more firmly convinced Helen that her suspicions were correct—that Annie knew much more than she chose to tell.

At last the opportunity, which she had so long wished, presented itself. Their music-teacher gave them a duet to perform together, and, during their first hour of practice, Helen began—

"Now, Annie, I just want you to unravel that whole mystery about Christine."

Annie trembled from head to foot, for she imagined that Helen had found the clue. "I knew it would all come out!" she gasped. "What shall I do? What shall I do?"

In an instant, a light flashed on Helen's mind; Annie was concerned in it, whatever the fault was. She was determined to sift it thoroughly.

"I understand it all," she said, "I have seen Christine."

"But, she did not tell you," interrupted Annie, eagerly. "She promised! She would not break her promise!" then, suddenly seeing that she had betrayed herself, she paused, and burst into tears.

"No, Annie, she did not speak to me; but you must tell me all about it now. What have you done?" continued Helen, calmly.

"Nothing!" replied Annie, sullenly, resolved to withdraw into denial.

"That answer will not do, Miss Annie; I am resolved to get at the truth—and, if you will not divulge it voluntarily, I know of other means to be employed. You have already committed yourself. I shall call in Mrs. Frothingham, and see if she can find out the truth."

"Oh, Helen, have mercy. Do not call Mrs. Frothingham, I beg of you!" gasped Annie, her countenance betraying her terror in every lineament.

"Then, confess of your own free will," was the stern reply. "Nothing else will save you."

Annie obeyed. In a broken voice she told the whole story. Helen listened with the deepest interest.

"Poor Christine!" she exclaimed, "and, poor Annie, too!" as Annie finished her relation of the circumstances. "And now, Annie, there is but one thing to be done," continued Helen, "and that is—" she paused, while Annie looked at her like a convicted criminal on the face of the judge who is to pronounce his sentence "—and, that is," repeated Helen, slowly, "for you to go to Mrs. Frothingham yourself—tell her the story you have told me, as you have told it to me; do not omit your own sufferings, and she cannot fail to be touched, as I have been."

"Oh, I cannot—I cannot," repeated Annie.

"But, you must," returned Helen, "and at once."

Annie wrung her hands, despairingly.

"Go, or I shall do so!" continued Helen. "That poor girl shall not be wronged another day. Decide at once! Will you go, or shall I?"

She rose, and proceeded towards the door.

"Helen, I will go," gasped Annie, "but, do go with me! To the door of her room, if no further!"

"Come, then!" said Helen, and, half-supporting her, she led her to the room where Christine had received her sentence.

"Oh, Helen, let me go! I cannot!" gasped Annie, as she paused to gather courage.

A rap on the door was Helen's only reply—she glided away, leaving Annie alone. The door opened, and Mrs. Frothingham stood before the terrified girl. Her first impulse was to speak sternly to Annie for coming thus unceremoniously to her room, she who was so punctilious in regard to her intercourse with her pupils, but a second glance at the pale girl before her, changed her proposed reproof to a kind inquiry—

"What brings you here, Miss Murray? What is the matter? Come in, and tell me all!"

Annie, somewhat reassured by her kind reception, did as she was commanded, but no sooner did she find herself seated alone with her teacher, than all her fortitude gave way, and she wept bitterly.

Mrs. Frothingham looked on in surprise for a few moments, then, as Annie still seemed unable to check her tears, she spoke rather sternly, "What is the meaning of all this, Miss Annie?"

"Christine!" ejaculated Annie, and again sobs impeded her utterance.

Mrs. Frothingham was all attention.

"Christine!" she reiterated. "And what of her? Say on!"

Annie fell on her knees before her teacher, and, with clasped hands and streaming eyes, began to tell her story. As she went on she gathered courage, and there was a great deal of simple eloquence in her brief narration. She did not attempt to palliate her own guilt, or to offer any excuses; and Mrs. Frothingham's eyes were suffused with tears, as Annie concluded.

"I have been very unjust," said she, rising, "but, I did it for the best," she went on, apparently forgetting Annie's presence; suddenly she recollected herself.

"You have done very wrong," she said, "and have been the cause of much injustice; but your voluntary confession, tardy as it is, inclines me to forgive you."

"Oh, Mrs. Frothingham," sighed Annie, stooping still lower till her fair curls hid her face entirely, "Let me confess all! I am so weak, so cowardly, that, even now, neither poor Christine's hard fate, her sad face, nor my own dreadful self-reproaches, would have driven me to tell you all, if I had not been discovered by one of the girls, who would have told it, if I had not. It is not a voluntary confession, but I am glad it is known. I am willing to receive the punishment I deserve. Do with me as you choose."

"Rise, Annie," said Mrs. Frothingham. "I believe you have already suffered sufficiently, without additional punishment. Come with me!" and she led the way to her niece's apartment.

Christine had been sitting listlessly there the whole morning; the merry sounds of blithe voices had occasionally fallen upon her ear, and merry peals of laughter that had seemed like mockery to her.

"How long is this to last?" she uttered, half aloud. "I cannot bear it much longer. My own thoughts torture me! They will drive me mad!"

Was it the answer of her own heart, or did she hear a voice, "Courage! Deliverance is at hand!" The door was ajar, and she imagined she saw a fluttering dress pass by. She rose hastily and looked out, but no one was to be seen, and, half inclined to think it something supernatural, Christine sat down, with a beating heart, to ponder on those inspiring words, for, little as it was to build hopes upon, it did cheer her and give her new courage. She had a friend, at least; who could it be? She little thought of Helen, yet she it was who could no longer refrain from giving her a word of encouragement, when Annie had really entered the room of Mrs. Frothingham. Christine's hopeless attitude had touched her, and she uttered those words and hurried on to her own apartment, with a glad heart.

Christine was yet pondering over this circumstance, for trivial as it was, to her, in her monotonous life, it was an event, when the door opened, and Mrs. Frothingham, accompanied by Annie, entered. One glance at Annie's tear-stained face was enough; she felt that all was discovered, and even in her gladness that she was cleared, came the pang of Annie's approaching fate. She sprang forward.

"Oh, Aunt Julia!" she exclaimed, "forgive poor Annie! She has suffered—indeed she has. Have mercy on her!"

"Christine, she is already forgiven. She has told me all."

"Oh, Annie!" exclaimed Christine, in a tone of the most heartfelt joy, stretching out her arms towards her.

Annie drew back from the proffered embrace. "I am not worthy," she said, in a sad, low voice. "I did not tell of my own free will," and rapidly she detailed the circumstances. "Can you forgive me?" she said, humbly, as she finished her story.

"Dear Annie!" was the only reply, but the tone was enough.

Christine could not now have harbored malice had she wished, her heart was too full of happiness, and she listened to Mrs. Frothingham's words as in a dream.

"Christine," she said, "I do not ask you to forgive me. I did what I deemed right, but as you have been unjustly punished, and your disgrace has been public, so must your reinstatement be. Prepare for your supper with the rest of the pupils."

She turned and left the room, leaving Annie and Christine together, to talk over the weary past, and to rejoice that again all promised fairly in the future. Christine listened to Annie's self-reproaches, for she felt that it was a relief to her to humble herself, and assured her again and again of her forgiveness. At last she said:

"Now, Annie, say no more, all is forgiven; let it be forgotten."

What a joyful meal was that supper. Once again one of the family, Christine sat at the table; she was too happy to eat, yet never had she enjoyed a meal so thoroughly. The pupils cast shy and curious glances at her, but she heeded them not; she only replied with smiles to the kind looks that seem to welcome the poor girl back, and recognized the kindness that prompted the sending of dainties to her from different parts of the table, by one and another, though she declined them all. At the close of the evening meal, Mrs. Frothingham requested teachers and pupils to assemble in the parlor, and when all were seated she called Christine forward, and taking her by the hand, in her silvery voice she spoke:

"As my niece has been in disgrace before you all, it is but just to her to inform you that she was innocent, though I supposed her guilty. I have recently been made acquainted with facts which completely exonerate her from all blame, and take pleasure in restoring her to all the rights and privileges of which she has been deprived."

She pressed the hand which she held warmly, and dismissed the assemblage. The girls crowded round Christine, vying with each other in declaring their pleasure, and she happy, so happy she could not express herself, stood looking on, her eyes suffused with tears, and smiles flitting over her face. That warm pressure of her aunt's small, soft hand; she felt it yet, and more than all the words she had uttered more than the kind voices of her schoolmates, more even than Miss Durand's warm congratulations, did that fill her heart with joy. She cared not for all that she had suffered, if, through it, she might find the way to her aunt's heart; to be allowed to love her, to caress her. Oh, what would she not suffer to gain that privilege!

She looked around for Annie: she stood at a little distance, gazing at the scene, as if she were unworthy to participate in the universal gaiety. Christine approached her.

"Oh! Annie," she said, "this more than pays me for all. Do not let your sad face spoil all my happiness. Forgetting those things that are behind, let us press forward," she whispered, and drew her into the gay circle.

Gradually Annie regained her cheerfulness, and ere the evening had passed, her laugh rang out full and clear. No sound could have given more pleasure to Christine. She was not merry, but quietly happy to all appearance, though that calm exterior hid most tumultuous emotions.

That evening she never forgot. It was an epoch in her history.

CHAPTER TEN

Theory and Practice

Again Christine was free to mingle, in the hours of recreation, with her schoolmates, to join their walks, and to listen to their merry chat, and to express her sentiments in return. At first, all this was very amusing, but gradually she wearied of the recurrence of the same themes, more particularly since she was unable to bear any part in the discussion of them. She cared nothing for dress, knew nothing of the society of which they spoke, and grew tired of the catalogue of beaux, and the glib enumeration of youthful flirtations which seemed to constitute the chief topics of conversation.

She joined the groups of girls less and less frequently, and withdrew still more to the solitude of her own room, where she found a quiet pleasure in reading and in study.

In this chamber, surrounded by her books, she lived in a world of her own; she forgot, in the stirring scenes of the past, all the trivialities of the present, and half imagined herself an actor in the histories she read. She wrote, too, and was never happier than when pouring out her wild fancies and bewildering thoughts on paper. It seemed to give her restless mind relief. She felt that she must express herself, and this was the only possible way. She felt that it would be profanation to bring forward all that she held sacred to the scoffing gaze of most of her schoolmates; and though her constant friend, Helen Harper, perhaps, would not have made a jest of her, yet there was a mocking expression in her cool, calm eye, as she looked steadily at Christine in her occasional outbursts of enthusiasm, that sent a chill over her, and induced her to endeavor to check any expressions of a similar character in the future; yet Helen's regard was very precious to her, and for this very reason she kept back her most secret and highest feelings from her inspection. It was Christine, the fine scholar, the strong spirit, that Helen prized, and Christine, the dreamer, shrank from displaying those restless, far-reaching, and tormenting, because unsatisfied, yearnings that she well knew would only be considered as so many proofs of her weakness by her friend.

But this withdrawal from their society, and disrelish of their favorite themes, was not at all liked by her schoolmates.

"Birds of a feather flock together," Rowena said, looking after Helen and Christine, as they walked together in the garden, where the fall flowers lifted up their sturdy blossoms amidst the dropping of the withered leaves, like cheerful and brave spirits unaffected by adversity. "There go the precious pair, and well matched they are. I declare," she continued, "it is amusing to draw Christine out, as I have done sometimes. She is as fresh and ignorant of the world as a baby. You should have heard her the other day, when I was joking her about lovers. She looked at me for a while, as if she had no idea what I meant, and at last said, 'why, Rowena, I never thought of such a thing; I never had an admirer in my life.' I believed her fully. I don't believe the child thinks or cares about a lover, and, if she did, I'm sure nobody would ever think of falling in love with her. But just imagine her listening to Philip Armstrong's nonsense. How she would stare at him! At the next soirée I mean to introduce him to her, just to see the fun," and she burst into a peal of laughter at the idea in anticipation.

Meanwhile, Helen and Christine were still walking in the garden, Christine stopping, every now and then, to pluck here and there a flower, which she added to a bouquet she held in her hand. At last she spoke:

"How different people are," she said, "and yet it is as unreasonable in us to find fault with, and try to make them over, because they don't have the same aims, and understand our feelings, as it would be to find fault with these chrysanthemums and china asters, because they are not roses. So we ought to take people as we find them, and be satisfied, for God has made them so."

"That's one of your nonsensical ideas," replied Helen. "God hasn't made them so. Do you suppose that He ever intended that any created being should be so vapid, and empty, and useless, as the most of those creatures that are called in society 'young ladies'—things like Rowena and her set?"

"He made the butterfly," returned Christine, "as well as the bee; and it seems to me one of the lessons that Nature teaches us, that each does God's will, in his own sphere, in God's appointed way. There are the thinkers in this world, and the workers—they do well to toil and to struggle onward, but there are the human butterflies, too—they are needed to make earth pleasant, to be brilliant and beautiful, and they discharge their duty just as well, in being merely pleasant to the sight, as the workers do, in their way. The pretty creatures refresh the laborers by their very beauty. Oh, wouldn't the world be barren, and dark, and dull, if only the laborers dwelt here?

"Wouldn't it be a dreary sight if everywhere we met only the stern, earnest, care-worn faces, and nowhere could see any joyous, careless idlers? Why, it would be as bad as if the world was one great granary, where the fruits and grain were ripe, but without any of the green leaves and flowers that make them so beautiful when they are out in the broad fields coming to maturity."

"All that sounds very well," said Helen, "but, please to remember that the beautiful flowers and green leaves have some use as well as mere beauty, and that even the butterfly uses all the powers that God has given it. Let the human butterflies do the same! There never was a human being who had not undeveloped faculties that it is his duty to cultivate; and, if God had meant for our butterflies to do nothing but look pretty, he would have let them, like their insect types, flutter a while, and then, before their beauty goes, die; but it isn't so: beauty goes, life remains, and, what then?—a soul is left, too, an undeveloped, distorted thing—a torment to itself and all around. And, what if this soul is linked to a worker, an earnest spirit, as is often the case? What can come of it but unhappiness? Oh, Chris, in Nature, the butterflies don't mate with the bees!"

"Do you know, Helen, I often think of all this," replied Christine, "when I hear the girls talking, as they do, so much of marrying. I think of them as wives and mothers, something that don't seem to occur to them at all, much as they talk of marriage—I think, how different from the women of Sparta, the mothers of heroes—and, I ask, are these frivolous beings fit to train the children that God gives them?"

"Ah, my dear, how old-fashioned you are! You haven't an idea of what a marriage is now, or of what the ambition of these girls is. It isn't to cultivate their minds or hearts; it isn't to make whole-souled, true women of themselves; it is their end and aim to marry well, that is, rich—to be Mrs. somebody; and, then the one object is to have the finest house, the finest carriage, the most servants, richest dress—in short, to be the most fashionable, a leader of the ton. Isn't that a high destiny for a being with a soul?"

"Oh, I've puzzled over this," said Christine, musingly. "I've thought of it, and wondered what the reason was that it was so, till at last I thought that I had got it. I thought that I had found the clue when I began to talk of the use of the beautiful; for it must be right, if we could only see it as God sees it."

"It isn't right! It's all wrong—all wrong!" exclaimed Helen. "Don't go on crying, 'peace, peace, where there is no peace.'"[16]

"Wrong!" repeated Christine. "It does seem so—but, what is to be done?"

"There comes out the downright Yankee, ready to do at once," cried Helen, laughing. "Do? Nothing! It would be of no use, my dear female Don Quixote, to run a tilt against existing things. Just scold as much as you please, or laugh, if you please, at the world, and let it wag on. That's the wisest thing you can do; and now, let's go in—it grows damp and cold. Enter, my dear busy bee!" she added, holding open the door for Christine to pass, "and don't trouble yourself any more about the butterflies!"

But Christine could not so easily do this. It seemed to her that it was wrong for her to keep silent when she saw the right so clearly, and she resolved, at the first opportunity, to endeavor to lead forward those around her in the true way.

Opportunities are not slow to present themselves when one is in earnest in desiring them; and when, as often happened, she was surrounded by a bevy of girls, some begging for assistance in this or that study, or asking her to write their compositions, and similar favors which she had often granted; she spoke timidly at first, but, growing interested in her subject, she went on with more and more enthusiasm, to speak of their duties to themselves and to God. She was quite absorbed in her theme, and had almost forgotten where she was and to whom she was speaking, when she was recalled to herself by the clapping of hands, and an ironical "hear, hear!" from Rowena, while a universal titter ran round the circle.

"Have we a preacher among us?" asked Agnes, in an irresistibly comic tone, while Sallie sprang up and made a ludicrous address, expressing the united thanks of her companions, and exhorting Christine, with the strongest kind of arguments, and in a nasal twang, to "go on, and never more to hide her light under a bushel!"[17]

Christine hardly knew whether to laugh or cry; she stood in an attitude of surprise and bewilderment, looking on with a sense of deep mortification that she had made herself so ridiculous, for she had a great dread of ridicule, hardly knowing what to say next.

Helen Harper had heard it all, and coming out of her room at this moment, she looked, with a half-pitying, half-comic glance at the girl, then whispering in her ear, "So you have been casting your pearls before swine, have you, my dear Don Quixote," she passed on.

Rallying herself at these words, Christine joined in the laugh against her, and began to assist those who desired it, and, as soon as this was over, gladly escaped to her room. She had had enough of pointing out the noble and the true, and, for a time, at least, felt far inferior to those she had endeavored to guide.

"What am I but an awkward, ignorant country girl, and how should I attempt to show these elegant, high-bred girls what to do. Fool that I was, and presumptuous as foolish!"

She dreaded to meet her audience again, and when she did venture out, she shunned them as much as possible; but it was of no use, the nickname of "the preacher" was fastened upon her. It was a sore subject to her, but she was doomed to hear many jests and jibes upon her sermon. Even after she thought it had been forgotten, in the midst of some long discussion on dress, Sallie would draw down her visage, and drawl out, with a side glance at Christine, "Vanity of Vanities, saith the Preacher."[18] But Christine bore it good-humoredly, laughing as merrily as the rest, and saying nothing, but inwardly resolving never to be placed in such a position again.

CHAPTER ELEVEN

New Acquaintances

Examination day was drawing near, and all was bustle and excitement in preparation for it. It was a great day, not only for Mrs. Frothingham, but for the towns in the vicinity. The good people of the village were, at this time, always favored with visitors who came to attend it, and the friends and parents of the pupils were always present in great numbers, not only at the examination, which might more properly have been called an exhibition of the accomplishments of the pupils, but at the soirée which followed, and which was always the most brilliant of the season.

The large school-room was crowded to its utmost capacity on this occasion; the young ladies, dressed simply but tastefully, looked most fresh and smiling, as if well pleased to be the centre of attraction to the large and fashionable audience, while Mrs. Frothingham, the very personification of beauty and elegance, presided with dignified grace.

The examination of the ordinary branches, such as the mathematics and the sciences, was rather hurriedly passed over, but the music was a prominent feature. Most admirable performances on the piano, harp, and guitar, and singing that would have done no discredit to many a public vocalist, enchanted the audience, and applause as well as flowers were the tribute of the gratified listeners to the young ladies, who, with modest but perfect self-possession, received this gracefully as their due.

The reading of compositions commenced, and each one in turn stood alone before that assembly, hushed to breathless silence to hear the reader's production.

Christine's turn had come, and rallying all her courage, she walked upon the platform. It was a trying ordeal for one so unused to attention as she to feel that hundreds of eyes were fixed upon her, and the hot blood rushed to her cheeks. She hesitated for a moment, and glanced around the apartment.

It was terribly still, and, for a moment, she felt that it would be impossible to proceed; her aunt's eye met hers; a glance at once full of encouragement and command, and controlling herself by a great effort, she began to read her composition.

It was a weird-like tale, full of deep and hidden meaning, yet simple in its style, and touching in its narration of the struggles of an earnest but weak spirit; as she read on, she forgot all about her. Her sweet voice rang out full and clear, or melted to pathos. It thrilled to the heart of every person present, and more than one tear-suffused eye testified to her powerful but unconscious eloquence.

Those simple words carried each back to his childhood, and those pure and holy aspirations thrilled to every heart, bidding the longings for the good and true that lay buried there, deep under the loam of selfishness, to come forth to a new resurrection.

When she concluded she was greeted by long and loud applause; she stood blushing and confused for a moment, as showers of flowers fell upon the stage, then, with simple grace, she gathered them up, raised them to her lips, curtsied gracefully, and disappeared.

It was her first triumph, and those flowers were more precious to her, as the tokens of it, than anything that she could have desired. She had gone through the ordeal well, and needed no assurance of it, though she was gratified by the evident pride with which her aunt regarded her.

It had indeed been a surprise to Mrs. Frothingham to see the self-possession of her unsophisticated niece; her graceful demeanor she attributed to her own teachings, but the soul, the power, and the eloquence which she had displayed, astonished and electrified her as much as it had done the audience who had little expected it from the plain though graceful girl.

No school had given her those pure, unsullied thoughts; no teacher had given her the enthusiasm which sparkled in her speaking face; nor had art taught her the graceful gestures or the soft modulations of her voice, which added so much to the effect of her beautiful story.

It was a happy day for Christine. It gave her a new consciousness of her own powers, an assurance of her own strength, which banished, for a time at least, the painful doubts that she had felt of her ability to make known to others the thoughts that struggled for utterance.

"I am understood at last!" was her inward cry; "thank God for that."

Ah, it was more than gratified pride that lent the flush to her cheek, the lustre to her eye, and the lightness to her step, as she mingled in the gay assemblage that evening, in the splendid parlors of her aunt's dwelling. True, she was comparatively unnoticed, for exile from the soirées of the session had been a part of her undeserved punishment, and she was unacquainted with the guests; but it was exhilarating to her to look on at the gay scene, to hear the fine music, and to watch the graceful girls as they glided through the dance, or to look around at the groups of animated talkers, to watch their faces, and imagine what they were saying; or to hear the light laugh echoing from the hall, where, two by two, ladies and gentlemen promenaded, as quietly Christine leaned back in an alcove and looked on.

Heavy curtains swept around her, and she shrank back out of the glare, and began to fall into one of her reveries.

She was thinking how much Bessie would enjoy this brilliant scene, and looking intently around her, to be sure that nothing should escape her observation, so that she might at least give her sister a faint idea of this brilliant party, when her aunt approached her.

She was accompanied by a lady of considerable beauty. It was a countenance that struck Christine's fancy at once, not so much from the regularity of feature or clearness of complexion, as from the severely intellectual expression of the whole, and the depth and brilliancy of the large dark eyes. She was dressed in a rich blue brocade; her neck and arms were covered only by a thin lace, through which gleamed white shoulders and beautifully moulded arms. Her figure was of about the medium height, but well proportioned, and she bore herself with graceful dignity. She was certainly beautiful, but it was not her loveliness which first struck one on gazing at her.

Christine recognized her as one whom she had been watching for a long time, when she had been engaged in conversation. She looked at her still, and thought that even in that rare assemblage of beauty and elegance, her aunt, in her costly dress of velvet and diamonds, and her companion, might challenge them all without fear of being rivalled in loveliness.

"What a beautiful picture they would make!" she thought, and with an artist's eye she gazed at them as they were passing by. Suddenly her aunt looked up. "Ah! there she is," she said, and in a moment she presented her niece to Mrs. Warner, the beautiful woman at her side, and with a few words left them to go to another part of the room, and, ere long, Christine saw her the centre of a gay circle, entertaining them all without apparent effort, looking a very queen surrounded by her courtiers.

She saw this at one hasty glance, for Mrs. Warner immediately entered into conversation with her; a few common-place remarks at first elicited the usual replies, but ere long, drawn on, she hardly knew how, Christine found herself expressing, as she had never done before to any mortal, her inmost thoughts to this stranger.

There must be magic in that bright eye, she thought, to be able to see the secrets of the heart, and bid the lips reveal them; but there was kindness in the smile of the stranger, and she evidently understood, if she did not sympathize with, Christine's ideas.

"We must see more of each other, my dear young lady," said Mrs. Warner, after they had been conversing for a long time. "You must excuse me for confining you so long in a corner, with a married woman talking to you, while this dancing is going on."

"I did not think it had been long," replied Christine, "and I have enjoyed it far more than dancing. Indeed it is not at all likely that I should have danced. I know no one here."

Mrs. Warner beckoned with her fan to some one across the room; a young man obeyed the summons, and worked his way to her.

"Your humble servant waits your commands," he said, with a low bow.

"Allow me to introduce to you, Mr. Armstrong, Miss Elliot," said Mrs. Warner.

Another low bow to Christine, and he began a strain of light badinage, to which Mrs. Warner replied in the same tone. Christine spoke only when directly appealed to, but this occurred so often that she felt not at all overlooked.

"Shall I have the honor of dancing with you, Miss Elliot?" suddenly said Philip Armstrong, as he observed that a cotillion was forming.

Christine bowed assent and they took their places in the set; it happened that her vis-à-vis was Rowena. She started as she saw Christine and her partner take their places, and exclaimed, half aloud, to the young lady next her—

"How on earth could Phil Armstrong have got an introduction to Christine? Mrs. Frothingham don't like him, and she would never have thrown her in his way if she could help it. Well, we will see if he plays the devoted to her, as he does to every new face."

And, in fact, he did pay Christine the most assiduous attention, apparently becoming so much absorbed in the brief snatches of conversation that the pauses in the dance allowed that he would forget to go through the figure when it again became time to do so, until recalled to his duty by Christine. When the dance was concluded, instead of leading her to a seat, as soon as politeness would allow, he continued to promenade with her for a long time; then, as if fearful of wearying her, he drew her into a corner, a little aside from the crowd, and seating himself by her side, continued talking to her with the greatest apparent interest.

By degrees the conversation turned upon beauty, and Philip gave a brief description of the various styles of different nations. He had been something of a traveller, and led on by the rapt attention which Christine paid him, and by her occasional questions, he gave her a glowing account of what he had seen in Italy and in the Holy Land. He had great powers of description, and his vivid word-pictures placed the scenes of which he spoke distinctly before her.

Nothing could have been more flattering to him than the sparkling eye, the glowing cheek, and half-parted lips of his listener, who had quite forgotten, in the scenes which he had portrayed, all that was passing around her.

"But I am wearying you, I fear," he said, at last, "by my long tales; what I was going to say when I began, though I have, I know, digressed considerably, was this—that, notwithstanding all that is said of the beautiful women of foreign lands, I am confident that America can produce more fair women of various styles, yet each one perfect in its way, than any other country. Look around you now, Miss Elliot. Is there not here an assemblage of beauty that ought to content the most fastidious?"

"There is, indeed," replied Christine, "but, were you a second Paris, and obliged to give the apple to the most beautiful lady present, to which would you award it?"[19]

"First tell me, Miss Elliot, which you consider most beautiful, that I may see if our tastes agree."

"I hardly know," returned Christine, "which I admire most, my aunt or Mrs. Warner. I can hardly imagine anything more lovely than Aunt Julia, and yet there is an expression about Mrs. Warner's face that pleases me equally as much as the more perfect loveliness of Mrs. Frothingham."

"They are very lovely women, Miss Elliot. You display good taste in your selection; but, since you cannot decide in favor of the superiority of either, let me ask whom you will select among the young ladies?"

"Then, I must pronounce Agnes Chotard the most beautiful. Look at her now, as she stands under the full blaze of that chandelier! What more could you desire?"

"Expression," replied Mr. Armstrong. "She is a beautiful statue. I tire of her monotonous beauty."

"Let me see your selection, then," said Christine, "I have performed my part of the compact."

"I will show her to you," he said. "There," and he held her fan, containing a small mirror, directly before Christine.

One glance was enough. Her eyes flashed fire, for she was peculiarly sensitive to her personal appearance.

"Mr. Armstrong, you are ridiculing me," she said. "I know as well as you do that I am hopelessly ugly."

Philip was silent, racking his brain for some suitable reply.

"Confound it!" was his mental observation. "I never knew a woman to be offended before, however ugly she was, at being told she was handsome. But, there must be exceptions to all general rules. How shall I get out of it?"

"Pardon me, Miss Elliot," he said, aloud; "whatever my opinion is, and since it has given such offence, I will not again express it—I ought to have known you better, than to suppose any compliment on mere personal beauty would be acceptable. It only shows my poor knowledge of human nature. Miss Elliot is above the ordinary weaknesses of her sex."

"That will make it all right!" he mentally added, as he looked at her to see how she received his apology.

He read in her countenance only increased displeasure; she turned away without making any reply.

"Still unforgiving!" exclaimed he. "What can I do, Miss Elliot, to reinstate myself in your good opinion? Believe me, I would not willingly lose it."

Christine looked at him with a penetrating glance, as if she would read his thoughts; he was evidently sincere, and she replied—

"Treat me with sincerity, then. Pay me no more mock compliments. I am a novice, I am well aware, in the ways of society, but that should be no reason why a gentleman should turn me into ridicule."

"Believe me, nothing was further from my thoughts," replied Philip. "You are a novice, indeed, else you would not have taken a few idle words to heart, which I might have uttered to any other lady in the room, pretty or ugly, without giving offence. You see, I begin with sincerity. Am I forgiven?"

Christine extended her hand in reply. He took it, pressed it warmly, and went on—

"In all sincerity, I hope that we may henceforth be friends. But, I see a gentleman coming with your aunt, bent on an introduction and on inviting you to dance. Will you promise me three sets, at least, this evening, as an assurance of full and free forgiveness?"

"Yes," replied Christine. He bowed, and turned away just as her aunt reached her.

Philip had guessed aright. Mr. Griswold, a foppish youth, all bows and smiles, perfumes, ambrosial curls, and jewelry, begged the honor of her hand in the next dance, and, as he conversed with her, Christine could not forbear contrasting his vapid, common-place remarks with the eloquence of her former partner, against whom she no longer cherished any displeasure. Her eyes followed him as he crossed the room; but she could not look at him long, for she found that he had taken a position where, though apparently devoting himself to Rowena, he could also see her every movement; and, whenever she glanced that way, she caught his eye bent on her. He managed to be in the same set with her, and whenever he took her hand in the dance, pressed it softly, and urged her not to forget her promise for the next quadrille. At the close of this set, she was besieged by applications to dance—for, whoever Philip took up was sure to be the fashion—and all were anxious to see what there was about this pale-faced, dark-eyed girl that had so attracted the critical and fastidious Philip Armstrong.

Mrs. Frothingham looked on uneasily at the assiduous devotion of the young man to her niece, and after she had seen him dancing with her so frequently, she took Christine aside, and said: "It does not please me to see you with one partner continually, neither do I like the gentleman; so do not dance with him again, should he ask you to do so."

She turned away without waiting for a reply, and at the same moment Philip again approached, and asked Christine to dance with him.

"No; I cannot," she replied.

"And why not?" he asked.

"Because Aunt Julia does not wish me to," she said, without hesitation.

"Well, then, grant me this favor—do not dance with anybody else," he said. "Will you not make this little sacrifice for your friend, and talk with him instead of dancing?"

"Oh, yes," replied Christine. "It will be no sacrifice; I am sure I had rather talk with you than dance with any one else."

"Let us sit here by this open window, then," said he, drawing her arm through his, and walking slowly towards it. "Now we will have a fine long chat," he said, when they were seated together, but they were doomed to disappointment.

Mrs. Frothingham again appeared to be making her way towards them; she did not come on directly, and Christine did not observe that she was doing so; but Philip's quick eye detected that though she paused to exchange a few brief sentences with this or that group, she was steadily drawing nearer.

"If your aunt comes here with any more stupid partners, Miss Elliot, remember that you are engaged to remain here with me."

"I will remember," replied Christine. But she was spared declining to dance.

Mrs. Frothingham only remarked, "Mr. Armstrong will excuse my niece, I am sure, as I wish to introduce her to some of my acquaintances."

"Allow me to assist you both through the crowd," was the reply, as he gave an arm to each, and made way for them to pass.

"Thank you," said Julia, when they had reached the lady whom she wished to see, with a bow that was intended as a token of dismission, but he only stood quietly by, and entered into the general conversation that followed.

Mrs. Frothingham bit her lip in annoyance.

"May I trouble you, Mr. Armstrong," she said, "to bring me my fan, which I must have dropped near that alcove where you were sitting a few moments since?"

He could not do otherwise than to go, but he cast a look at her, in which she read defiance, as well as a perfect understanding of her motive, as he disappeared.

"It's a pity if I am not more than a match for him," was her reflection, as she looked after his tall figure as he moved away.

"He is indeed handsome, elegant, and fascinating," she thought, "and, for these very reasons, all the more dangerous to a young and inexperienced girl. Who could imagine that such a fair exterior hid such a depth of falseness? that under that broad, open brow, shaded by soft, waving brown hair, that clear blue eye and smiling mouth, lurked only treachery and deceit? He is thoroughly unprincipled, and Christine shall not be exposed to his influence," was her conclusion, as her glance fell on his undeniably handsome face and figure, and to this effect she hovered near her niece during the remainder of the evening, and surrounded as were both by an admiring circle, Philip found no opportunity to say more to Christine, unobserved by her Argus-eyed guardian.

This very opposition served to strengthen him in his purpose. Christine's enthusiastic admiration of his talents, as well as of his beauty, which he easily saw; her freshness and simplicity had attracted him, and to one wearied, as he was, of pretty faces, to whom he had been obliged to pay his court, her very lack of beauty, and her dislike to broad flattery, had been attractions; then if it displeased her aunt, against whom he had a secret enmity, so much the better. He would win Christine's heart. Mrs. Frothingham should find that her will, powerful as it was, was no match for his. He would triumph over her, and with this resolution he bade her good-night.

"It is strange," soliloquized Mrs. Frothingham, after her guests had dispersed, as she sat in the solitude of her own chamber, "that, of all the people here to-night, Christine should have been singled out, by the only two persons that I should have wished to pass her unnoticed—Mrs. Warner and Armstrong. I must keep her from the influence of both, if possible." Revolving plans of this kind, Julia fell asleep.

CHAPTER TWELVE

The Aunt's Caution

The next morning early, Mrs. Frothingham tapped at the door of her niece's room.

Christine was an early riser, and was already dressed and at her window; she was not a little surprised to see her aunt at this hour, and waited with some impatience, to hear what had brought her there; but this was not Julia's manner. She talked of the party, the music, and a thousand similar nothings, to all of which Christine listened uneasily, waiting for the main subject. At last it came.

"I do not know what induced Mr. Armstrong, professed admirer of beauty as he is, to devote himself, as he did, to you, last evening. I was not surprised that you found him agreeable, for he has most dangerous powers of pleasing, which he exerted to the utmost; but I must tell you what he is—a villain, thoroughly unprincipled, making his boasts of the hearts he breaks."

"Oh, Aunt Julia, impossible!" cried Christine.

"It is strictly true, Christine. He is an infidel, scoffing at all religion, and making use of his talents, his wealth, and the time that he has to draw young men into the same vices that he indulges in."

"Can this be true?" asked Christine; then suddenly turning to her aunt, she went on: "And if it is so, for I must believe you, how can you introduce such a viper into the midst of young and inexperienced girls? Why is he tolerated by society? Why is he smiled upon and treated with such politeness and attention by virtuous ladies? Why is he not shown the abhorrence with which he is really regarded?"

All this Christine asked rapidly and earnestly; she looked at her aunt fixedly, and was shocked to see the smile that lurked around her mouth.

"You are so inexperienced, child, that I cannot help smiling at you," replied her aunt. "But, to tell you the truth, it is his wealth and position that causes him to be retained in society. He is immensely wealthy, and his family are among the most aristocratic in the State, and so, as he is a finished gentleman, he is allowed entrée into any circle he chooses."

"Then the people who encourage him to go on in his sinful courses, by taking no notice of them—treating them as if they were of no consequence—are, in God's sight, as guilty as he," replied Christine, solemnly.

"Take care, then, that you are not one of those guilty persons," answered her aunt. "Show him that you, for one, abhor his crimes. Treat him with the contempt he deserves."

Christine made no reply, but Mrs. Frothingham read in her speaking countenance all that she desired.

"How did you like Mrs. Warner?" she asked.

"I admire her," exclaimed Christine, enthusiastically. "She is so lovely, so gentle, so good—for I know, Aunt Julia, that nothing other than pure and true thoughts can give her that beautiful expression. I could not believe her false, even if you were to tell me so."

"That is quite enough nonsense," interrupted Mrs. Frothingham, coldly. "She may be good enough in her way, but she is a perfect enthusiast, a dreamer—always engaged in some foolish scheme or other, to bring about some fancied blessing to the world. Always riding some hobby to the disgust of her own family, and making herself a laughing-stock for all the town. She has some talent, but no common sense; there is nothing practical about her, and, as she seems to have taken a fancy to you, I must tell you beforehand that I disapprove of your having any more than a ceremonious acquaintance with her. You are already too enthusiastic, too flighty, and need none of her Quixotic schemes to make you more so. You need to have this part of your nature repressed instead of cultivated, and, for this reason, you will see the justice of my checking in the bud any intimacy between you and Mrs. Warner."

Christine heaved a deep sigh. Mrs. Frothingham went on.

"It is because of the danger that some day you may become like Mrs. Warner, for you have the same faults of temperament that she has, that I so earnestly desire you to check your dreamy enthusiasm, that you may become a practical woman."

"Oh, Aunt Julia," exclaimed Christine, "do you not see that it is wrong to crush out all those high aspirations after something holier and better that fill us with such a restless desire to go on in the way that leads to life eternal. Are not all the trials that we make here to become holier, even though we are often well-nigh discouraged, steps that lead us nearer to the infinite life beyond, and will it not be the highest joy in Heaven that we can attain to what we have so striven for here? Oh, do not bid me to crush the highest, the noblest powers that God has given me! Rather give me physical than spiritual death!"

"Nonsensical!" exclaimed Mrs. Frothingham. "Christine, I really am at a loss to know, sometimes, whether you have the usual quantity of good sense or not. Never let me hear such a rhapsody again! Aspirations! Spiritual death! I can almost imagine it is Mrs. Warner herself. All this fol-de-rol will only unfit you for the common duties of life, and I am more and more convinced of the necessity of keeping you away from that crackbrained Mrs. Warner's influence.

"You may think it very hard, now—but you will thank me for it some day—but, whether you do or not, I will not, if I can help it, have a second edition of Mrs. Warner in my family."

The breakfast-bell here interrupted the interview, and Christine accompanied her aunt to the dining-room.

After breakfast she was assailed by a perfect storm of raillery from the girls on her new conquest; the manner would, at any time, have been distasteful to her; but, after what she had heard of Philip's character, it was doubly disagreeable; and she was glad when preparations for departure for the vacation relieved her from the annoying jests of her schoolmates.

The house seemed very lonely after the departure of the young girls, whose light step and merry laughter had re-echoed through the spacious halls. It seemed so terribly still to Christine that she could not bear to remain in-doors. It was as if there had been death in the house, and she wandered restlessly up and down the garden walks, thinking of home, and feeling a longing she could hardly repress, for one loving word—one fond kiss.

Her aunt was kind now, but still cold; she felt an interest in her because she was her niece, and that was all; it could not satisfy her craving heart.

Helen and Annie would not return; they had graduated. Perhaps she would never see them again. It was a sad thought, for they alone, of all the girls, had seemed to feel any affection for her; and, though Annie's had cost her dear, yet she had valued her humble, dependent love, more than she herself knew, till she realized that it was lost to her. The monotony of her vacation-life was one day most pleasantly interrupted by a call from Mrs. Warner.

If Christine had been pleased by her at the party, she was delighted with her at the second interview. Her conversation was so much above that of the most of the ladies who had visited Mrs. Frothingham that it was really refreshing to be with her.

True, she had many novel ideas which somewhat startled Christine, and which Mrs. Frothingham listened to with polite indifference.

When Mrs. Warner took leave, she begged Mrs. Frothingham to come soon to see her, and requested her to allow her niece to visit her frequently. Julia expressed, in a few words, the pleasure it would give her to accept her invitation, but inwardly resolved that it was a pleasure she would not avail herself of very often. She had seen the kindling eye, the eager attention of her niece, and read in these signs the power that Mrs. Warner possessed over her.

She was not a little annoyed, therefore, when invitation after invitation came to Christine, from that lady, to spend the afternoon with her. On various pretexts these were declined; but, nothing discouraged, they were repeated again and again. At last, without absolute giving of offence, they could be declined no longer—and, with rather a bad grace, Mrs. Frothingham gave her consent—for Mrs. Warner's family was an influential one, and Julia, always politic, did not wish to give any occasion for misunderstanding with them.

CHAPTER THIRTEEN

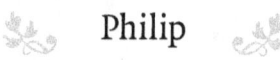 Philip

It was with a light heart that Christine wended her way through the streets of the pretty town, which she must traverse to reach her destination.

She walked briskly along, not even tempted by the staring announcement that goods were "selling at cost," in nearly every store on the principal business street, nor did the cloths hung out, labelled "great bargains," and giving their prices, even gain from her a second look, for dry goods had very little charms for her.

She went steadily on, her eyes a little downcast, and her brain busy in shaping into form a string of rhymes, as she called it, the ideas of which had been vaguely floating through her mind for several days; and it was frequently the case that, in her walks, these wandering thoughts received shape and dress. She had just completed the last verse to her satisfaction, when suddenly a quick footstep was heard behind her, and, in a moment, Philip Armstrong was at her side.

He seemed very happy to see her, but she replied to his greeting very coldly.

"I am delighted to see you out," he said, "after your illness. I feared it might prove something serious."

Christine looked at him in surprise.

"My illness!" she repeated. "I have not been at all sick!"

"Indeed!" returned Philip. "Your aunt informed me that you were too much indisposed to see me, when I called at her residence last week; but I see it all, Miss Christine. She has an unfounded and unreasonable prejudice against me, and is determined that I shall have no opportunity of cultivating your acquaintance—but you will not be so unjust. You will not be so tyrannized over?"

"Mr. Armstrong," interrupted Christine, "you are quite mistaken. There is no tyranny in the case. My aunt is, indeed, unwilling that I should have any further acquaintance with you, for reasons that you very well know, and I think she is right, and agree with her fully in desiring that we may meet only as strangers. I tell you this frankly, that you may relieve yourself and me from the annoyances that would arise from an opposite course. I might have shunned you without giving any explanation, but I think the straightforward course the better one; and after what I have said, you need not subject yourself to the cool reception which I shall certainly give you if you do not choose to pursue the course I request—to look upon me as a perfect stranger. Good afternoon, and good-bye, Mr. Armstrong," she concluded, turning down the street which led to Mrs. Warner's.

"Good-afternoon!" replied Philip, raising his hat; "but not good-bye," he muttered between his teeth. "Pretty well done for the unsophisticated country-girl," he soliloquized; "and cold and severe as she was, I like her all the better for it. She looked almost handsome, her eyes were so bright and piercing, as she administered her shower-bath to me. However, thanks to her truthfulness, I see just how the case stands. I have one strong point, her liking for Mrs. Warner, for she is a true friend to me. I will call there this afternoon."

No sooner resolved than done; and Christine had not been seated in Mrs. Warner's cozy sitting-room more than ten minutes when Mr. Armstrong was announced. Christine's first feeling was one of indignation, as he entered with easy assurance, bowed to her and raised Mrs. Warner's hand to his lips.

She did not even make the slightest inclination in reply.

Philip only cast a sorrowful look at her, and flung himself on a low seat by Mrs. Warner's side.

"I did not know that you had company," he began, "or I should not have ventured to disturb a tête-à-tête between you and Miss Elliot."

"You know that you are always welcome, Philip," replied Mrs. Warner; and Christine looked up a little mollified.

He had not then come because she was here, in a spirit of bravado, as she had supposed; she had been unjust to him. She did not glance at him, however, and he went on.

"You know when I get into one of my dark hours, I always come to my good angel, my dear Mrs. Warner, and to-day I am in the very blackness of darkness. Lead me out into light." He took her soft, white hand, as he spoke, between his, and looked at her imploringly.

Mrs. Warner raised the heavy masses of hair softly from his brow, and laid her hand lovingly upon it.

"My dear Philip," she said, in tender tones, "I have given you a better guide than I or any erring mortal can be. Have you read the words that fell from the lips of the compassionate Jesus?"

"Yes," replied Philip, bitterly, "I read of the prodigal son, who was received, after all his wanderings, to his father's house. I read that 'there is joy in Heaven over one sinner that repenteth, more than over ninety and nine just persons that need no repentance.'[20] I read all this, and far more that teaches the same lesson, and, with a lighter heart, I think I see the dawning of a brighter day. These are the teachings of one who has many professed followers, who revere his lightest word—they will help the wanderer to return, they will bid him God speed, I say to myself—and longing for words of encouragement, I draw timidly near to some one on whose face I think I read the spirit of the Gospel, peace and good-will to men; but as I approach that kind look changes to one of disgust and loathing—that gentle voice, instead of saying, 'Go and sin no more,' exclaims, like the Pharisee, 'Stand aside, I am holier than thou.'²¹ Even woman, whose province it is to bind up the broken heart, draws her garments closer around her, as if fearful of pollution from the touch of her hem to such as I, and passes by on the other side.

"Then, in bitterness of spirit, I exclaim, where is the boasted power of the Gospel? Where is the influence of those teachings, which, men say, can never die?

"I see myriads of church spires, and hear much of Christianity, but where are the fruits?

"Jesus told those who came from John, when he asked, 'Art thou he that should come, or do we look for another?' 'Go tell him what ye see, how that the blind receive their sight, the dead are raised, and the poor have the Gospel preached to them.'²² Try the church now by this. The blind are leaders of the blind, the dead in sins find no resurrection, and the poor—where is the Gospel preached to them? In yonder tall building, where, every Sabbath, kneel the rich and prosperous in this world's goods, are the poor side by side with them?

"The form is here, but the spirit of godliness is nowhere to be found. Then I close the book from which springs all this so-called Christianity, and say, it is a beautiful theory, but it cannot be put in practice. It shares the fate of a thousand philosophies before it. If it were of God, it would not come to naught. The light has faded out, and I stumble on again in the thick darkness, with no faith in man, woman, or God."

Christine had listened, with her whole soul in her eyes, to these outpourings of a bitter spirit. How often had similar thoughts filled her with unhappiness! She could not but sympathize with the young man before her, and her heart smote her for the injustice she had done him.

"I held my garments closer, and passed by on the other side. I thrust him down into the pit from which he strove to climb. God forgive me for putting one stumbling-block in the way of a poor wanderer, striving to ascend the narrow path."

She could hardly refrain from crying out, "Forgive me!"

Was Mrs. Warner never going to speak to him? Had she no words of comfort to offer?

She sat there still, stroking his hair with all a mother's tenderness, and at last she spoke:

"My dear boy, do not look at poor, weak mortals like yourself. Lift up your eyes 'to the hills whence cometh our help'—to our Saviour.[23] He alone can show you the true path. He is the Way, the Truth, and the Life. His teachings are no mere vain philosophy—else where were we? What would become of us? But no, 'I know that my Redeemer liveth,' and no shortcomings of man can affect the eternal and life-giving truth.[24] There is a revelation made to all, and each for himself can find the truth, which will be in him a well of water springing up into eternal life.

"Still, I bid you look into the Gospel, not around you, and all will be well. Come to me, my dear boy," she continued, "as you would to your mother; you never weary me. I never tire of hearing all the thoughts that oppress you."

"My ever kind friend," replied Philip, warmly; then, after a pause, he said, "and now will you not give me some music to exorcise the evil spirit entirely."

She rose, opened the piano, and played one of Haydn's symphonies, with a depth of expression that thrilled to Christine's heart at least. When she ceased, she requested Christine to play also. She complied, and sang a simple song.

Philip bent over her as she concluded, and said, in a low voice, "Is not this a token that you retract those harsh words—that hard sentence?"

"Forgive me," said Christine, "I did not understand you. Far be it from me to add one feather's weight to the load of sorrow that crushes you. I bid you God speed in the upward path."

"How can I thank you enough for those cheering words?" he answered. "May I venture to hope that you will be one of my few friends?"

One glance at her expressive face was enough.

"God bless you, sweet Christine," he said, in a voice so low that it reached her ear alone, and, bidding both adieu, he left them.

"The victory is won!" was his mental exclamation, as he rapidly walked down the street, and he almost wondered at the exultation which he felt. Why did he feel such a deep interest in this girl? Why was it that he felt that her love would be all the world to him? Never had he experienced the same emotions before, as often as he had fancied himself in love. Not all the beauties he had seen, had power to move him as this plain and simple girl.

"She shall love me," he said to himself, "as she can love, with a depth and strength that few women are capable of. She shall give me that pure, true heart!" and, exulting in his fancied victory, Philip Armstrong walked on.

CHAPTER FOURTEEN

The Seed Sown

No sooner had Philip departed, than Mrs. Warner began to talk of him.

"Poor fellow!" she said, "His is a noble nature, but he has been thrown under unfortunate influences. He is an orphan, and his is not one of those half-way characters that are neither good nor bad. He has had no restraining hand to check him in his mad career, to point out his follies, and to guide him gently back. If he had but known a mother's love, what might he not have been spared! But, he is not wholly lost. I have great hopes of him yet: that he may be the means, with his fine talents, of leading others on in the right way, I feel almost sure; and, let people say what they will of him, he shall never want a friend in me. I know he has faults, great ones. His ardent temperament leads him, even now, into a thousand follies which a little reflection would prevent his committing—but, then, his remorse is so great that I can never find it in my heart to censure or reproach him.

"Oh, Christine! it is worth a great effort to save such a soul as his from wreck and ruin; and how guilty are they who look at all his attempts at reform with distrust!"

"Oh, who could doubt his sincerity!" cried Christine. "I pitied him from the bottom of my heart, and I had said such cold words to him just before he came in!"

She went on to tell the whole story. Mrs. Warner listened with the deepest interest.

"Christine," she said, "I foresaw that you would have great influence over him. You may do even more than I to save him. Will you not endeavor to do so?"

"I will, Mrs. Warner. I solemnly promise to do all in my power to help him to become what he may be, a noble and true man."

Mrs. Warner smiled.

"I was not mistaken in you," she said. "I read you at the first glance, and loved you as soon as I began to talk to you. But now I must set about this pile of sewing which Philip's coming in has so grievously interrupted. I must make my needle fly quickly, else the poor baby there," she said, glancing at the occupant of the cradle, "will have no new gown this week."

"Let me help you," said Christine, drawing near the large workbasket, which was heaped with garments of all sorts and sizes, some in a half-completed state, and others only cut out.

"Ah me," she continued, "when do you expect to get this all done?"

"When shall I ever get out of work? Never," replied Mrs. Warner, cheerfully, "while I have five little ones, and a lord and master, to sew for. Stitch, stitch, stitch, is my life-long task. But, some of this work in the basket I am going to get done for me. Would you be willing to go with me to the place where I am to get the work done? It is not far from here—but, before we go, let me tell you something about the people.

"There are two maiden sisters, the relics of an old and once very wealthy family, who, now that all their riches have gone, are left to support themselves by the needle.

"They are as proud as ever were mortals, and, though nearly everybody knows that they must sew for a living, yet they never allude to it, and are always telling pitiful falsehoods to account for the number of garments that they may be seen to be at work upon. They are making a set of shirts for the minister, as a present, they will tell you, or they have a great deal of sewing to do for themselves. Even when I carry work to them, I never say anything about it, as I would to an ordinary sewing-girl. I tell them that I am going to send a package down this evening. They are much obliged, and, after dusk, I do send it, putting my directions inside on a paper. It is done, and returned after dark, but without a bill. They never set any fixed prices. It is understood that they are to receive a present in return, which all their friends take care shall be amply sufficient to remunerate them for their services."

"I cannot understand such feelings," said Christine. "How much more noble it would be now, to come out openly and say, we are poor, but we are independent; we will earn our own living, and ask, with a clear conscience and open brow, for the money for which we have toiled so hard and so honestly."

"Yes, it would be far nobler, and would command more respect from everybody if they were to do so, instead of keeping on telling these foolish stories that deceive nobody. However, so it is; this is their weakness, and it would be a most terrible blow to Miss Patience or Miss Tempe, did they discover that everybody is not blind to the fact of their working for a living."

"It's a pitiable weakness," said Christine.

"It is, indeed; yet they are not to be too much blamed for it. It is owing to the wrong basis on which society rests—owing to that false reasoning which would assume that labor is degrading; and not so much the labor either, for young ladies may sew, and work like servants, for a fair or a levee, and that is all right; but to do anything for pay—to receive the just equivalent for labor done, oh! that is dreadful.

"It is horrifying to fathers, husbands, and brothers, to have the females of the family do anything which may add something to the common stock. They will make slaves of themselves; yes, toil day and night to keep them from doing anything to make money. Not that it is considered out of the way to do sewing for themselves, or sometimes kitchen drudgery, but if they should think of entering a store, where, by lighter labor they might earn enough to hire a good, stout girl in the kitchen, they lose caste at once. Oh, she is only a milliner, a dressmaker, or she has gone into a store, is the sneering remark. What could have induced the family to allow it? All this has its natural influence, and girls shrink from encountering these remarks and glances as well as from losing their position.

"Another evil effect is this. These girls, feeling that they are a burden to their over-worked father, live with one aim, that of marrying, and of marrying well.

"Oh, how many a girl has, without one spark of true affection, married a man for a home.

"Oh, if it could but be changed! If girls could only be brought up like boys, with the idea that, when at a suitable age, it was their duty to earn their own living, how much more self-respect they would feel. Then they would not live for so paltry an aim as merely to become a wife, nor need they hesitate if love should lead them to wed a poor man. Then might a wife indeed prove a helpmeet to her husband, or should a woman live single, she might escape the sad doom of the poor and dependent old maid. Then would marriage be what it ought to be, a union of loving hearts, instead of, as is increasing every year in our land, a mere legal partnership, a marriage of convenience.

"Now, if here and there an independent girl will assert her right to earn her daily bread, there are only open to her two things, teaching and the needle, both overcrowded, and of course the competition is so great that the pay is small."

"But, what can be done?" asked Christine.

"Public opinion can be changed," replied Mrs. Warner. "It will be a hard labor, but a glorious work; and who would not be a partaker in it? Who would not for such a need to become a benefactress of her sex, suffer for a while all the contumely which she must experience?

"A day will surely come when she will be called blessed, and her works shall praise her."

"But, my dear Mrs. Warner, are you really a woman's-rights woman?" asked Christine, timidly, for she had heard this name applied to her friend with every kind of ridicule heaped upon her.[25]

"Yes, my child, I am, and I glory in the title. I know very well how much I am scorned in consequence, and how many sneering remarks are uttered against me, how many falsehoods told of me, and how many who, in their hearts, believe just as I do, laugh me to scorn. But what of that?

"'Blessed are ye when men shall revile you, and say all manner of evil against you falsely, for my sake.'[26] But I am wearying you, Christine."

"Oh no, go on, Mrs. Warner," replied Christine, who had been gazing with admiration on the glowing cheek and sparkling eye of her friend.

She sympathized with her in her lofty enthusiasm, though the subject was new to her, and longed to hear more.

"Some other time, Christine, we will talk more on this matter; but, now, if you will excuse me, I must see what my handmaid, Biddy, is about, for she requires constant overlooking, and if I did not pay a visit to the kitchen, though she has made soda biscuit fifty times at least, she would be quite as likely as not to forget flour, butter, or some other equally important ingredient; she certainly never would be equal to remembering them all.

"You should have seen her first experiment in pastry-cooking. I was just about to make some pies when I was interrupted by company, which put my doing so quite out of the question, yet I was very anxious to have them made.

"Biddy saw my perplexity, and being a good-natured soul, she begged me to allow her to do it for me. I hesitated, but she insisted that she could do it.

"'Faith, ma'am, and haven't I been after seein' yez do it more nor a hundred times, and isn't it myself that'll be doin' the same? Do jest thry me, mistress, darlin'!'

"I consented at last, first repeating to her the entire process over and over again, and left her to do 'her endeavors,' as she said. By-and-by I was summoned into the kitchen by Biddy, who solemnly informed me that, 'Sure the divil must be in the flour, for she had been bakin' the pies for four or five hours, and the outside of them wouldn't get done, let her put nivir so much hate to um.'

"I looked in at the oven, sure enough the crust was only a sticky paste.

"'Did you do just as I told you, Biddy? Rub in the butter, and mix with water?'

"At the mention of water, Biddy started.

"'Och, the wather!' she exclaimed. 'Divil a sup of that did I put in, at-all-at-all. Troth it's that same that I'm after forgittin' intirely.'

"And so ended Bridget's first lesson in pastry-cooking."

Christine laughed. "But why do you keep her," she asked.

"Oh, she is a good-natured creature, honest and faithful, and if she were to leave me, I might get a worse one in her place; indeed, I feel an attachment to the simple thing, and the baby loves her very dearly. She will dance Irish jigs and sing wild Irish songs to him by the hour together, and he will look and listen, as if it were the most charming performance in the world. But it grows late. I must to the kitchen," and Mrs. Warner vanished.

"How false are the charges," thought Christine, as that evening she wended her way homeward, "that her enemies bring against this noble woman, that she neglects her family duties for her hobby, woman's rights." And a closer acquaintance with her only increased Christine's indignation at the utter want of foundation for these reports. Never had she seen a woman with a more universal genius or more untiring energy.

Whether it was cutting and making coats and pantaloons for her boys, shirts and vests for her husband, preparing food for the family, dainties for the sick, or writing an article on her one grand subject for the press, she was equally at home and equally successful. Besides all this she was a frequent and welcome guest in the dwellings of the poor, assisting them when in distress, using all her influence to get work for them, and lending a sympathizing ear to their troubles. Never was there a more unselfish nor devoted friend, and every new trait in her character which Christine discovered, only increased her love for and admiration of her new friend.

Her husband was a sea-captain and much away from home, so that the care of the family devolved principally upon her; his absence, too, made home rather lonely to her, and often, work in hand, she would come to Mrs. Frothingham's, and sit hour after hour, talking of the schemes for the emancipation of woman that filled her heart and mind.

"I cannot endure this any longer," said Mrs. Frothingham, after one of these visits. "If Mrs. Warner must see you, either here or at her house, do go there. I dread to see her enter, and almost wish myself deaf that I might escape her continual talk on woman, woman's rights, woman's needs, woman's wishes. I have all the rights I want, except the right to forbid her coming to my house; but do you go there."

"I'll try homeopathic treatment, now," she added, mentally. "If Christine does get infected by her dogmas, she shall hear so much of them that she will become disgusted with them. The hair of the dog that bit will cure."

Julia judged her niece by herself, but she forgot that their characters were essentially different, and the very enthusiasm which she despised thrilled through Christine's soul. Her heart burned within her at the wrongs which she learned from Mrs. Warner's recital, and the arguments to which she listened seemed conclusive to her. The pupil bid fair to outstrip the teacher, in her zeal.

CHAPTER FIFTEEN

The Betrothal

Christine had long since related to her aunt all that had passed between Philip and herself, on her way to Mrs. Warner's on her first visit, his call, and the words he had uttered.

"Consummate actor!" was all the reply Julia vouchsafed to give to this account—and, when Christine indignantly exclaimed, "Had you seen him, you would not have doubted his sincerity," Mrs. Frothingham only replied:

"He is an adept at reading the human heart, and sees your weak point, at once. It only confirms me in my opinion of him."

"Unjust!" was Christine's inward thought, and she resolved that she would redeem her promise of remaining his friend.

Mrs. Frothingham read this in her face, and judged it best to place her upon her honor with regard to the acquaintance which she saw she could no longer prevent, except by strict commands, to which, with Christine's temperament, she thought it unwise to resort.

"You know my wishes," she said, quietly; "you know my opinion of young Armstrong, yet I place no restrictions upon you. I trust to your honor and your frankness that you will receive no visits or other attentions from him which you would conceal from me."

"Thank you, dear Aunt Julia," replied Christine, with ardor. "You may, indeed, rely on me."

Philip Armstrong was a constant visitor at Mrs. Warner's, and it was almost universally the case that Christine met him there; at first she had merely considered it accidental, and took no notice of it, but gradually, as his looks and words showed her unmistakably that it was her presence which drew him there, though it sent a thrill of delight to her heart, she felt that it was wrong.

Was not this a breaking of the tacit compact entered into between her aunt and herself?

Did it not savor of clandestine intercourse?

She had at first thought it too unimportant to mention that he was a visitor at the house of her friend, for her aunt was aware of this; but now, when she never failed to meet him there, she could not conceal from herself that it ought no longer to continue.

She resolved to put a stop to it at once, and when left alone with him, as was often the case, she turned to him, and said—

"It may be unintentional on your part, Mr. Armstrong, but it has so happened that we meet here very frequently. You know that my aunt disapproves of our acquaintance, and though she has not positively forbidden it, yet she expects me to regard her feelings, and I have promised to do so.

"I am your friend. You must not doubt that when I tell you that, if I am to find you here every time I come, I shall visit Mrs. Warner no longer."

"You call yourself my friend, and yet shun me in this manner," replied Philip, in a reproachful tone.

"I am, indeed," exclaimed Christine. "I do feel a deep interest in your welfare, but I cannot do evil that good may come. This has the appearance of clandestine meetings, a thing which, were I to permit, would destroy all my self-respect.

"No, Mr. Armstrong, this must not continue. This is our last interview in this house; but, believe me, I shall watch your progress with the deepest interest, and always remember that you have one true friend in Christine Elliot."

She rose as if to leave the room, but he detained her.

"Christine, dear Christine!" he exclaimed, "we part not thus. Not before you hear me declare that—I love you!"

A score of times before he had uttered protestations of undying affection, in words that he had flattered himself were irresistible in their eloquence; but now, when he would have given worlds to have been able to express the depth of his affection, he felt that it would be profanation to address to her the rhapsodies he had so often poured into willing ears. He could hardly utter even "I love you," and yet those simple words, in that tone, were more eloquent than anything he could have said.

Christine stood an instant with downcast eyes and glowing cheek, without reply.

That instant seemed an age to him; on her next words hung his fate, and he hardly dared hope that they would be what he wished. She was so far superior to him, so pure, so good; could she love such a wretch as he?

Christine sunk into a chair, and burst into tears. He saw it all.

"You pity me!" he exclaimed, "but you cannot love me. Fool that I was to hope it! Forget me, Christine. Forget the wretch who dared to love you, or, if you remember him, think that he had yet one redeeming trait, since he loved one all purity, though he was himself a sinner. Farewell!"

He took her hand and raised it to his lips, then turned to leave the room.

"Philip!"

That voice—that tone! Did he read it aright? One glance was enough. In an instant, she was clasped to his heart.

"But my aunt," whispered Christine, endeavoring to extricate herself from his embrace.

"Trust to me," was his reply. "Sure of your love, I am confident of all the rest."

"I hear a footstep," said Christine. "Dear Philip, release me!" and she slipped from his arms as Mrs. Warner entered; she looked from the agitated girl to the smiling Philip, and half read the secret, for she had long been aware of the love which he felt for Christine, and had guessed, even before Christine was aware of it, that it was reciprocated.

"Congratulate me, Mrs. Warner," exclaimed Philip. "Only one obstacle is in the way of our perfect happiness, Mrs. Frothingham's consent, and that is but a mole-hill."

"I do rejoice with you most sincerely," replied Mrs. Warner, "and hope that you may find Mrs. Frothingham's prejudices as easy to be removed as you seem to imagine."

"Never fear," he returned. "I am going now to beard the lioness in her den. Farewell, Mrs. Warner. *Au revoir*, my Christine!" and he was gone.

"Have I done right?" asked Christine, timidly, as her answers to her friend's questions drew from her the scene that had just passed.

"You have saved him, dearest," was the reply. "His love for you has changed him entirely. Your influence has roused all that was noble in his nature, and it rests with you to make him all that God intended him to be. I have no fears for the future. I do not doubt him."

"Doubt him—who could do so?" exclaimed Christine, quickly. "I never thought of that—of fearing for him! But will he always love me—he, so beautiful, so talented, and I, so plain, and so far beneath him?"

"Give yourself no uneasiness about that, my darling," returned Mrs. Warner. "You under-estimate yourself. You are every way his equal. I only hope that he may prove himself worthy of you. And now, my dear, will you accompany me to see Miss Patience and Miss Tempe Minor; or has this put the poor old ladies quite out of your head?"

"I had forgotten them," replied Christine, blushing, "but I am quite ready to go."

It was a small cottage that they entered, after the short walk that led to the place of their destination.

They were ushered into the parlor by Miss Tempe, who apologized for her appearance then by saying that the servant had just gone out. Mrs. Warner took no notice of this stale and stereotyped white lie, but seated herself on the hard, old-fashioned sofa, which, like its owners, had seen better days. The floor was covered by an old and faded Wilton carpet, which bore the marks of care, in the shape of many darns; and the very colors of the old pictures of stiff and antiquated ladies and gentlemen, which adorned the walls, had faded and grown rusty, as if sympathizing with the fallen greatness of their family.

The whole room had a shabby-genteel appearance, from the scanty curtains that draped the small windows, to the straight-legged and rickety old piano, which, in its day, had been the admiration of all the townspeople, who had listened with delight to the performance of Miss Patience upon its keys; but that had long since passed, though still Miss Patience rattled its keys, and sung the old songs in a shrill, high voice, which had won such rapturous applause from crowds of admirers, when she was the youthful heiress.

It was as pitiful as ludicrous a sight to see the ancient damsel at her ancient instrument, playing off the ancient airs and graces that suited so illy with her withered visage; the tossings of the head that shook the bunches of false curls till they seemed in danger of leaving her, the smile that had once been fascinating now only served to make the caricature of a belle more complete.

Miss Tempe had taken advantage of her sister's entrance to retire, and now appeared, dressed in a scanty and rusty black silk, with an additional cluster of cork-screw curls on each side of her attenuated face. She had not so many airs as her sister, for Patience had been the beauty and pride of the family, and could not forget it, and Tempe, still, from force of habit, yielded to her in all points of difference, and insisted on her having the new garment, or going to the party, when it was ascertained that only one could have this gratification.

"Had you heard that we have another member in our family?" asked Miss Patience.

"No," replied Mrs. Warner. "You know I am always behind all the rest of the town in learning the news. Who is it?"

"It is my brother John's only daughter, an orphan, poor thing!" continued Patience.

"John," mused Mrs. Warner.

"Yes," answered Tempe. "You remember he married rather unfortunately." Here a severe glance from her sister checked her in her intended communication.

Miss Patience did not trust her sister to proceed, but went on, "Her mother died some time since, and she lived with people who were not over kind to her. We heard of it, and sent for her. Call her, Tempe."

"Grace! Grace!" cried Tempe, and in a moment a young girl entered.

"She is hardly seventeen," said Miss Patience, after introducing her, and she looked even younger.

She was very slight and very fair, had a profusion of wavy, brown hair, a rosy mouth, and deep-blue eyes. She was not strictly handsome, but yet there was something very attractive about her and her every movement was grace itself.

She seemed a little shy, and said nothing, except when directly addressed, but her aunts seemed to look upon her with a great deal of pride and fondness.

She listened with a mischievous smile to the descriptions which Patience gave of imaginary new dresses, and seemed half-ready to expose the untruths she was telling; she restrained herself, however, and only tapped her little foot impatiently as the recital went on.

Mrs. Warner and Christine at last took leave, declining the invitation to remain to tea, which both sisters united in giving, and half-inclined to laugh, though feeling a pity for the old ladies, Christine walked slowly homeward.

"It is very kind in them to take that niece of theirs home," said Mrs. Warner, musingly. "I must try and see if I cannot help them and her, poor little thing. A pretty, fairy-like creature, she is, isn't she, Christine?"

"Yes, she is," was the half-absent reply, for now her mind was filled with her own affairs.

Had Philip seen her aunt? What had she decided upon? She longed to get home, and after leaving Mrs. Warner, hurried onward.

She had just reached her room, and thrown aside her bonnet and shawl, when a servant requested her to go to the parlor, and, with a beating heart, she entered that room.

"My dear Christine," said Mrs. Frothingham, as the girl glided to her side, "Mr. Armstrong has just been here to make a formal demand for your hand in marriage."

"And what did you say?" asked Christine, eagerly.

"That if he could gain your consent, I gave mine willingly."

"Oh, Aunt Julia," exclaimed the girl, with a flash of joy in her eyes that told at once that her consent would not be withheld, "I hardly hoped this. You have seemed to dislike Philip so much."

"I did warn you against him," said Mrs. Frothingham, "because I knew him to be a trifler, a male coquet, and feared that he was trying to gain your affections merely to while away the time, which hung heavily upon his hands; but I give you credit. You have played the game well; for, do you know, Miss Christine, all the beauty, and fashion, and wealth of many a girl has been unable to effect what you have done—he never before offered marriage to any one. Christine, I did not give you credit for such skill."

"My dear aunt, you pain me," replied Christine. "I never tried to gain his heart, and why he loves me I do not know. It is surprising to me that he should have chosen me; but he does love me, and I am very happy."

"I shall write to your father," returned Mrs. Frothingham, taking no notice of these words, "immediately. He will make no objections, I am sure. The match is unexceptionable. Philip is handsome, elegant, and rich.

"He will be here this evening, my dear, to see you, so go to your chamber, and make yourself presentable."

Christine vanished, and Mrs. Frothingham took her pen to inform her brother of the great event in Christine's history.

Never were there two happier beings than the young couple who sat that evening in Mrs. Frothingham's parlor. Julia sat on a sofa, at a distance from them, while, half-forgetful of her presence, Philip talked to Christine of the past, and the future, and whispered words that called a blush of pleasure to her cheek.

He, as well as Mrs. Frothingham, had written her father, and no cloud dimmed the picture, which he painted, of their future. They would go to Europe together; she should see all that was beautiful, in nature and art, in that grand Old World, all she had dreamed of so often, all that he had described, that she had read of. After this they would return, and would have a beautiful home where she should be mistress, and where he should find all the happiness that earth can give.

From these, and a thousand similar plans, he returned to herself; made her tell him all about her own dear home, describe father, mother, and sister, and from that led her on to speak of her own thoughts.

He listened to her with pleasure, and every glance that her simple narrative gave him into her pure heart increased his admiration of her. She was so different from any woman he had ever met, so frank, and free from coquetry, so earnest to know and do the right, so free from any of the petty aims of her sex, that he wondered how he had ever gained her heart.

He would never have wearied of listening to her, and it was an unwelcome sound, indeed, when Mrs. Frothingham said: "It is after eleven o'clock, Mr. Armstrong"; but he submitted with a good grace to the hint, and bowing to her, and raising Christine's hand to his lips, he bade them good-night.

No day passed, during the vacation, that Christine did not see him. She took rides and walks with him, accompanied by her aunt, went to concerts, to the opera, and the theatre; in fact, no wish of hers was ungratified.

The books she casually mentioned a desire to read, the flowers she most loved, were hers, as if by magic, and nothing seemed to give him so much pleasure, as to see the joy that sparkled in her eyes at these renewed proofs of his devotion.

When school again reopened, their interviews were less frequent, for Mrs. Frothingham would not allow it, but Christine wished him to resume the profession of the law, which he had abandoned; and, as his talents were well-known, business began to occupy him.

The consent of Mr. Elliot had been readily given on his sister's representations, and Philip urged a speedy union.

"In the spring," at last Christine said, and so the matter was decided.

Mrs. Frothingham desired the marriage to take place at her house, and as Mr. Elliot wished Christine to come home before the wedding, she decided to go and spend the three months which were to intervene, there, in making preparations for the nuptials. Mrs. Frothingham desired it to be kept as private as possible, in which both Philip and Christine agreed.

Philip accompanied her to her home, and she was delighted to find that he appreciated the sterling good sense of her father, and admired Bessie as much as she could desire, while all the family were equally pleased with his elegance and evident fondness for Christine.

CHAPTER SIXTEEN

The Old Homestead

It was winter—the dreariest season of the year in the country; and yet as Christine stood by the window the morning after Philip's departure, and scraped off with her finger the delicate tracery of the frost upon the panes, the scene upon which she gazed did not look dreary to her.

Wide plains of snow, interspersed here and there by clumps of evergreens, lay outspread before her; further on, her eye rested on the distant hills, on whose bold summits fell the first beams of the sun, which laboriously worked its way up from grey clouds that looked as if they were heavy with fresh snows; the farmhouse, with its low wall, surrounded, as by a rampart, with banks of snow, its yard, where, close to the orchard-fence, stood the heavy wood-sled; while a little further on were piles of wood, which it was a part of winter's work to haul from the neighboring forests; and the barn-yard, filled, as it was, with cows, horses, oxen, and sheep, who crowded around the large tub, from which James Cameron was cutting the ice, that the cattle might take their morning draught, added life to the still picture.

It looked very pleasant to her; even the bare skeletons of the orchard opposite inspired her with no gloomy thoughts. They only reminded her of a hale old age; she had seen them in their promising spring-time, when the young leaves and buds had covered their dry branches, in a very luxuriance of beauty—she had seen them in their strength, in summer, when those buds had given place to growing fruit, when the birds had built their nests there, and sung there their sweetest songs; there, in the autumn, she had seen those limbs weighed down by the rosy fruit, which, in its perfect maturity, had well fulfilled the promise of the spring-buds and summer-birth, and now the task was done—the orchard rested from its labors, but in those dry limbs she knew that there was life; it was only now in a quiet sleep, ere long to be succeeded by a fresh awakening, a renewal of youth, a yearly resurrection.

No, there was nothing dreary in winter, and, with a light heart, Christine obeyed the call of her sister to come to breakfast.

She held her aching fingers over the cheerful fire that roared and blazed in the huge old fireplace, for a few minutes, and then moved aside for James, who came in shaking the snow off his mittens, and stamping the same from his boots on the wide and glowing hearth; then he rubbed his ears, which were very red, and declared that it was cold—a proposition which there was no disputing, and which made the breakfast-table, with its smoking viands, all the more inviting.

The low walls and homely furniture of that farm-house formed a striking contrast to the elegances that had, for the past two years, surrounded Christine; but rough as it was, every plank in that old house was dear to her. She thought no longer of anything unpleasant in the past, but remembered only its joys.

She busied herself now through the short days in assisting her mother and sister in their household tasks, laughing with them at her awkwardness, or sat at her work, plying her busy needle, and carolling merry songs. Every stitch was one link that drew her nearer to Philip; these garments were for Philip's wife; and so the task, which otherwise would have been a weary one, was pleasant to her.

"I declare it really does me good," said Farmer Elliot to his wife, "to see the gal so chipper, more like other folks. It was a good idee lettin' on her go with Julia."

"Waal, I was alwus in favor of it, you know, father," replied his wife, "and it has turned out well. She isn't like the same girl she was two year ago."

Those two years had, indeed, effected a marvellous change in Christine. She was not beautiful, she never could be, except to loving hearts, who could read the beauty of her soul in her deep eye and in her changing countenance; but there was a charm about her, whether in her sweet, clear voice, her gentle, dignified, and easy manners, in the grace and lightness of her step, or in the refinement and delicacy that breathed in her every gesture, or in all together, it would have been difficult to decide, but which insensibly attracted all who came within the sphere of her influence; a charm which was all the more powerful that she herself was quite unconscious of possessing it.

Every week during that winter did she and Bessie ride down to the village, for the mail was only weekly there, and never was she disappointed in receiving the expected letter; letters, the perusal of which filled her heart with a gladness that leaped to her eyes, and sparkled there, and she read them over and over again, till she knew them by heart—by heart, indeed, for the heart more than the memory had to do with her remembrance of them.

Then the magazines, new books, and papers that came, were more than enough to supply her with reading during the long evenings. Never had there been such mails at Amity Mills, and, as the postmaster examined them, and read, "Miss Christine Elliot" on package after package, he raised his eyebrows, and gave utterance to a long, sharp, but subdued whistle, his usual method of expressing his astonishment or his conjectures.

"All this hain't for nothin'," was his shrewd decision, and, as he related his suspicions to his wife, she in turn to her friend

Mrs. O'Reilly, and she to hers, all under the solemn assurance of secrecy, it was soon known over the village that Christine Elliot was going to be married. All agreed on this main point, though there was a slight difference in other particulars—some avowing that the bridegroom elect was a doctor, others, a minister, while still others were as certain that he belonged to various other professions.

All this extreme anxiety as to her affairs, the settlement of this and other questions of similar importance, though it kept the villagers busy, troubled Christine little. During the long evenings, she read aloud to an audience, consisting of her father, who sat smoking at one side of the pine table, which was pulled out into the centre of the floor before the huge fire, and her mother, who rattled her busy knitting-needles on the opposite side, Bessie, who kept her blue eyes fixed on her sewing, conscious that James Cameron, who was fashioning an axe handle, or who was engaged in some similar work of architecture, was, in fact, watching her every movement, and blushes deepened the roses on her cheek, while her fingers flew all the faster under this scrutiny. The silence was only broken by the reader's sweet voice, the click, click of her mother's needles, or the occasional fall of some burned log, letting a whole pile of blazing sticks and brands roll here and there on the hearth, or the noise of the tongs in replacing them.

Then followed the comments of the listeners, as the apples, which had been warming near the fire in the japanned tray, and the pitcher of cider, was discussed—interrupted, perhaps, by a laugh at Bessie, who, thinking herself unobserved, had succeeded in paring an apple without breaking the skin, and had slyly flung it over her head, and was endeavoring to discover the letter which it formed, while James declared it to be a perfect C.

Often there was a little lamb, which its mother had refused to own, lying in a basket near the fire, whose feeble cry was hushed by warm milk which Bessie administered.

There was never any lack of topics for conversation, farming and politics rivalled each other, till nine o'clock rung out from the old wooden clock; then came the family prayers, for Mr. Elliot was a devout Methodist, and, though the long prayer he uttered was essentially the same he had offered every night for twenty years, yet it came from a sincere heart, and were not their wants the same?

So three months passed.

The March winds were howling over the earth, though now and then a spring-like day gave an earnest of what was to be; the snow had scarcely gone, and the farmer's work had begun, the wood was to be chopped which was to supply the next winter's fires, the dressing to be got ready for the fields, and the fences to be repaired or rebuilt.

It was April when Christine returned to Woodland Vale. The buds of the willows were swelling and ready to burst forth; the winter wheat was just peeping from the ground, and all Nature seemed rousing herself from her long sleep; Spring had got there before her; everything around her aunt's dwelling betokened her presence; the first hardy flowers were unfolding their soft petals, the leaves danced on the trees, the air was soft and balmy, the birds had returned from their southern pilgrimage. In everything she recognized the magic touch of Spring.

Her marriage was to take place in May, and all the family were to be present.

Mrs. Frothingham was in her element in planning the festivities. She had taken care to select the wardrobe of the bride, and had set the nimble fingers of divers seamstresses at work on articles of wearing apparel for her niece.

All was happiness and light around her; it was spring-time in her heart, and though sometimes a shadow flitted over her, as she thought of the Spanish proverb, "It is not always May," it was as fleeting as dark, for love's sunshine speedily dissipated it.

She was one day paying a visit to Mrs. Warner, and had been telling to that kind friend some of the bright visions that rose before her, to which Mrs. Warner's only reply was a deep sigh.

"Why do you sigh?" asked Christine.

"It is not that I do not rejoice in your happiness, my child, and pray that it may be lasting, though in this world sorrow must come to all, but I selfishly grieve sometimes at the downfall of all my hopes. I had looked forward to such a future for you. I imagined you toiling in the great work-field, and returning with rich sheaves, the fruit of your labors, to the garner, and, alas, your eyes are so dazzled by love's sunlight that you see nothing but brightness in the world.

"You heed not the fields that are to be brought in from the wilderness of the world, that they may sometime be white for the harvest."

"Oh, do not say so, Mrs. Warner!" exclaimed Christine. "I confess I have for a time been forgetful of all but my own happiness; but may I not rejoice in the good gift that God has given me, and do you not see that, instead of losing me, you have gained a laborer in Philip? Together he and I will toil on, cheering each other."

Mrs. Warner shook her head sadly.

"It cannot be," she said; "your duties will confine you to a narrower field."

"But not less noble," interrupted Christine.

"True," replied Mrs. Warner. "But I had hoped so much of you. I hardly knew how much, till I now see you about to enter on the common lot of woman. Christine, your field is the world."[27]

"Do not fear, my friend," interrupted Christine's sweet voice, "that I shall forget my duties to my fellows in the narrower circle around me. I will do what lies nearest me first, and not leave the rest undone. I will write! I can write—I am sure of it—words that will reach the hearts of men, and find an echo there. Do not feel so disappointed; I can do much yet."

"And when shall I read your essays, my dear?"

"Perhaps never. Essays are too often read by those who do not need them. Christ did not disdain to convey truth in parables. I will write in a form that will bring my words to all—the good who seek for the right and true, wherever it may be found, will hear me, and to the careless, who would never seek for truth, I will whisper lessons so gently that they cannot offend, and yet, that may bear with them seeds which may spring up in the heart."

"But Philip may not wish you to do so."

"You do not understand Philip; he would only urge me on to do all that I can in this short life."

"Christine," said Mrs. Warner, as her friend rose to go away, "I may have said too much. You have still high aims. You will make a noble wife and mother, and there are few enough of them in this world. In those duties you will find enough to employ all your powers. God is leading you into that path. I had hoped that you were she, who, like Miriam of old, should be one of the leaders of the down-trodden into the land of freedom; but, in His own good time, He will raise up a prophetess."[28]

"Yes, in His own good time," replied Christine, as she bade her friend good-bye, and walked to the lake where she had promised to meet Philip.

 Grace

It was before the time that she had appointed, but it was very pleasant to sit under the tall trees that waved their leafy branches near that beautiful sheet of water, to look into its crystal depths, and see the same beautiful picture reflected there, only in softer tints, that lay around her; the fleecy clouds, the waving trees, were mirrored below her, and she could almost imagine that she had a glimpse into the dwellings of the Naiads.[29]

She leaned back, at last, against a tree, and letting the soft air play on her cheek, she sunk into a reverie.

Mrs. Warner's words had roused her. She would awake from her slumber. She would work. A quiet smile played round her mouth, and a deeper light filled her eyes, as she marked out her future course.

Suddenly she heard voices near her. Surely, one was familiar to her—but no, a clear, girlish voice replied; it could not be Philip's tones, though strangely like them; it was probably some couple who had been tempted by the beauty of the day to sail over the still waters of the lake.

The voices came nearer. She was about to change her position when the words arrested her attention, and rooted her to the spot.

"Philip, dear Philip. Tell me; it cannot be so!"

The voice was sweet, but pitifully earnest and mournful, and every tone fell on Christine's ear as clearly as if the speaker had been at her side, yet she could not see her, separated, as they were, by clumps of trees.

"Why have you followed me thus?" returned a voice she well knew, but in a stern and harsh tone she had never before heard. "Why do you dog me in this manner?"

"Oh, Philip, do not speak so coldly, and forgive me, but I had just heard words that maddened me. I saw you, and I could wait no longer. I must hear denial from your lips! It cannot be that you are going to be married. It cannot be true."

"Yet, it is true," he replied.

Christine could bear suspense no longer; she leaned forward and saw, through the trees, her lover and a young girl, whom she instantly recognized as Grace Minor.

Both were turned away from her, and she could see distinctly the slight figure of Grace, who, at these words, had sunk on the ground, and was wringing her hands convulsively.

"Then it is true. I have been sewing, wearily and in sadness, on the garments of your bride! But, as your bride, she shall never wear them!" she exclaimed, checking her sobs. "I will go to her. I will tell her all."

"Do you dare to threaten me?" he interrupted, stamping his foot, and speaking in a fierce tone. "Dare to do as you have said, and I never see you more."

A fresh burst of sobs was the only reply.

At last she spoke, in a voice choked with emotion—

"Tell me, then, one thing. You do not love her?"

Christine held her breath almost suspended to hear the reply. She felt almost guilty at the exultation, which she experienced as he spoke.

"Love her?" he exclaimed. "Better than my own life—better than my own soul. She is the only woman that I ever loved!"

"The only woman! Oh, Philip, unsay those cruel words. It cannot be. She so—"

"Hush!" he interrupted. "Do not take the name of that pure being upon your lips. She, so far above all the world—she, the first of her sex that I ever respected—she, who endeavored to lead me into her own heavenly way. Do not bring her image into comparison with you," he added, sneeringly.

"But who made me what I am?" exclaimed the girl. "Was I not as pure as she, till you came with false words and smiles?" she paused, overcome with emotion. "Oh, God!" she ejaculated. "What am I now? He, who, of all the world, should pity me, spurns me with contempt. Tells me that all these months, in which he won my heart and wrought my ruin, he has been betrothed to another—that he never loved me!

"Philip Armstrong, the world will smile on you—it will crush me under foot, but, in the sight of heaven, you are guiltier than I. God judge between us!" and, turning away, she was soon lost to sight.

Her departure recalled Christine to herself.

She could not see Philip then, and rising, she leaned against a tree for a moment to recover her strength, for she could hardly support herself; but Philip might come that way and discover her, so, controlling herself by a strong effort, she managed to gain her home, and enter it without being observed.

She flung herself on her bed and gave herself up to her agony.

What a change had the last few hours made in her fate. As she contrasted the bright visions that had filled her with happiness, with the present, she groaned aloud. A few hours before, and the thought of his death would have seemed to her the most terrible blow that could have fallen upon her, and now how much rather she would have stood by his open grave, and would have heard the heavy sound of the clods falling on his coffin, than to see him, as she had, with the flush of youth and health upon his cheek, spurning from him his suffering victim.

Could it be that he, whom she had imagined so noble, true, and generous, was so treacherous, false, and vile?

Was it not a horrid dream? Alas! it was all too real.

Her eyes burned painfully—the light seemed to scorch them; her temples throbbed; she could not weep; she only laid still on her couch, with an aching at her heart, a dull, heavy pain that she could not escape; it seemed to her that her senses were unusually acute; every light step through the hall seemed to jar her aching head, and she could hardly bear the flutter of the white curtain, which the breeze, that blew in at the open window, caused. Just then she heard a ring at the door-bell—a step—Philip's step, his voice, and her aunt's in reply, and then his clear, ringing laugh.

How discordantly that sound fell on her ear. He could laugh, and she, could she ever smile again?

She knew that Philip had come to see why she had not met him at the lake, and she heard the step of the servant who was coming to her room.

She rose, and with trembling fingers, pencilled these words on a card:

"Philip, I was at the lake, and saw and heard all. Farewell."

She gave the card to the girl, who gazed at her pale face compassionately, and shut the door gently, pitying her evident suffering.

"Miss Christine is sick," said the servant, entering the parlor, and giving Philip the card.

He glanced at it and turned deathly pale.

Mrs. Frothingham noticed his sudden change of color, and with a light laugh, began to assure him that there was no occasion for alarm; that it was probably only one of her niece's usual severe attacks of headache.

"But I will go to her," she concluded, "and bring you an exact account of her health, and tell her what a model lover she has, who grows pale at the thought of her illness."

"Go, Mrs. Frothingham," exclaimed Philip, eagerly, "and beg her to come down, if but for a moment. Tell her I must see her."

"I will tell her," replied Julia, smilingly, as she left the room, and Philip paced up and down the apartment in a fever of suspense.

Mrs. Frothingham, meanwhile, entered her niece's apartment

"You are feverish, my dear," she said, putting her soft hand on Christine's burning forehead, "but you should see Philip. He is half-crazy about you," and she delivered his message.

"Oh, Aunt Julia!" exclaimed Christine, as she ceased speaking. "Tell him I cannot, I cannot!" and, with a quick sob, she fell back on her pillow insensible.

Mrs. Frothingham rang for a servant, and applied cold water profusely to the sufferer, and ere long she recovered her consciousness; when all was done that could ensure her comfort, Mrs. Frothingham returned to the parlor.

"She would not come!" was Philip's exclamation, as he saw her enter alone.

"She is very ill," was the reply. "It is a sudden attack, for she was quite well this morning; but she will be better soon. I shall send for Dr. Hubbard, immediately. Excuse me now, I must return to her."

"I have killed her!" muttered Phillip, bitterly, rising as Mrs. Frothingham left the room, and walking out of the house.

With his hat drawn moodily over his eyes, he strode on towards the cottage of Grace Minor.

It was growing dark, and he heeded no one he met; suddenly he felt a light touch on his arm, and a joyful voice exclaimed—

"Oh, Philip, I knew you would come—I have been watching for you, and came out to meet you."

He flung off the little hand that rested on his arm, and cast a fierce glance at the girl that made her shudder. Its meaning was unmistakable—all hope died out in her heart.

She sighed, a long-drawn, quivering sigh that was half a sob.

"Oh, Philip," she cried, "is there no spark of love for me in your heart? Do you hate me?"

"Yes, I hate you," he hissed through his shut teeth. "You have killed her, my bride—my wife. You are the curse of my life," and, as if maddened, he went on to overwhelm her with bitter curses and revilings.

She listened to it all, without a word in reply, only standing there with her hands pressed tightly over her heart, as if every word was a dagger that pierced to her very life; when he ceased, she only murmured—

"Would to God that we had never met!"

"You cannot wish it more devoutly than I," replied Philip, coldly. "Your presence is hateful to me!"

"I will relieve you of it," answered the girl, with a strange calmness. "Will you not say one kind word to your little Grace before she bids you farewell?"

She took his hand timidly, and went on—

"Call me Grace once more! Tell me that you do not mean all those cruel words you have said. Speak to me once as you used to do. I will trouble you no more!"

Her gentleness only seemed to irritate him more and more.

"Will nothing rid me of you?" he exclaimed, fiercely. "Have I not said enough, that you cling to me still? I could find it in my heart to strike you!" he muttered.

"Oh, not that, not that!" exclaimed Grace, wildly.

"Begone, then!" he said, contemptuously turning his back upon her. When he looked around, she was gone.

Rapidly she went on, her long hair floating in the wind, her shawl held tightly over her breast, whither she hardly knew. She had plunged into the forest—the underbrush clung to her garments, as if to hold her back—she only hurried on, leaving fragments of her dress in its friendly grasp—on, on, till she reached the borders of the lake, close to the very spot where Philip had told her that he never loved her.

"May God have mercy upon me, for man has none!" she said, wildly, and with all the calmness of despair, she laid aside her shawl, walked out on a fallen tree that, half-supported by those near it, was suspended over the clear lake.

There was a plash in the deep waters, a few faint, instinctive struggles, a gurgling cry—then the circling ripples grew wider and wider! All was still again, save the gentle washing of the waves against the shore, naught to tell of the fearful tragedy that had been enacted there—and the spirit of Grace Minor was with its God!

CHAPTER EIGHTEEN

Heart Struggles

As Philip Armstrong grew calmer, he despised himself for the harshness and cruelty of his words to Grace, though he could not clearly remember all he had said. He resolved to see her, and to do all in his power to atone for it; and, with vague plans for sending her far away, where her pale, suffering face should haunt him no longer, supplying her bodily wants, as if money could bind up the broken heart, he wended his way to her cottage-home on the following morning.

He found the old ladies in great anxiety about her, as she had not been at home during the night.

A vague foreboding, too horrible to be put into words, rushed over the young man.

The village was aroused, and ere long the lifeless corpse of Grace Minor lay in the little parlor, where first she had listened to the voice of him who had wrought her ruin. Who could read the agony, the remorse that filled Philip's heart, as he stood by her side, apparently calm, looking at that girlish face so bright and cheerful when he had first known her. What would he not have given to restore her to life? To recall those last interviews with her? How her last sad words haunted him. He felt that he was her murderer—and Christine, too, lay ill. He had killed her, too; no wonder that he looked haggard and wan. He shut himself up in his room, only going every few hours to learn how Christine was, for he could bear suspense no longer.

"She was better, though still suffering," her aunt said.

He felt a thrill of joy at these words. Her blood, at least, was not on his hands.

How he longed to see her, if but for a moment, to tell her he should never cease to love her, though she was lost to him forever.

The toll of a bell struck heavily on his ear. All that was earthly of Grace Minor was on its way to the churchyard. It was as if every stroke fell on his heart.

It roused Christine from an uneasy sleep. She started up, and asked her attendant, eagerly, who was dead?

The girl related all, the search for the poor Grace, and the finding of her dead body.

Christine listened to the tale with wild, flashing eyes, and parted lips—her curtain blew aside, and she saw the black procession slowly winding by. She uttered one deep groan and fainted.

Swoon succeeded swoon, and when, at length, she recovered from these she was in the wildest delirium.

For weeks her life hung as upon a thread, while she was unconscious of all about her. When, at last, she opened her languid eyes, no longer sparkling with the brightness of fever, and spoke a few words feebly, which showed that she was herself once more, her friend, Mrs. Warner, who sat by her side, could restrain herself no longer; she burst into glad tears that fell on the thin hand that rested on the white counterpane.

Christine looked bewildered.

"Where am I? Do not weep. What has happened?" she said, feebly, with a vague remembrance of something painful.

Mrs. Warner recollected herself, wiped away her tears, and telling her that she had been very sick, lifted her gently, shook up her pillow, and bade her compose herself to sleep.

But she could not sleep; it wearied her; yet she must think; what had happened? Gradually it all came back to her.

"Philip?" she whispered, inquiringly.

"Well," returned Mrs. Warner; "and here every few hours to ask for you. He sent you these flowers," she added, lifting a vase that was filled with the choicest blossoms. "Would you like them nearer?"

"No," replied Christine, faintly; "but tell him I thank him, and I am better."

Mrs. Warner faithfully delivered this message, and marked the flash of joy that irradiated his countenance.

"She is an angel," he said, and in his heart arose the hope, that had well-nigh died out, of a reconciliation.

Slowly Christine regained her strength, and, at last, she could sit up for some hours at her window; she had steadily refused to see Philip, though he had begged her to do so in eloquent notes, again and again.

"I cannot yet," had been her unvarying reply.

It was the morning that was to have been her wedding-day, and she sat by the open window, attired in a simple, white dressing-gown, her dark hair put smoothly back from her fair brow, and her dark eyes looking preternaturally large and bright, contrasting as they did with the paleness of her cheek.

Mrs. Frothingham sat there sewing by her side.

Christine, at last, broke the silence.

"You have written home, have you not?"

"Yes, regularly. I did not tell them how ill you were, for it would only have distressed them unnecessarily. You had every attention, and in your delirium would not have known who were your attendants."

"Do you know what day this is?"

"Yes," replied Mrs. Frothingham, cheerfully. "It was to have been your wedding-day."

"If Philip comes to day I will see him, and alone, if you please, Aunt Julia."

"Very well," was the reply, and, almost before the words were spoken, a servant brought in a bouquet of flowers from Mr. Armstrong, and a card, on which were pencilled a few words of entreaty to see her.

"Tell him I will see him, Aunt Julia."

Mrs. Frothingham left the room, returned with Philip, and immediately withdrew. Christine sat silently by the window, and Philip hesitated a moment before approaching her; she extended her hand, and, almost reverentially, he took it, pressed it to his lips and his heart. Tears were in his large, dark eyes, his cheek was thin, and the blue veins that threaded his brow were fearfully distinct.

"Poor Philip!" said Christine, softly.

"My own! My wife!" he exclaimed, kneeling before her, and, putting his arms about her waist, he pressed her to his heart. "Your gentleness pierces me to the heart. Your kindness is more than I can bear. Overwhelm me with reproaches as I deserve."

She gently disengaged herself from his embrace.

"I have no reproaches to make," she said. "You have suffered. I see it."

"God knows," he bitterly interrupted, "if suffering can expiate a sin, that I have endured enough to atone for mine, dreadful as it is."

Christine made no reply to this, but went on —

"It was not for me to add to your misery, and that is why I have sent for you to-day, to tell you that I have pitied you, and that I never have felt harshly to you through it all. I knew that it would be a consolation to you to hear these words from my lips, that I forgive you for any suffering I have felt, and that I grieve for you even more than for myself, that this day, which was to have been our wedding-day, should, instead, separate us for ever."

"Oh, Christine!" interrupted Philip, in a voice of agony, "you cannot mean it; you who are already, in God's sight, my wife! Oh, Christine, do not abandon me!"

"Hush, Philip!" she replied. "Do not urge me to this sin. Her form would glide ever between us—her memory poison all our future lives; even in my prayers for you, she would stand between me and God, reproaching me that I prevented your doing her justice, that I drove her to despair, and unbidden into the presence of her Maker, and then took her rightful place by your side. Every step to the altar would be through her blood!" she shuddered as she spoke.

"Christine, do you know what you are doing?" cried Philip. "Do you know that you will drive me mad? Do you not see that you are breaking the last strand that holds me out of utter ruin? That you are sacrificing me to a morbid scruple? Christine, you alone can save me! You alone can lead me in the right way!"

"That was my error," she said, unheeding his wild words—but as if thinking aloud. "I thought to take God's work into my puny hands. He has shown me how weak, how presumptuous I was. Philip, I sinned in that I tried to do it. It was like Uzzah's sin of old in steadying the ark, and I must submit to my punishment.[30]

"You were my idol, too. I loved you, oh, how wildly! God has smitten me for that. Let me submit, lest a worse thing come upon us. Farewell, Philip. I commit you into His hands who is able to guide you. All I can do, I will do—pray for you always. Go now, and may God bless you!"

"I cannot leave you thus!" he cried. "Christine, my own, I cannot lose you! It is not the voice of God that bids you thrust me into utter darkness," he went on, growing more and more violent: she fixed her eyes steadily upon him—that quiet, firm, and loving glance calmed him.

"Go, dear Philip," she said, "and, if you love me, spare me further pain. I am very weary."

He saw that she was, indeed, growing paler, and with one parting pressure of the hand, he left her to seek her aunt, and endeavor to obtain her influence in his favor.

He did not disguise from her the facts relating to the death of Grace, but begged her to use her utmost endeavors to gain Christine's consent to their union. His remorse was, indeed, great; and much as Mrs. Frothingham was shocked, she yet agreed with him that Christine was morbidly sensitive; she could not, without a pang, see so brilliant a match slip through her niece's fingers.

Like all the world, she blamed the victim. She had no pity for her weakness; she had done the wisest thing, the only thing left her. What could she expect, she asked herself.

How many who may be ready to condemn Mrs. Frothingham as heartless, do not in their secret hearts feel the same? Who cannot recall the fate of some weak sinner, like Grace, who has suffered a living death; by one false step sunk into utter ruin, without hope in this world. All her efforts at reform looked upon coldly—no society open to her, save the vicious—only cold words and averted looks from the virtuous—what is left her but death? What wonder that despair finds her a ready victim—that she plunges into deeper degradation?

Mrs. Frothingham was not heartless, but she was worldly, and she resolved to do her utmost to show Christine her folly. So, ere many days were passed, she introduced the subject: she ridiculed Christine's ideas of her own agency in Grace's fate—dwelt on Philip's remorse—and, at last, assailed her on her weakest point, his future reformation.

Christine was greatly agitated, but firm, and only replied, "Our union would only bring unhappiness. He has deceived me—that, I forgive him, but I could feel no confidence in him, and without that both he and I should be wretched. Then, too, he would cease to respect me, did I yield to his request, and I should lose all influence over him. I cannot lose that. It would kill me. No—if the knowledge of my love, the memory of what has been, cannot save him, I, weak mortal, could do no more! Aunt Julia, do not urge me further. It is hard enough for me to do right. There is a voice in my heart that urges me to do what I feel is wrong; do not lend the weight of your eloquence to my temptations."

"She wavers," thought Julia, "I will leave her to herself for awhile"; but she mistook.

No persuasions could induce her to alter her determination; she would not trust herself to see Philip; and though Mrs. Frothingham at last grew angry at her continued obstinacy, which she declared most unreasonable, Christine only fortified herself with endurance, and braved it all.

Julia, indeed, did think her very unnecessarily obdurate, for once enlisted on Philip's side, she made so many excuses for him to Christine that she finally worked herself into the belief that he was a very ill-used individual.

CHAPTER NINETEEN

Consecration

"Well, Christine, I hope you are satisfied, now," exclaimed Mrs. Frothingham, entering the library, where stood her niece in the act of drawing down the *Essays of Elia;* "you have driven Philip away, he is gone."[31]

"Gone!" repeated Christine, tremulously, and growing ashy-pale.

"Yes, gone to Europe, perhaps never to return, and what have you to say to that?"

"That it is the kindest and wisest thing he could have done," returned Christine, regaining her composure.

"You are the most provoking girl I ever met," exclaimed Mrs. Frothingham, who had hoped much from her evident emotion, and was not at all prepared for such a reply.

"Let me tell you," she went on, "that you have thrown away what many a girl, vastly your superior, would have thought herself only too happy in securing, and if you think that such matches are to be had every day, you are grandly mistaken. You are not so beautiful and so bewitching that you may expect to obtain perfection, even if perfect people were common. Philip, bad as you think him, is as good, if not better, than the majority of young men. He had so many qualifications combined that are essential in a husband, that I confess I have no patience with you for rejecting him for one error. I am sure if there was ever a sincere penitent in the world, he was one; and through your ridiculous and obstinate sentimentality you have lost him. You will one day see your folly as clearly as I do, and regret it as much, but your regrets will be too late."

Christine had listened to all this without interruption, but now she spoke.

"It is useless for me to say more on this painful subject. I cannot hope that you will look upon it in the same light that I do, but I do not regret what I have done, nor shall I ever do so. I have tried to do what was right. It has been hard for me to persist in it; to feel that I was going directly contrary to your wishes, you who are so much older and more experienced than I; but, Aunt Julia, God has shown me the right path very clearly, and it would have been willful sin had I done otherwise than to walk in it. I have lost much, indeed, in losing Philip, but, believe me, all that you seem to value so much, never for an instant influenced me in his favor. His wealth! What did I care for that? Would I not have gone forth, hand in hand with him, to suffer all the ills of life, and thought myself only too happy in sharing his sorrows. But it was not so to be. God's hand was in it all, and, even more for Philip's sake than my own, am I glad that strength was given me to go through my trial unshrinkingly. Believe me, my motives were pure; no anger or revenge had part in them, nor will I deny that I have suffered in obeying the voice of duty. But it is past now, Aunt Julia, let us speak of it no more. Any renewal of the subject between us can only cause unpleasant feelings."

"You are right, Christine. All your nonsensical notions only make me more angry with you. Let me tell you that the voice of duty and God's hand had nothing to do with it. I attribute it all to your own obstinacy, though you may prefer to give it fine romantic names; and as you wish me to do you justice with regard to your utter carelessness about Philip's worldly matters, I will do so, though it by no means elevates you, in my opinion. The whole affair only confirms me in my estimate of your character, which is this, that, for a girl with more than ordinary talent, you have the least good, practical common-sense of any person I ever met; and much as you may despise this humdrum quality, had I the power I would give half your talent for a few grains of good sense," and having finished speaking, Mrs. Frothingham rose, and without waiting for a reply, swept out of the room.

Christine sank down on a lounge near, and buried her face in her hands; her aunt's words had involved her in painful doubt as to whether she had done right. What if she had mistaken the voice of God in her heart, and had flung away her own and Philip's happiness? The thought was agony, but it was only momentary. She reviewed all that had passed, and felt an assurance that she had done what was right. She laid gently on the lounge, and, though her lips syllabled no words, yet her heart went out to God in that voiceless prayer which is often more eloquent in its sincerity than any form of words could be. As she prayed, she grew calm. Into His hands she committed herself, and one dearer than self, with the trustfulness of a child.

"I am His; let Him do as seemeth Him good," she said, half-aloud, as she left the room.[32]

Not long after she entered the dwelling of her friend, Mrs. Warner. That good lady sat in a low easy-chair, in her cozy sitting-room; her baby laid across her lap, while she was endeavoring to mend a ghastly rent in her oldest boy's pantaloons. She looked up with a smile of welcome as Christine entered.

"You are skilled in angles," she said, cheerfully. "What kind of a figure is that?" and she held up the rent in full view. "Is it a rhomboid, my female Euclid?"[33]

"I think it would defy geometry to give it a title," answered Christine; "but let me take the baby while you mend it, as you seem to be intending to do."

As she spoke she held out her hands to little Willie, who extended his dimpled fingers joyfully, and in another moment she was in full possession of him. Mrs. Warner busied herself in repairing the unfortunate pantaloons, talking cheerfully to her visitor.

"It is like coming out of darkness into sunshine to be with you, my dear friend," said Christine. "It does me good. I feel stronger every moment. I have not been very happy of late. I thought a few months ago that I knew just what my duties were; but God has closed the door through which I was about to enter the work field, and I see no other open. I am willing to work, but it is the study of a lifetime to find just the right place."

"No, there you err. We are in the right place always, and there, too, are our duties, though many looking forward, and far away, overlook what lies nearest them, and grieve that they cannot find their appointed place.

"'They also serve the Lord who stand and wait.'"[34]

"Is it for me, then, to stand and wait?" said Christine, rather sadly. "If so, I submit; but I need a life of action. I long for it. It seems to me that I have powers which ought to be exercised—but this may be only restlessness."

"No, Christine, it is not. I see clearly your duty. Do you not remember our conversation when I gave you up to woman's usual life—when I told you of the high hopes I had for you? God has taken you from that sphere. It is a mysterious thing to you, but I read it distinctly. He destines you for a higher calling.

"Christine, it is yours to be the champion of your sex. The pioneer in the march of progress. You are to rouse the indifferent—to give voice to the suffering of your sex. This is God's will. Happy are you if you shrink not from it."

"How? How am I to accomplish all this?" exclaimed the girl, who had been listening eagerly.

"You are to speak in words of power. You, who could so electrify an audience of worldly fashionables that, at your words, their sleeping souls were roused, that they forgot themselves for a few brief moments, and felt that they were indeed immortal, what might you not do if you would but speak for your sex?"

"Do you mean that I could lecture, that I ought to do so?" gasped Christine.

"I do," replied Mrs. Warner.

"Oh, I cannot! I cannot!" exclaimed the girl. "That cannot be what I ought to do."

"Just now you longed to enter on your mission. When it is pointed out to you, you shrink back. How little we know ourselves! You were willing to do God's will if it chimed in with your own."

"Oh, Mrs. Warner, it is so different—all is so changed!" and she burst into tears that she could not restrain.

"Do you regret your decision?" asked Mrs. Warner.

"Oh, no, no. But let me weep over my perished hopes; let me be forgiven, for I am human. I cannot see all that is beautiful crushed out of my young life without a pang."

"All that is beautiful!" repeated her friend. "I had not thought to hear such words from you, Christine. Is there nothing more beautiful than a life of ease and self-indulgence? Is there no beauty in self-denial, in proclaiming God's great truths, in elevating those around you, in teaching others all that you hold most sacred? What could you ask for more than this? To what holier aim, to what loftier task, could you consecrate your powers?"

"Let me think of it awhile," said Christine, looking up through her tears. "It is so new to me that I am not now prepared to accept it."

Mrs. Warner said no more; indeed, little was said during the remainder of the afternoon. Christine was thoughtful and absent, and her friend was too well accustomed to her moods to disturb them.

The twilight was deepening when Christine took leave, but instead of going home she walked on to the pond. It had been a favorite walk of hers and Philip's, and every step was associated with him. As she walked on, the sadness which these memories caused her gave place to other feelings.

"It is weak to grieve over the past," she said, and her thoughts reached forward to the future. Mrs. Warner's words returned vividly to her recollection. She thought of all that was pitiful and weak, in her sex; of the worldliness of nearly all about her; of their low and grovelling aims. "This poverty of the heart and mind, is more dreadful than anything else of which woman can complain," she said, half aloud.

But how raise her from her moral degradation? She must be first aroused to it. Was it not, as her friend had said, a glorious task to do this?

Her cheeks burned, her eyes sparkled, as she thought of this, and of a thousand reforms that she had longed to see accomplished through her instrumentality. She would enter upon this great work, and she thanked God for giving her so noble a task, one that would require all her powers—all her soul. She had reached the pond. The moon had risen, and its clear beams fell on the waters till they gleamed like silver; all was still, save the whispers of the wind through the leaves, the chirp of insects, and the plashing of the waves. It filled her heart with an indescribable sensation, a pleasure that was not unmingled with pain, a peace that filled her whole being, and yet a vague unrest, a yearning for something more.

She fell on her knees, and vowed a solemn vow to spend her life and her talents in the one great work of the elevation of her sex.

Filled with a lofty enthusiasm, and seeing already accomplished the great ends she sought, she walked homeward, and went directly to her chamber, for she was in no mood now for anything but solitude.

CHAPTER TWENTY

 The Field Is the World

The next morning, as she thought of her last evening's vow, she almost shuddered. What had she done? The glow of enthusiasm had faded away; she saw now that she had committed herself to a cause which was ridiculed by many and supported by but few. What could she do, a weak woman, single-handed and alone? "No, not alone," she exclaimed. "God will be with me."

But this thought could not prevent her from seeing that it was a difficult undertaking to which she had devoted herself. She knew she must experience the opposition of her friends, the hootings and revilings of the mob, the sneers even of those for whom she was laboring.

Could she endure all this? For a moment her heart sunk within her; but she despised herself for her momentary discouragement—all this should not daunt her, and with a firm purpose, she went to see her friend.

"How is it, Christine?" asked Mrs. Warner, "Are you ready to lead the way, to be the voice of 'one crying in the wilderness?'"[35]

Christine's only reply was to put into her friend's hand the following lines which she had composed the preceding night.

We have loved, and we have parted,
    That bright dream is in the past—
Yet I am not broken-hearted,
    Life is not all overcast.
True, the present gives no promise
    That the star of love shall rise,
Gleaming with its olden radiance
    In the future's cloudy skies.
Hope, the flatterer, long hath left me,
    She who lingers to the last,
Yet my heart repeats, not sadly,
    It is over—it is past.
It is past. For me no longer
    Shall love's fragrant blossoms bloom;
Those I gathered long since faded,
    Long since lost their sweet perfume.
Yet I bless that star which lighted
    For awhile my young life's sky—
And I bless those flowers, though blighted,
    That around me withered lie.
Ah! those words—I love, I am loved,
    Once had power my soul to thrill,
And I know that of earth's pleasures
    Then my being had its fill.
It is past! and I am grateful
    For that wild, bewildering draught;
Now I fling aside the chalice,
    All whose waters I have quaffed.
Onward now I press, perceiving
    That love is not all of life,
And, with heart and soul undaunted,
    Haste to join earth's din and strife.
I have taken up my burden
    Which I shrank from far too long—

Labor leads to life eternal,
    Is my battle-cry and song.
And the star which lights my pathway,
    Is the star of faith in God;
And white flowers of peace are springing
    In the parched ground where I trod.
God hath given living waters,
    That have made my thirst to cease;
Over rough ways, He hath led me
    To the path of perfect peace.

Mrs. Warner read the stanzas, and, as she finished their perusal, she exclaimed, in a tone of the greatest enthusiasm—

"I have not lived entirely in vain. Christine, you will go on from height to height. Your clear voice will ring out words of power that will startle the sleepers—words of encouragement that will cheer the toilers who strive to reach your high eminence. People will call you blessed! They will reverence you as one who walks with God; and, though no one will think of her who led you to the altar and consecrated you as a priestess—though no one will know whose voice made clear to you the oracles of God in your own heart, yet is my silent triumph none the less great. I shall rejoice in all your successes! My secret labors have not been unseen. His eye, from whom no secret is hid, has marked them all, and blessed me in seeing the fruit of my labors."

Christine looked at her friend's kindling eye and heavenly smile. She could not bear to check her high hopes, her lofty enthusiasm; but before her rose all the difficulties of the rugged road over which she was to pass, and the dark side of the picture, whose brightness was all that seemed to meet the vision of her friend.

"God grant that I, too, may see the fruit of my toils before I am called out of the vineyard," she said; "and now I must go to acquaint my aunt with my determination."

It was with a faint heart, though, to all appearances, outwardly calm, that Christine entered the library, where Mrs. Frothingham was seated.

How could she tell that lovely woman, who had so schooled herself in the ways of the world that any deviation from its strictest proprieties she regarded almost as a sin—that she, her niece, was about to break through all conventionalities—that she was about to devote herself to what her aunt would consider the most absurd of all Quixotic schemes? But it must be done, and, in a few brief words, Christine announced her determination.

Julia looked at her a moment, fixedly. "What did you say? I did not fully understand," she said—and poor Christine was obliged to repeat all that she had before uttered.

"Christine Elliot, you are insane!" was Mrs. Frothingham's reply. "You are fit for nothing but a lunatic asylum. A lecturer! A woman's rights' lecturer! What wild notion will you get next into that foolish head of yours?" and she laughed, a scornful laugh that abashed her niece not a little.

"You, with your pale face, now crimsoned with blushes, and your slight figure, trembling with agitation before one auditor, you think of facing an audience and lecturing them? Poor baby! Let other women unsex themselves if they will, do you banish all such thoughts from your mind, and I will forget all this rhapsody, and some of these days you will laugh with me at your crack-brained scheme."

But Christine, during this time, had recovered herself, and again firmly declared her fixed determination to devote herself to this work. She grew excited, as she went on to speak of the hardships of the poor, the few employments open to women, and the injustice of the small pay they received; she pictured the idle, aimless life of the rich, and then contrasted all this with what might be. She drew up her slight form to its fullest height, her eyes flashed, her voice rung out full and clear, as she described the woman of her imagination, a being fully developed, mentally, morally, and physically, as God intended her to be.

Even Julia was astonished at the eloquence of her words; new thoughts filled her mind, but she would not allow her niece to see the impression she had made.

"I see," she said, "that your mule-like obstinacy, with which I have already had sufficient experience, has settled on this hobby. It is useless for me to argue with a young lady who considers herself infallible—who has voices in her heart, and sees paths of duty in which she must walk! Who should presume to dictate to such a highly favored young woman? No, Christine Elliot, I have done with you for ever," she went on; "you have been a constant annoyance, a thorn in the flesh to me, ever since we met. You have gone contrary to all my wishes, thwarted my plans, disdained my advice—and to what has it brought you? To what you may consider glory, but which, in the eyes of an unfortunate person like me, unvisited by spiritual inspiration, is disgrace. I wash my hands of it. I shall send you to your father, and let him do what he can with his prophetess; but in my house you shall not remain another week. Go, ungrateful, headstrong girl; but be assured that you are walking rapidly on in the road that leads to destruction."

Christine's eyes flashed; bitter taunts rose to her lips in reply, but with an effort she refrained from speaking, and obeying her aunt's imperious gesture, she left the room, unshaken in her determination.

She had a week, then, before her, and in that time she would enter on her mission. She held a consultation with her friend, Mrs. Warner, who was fully as enthusiastic as herself, and it was decided that she should deliver a lecture in a few days.

Meanwhile, Christine worked day and night on her essay, and to Mrs. Frothingham's unspeakable horror, placards, posted upon the walls and fences, in a day or two, announced the forthcoming lecture.

All the town was in a ferment, and most assuredly Mrs. Frothingham would have laid violent hands upon her niece, and put a stop to the lecture by summarily sending off the lecturer, had she not prudently taken refuge in the house of Mrs. Warner.

Mrs. Frothingham was almost frantic with passion, but what could she do? She could not drag her from Mrs. Warner's, though she felt like doing so; she must let her take her own course.

CHAPTER TWENTY-ONE

Disowned

The appointed evening came. It was a free lecture, and the house was crowded.

As Christine, dressed simply in black silk, stood before that audience, her cheeks and lips deathly pale, Mrs. Warner trembled for her; but though her first few words were indistinct, and her voice faltered in the commencement of her address, she gained courage as she grew accustomed to her own tones; her color returned, and, forgetting all but her subject, she went on with an enthusiasm and resistless eloquence, which enchained her audience completely; she seemed to possess the power to sway her hearers at her pleasure.

Tears rushed to the eyes of her listeners, to be chased away by the smile that her strokes of humor or sallies of wit elicited. Even the most conservative forgot, for the present, his abhorrence to so startling an innovation upon old time customs, and "those who came to scoff," remained, if not "to pray," at least to confess the power of eloquence, which, like genius, knows no sex.[36]

For a short time all were carried out of themselves, and forgot their prejudices—all save the thrilling words of the speaker;

but when she ceased to speak, and her voice no longer fell on the ear, the spell was broken, and each returning to consciousness again, wondered that he had been so carried away.

Friends collected together, as the audience dispersed, talking of what they had heard; old men declared that, after all, there was some truth in what the girl said, and though the women said but little, or that little jestingly, yet, in the heart of many a young girl, the words inviting her to do, to take some part in life other than that of a mere animal, found an echo.

Mrs. Warner had waited at the door for her friend, and after the last stragglers had dispersed they walked home together. Christine listened languidly to her friend's praises and words of encouragement; they only humiliated her; she had fallen so far below her ideas in the expression of them that it pained her to think of it; but when Mrs. Warner went on to speak of the great good she must achieve, then her heart throbbed with ardor, and she longed to go on doing with her might what her hands found to do. She had committed herself to her appointed work, and, now that she had done so, she was willing to comply with her aunt's wishes and go to her father's house.

Mrs. Frothingham made no allusion to the last night's oration, other than the brief remark that, "she had succeeded in making a fool of herself," and treated her with a chilling formality, from which Christine was glad to escape.

She was, therefore, very glad to be on her journey home, though everything reminded her most painfully of the last time she had passed over that route; how perfectly happy she had been, sitting by Philip's side, under his protection, and feeling that this was only the beginning of a happy life with him—happiness such as she had hardly dared, in her wildest dreams, to hope for—now how all was changed. She resolutely kept down the rebellious thoughts that would arise, and choked back the tears that would start as she thought of the past.

She tried to raise herself above all depressing influences, by thinking of what God had given her to do; but there are times when, with the most resolute self-control, the heart will assert itself, and Christine had loved Philip too devotedly to be able to think of losing him without a pang. Even his unworthiness, which, perhaps, ought to have steeled her against him, added to her grief; to have lost him she could have endured—to be forbidden to regret him was harder yet to bear.

As she drew near her home she began to think of the surprise it would be to her parents to see her, and pictured their delight; but, as she reached the yard, she saw that she was expected, and, in the midst of their greetings, she imagined there was a suppressed displeasure.

She was right. A letter from Mrs. Frothingham had preceded her, giving an account of her obstinacy in persisting in Philip's rejection, his departure, and, next, her new plan, and equal obstinacy in carrying it out, her lecture, and, finally, her departure for home.

No sooner was she fairly seated and settled, than this letter was put into her hands, while all the family watched her narrowly as she read.

"It isn't true, is it?" cried Bessie. "I knew there was some mistake about it. I told you so, father, didn't I?"

"Speak, Christine," said her father, sternly. "What is the meaning of this? Is it true?"

"It is," was her firm reply.

Farmer Elliot's brow grew dark, and Bessie, utterly unable to control herself, burst into tears, while Mrs. Elliot put in persuasively to avert the storm she saw gathering—

"Wait, father; you have heard only one side of the story. Let Christine tell hers!"

"What have you to say then?" exclaimed her father. "Say it quick! I don't kear so much about the match that's broke off, though, from Julia's account, it seems you treated the young man rather unhandsome; but this woman's rights business—this lecturing—what have you got to say about it? I guess it will puzzle ye to get out of that?" he concluded, with a short, angry laugh that his wife well knew betokened extreme passion.

She grew pale, and cast a beseeching look at her daughter. Christine sat quietly there, her dark eyes fixed upon her father's face, apparently not in the least frightened. "She never will give in," was her mother's thought, "she is too much like her father," and, with a beating heart, she turned again to her husband.

"You see, she hasn't got a word to say for herself," continued Mr. Elliot. "She has disgraced herself and us, and that's all about it. That's what comes of her eddication!"

"Father," replied Christine, calmly, though her eyes flashed, "I have not disgraced myself or you, though I have lectured before an audience, and though I intend to continue to do so."

"You intend to continer to do so!" repeated Mr. Elliot, in a voice of suppressed passion. "Then let me tell you, gal, that you have missed your calkerlations there. You won't continer to, or if you do persist in it, you are no child of mine."

"Oh, father!" interrupted Mrs. Elliot—

"I mean jist what I say. She may settle down here like other folks and go to work, if she likes, but otherways she is no child of mine. She may decide wonst for all."

"Not now," interrupted the mother again, for from Christine's flashing eyes and parted lips she had already read too clearly the answer.

"Let Christine have a little time. Let her think it all over. Wait till to-morrow, father!"

"Wa-al," he replied, "but let her understand that is my fixed determination."

He turned and left the room; no sooner had his footsteps died away, than Bessie's arms were flung about her neck, and her tears fell on her cheek.

"Oh, Christine," she sobbed, "you don't mean to be a lecturer, as Aunt Julia said. You won't go against us all, and go round the country so. Do give it all up, and we will be so happy here together."

"My dear Bessie," replied Christine, soothingly, "you don't know anything about it, when I explain it all to you, you will urge me to go on, just as much as you try to dissuade me from it now. Father is very unjust. He is prejudiced, and will not listen to reason."

"Christine, don't speak so. Remember he is your father, and he has been a good father to you," said Mrs. Elliot, who seemed to stand on middle ground between her husband and child.

"And if he is," returned Christine, "that is no reason why he should make a slave of me, worse than a slave, to prescribe what I shall think—to be conscience for me. No, mother, the mere fact of his being my father gives him no such rights over me. I shall do what I think is right. 'He that loveth father or mother more than me, is not worthy of me.'"[37]

Mrs. Elliot knew not what to say. She sighed deeply and left the room. Bessie soon slipped out and Christine was left alone, unshaken in her determination, and looking upon the prejudice and ignorance which would hold her back in her chosen career, almost with sovereign contempt.

She rose and looked out of the window. Heaps of apples lay scattered on the ground in the orchard, for it was the time for gathering that fruit, and busy workers were piling them in baskets, or shaking the trees, while those beneath rapidly escaped from beneath the shower of rosy and golden fruit.

Many of the neighbors were there with baskets and bags, for Farmer Elliot's fruit was famed throughout the region, and he was accustomed to sell it to those who came at the time of gathering.

While she looked, she saw coming down the road a wagon drawn by a bony old horse, and driven by a tall and athletic man in the prime of life.

Christine recognized him at once as Elder Wiggins, the farmer-minister, who was accustomed to preach in the vicinity. He had evidently come for apples, for bags were in the wagon ready to receive the annual present which Farmer Elliot was in the habit of making him.

His dress was not particularly clerical in its style. His pantaloons were of the blue mixed cloth which had been manufactured by the busy hands of his good wife, spun, dyed, and woven, and, finally, with no advice or assistance from tailor or tailoress, made into a garment for the Elder. His coat had rather more pretensions to gentility, though that too, had been in part the work of Mrs. Wiggins, who had prepared it for the final touches at the fulling-mill, which sent it forth the claret-colored broad-cloth which constituted her husband's Sunday best apparel. The Elder himself had by no means the appearance of a student; instead of the pale face and narrow chest of that class, he rejoiced in a healthy, sunburned complexion and broad shoulders, which would have done no discredit to the hardy sons of Anak.[38]

He looked like one better skilled in digging in the fields than at Greek or Hebrew roots, nor did he hesitate to confess his utter ignorance of any other language except his own mother tongue.

He held the whole race of "college larnt" ministers as but little better than the wicked. He considered any preparation for the ministry as contrary to the Bible. "Were not Peter and John and James fishermen at their nets when Jesus called them, and did they have to stop to go to college and to a theological school before they began to preach?" he was accustomed to say. "No, they went right off and went to preachin', and I guess they had as many souls given to them as seals of their ministry, and done as much good as these men that hev to study so long before they begin. Besides, don't it expressly say, 'Take no thought for what ye shall say. Open your mouth and I will fill it,"[39] and, armed by these passages of Scripture, Elder Wiggins went out triumphantly, prepared to put to flight, with the sword of the Lord and of Gideon, a whole army of learned professors with their dictionaries, did they venture to oppose his progress. But notwithstanding his lack of "college larning," Elder Wiggins was well versed in the knowledge of the Bible, and though perfectly independent of commentaries, had ideas of his own, and made expositions of puzzling texts, which, however startling they might have been to the authors of these ponderous tomes, suited him and his hearers. He was a thoroughly pious man, and not at all devoid of good sense; his sermons were rather apt to be rambling, but he did not consider them the worse for that. "Scattering shot hit the most birds," he was accustomed to say, and had his sermons been models of logical arrangement, beginning with his statement of premises, followed by his demonstrations, and ending by his conclusions, they would not have produced half the effect which his present style did upon his auditors. The good farmers were wont to get into a drowse while listening to him, but this could not be of long duration under the stentorian voice of the Elder, and waking from their nap, they would listen and pronounce it "a powerful sarmon."

But, during the time that we have occupied in describing him, Elder Wiggins had reached the house, had been kindly greeted by Mr. Elliot, and had seen his bags filled and replaced in the wagon, his horse taken to the barn to have his supper, and had decided himself to remain to that meal.

The Elder, always welcome, was now unusually so to Mrs. Elliot; she took Bessie aside, and informed her that "it really seemed providential that he had come, for he could talk with Christine. He could argy with her, and make her hear to reason," and she, therefore, told the good man all the circumstances of the case, doing justice to Christine's apparent conscientiousness in discharging her duty.

The Elder listened with no small astonishment to the relation of her lecture, which, with some mortification, Mrs. Elliot gave him, but replied—

"Waal, waal! I'll soon show her that she's goin' contrary to Scriptur', and it will be all right."

So, blowing his nose sonorously, he proceeded to the foreroom, almost shaking the house with his heavy tread.

"How are ye, my darter?" he said, kindly, extending his hand.

Christine replied with politeness, and shook his hand cordially; she inquired after his family, to which he made brief replies; but it was not his method to hesitate about doing what he had to do, so he plunged at once into the "subject matter."

"Your mother has been tellin' on me about your lecturin', and how you think you orter do it. Now, I like to see folks do what they think is right; no matter how sot they be, it's better than these half-way folks that never amount to nothin'. But, then, I s'pose you'd be willing to hear to reason, and, if you was a goin' wrong, you'd be glad to be sot right."

"Certainly, Elder Wiggins," replied Christine, "I shall be glad to hear all you have to say."

"Waal, that's fair. I knowed you would say so," replied the Elder, and continued, "If I understand it right, these new doctrines of yourn air, that the women air just as good as the men—and there I agree with ye—and that they have a right to do the same things as the men, such as learnin' trades, bein' doctors, and lawyers, and ministers, and, besides all that, votin'. Ain't that a fair statement of the case?"

"Yes, we do claim all this," was Christine's reply. "Whatever a woman can do, and do well, we say let public opinion open the door for her to do, and let her be paid for her labor as much as a man would be, for the same amount. Let her try to do whatever she thinks she can do—if she fails, it will be no more than hundreds of men have done before her. And let her vote. She is under laws—let her have a voice in saying what they shall be. She is taxed—let her have the benefit of the principle which our fathers fought and bled to establish, no taxation without representation."

"Listen to me now," said the Elder, as Christine paused— "You've forgot one thing. Way back in the beginning of the world, when Eve made Adam sin, God put this punishment upon her, 'thy desire shall be to thy husband, and he shall rule over thee,' and, ever since that time, it has been so.[40] The husband is the head of the woman, and so it will be till the end of the world, for not a jot or tittle of God's Word will fail; so, don't ye see, you're fightin' against God?"

"Mr. Wiggins," replied Christine, "the Hebrew word there means will as well as shall—and, if it read, he will reign over thee, it would be only a prophecy, which it is, and has been fulfilled. It is not a command at all."

"When you say that, I can't dispute ye," replied the Elder, "but I have alus found when you git anybody in a tight place they'll fly right off to Hebrew or some such stuff, where you can't follow 'um. Even the folks that know Hebrew can't agree; and I say, fur my part, the old-fashioned English Bible is good enuf fur me, and I'm willing to go by that."

"And so am I," returned Christine, "but we are under a new dispensation."

"Ah, waal, my darter, you're no better off there. Paul expressly says, 'I suffer not a woman to teach,' and, 'let your women keep silence in the churches, and learn of their husbands at home.'[41] What have ye got to say to that, my darter?" exclaimed the Elder, triumphantly.

"That it was written for the times, and has nothing to do with the present age at all, any more than the directions about plaiting the hair, and others of a similar character that he gives, or than the positive command not to receive young widows.

"It is not fair to put such stress on one set of directions, and leave the others unnoticed.

"Besides, there are texts in favor of woman's rights. Remember the description of the virtuous woman, who 'worketh with her hands,' 'considereth a field and buyeth it,' who is 'like the merchants' ships, and bringeth her food from afar'; 'she maketh fine linen and selleth it,' and 'openeth her mouth with wisdom.'[42] Don't you see, she was what would be called, now-a-days, a woman's rights woman?

"Didn't she act as farmer, merchant, and counsellor?

"So in the New Testament, Paul says in Christ, 'there is neither bond nor free, Jew nor Gentile, male nor female,' and, according to the golden rule, what right has man to rule over woman any more than over others?[43]

"Paul gave directions as to the covering of the head when women prayed and prophesied; so, you see, they did it then. He speaks too frequently of women as fellow-laborers."[44]

The Elder interrupted her:

"You are wresting the Holy Scriptures to your own destruction," he said, solemnly. "You are changing the truth of God into a lie. Take heed what you do, lest sudden destruction come upon you, and that right speedily."

"Have you given up argument that you resort to denunciation?" asked Christine, rather provokingly.

"She is perverse," replied the Elder, turning to Bessie and her mother, then saying to Christine, "I perceive that 'you are in the gall of bitterness, and bonds of iniquity,'" he rose, and turned away.[45]

Mr. Elliot had been seated in the next room, listening to the conversation; he now entered, exclaiming, angrily,

"Let her alone! 'He that being often reproved and hardeneth his heart shall be suddenly destroyed, and that without remedy.'"[46]

Christine was silent.

There was an uncomfortable pause, interrupted by an occasional sob from Bessie, who sat a little behind her sister. Mr. Elliot saw tears in his wife's eyes, as she left the room, and the sight of them seemed to increase his anger. Elder Wiggins rose, and muttering some unintelligible remark, of which the only words distinctly uttered were "go out," left the room also, and took the path that led to the orchard.

No sooner had he gone than her father approached Christine, and laying his hand heavily on her shoulder, exclaimed—

"You are a rebellious, undutiful gal! You've most broke your mother's heart, and here you set as calm as if you had been doin' somethin' to be proud on.

"I've borne with ye long enuf, and now I ask you wonst for all, ef you're ready to acknowledge that you've done wrong, and give up all your woman's rights notions, and go to work like somebody? Say yes or no, right off!"

"No," began Christine, "for—"

"Stop!" interrupted her father, authoritatively. "I don't want to hear anything more from ye. I expected it would be so. You're farm, and so am I! You're no child of mine, and this house is no home of your'n! Go, and jine yourself to them that's like ye, in despisin' the laws of God and man."

Christine stood up before her father, her eyes flashing, her figure drawn up to its full height, her usually pale cheek flushed with her emotion, and, in a tremulous voice that she endeavored in vain to render steady, she said,

"I am ready to go this moment. Good-bye, Bessie," she said, approaching her sister, who wept convulsively.

She bent over her and pressed a kiss on her heated brow; at the touch Bessie looked up, seized her sister's hand, and held her back as she was rapidly leaving the room.

"Father!" she cried, "you are not going to send her away tonight? You would not turn a stranger from your house at such an hour, and she is your own daughter! Tell her to stay!"

"She is no child of mine," sternly replied Mr. Elliot. "I lay no commands upon her. Let her go or stay, as she chooses, and ask no favors of me."

"I have asked none as yet, sir," replied Christine, haughtily, "and I beg you to give yourself no uneasiness on that score in the future. Good afternoon," and, with a graceful curtsy, she left the apartment.

Bessie followed her, wringing her hands, and sobbing bitterly. No tears were in her sister's eyes; she walked rapidly to the kitchen where she found her mother.

"Mother, I am going," she said. "Your husband has disowned me, and has bid me go. Good-bye; but be of good courage—you need never blush for your child. Good-bye, dear, dear mother," and she flung her arms around her neck, and kissed her again and again; at last she released her from her clinging embrace, saying:

"I must stay no longer. It grows late, and I have a long walk before me!"

"My child!" exclaimed Mrs. Elliot, holding her firmly by the hand. "Do not be so hasty. I will see your father; when he has had a little time to think it over, and get cool, he will be sorry if he has said too much, and you will remember that he is your father, and will acknowledge what you have done that is wrong, then it will be all right again."

"It is useless to cherish false hopes," replied Christine. "My father will never reverse his decision—I will never submit to his conditions. I shall go."

"But, my child, you have no money, no friends, and to go out into the world alone, what can you do?"

"Many a farmer's boy has done the same," said Christine, proudly. "I will show you what a farmer's girl can do."

Again Mrs. Elliot and Bessie united in urging her to remain, but she was firm, and seeing this, they at last gave over in despair.

She would not sleep another night under his roof, she declared with a look that betokened her firm resolution. It was with difficulty that she was persuaded to take, as a loan, a small sum of money which her mother had put away, little thinking to devote it to such a use, and to keep her wardrobe, which was in part the gift of her aunt. On condition that she might repay it at some future time, she at last consented, and decided to wait for Elder Wiggins, who offered her a seat in his wagon as far as the village.

It was evening when she left her father's house.

Her mother's and sister's tears were on her cheeks; their last, fond, sad words rang in her ear; she still saw her father's cold, stern glance, to which she had returned as proud and defiant a look, as she bowed to him with cold civility and bade him good evening.

Now the excitement was over, and she realized that she was a homeless wanderer.

She was in no mood to receive the words of reproach which Elder Wiggins felt it his duty to express, or to listen to his advice to humble herself and go to her home; but she knew that the good man meant well, and forbore to wound his feelings by harsh replies. At last he seemed to think that he had said enough on that subject, and began to give her good advice for the regulation of her future conduct, which was received as his reproof had been, in silence.

As they approached the village, the Elder invited her to go to his house to spend the night, telling her that the stage passed his door in the morning, and he would see that she was put on board. He was evidently sincere in wishing her to do so, and she accepted his invitation.

She was kindly received by Mrs. Wiggins, to whom the Elder told the story privately in the next room, but the partition was thin and his voice loud, so that Christine heard the whole, even his concluding words, that "the farmer had been rayther *hash* to her, but then, you know, John Elliot is a master-sot man in his way, and the gal is a chip of the old block."

Christine slept little that night. She rose the next morning with haggard looks and a dull, heavy headache, which her long ride in the crowded, lumbering stage-coach did not tend to lessen, so that when she got on board the boat that was to carry her to Boston, she was glad enough to sink into a berth at once, and try to sleep. She tossed uneasily on her narrow pallet, thinking of the future. She was going now to her only friend, Mrs. Warner, but she could not long remain there. What next?

It was a constantly recurring question for which she had no answer.

At last the weary night passed, and in a few hours she was at Mrs. Warner's door, and in another moment in her friend's warm embrace.

"You see before you, Mrs. Warner, an outcast," said Christine, "banished from her father's house. I have no home. Will you receive me for a little while?"

"Welcome, my own Christine, my brave spirit," was her friend's reply. "Never say again that you have no home—while I have a roof to shelter me or a morsel of bread, home and food are yours. I will be mother and sister to you, my child," she added, taking Christine's shawl, and leading her to her room.

"You are not well, my dear," she said, kindly. "Your hands are burning, and your eyes have a sunken, heavy look; lie down awhile."

Christine obeyed, and tears filled her eyes. Mrs. Warner's kindness was inexpressibly grateful to her. She could bear harshness, but gentleness disarmed her; she buried her face in the pillow and wept long and freely.

Mrs. Warner sat by silently. At last she spoke, not of Christine's own affairs, but of the sad case of a poor woman whose drunken husband, in a fit of intoxication, had so disabled her that she was unable to work, and was left destitute with four small children, as he had taken all the money she had been able to save for some time past.

She had the satisfaction to see that Christine became deeply interested in her narration, and in the sorrows of others had, in part, forgotten her own.

Ere long she sunk into a profound slumber, from which she awoke refreshed in body and mind. She was once more herself, energetic and ardent, and after visiting several poor families, to whom she was a welcome and well-known guest, she talked cheerfully with her friend of her future plans.

She must support herself, so she would ask a small sum for admittance to her future lectures.

It was decided that she should deliver one in Boston, and, ere long, she stood before an audience in that city. It was a large and mixed assembly, composed in part of those whom curiosity had led there, of some few who wished well to the new doctrines, and of many who came not to listen, but to interrupt, and disturb the speaker.

She had hardly commenced her address, when hootings and hissings from the galleries resounded on every side. For a moment she grew pale and hesitated, but, regaining her self-possession, she waited for the tumult to subside with folded arms, and a calm, resolute face, and then went on again. But the disorder increased, and it was a long time before she could be heard; at last there was a lull, and she spoke in a clear voice, "Geese have hissed before now," and then went on, rapidly and eloquently, to speak of all the great movements of this and former ages, reminding her hearers that this was not unlike them in their reception; even the Apostles had been mobbed in Jerusalem, and the great Author of the principles of Christianity had suffered the death of a criminal; "but it is not the new doctrines, that I advance, that you have just denounced, for you have not allowed yourselves to hear them. Is it, then, the mere fact that a woman addresses you that is so distasteful? Yet, not long ago, a woman stood here, and thousands listened admiringly to the tones of her clear voice, as the Swedish Nightingale poured out a tide of melody.[47] She was applauded, and lauded to the skies; no one thought it unwomanly or indelicate in her—nor was it so.

"A Fanny Kemble may read Shakespeare to admiring thousands.[48] A Sontag may carry you out of yourselves while singing the thrilling music of some great composer;[49] but when a woman dares to utter the thoughts of her own soul, to speak as God has given her power to do, then she is pronounced unwomanly, and met with hootings and revilings.

"Where is the consistency of this?

"This, too, is the modern Athens! In ancient times, in that old city, famed for all the refinements of civilization, there were not wanting female philosophers, and, with Grecian history, the name of Sappho is as indissolubly connected as that of Demosthenes or Alexander.[50]

"Modern Athens, going one step beyond its glorious old model in the march of civilization, makes of her women butterflies, to flutter with gaudy wings around the saloons of fashion, and overwhelms those who would make them something nobler and higher, with opposition.

"But it is not woman alone that ye wrong. Like all wrong-doing it has a double curse—it reacts on you.

"These are the wives and mothers who are to mould the infant mind; it is their hand which shall make its impress on a coming age.

"Are these effeminate, thoughtless beings to be the mothers of heroes?"

This, and much more, she said, interrupted, at times, with the loudest hootings, stamping of feet, and clapping of hands. When, at last, she ceased to speak, as she left the building, she was greeted with oaths, curses, and the coarsest abuse from half-drunken men.

She shuddered, and for a moment her heart sunk within her, but she rallied. She had expected all this, though the reality was hard to bear, and when she related all to her friend, she could not disguise from her that she was somewhat discouraged.

"Whoso putteth his hand to the plough and looketh back is not fit for the kingdom," was Mrs. Warner's reply.[51]

"I do not look back," returned Christine, "I am ready to go forward, and, if need be, to die for the cause to which I have devoted myself. I have entered on my work, and bravely will I go on with it."

CHAPTER TWENTY-TWO

Annie Murray

Bright lights gleamed from Mr. Murray's splendid mansion in Fifth Avenue; carriages rattled over the pavements, and deposited loads of ladies and gentlemen there, and bursts of music, that greeted the new-comers, as the doors flew open to admit them, involuntarily quickened the pace of the ladies as they hurried on to the dressing-room.

Within all was light and gayety. Crowds of elegantly dressed ladies leaned on the arms of gentlemen, attired in all the glory of fashionable-tailordom; yet quite obscured by the more brilliant costumes of the fairer sex; but individuals were hardly to be noticed here; as they were announced there was a slight stir near the door and then they were swallowed up in the mass, adding, perhaps, a little more brilliancy to the whole.

It was in fact pronounced the most brilliant affair of the season. Indeed all was dazzling; the glow of the chandeliers, the sparkle of bright eyes and of gleaming jewels, was almost enough to weary one with its unchanging brightness. Light feet kept time to the swelling music; sylph-like forms circled round to Strauss' wild waltzes, or to Strakosch's inspiring polkas and schottisches.

Beauty, youth, and fashion were there, and Mrs. Murray, as she received her friends, and exchanged a few words with those about her, was, as she looked, well satisfied.

Her eyes followed the graceful motions of her daughter, as she glided through the dance, with no little pride, and, in truth, Annie had never looked so beautiful as on this, her wedding night. Her eyes sparkled with excitement, her color went and came, and her gleeful laugh rung out full and clear; she looked a very sylph in her airy dress, for rich laces fell in such profusion over the soft folds of her white satin robe that she seemed almost clad in gossamer.

But why attempt the vain task of describing her dress? Did not words fail Madame Bosanquet to express her admiration of this chef d'œuvre of her forewoman's skill, and did she not content herself with a little scream of delight, as she raised her hands and eyes to heaven in mute adoration of her artist's taste? What her voluble tongue failed to express, it would be presumption in any other to attempt.

Mr. Howard, the bridegroom, was a stout, middle-aged man, who, unlike his bride, did not seem to enter with great zest into the festivities of the evening. He looked like one who had nerved himself up to a task and was resolved to go through it unshrinkingly.

He, too, had been got up regardless of expense for this occasion, as sundry bills, neatly filed away, might have testified, but, alas, this availed him nothing, for he shared the fate of all bridegrooms, and was completely lost sight of in the superior effulgence of the bride.

Indeed it is a singular but, nevertheless, indisputable fact that the bridegroom is considered a personage of comparatively no importance on such occasions; but let the fair partner of his joys enjoy her brief triumph, and let the neglected one solace himself with the reflection, "thank heaven a bride and a wife are quite different things."

At last, for all things must come to an end, the wedding-party was over, and morning peeped in upon candles flickering in the socket, overturned vases of flowers, broken dishes, pools of wine, little archipelagoes filled with islands of cake on the carpet, empty wine bottles, scattered corks, soiled gloves, disarranged furniture, and the like matter-of-fact realities, which one would hardly expect to be the concomitants of such a scene of enchantment as that of the preceding night. Yet so it was; and while servants were endeavoring to bring something like order out of that chaos, Annie Howard and her husband were whirled off to Saratoga, Niagara, &c., on a wedding tour.

Annie enjoyed this most heartily; not that she was very fond of seeing beautiful scenery, and as she said, "Niagara was nothing. She had seen it before"; but the excitement of travelling, the opportunity of displaying her elegant dresses and diamonds at the hotels, and the occasional meeting of old, and making of new acquaintances pleased her.

She was therefore a little astonished when one morning Mr. Howard abruptly proposed that they should start for New York on that day.

"Why we haven't gone half as far as we intended," she said, in an expostulating tone.

"I don't know where you thought of going, but we have gone further than I intended," responded her larger half, "and for my part, I'm tired of whirling about the country and of eating French cookery, of lounging about hotels and seeing rocks, and trees, and water, and all that sort of nonsense. I'd rather see one good pavement in New York than it all."

"Why, Mr. Howard, how can you talk so? Just as if you didn't care anything about nature!"

"Nature, Ann? Pshaw, you nor I didn't come to see that. We came because it's the fashion, and now we'll go home and settle down peaceably. So let your maid pack up, and we'll start this evening."

"I wish you wouldn't call me Ann!" was all the reply his bride vouchsafed to make.

"You didn't object to it before we were married," he answered, "and I think it sounds just as well now."

Mrs. Howard made no reply; she was a little sulky; her husband thrust his hands in his pockets and began walking up and down the room, whistling a favorite air.

"I wish you wouldn't whistle," exclaimed his lady; "it goes right through my head, and it's so vulgar."

Mr. Howard stopped in his walk. "Ann," said he, "we may as well come to an understanding, first as last. You have taken me for better or worse, as you may find me, and, once for all, I tell you that I have had quite enough of your dictation. In fact, I'm tired of it, and don't want any more of it. What I say, I mean, and you will find it so, when you know me better."

"I know you well enough now to find you a brute," exclaimed Annie, bursting into tears. "I wish I had never seen you!"

"That wish comes rather too late, my dear madam," returned her liege lord. "Don't sit there making a baby of yourself; it don't improve your appearance at all," and Mr. Howard left the room, whistling, as if in defiance of his wife's request.

As the door closed after him, his wife burst into a passion of tears.

The honeymoon was hardly over, and yet the young wife shed bitter tears. She was grievously disappointed. Had she not drawn the matrimonial prize, in the lottery of the last season? Had she not made an unexceptionable match? Had she not expected perfect felicity as his wife?

Not that she loved him very dearly. She had been in a flutter of excitement till she became engaged to him, and had been happy in her triumph over her rivals; she had anticipated perfect submission to all her caprices from him, and now thus early to be thwarted in her plans, to be spoken harshly to, was more than she could bear.

She gave way to her grief, or rather to her anger, for awhile—
then, perhaps, her husband's hint recurring to her, she bathed
her eyes in cold water, and gave herself up to her maid to be
dressed for dinner.

When Mr. Howard joined her in the parlor, he was unusually kind, and seemed to regret their little disagreement; Annie
received his advances coldly, though she was secretly rejoiced,
for she imagined that this was a tacit avowal of his readiness
to yield to her wishes in future. But she was mistaken; that
night, in spite of her unwillingness to return, saw them on
their way to New York.

A few months had passed, and Mr. and Mrs. Howard had
gone to housekeeping.

Nothing could have been more displeasing to the young wife,
who had anticipated entering upon the gay and exciting life at
a hotel, and had imagined herself already the belle of many a
ball and soirée; to have all these visions of gayety for the future
dissipated, and in their place substituted a hum-drum life with
Mr. Howard, who dreaded nothing more than a card, informing him that Mr. and Mrs. Somebody were to be at home on
a certain evening, and who never accepted an invitation if he
could, with any ordinary civility, decline it, was a severe blow
to Annie, and she had resisted the proposed measure with all
the energy of her character; but she had a stronger will than
her own arrayed against her, and with rather a bad grace had
been forced to yield.

When the arrangements were to be made, there had again
been a constant disagreement, degenerating into a positive quar-
rel, for it seemed to Annie that her husband consulted her taste
and wishes only to go directly contrary to them; and, in fact,
Mr. Howard was one of those men who have so great a horror
of being under petticoat government that they will hardly trust
themselves to do what they really wish, if it coincides with the

liking of their wives, lest it should seem that they have no will
of their own.

At last, however, they were fairly established in their new residence, and Annie found that she had but entered upon fresh
troubles. She was unfortunate in her servants, and knew nothing of domestic affairs herself. Mr. Howard complained, and
justly, of the ill-regulated state of the household, and imagined, perhaps not without reason, that his wife took a spite-
ful pleasure in repaying him in kind for his former disregard
of her wishes.

Every day this couple, united by bonds which death alone
could sever, and who, so short a time before, had taken upon
themselves such solemn vows to love, honor, and cherish each
other, were becoming colder and more estranged. Every day
the fetters which bound them seemed more galling, and con-
tentions grew more and more frequent. Each felt wronged by
the other, and neither would yield in the smallest degree, or
acknowledge the commission of an error.

Outwardly, all was smooth and fair. Mrs. Howard had an
elegant house, a fine carriage, and servants at her command,
fine apparel, and a gentlemanly husband. What was wanting
to make her happy? Contentment and self-control, and, without these, all this availed her nothing. There was a Mordecai
in the gate.[52]

How little did those who envied her, as she rolled by in her
luxurious carriage, decked in gorgeous apparel, and with
smiles wreathing her face, dream that under it all lurked a
restless, dissatisfied, disappointed spirit that poisoned all her
enjoyments.

Nor was she alone to be pitied; harsh and cold as was her
husband, he too had had visions of a home, where a fond wife
should make a perpetual sunshine, and to which he could turn
from the turmoil and harassing cares of life, there to find happiness and peace. How sadly had he been disappointed.

Naturally reserved and unsocial, he grew more and more so, till he was positively morose; by degrees Annie became really afraid of him, and this fear extinguished the last spark of affection for him in her heart.

He, in turn, looked upon her as the destroyer of his hopes. Had he married a different wife he might have had a home, and he almost hated her at times for standing between him and happiness, as she did. Both had sought in marriage their own selfish gratification, without thought of the duties owed to the other, and the result was what might have been expected, bitterness and disappointment.

CHAPTER TWENTY-THREE

Joined Not United

Mr. and Mrs. Howard were seated at the breakfast table. A frown contracted his brow as he tried one dish after another, and pushed each away in turn as unpalatable.

"This coffee is execrable, Mrs. Howard," he said, stirring the muddy beverage as he spoke, "and, in fact, there is nothing fit to be eaten on the table. The rolls are raw, the beefsteak dried to a cinder, the eggs hard as so many bullets. It's an insult, madam, to set such a breakfast before anybody."

"You are as well suited as I am," replied his wife; "I am enjoying the same luxuries."

Her calmness irritated him.

"Why don't you do something about it, then? Why don't you make a change?"

"Do!" replied his wife. "Haven't I been doing all the time? Discharging servant after servant, and reading scores of greasy recommendations? And as to changes, haven't we had seven cooks in a fortnight, who have departed, and with them some half dozen tea-spoons?"

"Then, madam, I should think it was time that you took some interest in your household affairs, instead of trusting them entirely to ignorant and dishonest servants—"

"What do you mean?" interrupted Annie; "do you expect me, sir, to go into the kitchen—"

"Yes, madam; you understand my meaning exactly, to go into the kitchen and superintend operations there. Better women than you, Mrs. Howard, have not considered it beneath them to attend to their domestic concerns. When I married, I expected to find in a wife—"

"A sort of upper servant, Mr. Howard!" exclaimed Annie. "With such elevated ideas of a wife's uses and duties, you should have married a cook."

"Any change could hardly have been for the worse," replied her husband, coolly.

"You are too flattering," said Annie, with flashing eyes.

"The truth, however complimentary, should not be styled flattery, madam," he said, taking up the morning paper, and turning his back directly upon her.

Suddenly he exclaimed, in a voice of anger:

"What does this mean? Listen, madam!" and he read on:

"'Defalcation.[53]—A defalcation has just been discovered to have been committed by Alexander Murray, President of the N. and M. Railroad company, of some hundreds of thousands of dollars. As the books have not yet been thoroughly examined, it is feared that the worst is not known. Murray is missing, and is supposed to have gone to Europe. This is the more astounding, as he has always been considered one of our most respectable citizens.'"

Annie sat listening with eager attention; as he ceased reading, she heaved a deep sigh, and exclaimed, "It cannot be—look at the name again."

"There it is, in black and white," returned her husband, holding the paper towards her.

She pushed it aside. "Poor, poor father!" she said.

"You had better say poor husband," returned Mr. Howard, angrily. "Good heavens! that I, whose proudest boast it has been that no breath of dishonor could attach itself to my name, should have married the daughter of a defaulter!"

He paced rapidly up and down the room, while Annie sat with her face buried in her hands, weeping bitterly. He stopped short before her.

"You can weep for poor father, who, with his ill-gotten gains, is on his way to another country, but you have no tears for your husband, on whom you have brought disgrace. Your father did well to keep his shame secret till he got you off his hands; no doubt he exults that he got so cleverly rid of you, and cheated me so nicely. Weep on, madam! it needs much to wash the stain away."

Annie looked up; fire flashed in her eyes as she exclaimed, "I had rather share adversity with him, than prosperity with you!"

"I very much regret that you cannot do so," was Mr. Howard's reply, as he strode out of the room.

No sooner had he gone than his wife hastened to her father's residence. Alas, it was but too true. Her mother, a proud-spirited woman, showed, in her tearless eyes and haggard face, her agony, as she busied herself in preparing all things to join her husband.

"Oh, mother!" sobbed Annie, "are you going, then, to leave me alone?"

"I must join my husband, Annie. What else is left me to do, did I shrink from it? But, I am glad that you are so well situated here. I can leave you with the less reluctance that you are so happily married."

"Happily, mother!" groaned Annie. "Would to Heaven that I could go with you! Oh, mother dear, take me along. I will work for you—I will do anything, only take me away from that man. He hates me, mother, I know he does. He never speaks kindly; he looks at me with those savage eyes till I actually shudder, and, if you leave me, I have no friend left. Dear mother, you will not leave your own Annie!"

All this she had said in a tone of the most imploring earnestness. Mrs. Murray listened to it, with a sad face; as she ceased, she exclaimed, "my child! my child, you will break my heart! This was all that was wanting. You, whom I thought I had nothing more to ask for, unhappy, and I powerless to assist you.

"I cannot take you. You must stay. Oh, Annie, Annie, this is more than I can bear!"

She sank down upon a chair, and sobs shook her whole frame. Annie wound her arms about her, and mother and child wept together. At last, Mrs. Murray spoke.

"My Annie," she said, "you must try to regain your husband's affection, else your whole life will be miserable. You can do it, darling," and she went on to give her words of counsel and of gentle reproof, to tell her that she feared she had been selfish, to speak to her of marriage and its duties as she had never done before; for, in the light of her great affliction, she saw the hollowness of her past life, and would fain have kept her child's feet from stumbling over the rocks on which she had well-nigh fallen. Words of truth, she whispered into her child's ear, but, alas! eloquent and powerful as they were, what could this one lesson do towards destroying the effect of the whole education and silent influence of example which, from her earliest childhood, had imbued her with selfishness and worldliness?

Perhaps the mother felt this, as she unwound her child's clinging arms from her neck, and read in her continued tears and sobs only her own misery, forgetting that the sight of her grief but added to her mother's anguish.

She dared not trust herself to look into her child's future, but, with a heavy heart, busied herself in performing the necessary duties before leaving home, endeavoring thus to banish the painful forebodings that would, despite of all her exertions, crowd in upon her mind.

With slow and reluctant steps, Annie returned to her home, and with a sinking heart entered that splendid dwelling, the possession of which she would once have thought would insure her perfect happiness.

The hours dragged heavily along, and she leaned back in an easy-chair, watching for her husband's coming; not like many a wife who listens eagerly for that footfall, which is music to her, and who springs to meet her husband with sparkling eyes and smiling lips, that speak more plainly than words can do her joy at his return—not so did Annie watch and listen. She started at every little noise, fearing that it might be her husband, and when at last he came, she did not even look up at his entrance, but sat silently in her chair, with half closed eyes, apparently unconscious of his presence, and he, with his hands folded behind him, and his eyes bent on the carpet, paced moodily up and down the parlor, casting an occasional glance, in which there was no affection, upon the young girl, whose happiness was in his hands.

Suddenly the door opened, and Mrs. Murray entered. In a moment Annie had sprung towards her, and was engaged in taking her bonnet and shawl, and even when that was done, and her mother seated, she still stood by her side, smoothing her hair caressingly, and stooping to whisper words of endearment.

Mr. Howard had greeted her with cold civility, and now looked at his wife and the demonstrations she made of her affection for her parent, almost with anger.

She had seated herself like a child, upon a low stool near her mother, and half reclined on her lap, holding her head, and talking in a low tone. Her golden curls, which she wore looped up in front, had fallen down, shading her cheek, on which glowed a faint flush, her eyes sparkled with joy, and her whole countenance beamed with animation. She was always graceful, and her attitude now was peculiarly so.

Never had Mr. Howard seen her looking so beautiful, and as he saw how lavish she could be of caresses and fond words, and contrasted her reception of her mother with her cold endurance of his society, he thought "she does not love me," and the pain that this reflection caused him but steeled his heart against her, and his pride forbade his attempting to win her affections. Ah, had he but given way to the pleadings of his heart, had he given voice to that yearning in his soul, which was urging him to cry out "Annie, my wife, give me your love!" how different might have been their fate.

But who could read his thoughts under that lowering brow, as he looked on his wife and her mother?

Mrs. Murray, at length, addressed him:

"I am going to Europe, as you already know, I suppose. Annie has, no doubt, told you."

"No, Madam. Ann has not favored me with any information relative to your plans."

Mrs. Murray sighed.

"I am going," she said, "to join my husband. I am his wife, and my place is by his side. I have nothing to tie me here, except my child, and her I have already given to you. Now I confide her to you again, as a solemn charge. You are to her now, at once, father, mother, and husband. You will be the only friend she has left. Oh, do not you fail her! Be kind to my child. She is very young—be tender with her. Oh, Mr. Howard, do not visit the sins of her parents on her innocent head."

At these last words, her husband darted an angry look at his wife; she had been complaining of him to her mother, then. It hardened his heart, which Mrs. Murray's words had begun to soften, against her.

Mrs. Murray was silent. He felt that she expected him to speak, and at last he did so.

"Madam," he said, "your child shall never want for anything while I have the means of procuring it."

"Oh, Mr. Howard, it was not of bodily comforts, I thought," exclaimed Mrs. Murray, sadly. "I do not fear that she will lack those; but there is a hunger of the heart that is worse than starvation; there is an inward yearning that no luxuries can still; promise me that she shall not suffer from that! Tell me that you love her—that you always will!"

There was a pause. Annie had buried her face in the sofa cushions, but, with intense eagerness, she waited for a reply. At last it came. Love, for Mrs. Murray's words had aroused all his old affection for Annie, and pride were struggling in his heart—pride won the victory, and he coldly replied,

"It is out of our power to control the heart."

Annie heard it; a deathlike faintness stole over her, and all hope that he might yet love her died within her.

Mrs. Murray groaned aloud.

"How can I leave her," she said, "so young, so inexperienced, in this world, exposed to all its temptations, without a mother's watchful eye, unshielded by a husband's love?"

"Take me with you!" cried Annie. "You see, he hates me," she whispered in her mother's ear.

He heard only the first words, and maddened by jealousy, that his wife should prefer to go with her mother to remaining with him, he approached her, and seized her firmly by the arm.

"You are my wife!" he said. "You shall not go!"

She withdrew from his grasp; her bare arm bore the marks of his violence, but she said nothing; she only trembled, and flung her arms around her mother's neck, weeping like a frightened child.

"She is your wife, Charles Howard," replied Mrs. Murray. "You have taken her from a mother's care, see to it that you watch over her. You have taken her from a mother's arms, see that yours shield her—and from a loving home, see to it that you supply its place; for, so sure as harm comes to my child, so surely will I require her blood at your hands!"

She tried to escape from Annie's close embrace, but the girl held her fast.

"Do not leave me, mother!" she repeated, again and again.

"Pray, remain," said Mr. Howard, coldly, and she did so.

The husband, angry with Mrs. Murray that she usurped his place in his wife's affections, left the room, and for hours the mother and daughter sat together in the darkened apartments. With a sad heart Mrs. Murray listened to Annie's pleadings to take her away from the man who hated her, declaring that he would kill her when she was left alone with him.

How gladly would her mother have complied with her request, or have assured her of his love—could she have done either. She could only soothe her as she would have done a child, and when she grew calmer, advise her to be gentle, loving, and attentive to her husband's wishes, that so she might gain his heart.

Meanwhile, Mr. Howard, pacing up and down his library, cursed in his heart the hour when first he had seen Annie, and was fully as unhappy as his wife could be.

It was with a feeling that she had lost her last earthly friend that Annie watched the steamer that bore her mother away, as it ploughed its way down the bay, and, with a sigh of despair, she sank back on the soft cushions of her carriage as it whirled away, resting her head languidly on her hand.

Her husband was by her side, but he looked fixedly out of the opposite window, though he could not have told even what streets they had passed through.

At length the coach stopped; he assisted his wife to alight, saw that she reached her room, and that her maid was at hand to supply all her wants, and then turned away.

What would she not have given for one word of kindness from him; but none was spoken, and with desperate calmness she looked the future in the face, and submitted to her fate, that of the unloved wife.

CHAPTER TWENTY-FOUR

Helen and Her Husband

More than two years had passed, during which the name of Christine Elliot had become known far and wide. She had toiled on unshrinkingly, undaunted by the obstacles that she encountered, and they were not few, sustained through all discouragements by the high hopes which she cherished of accomplishing her darling object, of seeing her sex placed, in all respects, on an equality with her brother man.

To this one aim she bent all her energies; on this one altar she sacrificed all personal considerations.

It had not been without a struggle that she had realized that she must lay all her home affections on that shrine, and again and again she had written letters full of the highest eloquence, because fresh from the heart, to the dear inmates of the old homestead, only to feel a keener pang of disappointment on receiving them again, with the seals unbroken. At last she had given up the hopeless task of effecting a reconciliation, and endeavored to bury all painful recollections under the weight of duties which crowded every day more and more thickly upon her.

Nor was her time alone occupied in preparing her lectures; she wrote, she studied, giving herself no relaxation, till her thin cheek and hollow eyes, told too plainly that she was over-tasking herself.

In the hours not devoted to study, she sought out the poor, the sick, and the sorrowing; she listened to their tales of woe—she poured the oil of consolation into their wounded hearts—she gave them of her penury, for she did not find it easy to get more money than she required for her expenses—and what was of more value even than material aid, she gave of her abundance, sympathy, kind words of hope and encouragement.

Her hand had withheld many from entering the road that leads to death—her voice had lured the despairing back to life and hope—and though all this was done in secret, known to none others than the grateful beings she had rescued from worse than death, and to her God; though she was met often with revilings and taunting advice, to help the poor who needed aid, rather than to seek impracticable and useless rights for women, by those who knew nothing of her secret labors; while she would have shrunk from giving publicity to her good deeds, merely to exculpate herself from base charges, yet she had a peace within her heart which passeth understanding.[54] Verily, she had her reward.[55]

The only painful thought that filled her heart was the knowledge that she could do so little, and with words of power she endeavored to inspire her hearers with the desire to seek out and relieve the distressed, as well as to press forward to claim the wider field which she pointed out as before them.

She heeded not the ridicule or the coarse and vulgar abuse that abounded in the columns of nearly every journal in the land; the shafts of malice glanced harmlessly aside; the filth of low ribaldry could not cling to her white garments, as pure and unsullied in reputation she walked on steadily to the goal which she was striving so earnestly to attain.

But powerless as was all this to wound her, it did reach the bosom of her relatives and rankled there.

Mrs. Frothingham read it with flashing eyes and compressed lips, and Farmer Elliot's stern brow grew black with fierce frowns, and through his set teeth he muttered words that were almost anathemas on his daughter, that she had placed herself and him in a position where they could be thus assailed.

He had disowned her, but he could not prevent a portion of her disgrace attaching itself to his good name.

His wife and Bessie did not dare to mention Christine's name to him; together they wept over her infatuation; together they read the comments of the press upon her, and were in turn grieved, shocked, and angered by what they read.

As the fall of the year again came around, bringing with it its golden harvests, its glory of many-colored forests and the softness of the hazy days of the Indian Summer, the inmates of the farm-house were surprised by a visit from Mrs. Frothingham.

She said little to Mrs. Elliot or Bessie on the subject of Christine's chosen career, but she was often closeted with her brother in close consultations, the subject of which the mother and sister could only guess, since they were not allowed any part in them.

Farmer Elliot would pace the floor during these interviews, his face working with the violence of his passions, while Mrs. Frothingham, cool and collected, would talk on in her soft, gentle voice, without ever raising her tones, yet uttering words that excited her brother to all the more fierce anger against his child.

His wife read this in his manner, which daily grew sterner and more cold; he rarely addressed her, and when she had resolved to speak to him on the one subject that engrossed the thoughts of both, his fierce looks would deter her from proceeding, the words would die away in her throat, and choking sobs that she could not restrain would take their place, as she turned away to weep on the bosom of her loving and sympathizing Bessie.

"Julia is only making bad worse," she would say. "John is growing more and more angry—oh, why will she harden his heart so against her. She is his child, she is my child, and, misguided as she is, we are still her father and mother."

"I wish she would go," was all the consolation Bessie could offer; and, at last, she did go, but Farmer Elliot accompanied her.

He made no explanations as to the object of his journey—but, with something of his old kindness and affection bade his wife and daughter, good-bye, telling them, as if they had been children, that he would bring them something fine from town.

With a deep sigh, Mrs. Elliot looked out after the wagon that bore them away, till a turn in the road hid them from sight, then walked away from the open door to exchange surmises with Bessie on the object of the journey, and whither it tended.

Meanwhile, Mr. Elliot and his sister journeyed on to Boston, where, as the papers announced, Christine was soon to speak. It was the day before the lecture was to take place that Christine, attired in her simple travelling costume, sat in the parlors of the Revere; she was feeling that sad sensation that is produced by being in a crowded solitude, an utter loneliness, a longing for one friendly or familiar face. She sat silently there, unconscious that she was an object of curiosity to the ladies in the room, who had whispered to each other that she was Christine Elliot—suddenly a whisper reached her ear—she blushed deeply, painfully; for, though she could stand before an audience, and, in her inspiration and utter self-forgetfulness, feel no hesitation or embarrassment, she could not be aware that she was the object of curious scrutiny, as if she were some curiosity, without painful diffidence. She longed to get away, yet hesitated to move, when all at once a bright face was close to hers, a small hand grasped her own, and a sweet voice cried—

"My dear Christine, how glad I am to see you!"

The new comer went on, in a sprightly way, to tell her that she had just heard, as she passed the house, a knot of gentlemen saying that Christine Elliot had come, and she could wait no longer, but came in directly to see her. She talked so rapidly that Christine could say nothing; she could only look at her friend with a gladness in her large, dark eyes that spoke volumes.

"And, now," concluded the speaker, "you must go directly with me, to my house."

"Why, Helen," replied Christine, "I thought your father lived in New York."

"So he does, my dear," said Helen, smiling, "but I am not Helen Harper now; allow me to introduce to you Mrs. Helen Linton, and then to take you to my house and show you my husband. Come, I shall take no refusal."

"I am not disposed to decline your invitation, my dear Helen," said Christine. "I am very glad to go to the house of a dear friend, and that friend, Helen Harper."

"Linton, my dear—don't forget my new name nor my new dignity—and now on with your bonnet, and we will be off directly. Your baggage shall follow. Please give your directions."

In a few moments more, they had left the Revere; and not long after, having laid aside her travelling dress, Christine sat in the little parlor of Helen's residence.

Small, indeed, it was; there were no mirrors, no elegant curtains, whose soft folds draped the windows, no costly furniture or magnificent carpet, all was simple and inexpensive, though tasteful.

There were, indeed, one or two fine paintings on the wall, and an elegant piano almost entirely filled up the small back parlor. Helen looked at her friend as she glanced round the room, and then, assuming a serious tone and manner, exclaimed, rather in answer to Christine's looks—

"Yes, my dear, I have made a bad match. I have married a poor man. The die is cast; poor we are, and very probably poor we shall always be. It is a sad fate, indeed!"

Her tone was solemn, but a gleam of mirth in her eye contradicted her words. Christine looked at her for a moment, then, in a tone as serious as that of her friend, she replied—

"Congratulations, then, would be quite out of place. Allow me to condole with you—to mingle my tears with yours."

"Not yet," said Helen. "Let me first show you my husband, that you may see the climax of my misery, and then you will better appreciate my feelings."

She slipped out of the room and soon returned, accompanied by a gentleman who was attired in a dressing-gown, and who still held a palette in his hand.

"My husband, Miss Christine Elliot," said Helen, and Mr. Linton bowed gracefully, and welcomed her warmly to his house. He apologized for coming thus abruptly into her presence, as he said Helen would not wait for him even to lay aside his palette, but dragged him along; and, after a few remarks on the ordinary topics, he withdrew.

Christine looked at him well. His was not a face and figure that could easily be forgotten. His figure and manners were undeniably elegant, but his face, perhaps, was not strictly handsome; his features were not perfectly regular, but there was a softness in his deep-blue eyes, and a lofty expression on his high, pale brow that would have seemed somewhat too far removed from ordinary humanity had it not been for the mirthful smile that played around his mouth, and lighted up his whole face with a genial expression. His hair was very beautiful; of that golden-brown hue, so rarely seen in real life, which some of the old masters used to give so often to the Madonna.

Helen had watched the countenance of her friend during her husband's presence, and, as soon as he had closed the door after him, she exclaimed, in a tragic tone:

"Shouldn't you think the society of such a man as that would be enough to make one woman miserable?"

"Have done with your nonsense, child," replied Christine, "I can see plainly enough that you are so proud of him that you can't express your admiration, and so are trying to get me to flatter you, by dilating on his perfections in my very best style. I won't indulge you. But tell me how it happened that you married him."

"How it happened I hardly know myself," said Helen, laughing; "but he had been painting my portrait—he is an artist, you know—and somehow it fell out that he took a fancy to me, though what he saw in me I don't know—he so spiritual, so noble, so unselfish, and I so matter-of-fact, for I am just the same as ever, Chris. Well, I can't just tell how, but you know when two people love each other they generally manage to make it known, and so, after a while, we were engaged. Father consented readily, though he didn't exactly like the idea of Will's being an artist; if he had been a grocer, or even a tailor, he wouldn't have objected, but painting he looks upon as fol-de-rol. He says 'it don't pay'; however I soon brought him round.

"But mother was terribly disappointed. She, like a good many other mothers, was ambitious for me to make a grand match. It rather touched her pride that I should marry, as she called it, beneath me. The idea of Will being beneath me!

"Well, after a long while, she did not positively refuse to give her consent, as she had done, and so we were married.

"You will like him, Christine, I know. He is just such a person as you are; just as full of plans for doing marvellous things—has a thousand and one reform hobbies that he rides in turn, and I look on, and laugh at him as I used to do at you. By-and-by, you and he, and a whole regiment of Don Quixotes like you, will get tired of running your tilts, but if it's any satisfaction to you to keep on, why I have no objections."

"I see you are the same Helen as when at Woodland Vale," replied Christine; "but I know that you see as plainly as any one the evils in society, and that, under this assumed lightness, you do in reality have a deep interest in efforts to remove them."

"I look on with deep interest, as you say," returned Helen. "I do not deny it; just as I should on the efforts of an alchemist to discover the philosopher's stone. It would be a fine thing if that should be discovered, and so it will be when you reformers find the moral philosopher's stone that will turn evil magically into good. Go on, my dear. Work away with your crucibles and retorts. I feel the greatest interest in your labors."

"But, Helen—" began Christine.

"Not a word now, my dear. I must go and attend to dinner, for you people who live in the clouds do drop down to earth three times a day, and with all the better appetites for your sojourn there—so I must see that something is prepared for you. Excuse me now. You will find books of all sorts lying round in all kinds of places here, and I know that I could not furnish you with company better suited to your taste.

"You are at home here. Do just as you choose; you needn't make yourself agreeable if you don't like; you may sit alone or have company; you may talk or be silent—in fact, you have the largest liberty. Make the most of it," and Helen was gone.

Christine threw herself on a sofa with a book, but though she had taken one of her favorite poets, Mrs. Browning, she did not lose herself in her pages.[56]

Helen's words had their old effect upon her, to plunge her into doubt as to whether she was not indeed disquieting herself for naught.

She looked back on her labors of the past two years. What was the result? Wearily she sighed. She could lie quietly no longer; she opened the piano and struck a few chords softly, and in a low sweet voice, she sang one of her favorite melodies. The music soothed her; she leaned her head on one hand, and allowed the other to stray over the keys—then, as her mood changed, she raised herself up, and a glad, triumphant strain burst from her lips. For a few moments she was as one inspired—her eyes were upturned, her whole face a glow of enthusiasm; and Will Linton, who stood in the doorway quite unnoticed by her, gazed with an artist's admiration on her kindling expression.

As she ceased to sing, he drew near—he would not have spoken to her of what he had seen; her emotions had been too pure and high to be a topic of conversation, but he felt that he understood her; and, sitting near by, he began to talk to her of her aims and aspirations, in a manner that convinced her at once that he did indeed sympathize with her.

Rapidly the hours passed, and they were quite unconscious of the flight of time, till Helen's gay laugh recalled them to reality.

"I must interrupt 'the feast of reason and the flow of soul,'" she said, "and offer you, in its place, a more substantial feast.[57] I have achieved a triumph. Come, and see what the united skill of Honora and I has produced," and she led the way to her dining-room.

All was in the nicest order, and, with no small pride, Helen presided at her table. When the dessert was placed before her guest, she announced that the lemon-pie was the triumph to which she had alluded, and, indeed, it did great credit to her culinary skill.

She listened, with evident pleasure, to Christine's assurances of its excellence, and replied—

"Yes, Chris, you can make better speeches than I, but I can beat you at pie-making."

"Perhaps you could at speech-making, if you were only to attempt it," returned Christine.

Helen laughed.

"You needn't fear losing your laurels through my rivalry there," she said. "No, thank you. It's a fine thing to be a general, but really it does seem essential to have an army as well as officers; and I don't care about being a leader, till there is something or somebody to lead."

"If all you are waiting for is an army, Helen," answered Mr. Linton, "you will not have to wait long. The movement has already many friends, and their numbers are increasing daily."

"A mere handful in comparison to its opponents!" said his wife.

"It is true," said Christine, "that at present we are comparatively few in number, but the seed must first be sown. Remember the parable of the mustard-seed, 'which is, indeed, the least of all seeds, but when it is grown is the greatest among herbs and becometh a tree, so that the birds of the air come and lodge in the branches thereof.'"[58]

"I'm afraid it will be a long time, Christine, before you see the realization of your hopes, in the verification of that parable."

"I may never see it," replied Christine, with a sigh; "but it must be; it will go on, for the truth must succeed, sooner or later. All reform movements are slow in their beginnings. They are like the avalanche, which creeps on so gently at first that its onward course is almost imperceptible, but gathering strength and velocity as it proceeds, it rushes on, bearing before it all that men had deemed most stable and immovable."

"I trust," said Helen, "that your moral avalanche won't bring, like its counterpart in the material world, desolation and ruin in its track. But, I don't fear it at present. Why, my dear Christine, do you realize that the most powerful opponents to your reform, are the very ones you are trying to benefit? How many women do you suppose there are who want their rights?

"It was only the other day that I was conversing with a young lady on the subject, and among other things I spoke of your doctrine, that every girl should be educated to expect, at the proper time, to earn her own livelihood, as her brothers did.

"'Goodness me!' cried the young lady. 'Those are a queer kind of rights! I'm sure I don't want to do as my brothers do.' She gave utterance to the almost universal sentiment of her sex. The idea of exertion was distasteful to her. Now a few energetic people like you, to whom action is life, have misjudged other people by yourselves.

"You reach out for a wider field—you would cast off the shackles that bind you, and then free others from the same, and lead them forward to the open vineyard—but they do not feel like you—they would not go.

"What do these women, whose whole pitiful souls are engrossed by dress and fashion, and who find no greater enjoyment than to fritter away their time in idleness, want of a wide field to work in? Work! That is low and vulgar. They would escape from your grasp, and return to their wallowing in the mire.

"So, Christine, I look on your efforts as hopeless. Even if you should gain all you desire, and entrust it to the keeping of those whom you are so eager to raise, it would be tossed aside as a useless boon. 'Who would be free, themselves must strike the blow.'[59]

"Oh, Helen, how can you speak so contemptuously of your sex?" cried Christine. "Woman is not the degraded being you represent her, or if, in some cases, she has become so, it is the result of her education, and the circumstances in which she is placed.

"God has given her a head to plan, a heart to will, and hands to do, and if custom has so forged fetters about her that she cannot develop the powers her Creator has given her, so much the more reason that she be assisted to escape from them. Let us not sneer or mock at her first weak, puny efforts when she is freed from her chains. In coming out of utter darkness, the light is at first painful; let us be tender with her, if she does at first shrink from its full glare."

"I see it is quite useless for me to waste my eloquence upon you," said Helen, smiling. "You are perfectly invulnerable, armed at all points. There is one thing certain; you have the three ingredients in your composition that go to make up the reformer: hope, energy, and perseverance; what a pity it is that they should be expended in battering away at imaginary evils, when there are so many real ones in the world."

Mr. Linton had been listening with great interest to the conversation, and before Christine could reply, he exclaimed—

"Think of the poor seamstress, who toils day and night with her needle, 'sewing at once, with a double thread, a shroud as well as a shirt'; see her, in her lonely garret, with thread-bare garments, haggard cheeks and hollow eyes.[60] Is there no reality in the dangers that encompass her?

"Oh, Helen, are you a woman, and does not your heart bleed for your poor, weak and weary sisters?"

"Ah, my dear Will," said Helen, "this is too much! Christine was fully a match for me, and here you deploy your forces and open such a battery upon me that you threaten to demolish me at once. I am a woman, and not heartless, as I think you must admit, but I confess I don't see how the right to vote or to hold their property is going to put bread into these unhappy creatures' mouth's. What good will equal political rights do starving wretches?"

"Do you not see," cried Christine, "that those rights are at the foundation of everything? It is the absence of them which has made society what it is. Give us those and all the rest will follow. Then will there be avenues opened, that women may not all crowd to the school, the needle, and the kitchen for support; then will there be made laws that will do justice to all—then will be removed that feeling, so universal, uttered coarsely by the low and vulgar among men, and made evident by the manners of the educated and refined, of the inferiority of woman.

"Then will the poor, toiling woman receive as much for her labor as her brother man, and then will the rich have something higher and nobler to employ her mind, some object better worth living for than to be a leader of the ton, the figure on which to display the skill of the dressmaker, milliner, and jeweller."

"But, Christine, granting that those objects for which the rich live are mean and paltry, would the substitution of the haranguing of caucuses, the rallying round the polls, and the scramble for office be any improvement? Politics even now are given up by many of our best men, in disgust; they have ceased to be active participants in them; shall a pure-minded woman desire to enter the path which they have turned from?"

"Her purity would restore the corrupt system to its original state," replied Christine. "For the very reason that it has fallen from its high estate, into the hands of the unprincipled, should noble men and pure women unite in taking again the reins of government.

"It is wrong for them to turn away discouraged and disgusted, when so great a task is before them. Let woman urge on her brother and work with him side by side. There is no fear of her losing her dignity. God has given her instincts which will keep her in the right way. She and man have, indeed, in many respects, dissimilar natures; she has her separate sphere, but it is the wide one that God has given her, in giving her powers to develop. Let her enter upon that, and let not man, in his ignorance and self-confidence, say, 'thus far shalt thou come, and no farther.'"[61]

"Remember one thing, Christine," said Helen. "If women are placed on a perfect equality with men, they must not expect all the little attentions that they now receive—the delicate preference of their comfort to that of the gentlemen—the giving of seats in crowded stages, halls, or lecture rooms—in fact, the thousand and one little things that speak so much for the regard felt for woman, as she is, gentle and dependent."

"I do not see the necessity for that," returned Christine; "as far as history goes to prove anything, it shows just the opposite results from the elevation of women. In barbarous nations, where she is little more than a slave, she is treated with contumely and contempt; as civilization advances, she rises in the social scale, and receives proportional respect—why, then, should one step farther in advance, the giving her those inalienable rights which we claim to belong to every human being, and the increased intellectual development which a wider field of necessity must give, cause her to forfeit that respect which is due to progress, and which has followed naturally in her upward course heretofore? But even did she lose these little attentions, would not her gain be infinitely greater than her loss?"

"You would be horrified if I were to answer no," said Helen, "and yet that would be the answer of an overwhelming majority of women who hug their chains and glory in what you would call their shame!"

"The old argument of the oppressor, the world over," returned Christine, "but no reason why efforts should not be made to show the oppressed their wrongs, and once awake to that, they will work their own cure."

"Well," answered Helen, "we have had a long argument, and, as is usually the case after a discussion, the result is that each is more sure of being in the right than when he began. But believe me, Christine, I appreciate your motives, whatever may be my differences of opinion. You see, my husband is such a radical, it is important for me to be a conservative to keep the balance true; but now let us adjourn to the parlor," and she led the way to that apartment.

Music and chat on various subjects—for Christine could talk on other themes than that of Woman's Rights—followed, and whiled away the hours.

Helen and her husband were evidently very happy. Dissimilar as they were, each prized in the other the traits of character not mutually possessed, and no differences of opinion could affect the strength and fervor of their attachment to each other. Neither Will nor Helen wished or expected to have their views on any subject accepted without investigation by the other; each well knew that no two minds can receive exactly the same impressions from any one thing, and each recognized the right of the other to receive and express the opinions resulting from the examination of any subject.

CHAPTER TWENTY-FIVE

The Insane Asylum

The evening was bright and beautiful on which Christine was to address the people of Boston on her usual subject. The stars shone brightly, and the moon's pale light fell softly on the leaf-strewn walks of that pride of the Bostonians, the spacious Common, as Christine, accompanied by Mr. Linton and his wife, crossed it, on her way to the Melodeon, where she was to deliver her lecture.[62]

The building was brilliantly illuminated, and a thrill of delight that did not spring from gratified pride filled Christine's heart as she stood before that audience, composed of the beauty and the fashion of the town. She contrasted it with her first lecture there, when crowds of low and brutal men had drowned her voice with cries, stamping, and hissings; and now, as she went on to speak, and found herself listened to with breathless attention, only interrupted now and then by murmurs of approval, and other tokens of applause; she felt, indeed, that a great victory had been achieved, and she rejoiced in it, as a sure token that the cause which she had espoused would yet succeed.

The thought inspired her, and never had she been more eloquent—never had her eyes beamed with a brighter light, nor her whole heart been more evidently in her words. She was in the midst of one of her most thrilling appeals to woman, and quite carried away by her own picture of the future, when suddenly she stopped, hesitated, and for a moment seemed unable to go on, for at that instant her eye had rested on the dark, stern face of her father among the crowd.

That fierce look pierced to her very heart; it checked the words she was about to utter, and quite unnerved her for a few seconds, but by a strong effort she regained her composure, and pursued her theme as before.

That night she seemed unusually dispirited, as both her friends noticed, though quite unaware of the cause. She seemed absorbed in thought, was absent and moody, and did not appear to notice the remarks addressed to her unless repeated. She went early to her chamber, but not to sleep, for the sight of her father had brought, in all its freshness, the fact of her homelessness to her mind. She had read in his face no softening towards her—no pride in the applause which she had received, though she had watched him narrowly; there he had sat, calm, cold, and stern during all of her speech; nothing that she had said, though the audience had been at times convulsed with laughter, or hushed and breathless, listening to her words with tearful eyes, had been able to vary the expression of his face; that black, fierce frown haunted her—she felt again that shuddering, chilling sensation it had caused her, when she had first encountered it.

The night wore slowly away, and Christine gladly welcomed the day. She longed to be away now, to see her dear friend, Mrs. Warner, her more than mother, and soon she stood in that quiet sitting-room, so rich in associations of pleasure and of pain. Here she had met and loved Philip; here she had sorrowed over his fall; here she had consecrated herself to her life's labor, and here she had found a home and a loving heart when all others had forsaken her.

Mrs. Warner met her with the same true affection; listened to her account of all she had done, and drew from her even her most secret thoughts; encouraged her, sympathized with her, and had the satisfaction of seeing her dark mood pass away—to see gay smiles take the place of the harassed look that had settled round her mouth, and the deep, thoughtful expression of the eye vanish before merry glances.

While Christine was thus recovering her lightness of heart, and enjoying the hours that were passing all too swiftly with her friend, Mr. Elliot and Mrs. Frothingham were seated in the parlors of the Revere.

"She is not here," he said, "though she did come here on her first arrival in the city; but she left to go to Mrs. Linton's, an old friend."

"Yes, I know," replied Mrs. Frothingham. "I had rather she had been anywhere else; I know Helen Harper well. However, we must go there at once."

"I have a carriage at the door," said her brother, and together they passed out of the room.

Not a word escaped the lips of either on their way. Farmer Elliot's looks did not invite conversation, and Mrs. Frothingham respected his mood.

"Is Mrs. Linton in?" she asked of the servant who opened the door, as they reached Helen's residence.

She was not, she had gone out to be gone all day.

"Very well," said Julia, in a tone of evident relief. "Is Mr. Linton in?"

He was, and sending up her card, she and her brother entered the parlors. Julia's quick eye read Mr. Linton at a glance as he entered the room, and, after introducing her brother, she exerted all her graces of manner to produce a favorable impression upon him. It was not in human nature to resist Julia, when she chose to exert herself; her beauty, great though it was, was far inferior to her grace of manner and powers of fascination; after she had been talking some time, quite uninterrupted by Mr. Elliot, who sat silent and moody, she addressed herself in a lower tone to Mr. Linton.

"Miss Christine Elliot is, I am told, with you."

"She has been," was the reply, "but is now gone for the day, to see her friend, Mrs. Warner.

"If she has been with you any time, it is useless to attempt disguise. You must have seen her unfortunate state of mind. It is indeed a sad blow to us—perhaps you are not aware that I am her aunt, and that he is her father," she said, casting a look at Mr. Elliot, and speaking still lower. "It has nearly killed him," she added, in a tone of the deepest apparent feeling.

"Indeed," replied Mr. Linton, rather confusedly. "I have not the slightest idea to what you allude. Is it her position as a lecturer to which you object?"

"My dear sir," interrupted Julia. "Is it possible that you have not discovered that her originally fine mind has lost its balance—that she is insane?"

"Impossible!" cried Mr. Linton, in horror.

"Alas, it is too true!" replied Mrs. Frothingham, pressing her handkerchief to her eyes. "Insanity is not uncommon in our family, and, for some time past, it has been developing itself in my unhappy niece. We wish to keep it perfectly quiet. It is grief enough to see her mind perfectly shattered, without the publicity which the press would give it; we shall take her away quietly and keep her in quiet, hoping that she may be restored. May we trust to you to keep her secret, if it is not already too well known?"

"Most assuredly," replied Linton.

"And may we count on your assistance, my dear sir," continued Julia, raising her fine eyes to his face and speaking in her softest tones, "to enable us to remove her without difficulty or force?"

"Certainly," replied Will, much moved by her evident distress. "But, what would you have me do?"

"Nothing more than when she returns, to let me know at once, and tell her that I shall be here to see her. I will come, then, and take her away."

"It is very sad," said Linton, "and singular, that I have discovered nothing of this."

"Have you not, then, seen anything strange about her, any apparent unconsciousness of what was passing, any wildness of the eye? These are the premonitory symptoms of her violence."

Linton sighed. He remembered her abstraction the previous night, and could say nothing. Mrs. Frothingham rose, her eyes were full of tears, her lip quivered, and her voice was tremulous, as she bade him good morning; and, with feelings of the deepest sympathy, he looked after the sad aunt and heartbroken father, as they drove away.

They had not been long absent when Christine returned; her interview with her friend had made her very cheerful; she was in high spirits, and laughed and chatted gaily with Mr. Linton: as he contrasted her manner with that of the previous night, he sighed deeply, for he had been prepared by Mrs. Frothingham to see signs of disordered intellect; and these slight alternations of manner, though they would, probably, have been unnoticed by him, unless put on his guard, now seemed only a verification of Julia's words. It is not to the jealous alone that 'trifles light as air are confirmation strong, as proofs of holy writ.'"[63]

Linton immediately dispatched a messenger to Mrs. Frothingham, and awaited her coming with no little impatience; she came at last; and telling Christine that her aunt had called to see her, and wished him to say that she would soon call again, he left the room as Mrs. Frothingham entered.

Christine sprang to meet her, and, reading kindness in her looks, could control herself no longer. She flung her arms around her neck, and sobbed aloud.

"This is very kind, Aunt Julia," she said, at last. "I have not dared to hope for so great a pleasure; with your co-operation I shall soon be restored to the hearts of my parents. Dear Aunt Julia, your visit has made me very happy. Last night, I felt that a reconciliation was almost hopeless, when I saw my father in the lecture-room—"

"You saw him, then," interrupted Julia, sadly, burying her face in her hands, and apparently much moved, "oh, my brother—my dear brother!"

"Has anything befallen him?" cried Christine, in great agitation. "Is he sick? Is he dead? Speak—tell me the worst at once. This suspense is horrible."

"Worse than dead, Christine," said Julia, and, sinking her voice almost to a whisper, she added, "he is insane!"

"Oh, heavens!" cried Christine, turning pale and sinking back into a chair, while an expression of the keenest agony passed over her face. "I have driven him mad!" she gasped, wringing her hands wildly. "Inhuman daughter that I am!"

Julia was touched by her evident suffering. She leaned over her, and kissed her brow.

"Poor child," she said, softly; then continued, "Do not take it too much to heart. We hope that it will be nothing lasting. He would go to hear you speak, and would come to see you to-day. I have succeeded in getting away from him for a few moments, and have come to consult with you. He is moody, but perfectly harmless; and, if he can be removed to a quiet asylum, far away from all old associations, for a short time, I trust he may recover. I have come to propose to you that you accompany him with me to the asylum in Augusta. Will you do so, or are your engagements such that you cannot? In that case, I can go alone."

"No engagements could interfere with such a sacred duty," said Christine, in a choking voice, for every word her aunt had spoken had been like a dagger in her heart. One thought alone filled her mind; her father was insane, and she had made him so. It was almost more than she could endure. She groaned aloud as she listened to Julia's directions for the journey which must be made immediately, and gladly availed herself of the assistance which she proffered in getting ready for her departure.

Mrs. Frothingham suggested that it was not worthwhile to expose her father's misfortunes to the Lintons, to which Christine assented, and left a note for Helen, telling her that unforeseen circumstances compelled her to depart thus unceremoniously, and thanking her for her kindness. Much the same thing she said to Mr. Linton, who bade her a kind farewell as she left his residence.

Mr. Elliot met them at a hotel, and assented quite readily to Mrs. Frothingham's proposition that he should accompany his daughter on a short trip for her health. He was very silent and moody; but Christine was prepared for this. She watched him with an expression of mingled sadness and affection in her fine eyes, and endeavored to pay him every little attention in her power, but he repulsed her, and seemed annoyed by her assiduities, so that she was obliged to desist. He even seemed to dislike to find her eyes resting on him, and she was forced to content herself with stolen glances at his face, when she thought herself unobserved. He had changed greatly since she had seen him; not that he had grown very much bent or grey, but that dark, stern, fierce look had settled down upon his face, and changed him almost entirely from the cheerful man he had once been.

At last they reached Augusta, and, apparently quite unsuspicious, he allowed himself to be carried to the asylum, where Mrs. Frothingham previously went to make arrangements, leaving Christine and her father at a hotel while she did so.

On reaching the asylum, the Doctor invited Christine to go and look at the rooms, and showing her two or three unoccupied, desired her to make a selection. She did so, and requesting her to be seated a few moments while he gave a few necessary directions to a servant, he left the room. Christine sat quietly there, lost in thought. Some moments passed and the Doctor did not come; she grew tired of waiting for him, and imagining he had forgotten her, resolved to go to the parlor; she could easily find her way, though she had come through rather winding passages.

She walked to the door and tried to open it. It was fastened on the outside. She heard footsteps in the hall. She knocked at the door; nobody paid any attention to her rappings. She cried out loudly to be released, that there was a mistake; a harsh voice bade her keep still. Half frantic, she ran to the window; it was high and barred. She looked out and saw, just turning a corner, a carriage, and in it she could plainly distinguish the face of her aunt Julia and *of her father.*

The truth flashed upon her at once. She had been deceived. She was a prisoner.

In the wildest excitement, she ran to the door. She screamed till she was hoarse for Dr. Lyman; she shook the door; she beat against it, for a long time to no purpose; at last footsteps approached, and Dr. Lyman appeared.

With flashing eyes, and in accents tremulous with passion, she began to tell her story, but he turned contemptuously away. She sprang towards him, and held him fast as he was about to leave the room, crying,

"I am not insane! Indeed I am not."

"Oh, no; I dare say not," replied the Doctor. "In fact, we haven't any insane people in the house."

"But, Doctor," began Christine, "I came to bring my father—he is insane. There is some mistake."

"Ah, well, I will inquire into it," replied the Doctor. "Sit down, now, quietly, and I will make it all right."

His words were soothing, but Christine saw that she was not believed. She would not let him go; she clung to him, determined to go out of her prison with him. He tried gentleness at first, then, growing weary, wrenched himself dexterously from her grasp, and in an instant was gone. The door was locked almost instantaneously, and she was again alone.

"I will not stay here," she cried, battering furiously at the door, and begging to be let out, again and again. Ere long her door opened, and admitted the Doctor, with two assistants, who, spite of her resistance, slipped on a straight-waistcoat, saying she was "as mad as a March hare." The Doctor then told her that unless she kept quiet she would be confined to a bed.

She saw her mistake; her violence had been so much against her, and, restraining herself, she began to tell him that she was Christine Elliot; but he turned away with a shrug of the shoulders, and, exasperated, she began to threaten him for his unlawful imprisonment of her. He made but little reply to her, and soon left her—sending a woman into the apartment.

She answered the inquiries that Christine made, so far as to tell her that the lady and gentleman who brought her had gone away, and listened quite kindly to the protestations of her sanity which Christine poured forth.

"Well, then," said the woman, "if you ain't crazy, don't act like a crazy critter."

The advice was good, and Christine determined to restrain herself that she might the sooner regain her freedom. Months passed, and as she had been uniformly gentle, after her first outbreak on her arrival, she was gradually allowed greater freedom; she mingled at times with the patients in a large hall and saw occasional visitors.

She had hoped that her quietness of manner might lead to a belief in her cure, and looked eagerly every day for some word from her physician's lips that might denote his perception of her recovery. None came.

She was sitting one day, as usual, in the hall, surrounded by insanity of all characters; there were the sad who wept and moaned, the gay, and the pompous, who deemed themselves some great personages; these and many others who walked about, paying little attention to each other, when a visitor entered.

Christine did not look up, but as the physician passed her, she heard him say "there, too, is a monomaniac, who imagines herself to be Christine Elliot; sane in all other respects, apparently—quite gentle, yet almost a hopeless case."

The mystery was then explained; she had been placed there under a fictitious name, and it was evident that she was to be kept there a long time. Her heart sunk within her; no gentleness of demeanor could contribute to her escape; a fierce hatred to the authors of her misery sprung up in her heart, she ground her teeth. "My turn will come!" she said, fiercely.

She now asked often for pen and paper, and wrote letters to Mrs. Warner, and Mrs. Linton, again and again. No replies came, for they never reached their destination, and sometimes fearing that she had no friends, sometimes guessing at the truth, that her letters were not forwarded to the persons to whom they were addressed, she passed her time wearily hoping for, but at times almost despairing of escape.

At times she feared that she might, indeed, become insane; she watched the operations of her mind narrowly, and was startled at the wild fancies that haunted her; she endeavored to control herself, to prevent the wandering of her thoughts, to which she observed a tendency, and the very effort to do so, seemed to increase, instead of checking the wildness and waywardness of her imaginings; then would arise the old bitterness with new power against those who had placed her where she was in such imminent danger of what she dreaded far worse than death; the fear that had haunted her early years, and which her life of action, by preventing her morbid dwelling on her own emotions, had, for a time, quite dissipated, now assumed new strength.

How long was this to last? There was no reply, save her own weary sighs.

She grew thin and pale, for she was experiencing the truth, that "hope deferred maketh the heart sick,"[64] and her heart-sickness prayed on her body.

CHAPTER TWENTY-SIX

Sweet Home

Nothing could have surprised and shocked Helen Linton more than the tale her husband related to her on her return. She read Christine's farewell note again and again, she reviewed all her conduct and remembered the opposition which she had encountered from her friends—as she thought of all this she grew indignant, and exclaimed:

"Will, it is utterly false—she is no more insane than I am!"

"Helen," replied her husband, "you are letting your feelings run away with your judgment. Her relations are the best judges of the matter, and what earthly reason could they have for making such a statement, if it were not so?"

"Because they mean to put an end to her public life, by fair means or foul—"

"Helen," said her husband, "you are unjust. Had you seen as I did, the grief of that sweet lady, her aunt, and the heartbroken father, you could not speak as you now do. Their sorrows are enough without the weight of unjust suspicions. Mrs. Frothingham's emotion was so great she could hardly express herself."

"Consummate actress!" was Helen's reply; "where did they take her?" she asked.

"I did not inquire," replied her husband, "nor did they tell me."

"It's all of a piece," cried Helen, "they mean to keep it a secret so that none of her friends can go and see her."

"They do indeed wish it kept quiet," returned Linton, "but I can readily appreciate their motives; it would be very unpleasant to have the fact, with the comments of every heartless scribbler who chose to make them, going the rounds of the press; and it was doubtless for the same reason that I did not ask, that they did not tell me where she was taken, namely, they did not think of it."

"Oh, you dear unsuspicious Will," replied Helen, "anybody can deceive you so easily! You are so frank and sincere yourself that you think everybody is like you."

"Is it owing to that unfortunate trait of mine, of being so easily deluded, that I got so taken in, when I married, Helen?" asked her husband, with a smile.

"You may thank your stars that you were thrown in my way," answered Helen, "for, if fortune hadn't favored you, in giving you your present admirable wife, I am sure, I don't know what would have become of you."

"You wouldn't insinuate that the Fates had anything *worse* in store for me, would you?" he replied. "My present lot is bad enough for any mortal—"

Helen put her hand playfully over his mouth.

"No more of your impertinence, sir," she said, "but just come and show me what you have been doing in the studio to-day."

Throwing his arm around her waist, he drew her into the room of which she spoke.

Pictures leaned against the walls or rested on easels, in different stages of completion. Helen looked at one after the other; they were mostly portraits; she pronounced several almost perfect, and others flattered, while her husband listened to her comments upon the paintings and the persons who had sat for them; he smiled a little at her brief, shrewd summing up of the characters of several, but ended, by a sigh—

"I am so tired of portrait painting," he said: "I want so much to paint what I have here," he added, tapping his forehead—

Helen did not ask him why he did not. She knew very well that his present business was far more profitable, and that he could not afford to dispense with this means of livelihood while absorbed in the work he desired to be engaged in. But she did not allow the sadness which she felt, to be visible in her face; she only said, "Some of our greatest artists are as well known through portraits as in any other way. The subject is not so very much—genius can lend a charm to anything. All in due time your great picture shall stand on the canvas—'learn to labor and to wait.'"[65]

"A hard lesson, Helen," replied Linton.

"Yet it is the secret of true greatness, my dear Will, and well worth learning; but now it is so pleasant here, just take a seat on this lounge, and let me read to you."

He did as she requested; half-reclining on the lounge, while she sat on a low stool close by. She began to read Mrs. Browning's "Isobel's Child"; her voice was clear and low; she read with deep feeling, and both she and her listener were quite absorbed in the pictures presented to their minds. Even after she had ceased to read, a soothing sadness, not unmixed with pleasure, filled the hearts of each as they sat there in the gathering twilight, in that silence which is sometimes more expressive than speech, and which is never wearisome to those who love each other.

At last the lights were brought in, and Will, drawing near a table, rapidly sketched three scenes; Isobel with her child sleeping on her knee, the light of earthly love and happiness in her face, as she rejoiced in the granting of her prayer for its life; then the babe, saying to her:

"Oh, mother, mother, loose thy prayer!
Christ's name hath made it strong;
It bindeth me, it holdeth me,
With its most loving cruelty,
From floating my new soul along
The happy, heavenly air!"

while her face betokened the struggle going on in her soul; lastly, the dead child on her arm, the grandeur in the mother's face.

Linton paused in his sketching.

"Ah, Helen, I cannot give that beautiful expression," he said—

"'Like one God-satisfied, but earth-undone.'"

"They are exquisite," returned his wife, looking with admiration at the sketches. "Some day you must paint them."

"Some day?" said Linton, with a sigh.

"Yes, my dear Sir Faintheart—so cheer up. I had my fortune told me once, and I was to have a great man for my husband. I'm tolerably well satisfied that I haven't made a mistake in the man, and I believe others will agree with me, some day—don't you?"

Her husband's only reply was a warmer pressure of the hand he held, but in his flashing eye, and glowing cheek, she read the passing away of the brief fit of despondency that had, for a time, had the mastery over him. He now joined with spirit in conversation with his wife, and merry voices and light laughter re-echoed through that pleasant room; the very portraits on the wall looked down almost intelligently on the youthful pair, who had forgotten all, save the existence of each other, while talking of their plans for the present, and their hopes for the future.

At last the quick strokes of a clock, on the mantel, recalled them from their pleasant air-castles to reality; for not in the old fairy-tales alone do the chiming of the hours have a magic power to dissipate the creations of imagination, and reduce them to blank realities. The miracle has been going on every hour, and there are few who cannot sympathize with the hapless Cinderella, in the suddenness of the change, by which they have been brought back from the ideal to the real.

"All this time," said Helen, as she rose to leave the room, "we have quite forgotten poor Christine, but I will go and see Mrs. Frothingham before long, and find out where she is, and how she is getting along."

"Very well," said Will, with a yawn, as he followed his wife from the apartment.

CHAPTER TWENTY-SEVEN

On the Rack

Mrs. Frothingham stood alone in her spacious parlors. She was looking out of the window, but, apparently quite oblivious of the landscape before her; she heeded not the budding beauty of the spring, the delicate verdure of the lawn, or the opening foliage upon the trees that, in clusters or separately, stood about her dwelling. Her eyes were fixed upon the distant hills that skirted the horizon, but she was hardly conscious that she was gazing upon them. The balmy, spring air tossed the heavy masses of curls that shaded her delicately tinted cheek, as if to call her attention to the loveliness around her on every side—but all in vain.

Very lovely she looked, as she stood there dressed in her elegant morning robe, which displayed the symmetry of her figure to full advantage—her little lace cap half hiding, half displaying the profusion and luxuriance of her hair, and one small foot peeping out from the folds of her garments, while her attitude was grace itself. She stood in the shade of the rose-colored curtains, with one hand supporting her head, while the other fell gracefully by her side, resting on the green silk of her robe, whose color enhanced by the contrast the pearly whiteness of the taper fingers that rested upon it. The thoughtful expression of Julia's face, though not its usual one, suited well with the calm repose of her attitude. Indeed, so motionless she stood that she might have fitly represented the beautiful statue of Pygmalion ere it had woke to life.

At last she moved from the window. "It is time," she said, half aloud, and seating herself at an elegantly inlaid writing-desk, she began to write a few words.

"The six months have elapsed, my dear John," so ran the letter, "and, according to my promise, I shall go directly to see Christine. I think we may indulge the hope that, though the remedy has been rather severe, yet a cure has been effected. At least, I am very sanguine in my expectations.

"I will write you immediately on my return, or, what will be better still, possibly I may come with our restored patient to your house.

"For the present I must say, Farewell."

Ere long the letter was dispatched, and Mrs. Frothingham on her way to Augusta. She went directly to the Asylum, and inquired for Miss Caroline Frothingham, as under this name Christine had been placed there.

The doctor spoke of her gentleness, but shook his head when asked if this was not a favorable symptom. He said that the patient seemed still to be in her unhappy delusion with regard to her personality, and that the letters which she wrote only confirmed the fact of her insanity, consisting, as they did, of declarations of the cruelty of her friends in enclosing her, though sane, in a lunatic asylum, begging the assistance of those to whom they were addressed in obtaining her release, and all signed Christine Elliot.

Mrs. Frothingham listened with a sigh, and then requested to see her niece.

With a glad heart Christine obeyed the summons to go to the parlor to see a friend; she had no doubt that at last her letters had reached her friends, and that either Mrs. Warner or Helen Linton had hastened to see her at once; with her old, elastic step, she passed quickly to the apartment, and with sparkling eyes and extended hand approached the lady, who stood a little turned away from her; at the noise of Christine's entrance she turned around, but the girl advanced no further; the flush of joy faded on her cheek, the sparkle of hope died out in her eye, and gave place to a look of fierce indignation; as Mrs. Frothingham would have taken her hand, she motioned her aside with a gesture of contempt, folded her arms closely over her breast, and turned, without a word, to leave the room.

The Doctor, who had followed her, observed Mrs. Frothingham's look of apparent distress, and said, in a low tone,

"Do not let this reception discourage you; nothing is more frequent than for persons in her situation to turn against their nearest friends."

"But I must speak with her," said Julia. "Bid her remain."

"I will not," said Christine, in reply to his command. "I will not remain in the same polluted atmosphere with a woman capable of such vileness."

"Remain!" said the Doctor, with a look and gesture that Christine well understood.

She hesitated; the first feeling of anger had subsided, and she did in reality wish to know what had brought Julia there, and with a hope, which made her heart throb exultingly, she turned and seated herself on a sofa.

"I presume you have no objections to my seeing my niece alone," said Julia.

"Certainly not," replied the Doctor. "If you should want anything, that bell will receive instant attention"; so saying, with a bow, he left the room.

Christine did not speak; she looked fixedly at Julia, who did not seem inclined to break the silence; at last she could wait no longer.

"To what am I indebted for the honor of this visit?" she said.

"To my interest in your welfare," replied Julia, calmly.

A flash of anger gleamed in Christine's eyes. "I ought to be deeply grateful," she said, "for an interest which has manifested itself in so many acts of kindness! This last debt of gratitude will, I fear, be more than I can repay.

"Have you any more favors of a similar character to heap upon me? I am already overpowered by the benefits I have received at your hands."

"Pray go on, Christine," said Julia, as she paused. "Say all that you wish. It is as rare as pleasant, in this ungrateful world, to meet with such appreciation of one's services; indeed, I am happy to find myself so well appreciated."

"Woman!" cried Christine, exasperated by Julia's coolness. "I do, indeed, appreciate your character fully, but I lack words to express my detestation of it and you; you, made up of treachery and deceit—a libel upon your sex—with the face of an angel and the heart of a fiend—I loathe you! You are beneath hatred, and fit only for contempt!"

"Go on, my dear," said Julia, in her softest tones; and, as Christine's anger prevented her replying, she added—

"I quite expected it all. This is your first opportunity to spit out the concentrated venom which has been accumulating for the last six months. Say on. When you have finished, I will speak; until then, I will be a listener."

Christine was silent for a moment. At length she said, shortly, "Say what you have to say, and begone!"

"Do you wish to leave this place?" asked Julia, without heeding her niece's anger.

Christine's eyes flashed.

"I am not surprised," she said, in a tone of bitter irony, "that you should doubt my willingness to leave a place to which I was so anxious to come, and where the society is so very agreeable."

"I regret, then, to deprive you of the pleasure of a longer sojourn here, since you have found it so delightful, yet that was my intention when I came here. I can hardly expect your thanks, however."

"Thanks!" interrupted Christine, bitterly, "and for what? For my unjust imprisonment, or for the tardy act of justice in my release? You do well not to expect thanks, madam. I will leave you now, and make preparations for my departure. When I am free, we will see if the law cannot reach you, who have dared to confine me thus."

"But you are not free yet, my dear," said Julia, carelessly, "and, even when you are, I imagine that revenge will not be so sweet to you as to lead you to have less regard to your reputation than we have had—that you will not care to publish your insanity to the world, who will be ready enough to believe it."

"I could hardly publish it more widely, than the fact of my being in an asylum would do!" exclaimed Christine. "It is already known, and I owe it to myself to prove that it is not so."

"I beg your pardon, Miss Christine, but the papers have long since announced the severe illness of Christine Elliot, and, of course, her necessary retirement for awhile from public life, and here, Miss Caroline Frothingham only, has been considered insane.

"So, as I said before, even when you are free, I should suppose that common prudence would dictate the policy of your keeping quiet. There are always people enough ready to believe ill of anybody, if there is the least occasion."

Christine was silent. She saw that Julia was right, and that the fact of her having been in an asylum would, if known, greatly lessen her influence. She bit her lip, and turned angrily away.

"Allow me to suggest to you," said Julia, in her mildest tones, "before you go to your room, as you seem to be on the point of doing, that there are certain conditions to which you must subscribe, before you leave this pleasant spot."

"Conditions!" repeated Christine. "Dare you propose conditions? No, madam. I demand release as an act of justice, and I will never submit to make terms with you."

"Very well, then," said Julia, coolly. "If that is your determination, I will resign Miss Frothingham to the care of her keeper," and she laid her hand upon the bell.

"Oh, heavens!" cried Christine, in the wildest excitement, springing forward and grasping her aunt's hand. "You cannot be so cruel! You cannot have meant to mock me with false hopes, only to plunge me into the deeper despair! Take care what you do. You will drive me mad!"

"It was your own choice," said Julia. "You can be free by the utterance of only one word. Only agree to the conditions; but you refused even to hear them."

"I am in your power," sighed the girl. "Let me hear them."

"You must promise, first, never again, by voice or pen, to defend the foolish doctrines of that ridiculous cause which you have espoused. Next—"

"Stop there," said Christine, raising herself to her full height, "and hear me now! I solemnly swear that never will I desert the cause to which I have pledged myself, till I am convinced that it has no foundation in justice or truth. Never shall any personal considerations, no matter of what nature they may be, influence me to give up what is more sacred than life—my convictions of what is right and true.

"I am in your power; but you may keep me here till death or madness in reality overtakes me, and the guilt will rest on your soul. Life I can lose, but never, never, so long as life lasts, will I be faithless to that duty to which God has called me. You have my answer."

"Then, remain!" cried Julia, fairly exasperated. "You are in your proper place! If this is not insanity, never was there a case. You shall return to your cell, and there shall you remain till you promise what I have required."

"That I shall never do," repeated Christine, for the moment quite elevated by her enthusiasm above all thought of the weariness of her imprisonment.

"Then *never* shall you be released," retorted Julia.

"Be it so," answered Christine; "but give me rather perpetual imprisonment, with none but these hapless wretches about me, so that my soul is unstained, than life in the free air, under God's beautiful heavens, with those I best love, if the price of that must be dishonor, and treachery to the highest and noblest instincts of my nature. I do not envy you, madam; hapless as is my fate, I would not exchange places with you. On earth we may never stand before a tribunal, but there is a bar before which we all must stand; there is a day of retribution—"

"I will hear no more," cried Julia, ringing the bell, violently.

A servant instantly appeared, and Doctor Lyman almost immediately entered.

"I had hoped," said Julia, "that I might have relieved you of your charge, but I find that she is yet unfit to be removed."

"You are saying what is false!" cried Christine. "You know that every word you utter plunges you deeper into perjury."

"Alas!" sighed Julia; "every sentence that she utters only makes clearer her misfortunes. It is painful for me to look upon her!"

"Well it may be!" cried Christine, "if you have yet a spark of conscience. Doctor, ask her if I am not Christine Elliot, and look well at her when she attempts to deny it!"

"Poor girl!" sighed Julia, softly.

"I see that the interview is injurious to her," said the Doctor. "She looks wild; her violence may return. I must put an end to it."

Mrs. Frothingham bowed her head in assent, and Christine, making no resistance, was again placed in her lonely chamber.

How her heart ached as she looked on the four walls that hemmed her in. She looked out of the window, and longed, oh, how ardently! for freedom. The air that kissed her fevered brow seemed inviting her to go out into the deep old woods that she so dearly loved. She almost imagined herself there, sitting, as she had so often done, on the soft carpet of moss, close by a steep ledge of rocks, while the giant trees, the growth of centuries, stood like sentinels around her, and the rustling of their leaves overhead had alone broken the silence. She woke from this pleasant picture with a start! Alas, how different was the reality! When could she ever, at her own free will, ramble where she chose?

"Oh, it is horrible!" she cried—"horrible that my young life must be extinguished in this prison—that all I have so hoped for should end thus! The birds of the air can soar as they will; the very lowest of insects are free, and I, a being with a soul, must pine away here, losing all my strength, all my energy, all my mind. Oh, it is unjust! Is there a God, and does he allow such horrible wickedness?"

She paced the floor in agony—she gnashed her teeth—she tore her hair, then suddenly catching a glimpse of herself in a glass, she stood still, horrified.

"Oh, God!" she cried, "I am indeed forsaken. I am losing my senses! Is not that being, a madwoman, indeed?"

A flood of tears flowed from her eyes; she sunk upon her knees, and in agony poured out from her whole soul, a prayer that she might not indeed become mad.

Exhausted at last by the violence of her emotions, with aching eyes, and throbbing head, she laid down upon her couch, and, ere long, sunk to sleep, to pass a few happy, because unconscious hours, only to wake to a new realization of the bitterness of her lot.

With her whole soul she hated her father and Julia; the very thought of them made her furious; she hardly trusted herself to resolve what she would do to revenge herself, were they in her power; but never did she regret her determination to adhere to her principles, never did she waver in her firm resolve.

As days passed, she spent her time in revolving plans for her escape; but she was too closely guarded to hope much from anything she could devise.

Three months passed slowly by, without any event to break the monotony of her weary life. She took no interest in the light tasks assigned her; she shrank from any intercourse with the unfortunate beings around her, and, in fact, seemed sinking into that state, the most hopeless of any kind of insanity, that of a gentle, but settled melancholy; a sad expression lurked around her mouth; her eyes were downcast—she rarely looked up at any disturbance, never voluntarily addressed any one; answered briefly, if spoken to by any one. Her health, too, was declining; she was growing weaker every day, and she rejoiced in this gradual decay which she felt stealing over her.

CHAPTER TWENTY-EIGHT

Suspicions Awakened

"It's the finest kind of a day for a ride," said Helen Linton, as she stood before her mirror, in her chamber, smoothing her hair. "The air is so cool and refreshing, and everything in the country must look so beautiful. It would do you good, Will, to go out."

"It would be very pleasant," replied her husband, who was leaning back, languidly, in a chair; his eyes were heavy, his cheek thin and pale, and when he rose, it was evident that he was much emaciated.

He looked like one just recovering from a severe fit of sickness, and, indeed, he had but recently been able to leave his chamber; for months he had been dangerously ill, and to the untiring care and attention of his wife, so the physician acknowledged, even more than to his remedies, he owed his life.

Night after night had she sat by his bedside, moistening his parched lips, bathing his fevered brow, and watching his every movement, anticipating his every want, and when he had sunk into an uneasy sleep, how often she had buried her face in the pillow, and wept noiseless but bitter tears, as she thought of the possibility of what might be in store for her; but night, alone, saw her give way thus to her grief; for the sake of her husband, she had hid her bleeding heart under a cheerful countenance, and spoke cheerfully of his recovery when she dared hardly trust herself to think of what a day might bring forth; now he was out of danger, and he seemed doubly dear to her since she had so nearly lost him.

She would have thought it impossible to have loved him better before his illness, but now she realized that, without him, life would lose all its charms to her.

"Well, then, if you would like it, let us go," she said; "let us see if the fresh country air won't put a little life into those dull eyes of yours, and put a little glow on your pale cheek. Fie! are you the handsome husband I was so proud of? Ah, this is a world where sooner or later justice is done to everybody. 'Every dog must have his day.' I am the beauty now. Come and contrast yourself with me in the mirror, and you will be forced to acknowledge it. Come," and she took him playfully by the hand.

"No, Helen," he said, stroking her hair fondly, and drawing her closer to his side; "if that is so, it is a heart-rending fact, of which I don't care to have ocular demonstration. But let us have breakfast, I am hungry."

"Who would think that three such commonplace words as those last, my dear Will, would sound so pleasant. Only four weeks ago, what would I not have given for the assurance that you would ever again utter that sentence? But come, I hear the tinkle of the breakfast bell."

"And where shall we go to-day?" asked Will, as he leisurely sipped his coffee. "Do you think of any place where you would particularly like to go?"

"I had thought of Woodland Vale," replied Helen. "It is not far, and the roads there are delightful; then, too, lastly—"

"And now comes the true reason," interrupted Will; "for a woman always put that last, as she commits the most important thing in a letter to the postscript."

"Well, lastly, then, my dear lord and master, I want to see Mrs. Frothingham, and inquire after Christine. Your sickness has put everything else out of my head, but I really want to know what has become of her."

"And so do I," said her husband. "She was a noble woman. Ah me, how sad it is that so many of our most gifted spirits have fallen under the curse of insanity."

"We will find out where she is, and go to see her, at any rate, Will," said Helen, as she left the table, "and now let us be off as soon as possible."

Not many minutes had elapsed ere they were on their way to Woodland Vale; a most charming drive it was. It was so pleasant to leave the dusty city, with its noisy murmur, its clattering pavements, and its crowded streets, and to go out into the broad country, under the blue heavens, to breathe the fresh, pure air, and to look on the varied beauty of the landscape.

It is a pleasure that none can more fully appreciate than those who have been confined for a long time to a city, where long rows of stately brick dwellings vie with each other in monotony, and even the few trees that stand here and there seem to have lost the fresh look of their country cousins, and murmur to each other tales and recollections of the beautiful forests.

Helen was very fond of the country, and her delight showed itself in a thousand fantastic ways; she talked and laughed gaily, she sang; she would drive rapidly, as if exhilarated by the rapid motion, or stop suddenly, to gaze about her, to point out the beauties of the scene to her husband, or to gather flowers that grew by the road-side, declaring that none of the cultivated pets of the hothouse could compare with the golden buttercup, the fragrant white clover, or the delicate fringe-like seed of the grass that she added to her bouquet.

Will looked on with delight equal to her own, though expressed in a quieter way; he was never weary of gazing up into the sky at the shifting masses of cloud, tinged here and there by the rays of the sun, or looming up from a base of shadows, till their soft, white tops rested on the blue, so delicate, in their fleecy beauty that one could almost imagine them the fit resting-places of some bright spirit.

At length they reached the shaded streets of Woodland Vale; all was quiet there, no rude noises or din of human industry broke in upon the beauty of the spot as they drove slowly along.

Mrs. Frothingham's residence looked the very abode of peace, as it peeped out from its profusion of trees and shrubbery; its gallery was almost entirely overshadowed by vines of all sorts, clustering roses, morning glories, and a troop of other climbers, and, when they were ushered into the parlor, all its adornings displayed the same exquisite taste; flowers were everywhere, from one simple moss rose, with its few buds, standing alone in its little vase, to pyramidal bouquets, standing conspicuously before the mirrors.

Mrs. Frothingham looked the fitting occupant for this fairylike place; dressed very simply, in white, with a few flowers in her dark hair, she glided in, and welcomed Helen and Linton with a cordiality that was apparently unaffected.

She had heard of Linton's illness, and at once introduced that subject; indeed, so skillfully did she manage to direct the conversation that nearly an hour had passed before Helen had mentioned the object of her visit. At last, rather abruptly, she said:

"Have you heard from Christine lately, and how is she?"

"I saw her not long since," said Mrs. Frothingham, "and regret to say that she is still in the same unhappy state as at the time when she left your house."

"Indeed," said Helen. "I had hoped that she was quite well by this time; for, do you know, Mrs. Frothingham, she did not, to my knowledge, betray the slightest symptoms of a disordered intellect while at our house."

"She has been very violent since that time," replied Mrs. Frothingham. "Indeed, we fear her case is almost hopeless."

"Where is she?" asked Helen.

"In a place of perfect retirement," said Mrs. Frothingham, "for her physician recommends that she be kept very quietly; indeed, she sees no one except her own family."

"Where did you say she was?" persisted Helen.

"Really, I am sorry to say that I am not at liberty to tell you; her father is morbidly sensitive lest it should become known that she is insane, and has charged me to be entirely silent as to the place of her retirement. Not that I should fear to acquaint you with it, my dear Mrs. Linton, but I am under a promise, and were it not so, as she can see no one, it would be of no service to you to know the place where she is. You must see how I am situated."

"It is very singular," exclaimed Helen, "that she should have become so violently insane all of a sudden, without any premonitory symptoms. There are those who, knowing the opposition of your family to her cause, might suspect your motives in withdrawing her from public life. You owe it to yourselves to make known the causes of her retirement and the acts which proved her insanity."

Mrs. Frothingham's eyes flashed, but instantly controlling herself, she said:

"I think no one who knows the facts could doubt our motives; and as it is kept so quiet, we are spared publishing her misfortunes to the world, who might wish to pry intrusively into her sad case."

"No one more than I," returned Helen, "would deplore the publicity which you seem to wish to avoid, but as I am her friend, would you not favor me with some account of the first symptoms of her malady?"

Mrs. Frothingham was silent, but Linton exclaimed, "My dear Helen, do you not see that the subject is deeply painful to Mrs. Frothingham? Do not press it further."

Julia cast a look of gratitude at him, and exclaimed, "Thanks for your forbearance. It is indeed a painful subject."

"I beg that you will pardon me for my seeming heartlessness," said Helen, "and believe me, it is my interest in Christine that has led me to this apparent forgetfulness of your feelings, for I confess I have had painful doubts as to whether you might not have been misled, by the excitability of her temperament and the enthusiasm of her nature, to suspect her of a disordered mind which she did not possess."

"I can pardon in you, what, from any other person, I should consider a gross insult," said Julia, with flashing eyes; "the supposition that we did not use even ordinary care in her examination before coming to a conclusion which justified us in pursuing the course we have taken. But even from my former pupil, Helen Harper, I cannot hear such implied suspicions on myself and the nearest and dearest friends of my hapless niece, without mingled pain and indignation."

"I assure you, Mrs. Frothingham," said Linton, "you have quite mistaken my wife's remarks; I am confident that she had not the remotest idea of casting a shadow of suspicion on the purity of your motives; and I am quite sure that she, as well as I, when she thinks more of the matter, will applaud the course that you have pursued as the pleasantest and wisest that could have been taken under the circumstances."

"You are very kind," said Julia. "Ours is a painful situation, Mr. Linton, and to feel that we are misjudged by Christine's friends renders it almost insupportable!"

"Give yourself no further uneasiness with regard to that," cried Will. "No one could be so cruel as to impugn your motives or, I think, question the judiciousness of your act."

Helen made no remark, but, satisfied that she could get nothing definite from Mrs. Frothingham on the subject, began to talk on other things, and after chatting a few moments very pleasantly took leave.

No sooner had she got comfortably seated in the chaise than she declared most positively her belief that Christine was no more insane than she was. In vain Will reasoned with her; in vain he showed the perfect justness of Mrs. Frothingham's words, still Helen declared that her opinion was unchanged, nay, rather confirmed by Julia's conduct.

"I never knew you to be so unreasonable," finally exclaimed her husband.

"And often as you have been deceived, I never knew you to be so completely blinded," returned Helen.

She insisted on seeing Mrs. Warner, and found her equally as ignorant as herself of Christine's whereabouts, but, being as unsuspicious as Linton, quite shocked and incredulous when Helen declared her belief in Christine's sanity.

"Oh no! nobody could do such a wicked thing!" she cried. "It is utterly impossible for a father and an aunt to be guilty of such a horrible crime."

"Helen, it is really wrong to be so suspicious," said her husband, while a look of pain crossed his fine features; "it is doing a positive injustice to Mrs. Frothingham, and it is painful to me to see you giving yourself up to such distrust of others."

"My dear Will," replied Helen, laughing, "you and Mrs. Warner forget that we are told to be as wise as serpents as well as harmless as doves—but time is flying, Will—ought we not to be on our return?"[66]

Her husband assented, and bidding Mrs. Warner adieu, they were soon on their homeward way. Helen said no more about Christine, for she found that her husband disagreed with her, and though at times she thought that perhaps she was in reality unjust, yet the conviction of her friend's sanity would force itself upon her mind and she resolved to find her out and see her for herself. Meditating on a thousand schemes for accomplishing this, she rode home in silence.

CHAPTER TWENTY-NINE

 Elder Wiggins's Plot

Christine was sitting in the listless attitude that had become
habitual with her, when she was roused by a summons to the
parlor to see a friend. She had long since given up all hopes of
seeing those she really considered her friends, and languidly
entered the parlor.

With a cry of delight, she sprang forward, and grasped the
hand of Elder Wiggins, who stood before her.

"I am so glad to see you!" she cried, and tears rushed to her
eyes as she asked, "How is mother? How is dear Bessie? When
did you see them, and how does the dear old farm look?"

"Poor creetur! Poor creetur!" repeated the Elder, rubbing
the back of his hand across his eyes. "You are looking dreadful slim and poorly. I do believe it would do ye good to get out
into the open air. It isn't nat'ral for any human creetur to be
shut up so long."

"Oh, Elder Wiggins, don't talk about me or my heart will
break," sobbed Christine. "Tell me about home. Tell me—"
but sobs impeded her utterance.

"There, now, don't cry, my darter; don't cry," said the good
man, pulling out his bandana and blowing his nose sonorously,

while he gulped down his emotion. "I'll tell you all about 'um. You see, I was there t'other day, and your mother had heerd that I was a comin' to Augusta to attend the Gineral Conference. Waal, she followed me out to my wagin, and sez she—'Elder, won't you go and see my darter, and let me know how she is?'

"'Where is she?' sez I. At that, she bust out a cryin', and, arter a spell, she told me jest how the case stud, and so here I be; and, hain't you got some comfortin' word or nuther, to send to your poor mother? She's took it to heart dreadful, I can tell ye."

"Does she believe I am—" the words stuck in her throat. "Does she think I am insane?" at last she forced herself to say.

The Elder was silent; he did not like to tell the truth, so he began, "She was dredful afeard that you might be sick or in need of suthin', and she give me some money to buy anything that you had got your mind sot on."

Tears streamed over Christine's cheeks.

"Oh, Elder Wiggins," she cried, "I am not insane! Listen to me. Let me tell you all about it."

Rapidly and distinctly she went on to narrate the whole of the circumstances connected with her entering the asylum, her last interview with her aunt, and the conditions on which she might be released. She told him, also, that, as he already knew, she was there under a feigned name, and that the physician was led to believe that her persisting in calling herself Christine Elliot was a proof of her insanity.

Her accent, her manner, her words, seemed to convince the good man of her truth. He well knew her father, and thought this consisted well with his character. Christine read in his face his belief in her story.

"You believe me!" she said, joyfully. "You will help me to escape! You will go and tell the Doctor all, and he will let me go free."

"Not so fast, my darter!" said the Elder. "Yes, I do think you've told me jest the hull state of the case, but now I must jest turn it

over in my own mind fur a spell. Ye see the Doctor wouldn't be
so likely to let ye out on my say so; he might think it would git
him into trouble; besides, he's paid for keepin' on ye here, and
'tain't likely he's over-anxious to get rid on ye, but ye shall be got
out somehow or nuther, or my name hain't Jotham Wiggins."

He sat a few moments in silence; at last he spoke.

"You hain't changed your mind about agreein' to your aunt's
conditions, hev ye?"

"Never!" exclaimed Christine, with a flash of her old spirit.

"Waal, waal, I didn't expect ye would. Ye know, I don't agree
with ye in yer notions, but then it's a sin and a shame to parse-
cute ye fur um; and I've got a plan in my head that will help ye
out. You jest write to yer aunt, sayin' that you hev thought over
what she said when she was here, and you rayther guess you've
come to your senses. Ask her to come and see you on a sartin
day; and then, when she hez cum, you jest git the Doctor to be
within ear-shot, unbeknownst to her, and hear what's goin' on.
I'll risk, then, but what he will see how the land lays."

"I see," said Christine; "but then she could fix it all up, and
explain it all away, so that I could do nothing. You don't know
anything about her, she has such powers of deceiving. If you
could only stay and listen, *too*, then it would be all right."

"I don't know as I kin," said the Elder, thoughtfully; "but
hain't ye got nobody that would come about the same time?"

"My friends have all forsaken me," said Christine, despond-
ingly; "they pay no attention to my letters."

"P'raps they never see um," said the Elder, "jest write to some
on um, and I'll carry your letters to the post-office myself, and
I'll stay if I possibly kin."

"Dear Mr. Wiggins, how shall I ever thank you enough?"

"Don't crow till ye git out of the woods, my darter. This is
a pooty kittle of fish, I'm gittin into," he added, musingly. "It
looks a mighty sight like doin' evil that good may come.[67] Here
I'm layin' traps and goin' into desate dredful strong!"

"But you will not desert me!" cried Christine, imploringly.

"No, no, you poor creetur!" replied the Elder, "though it does go aginst my grain to do such underhanded business. I hain't used to it, you see—but under the sarcumstances I don't see no other way. You'd better go now and write your notes, and I'll call and git um to-morrow. I'll see the Doctor then, and talk with him about it, too. And now good-bye, and may the Lord be with you!" so saying, the Elder laid his hand gently on her head, as if in the act of blessing her, and in another moment she heard his heavy steps as he was conducted to the outer door, while an attendant followed her to her chamber.

Christine at once availed herself of the opportunity to write to both Helen and Mrs. Warner, to come on the day that she had fixed upon in her note to her aunt, but charged them to keep their coming secret, and informed them what her assumed name was.

She waited impatiently for the next day. It seemed to her that never had the hours slipped away so slowly, but at last the night passed, and once more the Elder was announced.

"It is not customary," said the Doctor, "to allow the patients to see company so often, but this is an extraordinary case, and I observed that your visit seemed to arouse this girl from her usual apathy, which I consider a favorable symptom."

The Elder was on the point of telling the whole story, but restraining himself, he concluded first to get the notes she had written into his possession, and so quietly awaited the entrance of Christine.

She welcomed him most cordially, and gave him the letters at once, for she felt a feverish impatience to have them on their way.

"You haven't written to your mother, hev ye?" asked the Elder.

"No," said Christine; "you can carry my messages to her. But are you sure that she didn't have anything to do with my being sent here?"

"Sure!" said Elder Wiggins; "I'm as sartin on it as I am that I'm alive. Why, she didn't know for ever so long that you was in a hospital. She guessed at it from some things she over-heerd, and when she asked your father about it, he told her that you was crazy, and in an asylum, but didn't tell her where. She found that out by a letter from your aunt, Miss Frothing-ham, and I ain't sure that your father knows that your mother has found it out yet. No, my darter, you've got a good mother, and you hadn't ought to suspect her of doin' anything to your disadvantage."

"I know I ought not to do so," said Christine, "but I am afraid this long confinement, and knowing who have been the cause of it, has made me distrustful."

"Waal, I don't much wonder at it," said Mr. Wiggins. "Sech things is kalkerlated to raise the old Adam in ye; but keep it un-der, my darter; don't let it get the upper hands on ye."

"What time does the mail close?" asked Christine, after she had given many affectionate messages for her mother and sister.

The Elder laughed. "I see you are in a hurry to git rid o' me."

"Oh, no!" interrupted Christine; "but I feel so eager to have those letters go! When I had no hope of getting out, I felt a sort of indifference to the passing of time, but now that I see deliv-erance before me, I can hardly wait for the slow days to wear away, and it seems to me that the delay of one day would be al-most more than I could bear."

"Waal, you shan't stay here a day on my account," said the Elder. "I'll send the letters by this mail, you may be sure of that; and now I will go. Keep up a good heart; it will all come out right yet."

Before leaving the asylum, the Elder sought out the Doctor, and briefly told him the whole state of the case.

Dr. Lyman listened incredulously.

"My dear sir," he said, "you have been deceived by her plausible tale. When you have been engaged in the study of these diseases of the mind as long as I have, you will pay as little regard as I do, to what they have to say. They are perfectly sincere in thinking that all they say of the ill-treatment of their relatives is true, and their artfulness and skill in concocting stories is at times almost astonishing."

The Elder made but little reply; he rightly judged that it would not be advisable to acquaint the Doctor with the plan he had laid, for he saw clearly that he would not have lent himself to such a piece of nonsense, as he would have considered it, as well as insult to Mrs. Frothingham.

Nevertheless, he was determined to carry it through, and though at no inconsiderable inconvenience to himself, he remained in Augusta, and its vicinity, till the day appointed.

Both Mrs. Warner and Helen arrived at the time specified, and were met by Elder Wiggins, who explained the whole affair to them. Mrs. Frothingham soon after arrived at the same hotel, but the Elder took good care that she should see nothing of his accomplices, and hurried them off at once to the asylum. Here he unfolded his whole design to the Doctor, who at first was indignant at such a proceeding, and when soothed by Helen, who assured him that nothing was further from their thoughts than to question his sincere belief in the insanity of his patient, laughed the idea to scorn, and protested that he would have nothing to do with such a foolish business.

At last, however, through Mrs. Warner's and Helen's united influence, he yielded a reluctant consent to keep their arrival a secret from Mrs. Frothingham, and to join them in a room from which they could be unseen witnesses of the interview between the aunt and niece.

The Elder rubbed his hands with delight when this was determined upon, and could not conceal his exultation at the success of his designs.

Mrs. Warner, Helen, and the Elder, were seated near the folding-doors which divided the parlors, and through these they could distinctly hear all that passed in the front parlor, while a small aperture had been left open, through which they could see all that took place at the interview.

Mrs. Frothingham and Christine were left alone there, and ere long the Doctor joined the group of listeners in the back parlor.

"I suppose you were somewhat surprised on receiving my note," said Christine.

"Oh, no," said Julia, carelessly. "I concluded you would come to your senses at some time; we could afford to wait your pleasure."

"Then you were determined to keep me here till I would agree to your conditions, were you?" said Christine.

"Of course we were, my dear Christine," replied Julia. "As to having a Woman's Rights lecturer in our family, that your father and I decided we would not submit to, and until you promised to give it up, we had no alternative but to keep you here or in some similar place."

"Do you hear that?" whispered the Elder, triumphantly, to the Doctor, in so loud a voice that Helen trembled lest they should be discovered; she laid her finger on her lips in token of silence, as Christine went on,

"Well, if I sign the papers as you wish, will you tell Dr. Lyman that I have not been insane?"

"Certainly not," returned Julia. "I shall do no such foolish thing. It would not benefit you in the least, as Miss Caroline Frothingham will cease to exist as soon as she is removed from this place—and he need not be admitted into our family secrets at all."

"Well, if you will not let him know the truth, then, will you give me a paper, stating that your opposition to my course was so great that you and my father had me placed in an asylum for the insane, though well aware of my sanity, and set me free when your object was attained, my abjuring all further participation in public life?"

"No, my dear Christine," said Julia, calmly. "I beg to be excused from putting myself thus into your power."

"And yet you admit it is true. Haven't I stated the case just as it is?"

"Certainly, my sweet niece," returned Julia.

The Elder could hardly restrain himself.

"Aha!" he whispered. "Do you hear that are?"

Helen shook her head. "Hush!" she breathed, softly, as Mrs. Frothingham continued,

"Once, for all, let me assure you that you need expect no documents that you could use against us; your release is all the recompense you will obtain for giving up your wild-goose project. I have the conditions here; shall I read them?"

She read distinctly a solemn renunciation of all future participation in any way in the Woman's Rights Movement, and, at its close, said, drawing a pencil from her pocket,

"Sign this and you are free. I am ready."

"But I am not," returned Christine; "neither now, nor at any future time, will I sign such a document; on the contrary, so soon as I am free, I will devote myself, with all my energies, with heart, mind, soul, and strength, to that great cause."

The Elder rubbed his hands in great delight at this declaration; not that he sympathized with her enthusiasm, but he liked the spirit which dictated it.

"Girl!" exclaimed Julia, in a voice of passion. "What did you mean by bringing me here on a fool's errand? How did you dare to deceive me in this manner? Speak! What did you mean?"

"That I defy you and your power, Mrs. Frothingham; that it is my turn now to triumph, for much as you feared committing yourself, and excellent as were your plans, you *are* committed and your plans are defeated."

"That's a fact!" cried the Elder, in his loudest voice. "Bless the Lord, the wicked shall not always flourish, neither shall the horn of the ungodly be exalted for ever."

He flung open the doors as he spoke, and entered the apartment, followed by Helen, Mrs. Warner, and Doctor Lyman.

"Out of thine own mouth will I condemn thee," began the Elder, while Helen and Mrs. Warner, with the most heartfelt delight, embraced Christine again and again.[68]

Julia was horror-struck. She could not speak for a moment—she grew red and pale by turns, for she saw that all was discovered.

"Be silent, man!" she said, at last, to the Elder, who had continued to address her in Scriptural language, but not in the most flattering terms. "From such as you I might have expected nothing better than playing the part of a listener and spy, but I had hardly looked for such treatment from a gentleman like Dr. Lyman."

"It was with great reluctance, madam, that I lent myself to such a scheme," returned Lyman, "but the result has perfectly justified me in the course which I pursued. I need hardly tell you my opinion of the inhuman outrage to which your niece has been subjected, nor can you expect much sympathy from a man whom you have made your tool in carrying out your cruel plans. When a lady stoops to such base ends, and baser means, she forfeits all claims to be treated as such by a gentleman."

"Will Dr. Lyman order my carriage?" was Julia's only reply, as she rose from her seat.

He bowed, and withdrew. She approached Christine.

"In all this," she said, "I have sought what I considered your highest good."

A groan from the Elder interrupted her, but she heeded it not.

"You were in the broad road to destruction, and your father and I deemed it our duty, however unpleasant, to place such obstacles in your way as might check your downward career. You have broken through them, and will rush on headlong to ruin. Remonstrances are useless, but, in justice to ourselves, I have said thus much. We can do no more."

Without waiting for a reply, she turned, and dropping a profound curtsy, swept from the room.

"Waal, I declare!" exclaimed the Elder. "Ef that don't beat all!"

Helen broke into a hearty laugh, and Mrs. Warner's looks betrayed her astonishment at what had passed.

"Dear me, what an ungrateful girl you are, Christine," said Helen. "Here you have been placed in a position of perfect safety and peace, and yet struggle to get out of it, and, not only that, but worse than all, you haven't the slightest gratitude for such a blessed boon as withdrawing your feet from the downward path. Why, I'm horrified at such insensibility."

Christine smiled faintly.

"It's my opinion that the sooner you get out of this place the better you'll feel," said the Elder. "You are as pale as death, and one good breath of free air will do you more good than anything else—so we'll be moving."

He left the room to make arrangements, and Helen at once proposed to go to her friend's chamber, and do what little was to be done in preparing for the journey. Christine looked around her room, which she was never more to enter, and all that she had felt during her imprisonment rushed to her recollection. The weariness, the resentment, the despair that by turns had swayed her spirit were all as fresh as if she was again under their influence. She gladly left that spot, and most gladly would she have banished from her mind all that was connected with it.

Dr. Lyman expressed his regret at the occurrences which had led to her unjust imprisonment, but she stopped him.

"Do not allude to it, my dear sir," she said. "You did but discharge your duty, and I have to thank you for the uniform kindness which I have experienced at your hands. May I ask one favor of you, ere I go? It is this—that all this may be buried in oblivion; that neither my confinement here, the cause of it, or the means of my restoration, may ever be made public."

"You may rely on my secrecy," returned Dr. Lyman, as he led her to the carriage which was to bear her away.

Having seen Christine safely placed in the hands of her friends, Elder Wiggins bade her good-bye. She pressed his hand warmly, she thanked him again and again, she called him her deliverer, and seemed never willing to let him depart. Her gratitude evidently distressed the good man, and to her repeated exclamations, "How can I thank you enough? What can I do to show my gratitude?" he replied, "I'll tell ye, jest say no more about it—that's the only favor I'll ask of ye. Good-bye, my darter, now, and may the Lord lead you into the right way!" So saying, the Elder shook her hand heartily, and left the apartment.

A friendly dispute now arose between Mrs. Warner and Helen, as to which should first receive Christine as a guest. It was finally settled that she should go first to Mrs. Linton's, as she did not wish to see Mrs. Frothingham if she could avoid it.

Mr. Elliot's anger knew no bounds when he received intelligence of the failure of his plans, of which Mrs. Frothingham hastened to acquaint him, and Mrs. Elliot trembled lest he should discover her agency in it, but if he did suspect her, he made no such allusion but only manifested his displeasure by increased moroseness; he fairly gnashed his teeth with rage, on reading a newspaper-paragraph, which stated that Christine Elliot had regained her health, and would speak in Boston very soon.

He flung down the paper and rushed out into the open air almost choking with passion. Must he be thus thwarted by a mere girl?

"Would to God she were in her grave!" he ejaculated, bitterly, as he paced up and down in the orchard.

The stars shone softly down and the moonbeams silvered the path where he trod. All was peaceful there, but none of the influences about him softened his heart. He cursed her in the bitterness of his spirit as he strode fiercely backward and forward.

Mrs. Elliot had been a witness of his agony; her heart ached for him as she watched his tall form pacing up and down; she could bear it no longer—she stole softly to his side, laid her hand on his shoulder, and murmured, "Father!"

She could not have been more unfortunate in her address— Father! Was not Christine his child? He shook off her hand fiercely, and continued his rapid walk.

Mrs. Elliot leaned against a tree and wept bitterly. Her husband was touched: he really loved his wife and his heart smote him for the coldness with which of late he knew that he had treated her.

"Go in, wife," he said, in a softer tone; "this is no place for you!"

"John," returned she, "you are unhappy—it is my place to share your troubles. For thirty years we have lived together and have shared each other's joys and sorrows. Do not cast me from you now. Speak to me kindly once more, or my heart will break. What have I done that you should spurn me from you?"

Her husband took her hand in his; "Miranda," he said, "you have been a good wife to me. For thirty years you have toiled early and late with me—you have been all that any man could ask, and I honor you for it. I have not been all that I should have been to you—"

"Oh John, do not talk so," interrupted his wife.

"Of late," continued her husband, without heeding her words; "I have been harsh, but I was mad. She has made me so—she has made this once happy home a hell upon earth—she has turned me into a tiger—we have nourished a viper that has stung us. Do you wonder that I pour bitter curses on her head who has done all this?"

"Oh John," sobbed his wife, "do not say so—do not curse her. She is still our child; erring, misguided she may be, but never intentionally wicked. Oh, my husband, it is not well to cherish hatred in your heart against her!"

"Leave me, wife!" exclaimed Farmer Elliot, fiercely; "I cannot trust myself to hear you talk of her. Banish her from your speech, from your thoughts even."

"John, I am her mother."

"No more, woman!" returned her husband, fiercely; then in a softer tone he said: "Go in, Miranda—I will come by and by."

She obeyed—slowly she turned and left him alone with his bitter thoughts and with his God.

CHAPTER THIRTY

 Gilded Misery

Annie Howard sat in an attitude of deep dejection on a lounge in the library; her head was bowed down, and her hands pressed tightly over her brow; she sat silent and motionless—her eyes were tearless, but dark shadows were beneath them, and around her mouth an expression of hopeless grief had settled. That slight figure and youthful face, so expressive of melancholy, cast a gloom over the otherwise cheerful room.

It was a large and lofty apartment; its walls were lined with rare and valuable books; small cabinet paintings of great merit hung on the walls, and there, too, were statuettes of almost inestimable value, which Mr. Howard had imported from the Old World, for he had spared nothing in the decoration of his dwelling.

On a mosaic table, a gem of art itself, laid the latest works of the best writers on this and the other side of the water, magazines, and a portfolio which contained fine prints and engravings.

An elegant writing-desk laid upon a marble slab, which was supported by the four seasons, and a statue of Silence, with a finger pressed to her lip, and a cluster of roses falling gracefully from the hand that depended at her side, stood near it; while opposite, a slave in bronze held pens in one hand, and a supply of ink, in a shell-like vessel, in the other. A coal fire glowed in the grate and lent a cheerful aspect to the room, whose stained-glass windows shed a mellow light over all within it. The sweet breath of flowers floated in from the open door of a conservatory which led out of the library, and canary birds trilled out their sweet songs, revelling in a perfect sea of music, and yet Annie's face did not lose any of its sadness.

It would have been difficult to recognize in that wearied, care-worn countenance the beautiful Mrs. Howard, whose sparkling animation had been her chief charm, and who, during the past season, had been the reigning belle at Saratoga. No one who had seen her brilliancy there, her unfailing flow of spirits, upon which she had so often been complimented, and had heard her low, musical laugh, as she had flitted about, surrounded by a numerous circle of admirers, a thing all life, smiles, and gayety, as pleasing to the eye as the flowers or the sunshine, and seemingly akin to them, would have recognized in this dispirited, hollow-eyed, and faded woman, the sylph who had been the object of such admiration as well as envy. Yet so it was. She had lost the beauty and light heart of her girlhood, and in solitude she gave way to her weariness and despair, though in public she was still all she had ever been. The arts of the toilette, and elegant and tasteful dress, repaired the ravages sorrow had made; and excitement, and resolution to conceal her secret pain, lent a sparkle to her eye, and a feverish brilliancy to her spirits, that passed, with the unobservant eye of a crowd, for the spontaneous out-bursts of a glad heart.

But, what a hollow mockery was her life. In her pursuits her husband manifested no interest, even in public, and in private she received from him only bitter frowns and sarcastic words, or, worse still, a dogged silence which he would not break for days. He would return from his business, and seat himself in the library, with book or pen in hand, while she sat listlessly in a corner of the sofa; and so, without a sound, save the scratching of his pen, or the rustling of the leaves he turned, or a suppressed sigh from Annie, would the evening pass. How she dreaded those wearisome evenings. She would gladly have escaped from the library, but he would not permit this; often she had tried to steal away unobserved, but had as often been ordered to remain or requested to do so, with sarcastic compliments on the pleasure of her society—and so she would sink down again upon her seat, with a silent submission that irritated her husband more than words could have done. The very sight of her helpless, uncomplaining face angered him, and he felt at times hardly able to restrain himself from laying violent hands on her, that he might break that sullen silence, which was her most powerful weapon, and which no words of his could break. At first, her cheek had flushed and paled at the sarcastic bitterness of his expressions, but now, even her face had settled into the impassiveness of a statue, and he could not mark the effect of his stinging words, study her as closely as he might.

There was a singular mixture of love and hate in his heart towards her; he would have given worlds for one expression of tenderness from her lips, and yet at times he hated her intensely, from anger and jealousy that it was withheld from him. Annie feared and loathed him; the very sound of his footstep sent a cold shiver over her frame; she took no pleasure in the elegances that surrounded her—no pride in his wealth, except as it enabled her to triumph over her fashionable friends in display, and, of late, even this ambition had ceased to interest her.

There was, indeed, one drop of happiness in her otherwise bitter cup—her little daughter, her precious Rosa; and the thought of her child seemed to dispel the sadness that shrouded Annie's whole figure like a garment.

She rang the bell, and bade the servant who obeyed the summons, tell the nurse to bring Miss Rosa, if she was awake, to her mamma. In a few moments the nurse appeared, bringing with her a little child of some four years of age, who sprang joyously into her mother's arms, and returned the kisses that were showered upon her.

"You may go, nurse," said Mrs. Howard, and the woman disappeared, leaving mother and child together. Those little clinging arms were twined round her neck, that baby-mouth pressed to her cheek. She was not all alone. How precious to her parched and arid heart was that well-spring of love! She pressed her child to her heart, and tears rushed to her eyes and fell over her cheeks.

Little Rosa's soft hand wiped them away.

"Don't cry, mamma," she said, "*Rosa* loves you!"

With the holy instinct of childhood, she touched at once the cause of her mother's tears, and offered the sweetest consolation.

"Rosa don't love papa," said the child. "Papa is bad—he makes mamma cry."

"My darling must not speak so—she must love her father," said Annie, gently; but the child, with all a child's perversity, went on.

"No, I won't love papa—I don't love him one bit. I wish he was dead, and put in the ground, and then mamma wouldn't cry any more."

Annie was shocked—the feeling and the wish had half unconsciously lurked in her own heart, but to hear it syllabled by her child's pure lips, sent a shudder over her.

"Rosa makes mother feel badly when she talks so," she said. "She must be a good girl, and then her father will love her."

"No, he won't," said the child; "he looks cross at me, and he *pushes* me away sometimes. Rosa don't love him—she loves mamma, but not naughty, bad papa."

"Would you like to go away with mamma, darling—leave nurse, and go away off, all alone with mother?"

"Would father come too?" asked Rosa.

"No."

"Oh, yes, dear mamma, let us go. Put on my hat and let us go."

"Pretty soon, darling; I must write a note first to Mr. Elliston; be a good little daughter, now, and look at the pictures while I write."

Rosa slipped from her mother's knee, and obeyed, while Annie hastily wrote and dispatched a note by a servant. Her child's words had determined her on pursuing a course which she had long been thinking of, and with a lighter heart than she had had for many a day, she awaited the return of her messenger.

She talked to Rosa in a cheerful way of their new home; she told her stories as she lay cradled in her arms, and listened to her baby prattle with the deepest interest.

She did not name her father again; indeed, Annie felt a guilty pleasure in the thought that he could not rob her of her child's affection, nor did she wonder that Rosa feared, rather than loved, her father.

True, he had at times fondled her, and loaded her with playthings, but when she met him on his entrance with caresses, if, in his dark moods, he would speak sternly and repulse her coldly, so that Rosa now only stole timid glances at him when he appeared, and this apparent timidity, by making him very angry, had only increased the estrangement between father and child. She read his face, for children are excellent physiognomists, and withdrew still further from him, or burst into tears when he took her in his arms, at which he would break into a passion, and with angry words banish her to the nursery.

No wonder, then, that she shrank from him, and lavished all her young affections on the mother who idolized her, and who treated her with unvarying tenderness.

An hour slipped rapidly by, while the mother and child sat together in the library. Rosa had begged for a song, and during the singing, lulled by the soft melody, her black eyes closed, her breathing grew softer and more regular, and Annie gently laid the sleeping child on a sofa near, and bent over her, watching her treasure, with all a holy mother's love in her eyes.

As she knelt there, she was unconscious of the entrance of a tall, fine-looking old gentleman, who looked for a moment or two on the group with a pleasant smile, and then approaching and bending over Annie, kissed her softly on the brow.

She started; then said gently, "My dear Mr. Elliston, I am very much obliged to you for coming so soon. I know how busy you always are, but I did want to see you very much."

"Well, well, here I am. To be sure, I'm busy, but then I always will spare the time to come at the request of my little god-daughter. What's the matter, now? Has Rosa got a new tooth that you want me to see, or what other equally important affair is it?"

His manner was short and abrupt, but under it lay a world of kindness, and Annie only smiled softly.

"Guess again," she said, with some of her old playfulness, "but you might guess all day," she continued, "without success."

"Then I will not undertake it, so say on."

Her face grew serious again.

"It is on legal business that I want your counsel."

"Legal! Then you ought to have come to my office. It's just like you silly women, to think a man has nothing else to do but to come four or five miles, away from his office, when she has nothing to do at home, and might go to him as well as not."

"I knew you would come, my good god-father."

"Yes, yes, presuming on good-nature, as usual."

"Forgive me," said Annie, while tears rushed to her eyes, "but I wanted a friend, and where else could I go for kindness but to you?"

"Poh, poh, you silly child!" exclaimed Mr. Elliston as he observed her emotion. He laid his hand softly on her head—"Tell me what I can do for you? What is the legal advice you wish?"

Annie did not look up. "You know that I am not happy," she said; "I have dragged out these years of my married life, and they have taken from me youth, health, and happiness; all but life. You have often told me to bear it patiently, and I have tried to do so; but now I can endure it no longer. I cannot bear to see my sweet child lose all as I have done—to see her bright spirit sink slowly into the shadows that darken our home. I must have a divorce or a separation."

Mr. Elliston started. "Annie!" he said, in a hoarse voice, "what has driven you so suddenly to this determination? I have heard it whispered, but I scorned to heed it, that Harry Lansing paid you those attentions which you should receive from your husband alone. Look into your heart, and see if your motives are pure, or if you do not deceive yourself, and me, in the causes which lead you to desire this."

Annie lifted her blue eyes quietly to his face.

"Harry Lansing has been very kind," she said; "he has guessed at my sorrows, and he has sympathized with me; but no thought of him entered my mind when I thought of a divorce. I do not want to marry again. Let me live far away from Mr. Howard, in some quiet spot, with my child, and I ask no more."

"A divorce is impossible," said Mr. Elliston.

"Well, then, a separation. People do sometimes separate."

"And would Mr. Howard consent to this?"

"Consent? No, I dare say not; but I shall not ask him to do so; I shall resort to the law."

"And on what grounds, then, do you request a separation?"

"Can you ask me, my kind friend? Does not my husband treat me with unvarying harshness? Does he ever speak to me, except in sarcastic or bitter words? Does he not hate me? Oh, Mr. Elliston, he treats me sometimes with the coldest contempt; he will not speak to me for days together; he even humiliates me in the presence of my servants, so that they treat me with no respect; he is harsh to our child—he struck her brutally the other day, and when, wrought up to desperate courage by the blow, I snatched her from him, he raised his hand to strike me too."

"Did he do it?" muttered her companion between his teeth.

"No; but ten thousand times sooner would I have borne the blow that in his passion he dealt my innocent child."

"And is this all?" asked Mr. Elliston, as Annie paused.

"All?" returned Annie, "is it not enough?"

"Not to entitle you to a legal separation. So long as your husband provides you a good home, good and sufficient food and clothing, you have no choice but to remain; unless, indeed, he too should be willing for a separation; then, *without* the law, you could arrange it between you."

"He would never consent. Alas! there is no hope for me! But I can leave him, Mr. Elliston?"

"And what would support you?"

"The money my aunt Murray left me; it is not a large sum, but it would support Rosa and I."

"That belongs to your husband; there was no arrangement made before your marriage to settle it on you, and it becomes his by a union with you. More than all this, should you leave him, *he* has a right to the child. He could take her from you—the law would give her to him."

"Oh, cruel, unjust law!" cried Annie, "to tear my babe from my arms and give her to her hard-hearted father. What shall I do? What shall I do? I shall die if I live here longer. Every day it grows harder to bear his tyranny—every day I hate him more and more, and he crushes me every day deeper and deeper. Dear Mr. Elliston, save me from this horrible fate—how horrible nobody can know until they have tried it themselves. Ah, me! how many times has my heart bled when I saw happy wives leaning proudly on their husbands' arms, and when I have seen husbands looking kindly on their wives.

"For me there is no kind glance. But worse than all, my baby—I can bear my own sorrow—I have borne it—but when I see children climbing with loving boldness on their father's knee, and think of my darling, who will never know a true father's love, it drives me mad.

"I cannot have her grow up to womanhood under the influence of such a wretched home—and worse than all is the fear I sometimes have that, at some future day, he may estrange her from me—that some day she may treat me with contempt, as he does.

Oh, Mr. Elliston, you were my mother's friend. You have promised to be one to me! You will not let me sink back into this darkness of despair. You will save me! You will do something for me!"

"Annie, my dear child, most gladly would I help you, but, alas! it is out of my power. Had you no child I would take you from him at once, but you would not leave him if he retained her, and he would do so, most assuredly. I could not prevent it. I must only reiterate my old advice, bear it all, and try to be as cheerful as you can. Many a woman besides you, my darling, has had similar trials; they have borne them, and time, that great healer, has even brought them happiness."

"Happiness!" bitterly repeated Annie. "That will never be mine, this side of the grave."

"Annie! Annie, do not talk so! Hear me now, while, like a true friend, I tell you that, harsh as Mr. Howard is, he is not alone to blame. You do not try to make his home happy. You do not, I fear, try to suit yourself to his peculiar temper."

"Am I a slave, to bow to his caprices?" cried Annie, bitterly. "What should I gain but still further humiliation, were I to attempt to submit to his whims?"

"Annie, if you loved him as you ought, you would not speak so."

"If I loved him! But I do not. I might have loved him once—now I hate him. I loathe him, and ought I to remain the wife of a man I abhor?"

Her eyes were wild, her lips quivered, her features worked convulsively.

"My dear child, you are ill," said Mr. Elliston. "You had better go to your chamber and try to sleep."

"Then you give me up! You will do nothing for me!"

"I cannot; oh, how gladly would I, my Annie, if I could. Cold as my advice appears, it is the best I can give. Try and be a good wife, and in time you may meet your reward in your husband's love."

"Do you know what you are dooming me to?" exclaimed Annie. "To days of weariness and hopelessness—to the life of a slave, who hates and fears her master—to nights of wakefulness, to rest on pillows wet with unavailing tears—to utter loneliness, for even you, my only friend, shrink from me, because of interfering between husband and wife, and yet you can leave me to this fate, and promise me happiness. Ten thousand times rather would I say, give me death! if it were not for my sweet Rosa, who may, perhaps, one day, repay her mother's love with indifference."

Mr. Elliston paced up and down the room.

"Annie, Annie!" he exclaimed, "you distress me; but what can I do? I will see if Mr. Howard will consent to a separation; it is all I can now think of, to release you from what is, indeed, a sad fate. Now, good-bye, my daughter."

He pressed her to his heart, and left her.

A strange calmness succeeded Annie's emotion. She stooped over her babe, and whispered, "If no one else will help us, we will help ourselves, my Rosa."

CHAPTER THIRTY-ONE

 The Flight and Its Consequences

"Where is my wife, sir?" exclaimed Mr. Howard, entering the private office of Mr. Elliston, where that gentleman was seated alone. His face was pale with anger, and his voice choked with passion.

Mr. Elliston turned round in the arm-chair, in which he was sitting, and looked at him in silent astonishment. This only exasperated Mr. Howard still more.

"Speak, sir!" he cried. "Where is my wife? What have you done with her?"

"Done with her!" repeated Mr. Elliston. "Nothing!"

"It is a false—"

Mr. Elliston's eyes flashed.

"Stop, Howard!" he exclaimed. "Do not utter those words that are trembling on your lips. You are evidently under the greatest excitement. Sit down calmly, and tell me what this conduct means. Upon my word and honor, I know nothing of Annie." His voice trembled. "Tell me the worst," he said. "This suspense is unendurable."

"Do not imagine, sir, to blind me in this way!" exclaimed Howard. "I am not so easily deceived. The servants tell me that

268

you were closeted with her yesterday, and I have long known that your counsels induced her to rebel against my lawful authority. You came to me yesterday; you urged a separation. I indignantly refused to listen to your propositions. On my return, I told my wife of all that had passed between us. I told her, too, that I would never consent to such an arrangement, and this morning I find that she has gone—has taken her child and gone—no one knows where better than yourself. She slipped out, like a criminal, in the night, and sought your protection, sir! Where have you hidden her? Wherever it is, I will find her, and I will tear her from you."

Mr. Elliston leaned back in his chair, and groaned aloud. "My poor Annie!" he murmured, then turning fiercely upon her husband, he said—

"Would to Heaven that she were under my protection! Poor, helpless innocent! Charles Howard, you have much to answer for.

"Hear me man, for I will speak! You have tyrannized over her; you have driven back all her young affections; you have taken advantage of her unprotected situation to treat her as you would not have dared to do, had her friends been near her; you have forsworn yourself, for you have vowed to be all to her that a loving husband should be—father, mother, truest friend, and how have you kept your vow?

"When she had lost all others and turned to you, you failed her. You drove her to the resolution to leave you, and then you refused to let your slave escape. You returned to your home to heap triumphant, bitter, and insulting words upon your victim. I know it well. I can see you as you stood there, proud and exultant, riveting, as you imagined, new chains upon your unhappy young wife.

"Man, you drove her mad! You have shaken her faith in all that is good and true in humanity.

"She could look nowhere for rescue, and God only knows what has become of her!"

He groaned in bitterness of spirit.

"God pity her!" he cried. "Out in this cold, bleak world, with no one to shield her—a feeble young mother with her child!"

Howard had paced up and down the room, listening, with set teeth, to Mr. Elliston.

"You are an old man, and in your dotage," he said, "else you should not have uttered a tithe of the insults you have heaped upon me. I will not bandy words with you about that worthless woman. You say you do not know where she is, and I believe you. Now, it only remains for me to find her, and wherever she is, she shall return to me. Let me get her once again—" he paused, and ground his teeth fiercely.

"Man, I despise you!" these words trembled on Mr. Elliston's tongue, but, by a mighty effort, he restrained them, and compelled himself to ask—

"Did Annie take any money?"

"No, she had none; but she did take some of her jewels, and by those we can trace her. By heavens! she shall not escape me thus. I will find her, if I have to move the solid earth to discover her."

Mr. Elliston did not reply; he did not heed the husband's remarks. A gleam of joy lighted up his face, and he murmured, "Then, she did not go out, maddened, with her babe, to die."

"I, too, will try to find her," he said, aloud. "This very day I will begin the search."

But many days, many months even, passed, and she had baffled the search of her husband, urged on by passion and the desire of revenge, and of the friend who longed to throw around her his protecting arm.

Indeed, she had taken every precaution against the pursuit of which, she was well aware, she would be the object. She was haunted by the vague fear that her child would be taken from her; this had prevented her taking refuge with her good friend Mr. Elliston, when, stung to desperation by her husband's taunts and words of defiance, she had stolen out of her house, taking with her her darling. Had it not been for her, she would have taken nothing with her; but, as she gathered together her jewels, she had thought, "I am not indebted to him; these are not his gift, but a small portion of my own money of which he has robbed me!" and so, with a small bundle in her hand and her sleeping child in her arms, she stole softly out of the house.

She hurried through the dimly lighted streets, all fear of midnight ruffians swallowed up in the greater fear of being discovered by her husband.

On she went till she reached a street, or rather a lane, one of those crowded alleys that may be found in all large cities, where the poor are huddled together.

Here she had been, when yet living at home with her mother, to see the old mother of a trusty servant girl who had long lived with them, and she felt sure that old Mrs. O'Brien would receive her. Where else could she find so secure a hiding-place?

She hurried up the broken stairway and tapped at the door. There was no response. At last she rapped louder, and this time her summons was answered by the opening of the door and the protrusion of a night-capped head, whose owner, in no gentle tones, inveighed against this disturbance of her rest.

"Does Mrs. O'Brien, the old lady, live here?" asked Annie, timidly, and with sad forebodings.

"Och, thin, the old craythur is dead these five months."

"And where is Bridget?" asked Annie, faintly.

"She's out to sarvice," said the woman; "but what are ye after wakin' honest folks at this time o'night jist to be askin' them questions?"

Annie wrung her hands. "Where shall I go? What shall I do?" she murmured.

"Bridget O'Brien was in my house a long time," she said, "and I know she would not refuse a night's shelter to her young mistress now in her distress. I have nowhere to go now. I cannot go into the street."

The woman looked at her a little suspiciously, but her evident distress touched the warm Milesian heart.[69]

"Come in, ye poor craythur," she said; "I'm a poor widdy woman, and have but the one bed, but it's not Judy Macarthy that would turn a body into the strate, let alone the baby."

"God bless you, my good woman," said Annie, as she entered the apartment.

It was a very small room, and the furniture was scanty, but it was a place of refuge, and gladly Annie sank into the seat which Judy offered her.

"Faith, and I've no bed but the one, and myself and the childer slapes in that same," she said.

"I do not want a bed, my good woman," replied Annie; "let me sit here in this chair, with my child in my arms, and I shall be very comfortable. You are very kind, and I shall never forget it in you."

Mrs. Macarthy made no reply, but soon took Annie's advice, and crept to bed again, "with the childer," and ere long was sound asleep.

Annie, for a long time, was wakeful, but at last she too was overpowered by sleep.

When she awoke, her hostess was busy getting breakfast for her family, and ere long the children were scampering about; sturdy little creatures, who gazed at the stranger with mingled curiosity and shyness.

Mrs. Macarthy had examined her sleeping guest, and her pale, youthful face had quite won upon her. She offered her a portion of the meal she had prepared, and with no little delicacy forbore to pry into her affairs. No sooner was the meal dispatched than Annie informed the good woman that she had been unfortunate and had no home, and asked her if she knew of any room in the building that she could occupy. Fortunately, there was a vacant apartment next door to Mrs. Macarthy, and ere long this was engaged. Judy proved to be a kind and efficient friend; through her Annie found an old Jew, who bought some of her jewelry at less than a third of its value, and with the proceeds she fitted up her room simply, and supplied her wants.

For some days she did little else than to amuse Rosa and arrange her room; then she bought materials for plain garments for herself and child, and so occupied her time in sewing. But gradually her money and jewels disappeared; she could not see poverty so near her without the wish to relieve it; she had known nothing of the poor before she had been thus brought into contact with them, and while she had money her hand was open; in fact, they looked upon her as a rich lady, and came freely to her with the relation of their sorrows.

Annie was thoughtless and improvident, but the wasting away of her supplies brought her to her senses; she must do something for her own and her child's support. Again she had recourse to her humble friend. She could only suggest the taking in slop-work, as it is called—the making of shirts—which Annie gladly decided to do. She went to the shop to which Mrs. Macarthy directed her, and on leaving a small sum as pledge of its safe return, took a bundle of shirts home. It was her first experience in shirt-making, and here again she was forced to seek instruction from her neighbor; but she toiled on cheerily, singing at her work, comparatively happy, for her child was well, they were safely housed, and by and by Annie fondly hoped that they might go to her mother, when pursuit had grown hopeless, and she had earned money enough to go.

Poor child! a few months dissipated all these visions. Times grew hard, food and fuel were very high, and her little remaining supply of money was soon exhausted. Mrs. Macarthy had moved, and the loss of her friendly face was, indeed, no small grief to her.

Now indeed Annie knew what bitter poverty meant; day and night she toiled at her work; with aching eyes she sewed on, earning a mere pittance, but untiringly she plied her needle; on the thread it carried hung her own and her child's life.

She dreaded to go to the shop to get her pay, for of late the foreman had paid her fulsome compliments, and peered into her face with an expression of coarse admiration that both terrified and disgusted her, but go she must to get her money and a new supply of work, and so she endured his insolence, which every day grew more and more unbearable. She did indeed try other shops, but they had no work to give out was the brief reply, and discouraged she gave up further search.

Then to add to her troubles her darling child grew sick. It made her heart ache to feel that she could not devote herself to her entirely, yet the attentions she did give her delayed her work; she had a physician, but his remedies did no apparent good—day by day the fever raged more violently in her veins, and as Annie bent over her, moistening her lips and bathing her little aching head, she felt indeed that this was more than she could bear.

"Oh God, do not let her die!" she would cry. "Spare me my child! I cannot let her go!"

And her prayer was granted; the flush of fever left her cheeks, but pale and feeble she lay on her pallet, her little thin hands resting on the counterpane and her black eyes looking almost unearthly from their brilliancy, contrasted as they were with the marble paleness of her face; but her faint smile once more made glad her mother's heart—her sweet voice once more uttered fond words, not the wild ravings of delirium that had sent such a chill over her untiring nurse.

All she needed now, the physician said, was nourishing things; easily said, but alas, where was she to get them? Tears filled

Annie's eyes, as she thought of the father's wealth and luxury, and looked at her feeble child, on her narrow pallet, suffering for want of the comforts with which he was surrounded. At times she resolved to go to him, but the fear that he might take her Rosa from her, as a punishment for her desertion, deterred her. She should have all that her mother was able to earn, Annie determined, and taking her bundle she sought the shop. The foreman was unusually insolent. Annie was indignant, and declared that she would speak to the owner of the shop, and inform him of the treatment she received.

"Do, my lady," retorted the fellow, with a sneering smile; "and see what you get for it—no more work, I'll promise you!"

He flung the money to her as he said this, and with difficulty repressing her sobs, Annie turned away. She dared not complain, for fear of losing her only means of subsistence; she hurried on, and with her scanty earnings bought some few luxuries for her child. It was nearly the end of the month, and she had no money to pay her rent; she might be turned into the streets, but she could not deny her sick child what she so much wished, while she had any money remaining.

Little Rosa's smile, as she took the grapes her mother brought her, more than repaid her for all she had endured, and though faint and weary, she sat down by the bedside to her never-ending drudgery, her never-resting needle.

Another week had passed; she had spent her last penny, but her work was completed, and, nerving herself to her disagreeable task, she walked to the store of her employer. Her persecutor looked at the bundle contemptuously, and declared that the work was perfectly ruined. Annie trembled—she tried to remonstrate, but the brute, in an apparent rage, declared that she ought to pay for the material she had wasted, and when she ventured to suggest that he had looked at the wrong bundle, that there must be some mistake, and requested her pay, he swore at her, and ordered her out of the store. Annie would have left in anger, but the thought of her child restrained her; she demanded to see the proprietor. He was out of town, was the sneering reply.

Annie wrung her hands in agony. It was cold; she had no more fuel, no food for her child. She begged for her pay, in words and tones that might have moved the most obdurate. The brute enjoyed his triumph, but he did not relent.

"Next time you'll know how to treat a gentleman," he said, as she turned and went out of the store.

"What should she do? How could she meet her child?"

For one moment she half resolved to take her child in her arms and throw herself into the river. As she hurried on, her eye fell on a beggar.

She started—there was one resort, and with a breaking heart she crouched on a doorstep and held out her hand. Oh, Heavens! that she should come to this.

A few moments passed; it seemed to her like hours; every passing footstep startled her, no one noticed her, and, in utter despair, she was about to return to her desolate home, when a bevy of young men passed, and a coin dropped in her hand. It was a dollar, and with a throb of delight she rose from her seat, and hurried away. She stopped on her way to get a loaf of bread and an orange, then hastened to her child, for she had left her much longer than usual. On she sped, till she reached her wretched home, ran lightly up the staircase, and entered her room: as she turned to close the door, she observed a gentleman standing there. One look was enough.

"Annie Howard!" he exclaimed; "you here?"

She turned deathly pale. "Oh, Harry!" she gasped, and burst into tears.

He pushed the door open, and entered. For a few moments he did not speak, and Annie's sobs alone broke the silence. At last she checked herself.

"Oh, do not betray me to my husband," she cried. "You will

not be so cruel. He would take my child, and that would kill me, indeed it would."

"No, Annie, indeed I will not," he replied, soothingly. "I am your friend, and always shall be, sweet Annie. But, oh, to find you thus."

"I never begged before," she said, with a shudder, "but for my child, what would I not do?"

She went on, in a low voice, to tell her sad tale; sobs impeded her utterance, and her listener was deeply affected.

"But it led to your discovery, sweet Annie. That white, delicate hand had a strange attraction for me. I had held those taper fingers too often, soon to forget them, and though I could not think it was you, I left my companions and followed you; the figure, the step, both were familiar, and a glimpse I caught of your face, confirmed me in my suspicions.

"Weep no more, my sweetest friend," he said, softly. "Trust to me, and I will take care of you and your darling. You shall never want again."

"My more than brother!" cried Annie, with a burst of glad tears. "Oh, Harry, you were always kind."

"You will let me find you a better place than this," said Harry, "where Rosa's cheeks shall look like the red roses once more—where you shall give up this weary toil. Give yourself no further trouble. Trust me, will you do so?"

Annie laid her little hand in his, with a confiding smile.

"May God reward you," she said, "for your kindness to me."

That night Annie left the room where she had seen so much sorrow, forever.

CHAPTER THIRTY-TWO

The Convention

A bright and beautiful morning ushered in the day on which the Woman's Rights Convention, which had been for some time announced in the papers as to take place in New York, was to hold its session. From different parts of the country the leaders of the movement had come, and assembled in the Tabernacle, to take counsel together, and to cheer each other with reports of progress in their respective sections, as well as to set forth their views to the multitude. The house was crowded with a respectable and attentive audience; even the galleries were filled with the smiling faces of ladies, who fluttered their fans, and whispered comments to the gentlemen who sat by their side.

Upon the platform sat a group of ladies, the well-known leaders of the movement, young and middle-aged, dressed with neatness and simplicity. Most of them wore the ordinary costume, though among them might be seen the simple and quaint garb of the Quakeress, and even the Bloomer, though that was worn by but few. One or two gentlemen, who were sympathizers in the cause, completed the group. All was decorous in the extreme.

A quiet dignity characterized the business proceedings of the officers of the Convention, and the speeches that were made, were received with respectful attention.

The speakers could but contrast the present orderly and attentive audience, with the noisy, tumultuous throng, who, a few years before, in that very house, had received them with hoots, hisses, and yells of derision. Many of them spoke of the change, as a marked step in advance, and with enthusiasm congratulated each other on the progress already made, and urged the friends of the cause to go on with renewed and untiring efforts to advance it still further.

Christine sat among her friends, to whom she was united by a common bond of sympathy, and listened to the remarks made; but one who knew, and could read that expressive countenance well, would have seen that she did not share in the general enthusiasm of her fellow-laborers. Her eyes were downcast, her hands folded listlessly, and borne away in the train of thought which the speaker had suggested, she was hardly conscious of the words that fell on her ear, or of the curious eyes of the multitude, who gazed upon her with no little curiosity, whispering together, and pointing her out to each other, for none among that band of talented women could surpass, and few could equal, Christine Elliot.

Her genius and eloquence were admitted by all, even by those who had the least sympathy with her labors and aims; and whenever she was to speak she was sure of crowded audiences, who, drawn together by her fame and enchained by her eloquence, joined in the universal acknowledgment of her extraordinary powers as an orator; for this gift, unlike many others, never fails to be appreciated by all who come under its influence. If Christine had labored only for fame, she might have been well content with the meed she had obtained, but she had far higher ends in view. She was human, and not insensible to the appreciation of her powers, but at times she felt really humbled that, with her acknowledged talents, she had yet accomplished so little.

Now, sitting on this platform, she reviewed the past and contrasted it with the present. She thought of all that cheered her sisters, and sighed. True, they had large and attentive audiences, but the American people were like those of Athens, always ready to hear and to tell some new thing, and this did not so much encourage her. There was less uproar and disturbance at their public meetings, less untruthful and ludicrous reports in the public prints, but did the calm which had succeeded betoken a change of feeling, or mere indifference? What signs were there of change? What new laws had been enacted? What progress had been made in her darling project, which she deemed at the root of all other demands, the granting of universal suffrage? What new laborers from her own sex had joined the band? There were the same earnest spirits, none of them had failed, but they must pass away; where were those who would fill their places when they should put off their armor—where were those who now would join them in the warfare waged against evil?

Alas, it was no light task to divert old customs into entirely new channels; ideas which children had imbibed with their mother's milk, were not so easily dislodged from the mind. This, and much more of a similar character, floated through Christine's thoughts, as she sat amid her sisters; but, when she spoke, she would not check the ardor and enthusiasm of her friends by her own discouragement and sad forebodings.

She banished these from her mind; she gave herself up to the glorious principles of right, whose contemplation thrilled her whole being, and the words of burning eloquence that fell from her lips, coming, as they did, fresh from her heart, touched the secret souls of all her listeners. The perfect silence that reigned over the assembly was broken only by murmurs of approval that grew louder and louder as she proceeded, and swelled into thunders of applause as she stood a moment in silence after she had ceased to speak, with the light of genius in her eye, and the glow of enthusiasm on her cheek.

Thus, for a moment, she remained, as if entranced by her own visions, then recovering herself, she inclined her head gracefully and turned away.

The session was over, and warm congratulations and merry chat mingled with words and topics of deeper interest among the group on the platform.

Christine listened with a faint smile, and soon, accompanied by Mrs. Bond, who was a fine speaker and possessed of no inconsiderable share of talent, withdrew from the group, and walked slowly away. She could no longer keep silence; into her friend's ear she poured her gloomy forebodings.

"We have not yet, I fear, struck at the root of the matter," said Christine. "Of late, I have become more and more fixed in the conclusion that time alone will bring this matter right—*education* must do the work. It is that which is our greatest obstacle; if the effects of that were but removed—if we had fresh and unbiased minds to act upon, our task would be easily accomplished. I am willing to toil on; the seeds sown will not be in vain, but I have ceased to hope to see the results of my labors. With this generation we can do little, but with the next, if we could but reach them, much might be accomplished. It is to them we must look; do you not agree with me, Mrs. Bond?"

"There is, indeed, much truth in your remarks on education," returned the lady addressed. "It is our greatest and most powerful adversary, particularly one branch of it, to which you have not alluded, but which you might have referred to—I mean, religious education. Our women are bound in the fetters of slavish superstition, and those are the most difficult of all chains to break. The church, in all ages, has been on the wrong side in all movements of Human Progress.

"It is only when all the world goes over to the side of right that the church comes in, declaring that it has always been of that opinion too.

"When the church, with its narrow bigotry, is set aside, as it will be, like all old dead systems, sooner or later, then will dawn a brighter day."

"Oh, Mrs. Bond, I do not agree with you," said Christine, earnestly; "the church is *not* corrupt or dead, and the religious element in woman is one of the holiest attributes of her nature. She may fall into some errors, but the evil that arises from that is more than counterbalanced by the good.

"Should she ever lose that attribute, Mrs. Bond, she would lose everything. Without the religious element, society would relapse into a state of barbarism, and woman would sink again into tenfold deeper degradation.

"Nor do I think with you that the church always brings up the rear in the march of progress; the principles upon which it rests, lie at the root of all advancement and the elevation of the race.

"Did I not believe that the Bible sanctioned our movement, I for one would have none of it."

"That proves only the force of early education," replied Mrs. Bond, laughing; "you were born in Puritan New-England; you imbibed Puritan notions with your earliest breath and they will never leave you.

"When I see a woman of your strength of mind and otherwise liberal notions, still hampered by these fetters of bigotry, I am the more anxious that others weaker than you should be freed from them. I am surprised that you should wish the written authority of a book so obscure and indefinite that it admits of myriad different interpretations; on the subject of human rights and freedom, a subject as self evident as that two and two make four, what need is there of written authority? Besides, you are in the minority in thinking that the Bible is on our side.

"Not long ago in Indiana, on the occasion of the revision of the Constitution, there was a clause introduced to give to married women the right to their property. It passed; but by the influence of a minister was recalled. He appealed to the old superstitions of the members of the convention, and brought all the force of the Bible argument against the rights of woman, and so it was lost.

"What do you think of that?"

"That it proves nothing against Christianity or the church, but only shows the narrow-mindedness of the individual, and his false conceptions of the teachings of the book he reverences."

"It is nevertheless a singular and significant fact," answered Mrs. Bond, "that the teachings of that volume are understood by a large number of individuals to be directly opposed, not only to our reform but to all others; there is no lack of excellent arguments drawn from it, in favor of slavery, and against temperance; and had our good Puritan Bostonians gone to the Bible for their authority, when they converted their harbor into a tea-pot sooner than pay taxes, they would have been met with 'Render unto Cesar the things that are Cesar's';[70] and had the people, when they rose against the British yoke, appealed to the Bible to keep them in countenance, they would have been met with, 'Submit to the powers that be, for they are of God.'"[71]

"But, my dear Mrs. Bond," returned Christine, "you have fallen now into the same error, with our opponents. You are taking isolated texts, which were uttered in a different age, and, forgetting the occasion which gave rise to them, and the modifying circumstances attending their utterance, you are applying them to the present time, instead of taking the spirit and general maxims which are applicable to the whole world, as a guide. Let but the pure and glorious spirit of that sacred book have free course and its due influence on the hearts of men and there will be no further need of so-called reforms; they will all be included in the one great reform—true Christianity—like Aaron's serpent rod, that will swallow all the rest."

"I believe in perfect freedom of opinion," returned Mrs. Bond, "and, as I see plainly that I cannot convert you to my faith, and am equally confident that it will be impossible for you to induce me to accept yours, we must agree to disagree. But I must confess your character has always struck me, since I first knew you, as a most singular compound of the radical and conservative, which I can account for in but one way, that you were a radical by nature, and a conservative by education."

Christine laughed merrily.

"I a conservative?" she said; "that is the last charge that I should expect to have brought against me. I very much fear that the respectable band known as old fogies would lift up their hands and eyes in horror at the bare idea of possessing any trait in common with me—a few such conservatives as I amongst them would revolutionize the whole band."

Mrs. Bond smiled. "Nevertheless I persist in my declaration," she said, as they entered the house of a friend, where they found a home during their stay in the city.

CHAPTER THIRTY-THREE

The Midnight Summons

The afternoon and evening sessions of the Convention passed off quietly, to the evident satisfaction of all of its friends. In the evening, particularly, the audience was more than ordinarily large and brilliant, and the speakers were unusually eloquent. Christine had designed saying nothing, but at last, in answer to loud and repeated calls from the crowd, she rose, and addressed them very briefly, but so happily, that shouts of laughter greeted her sallies of wit, as she again resumed her seat.

The assembly dispersed in high good-humor, and, after the crowd had somewhat scattered, Christine, with her friends, left the building. As they walked down the passage that led to Broadway, a haggard, wretched-looking woman approached Christine, with the inquiry if this was Christine Elliot. Christine replied that she was correct, and, drawing out her purse, was about to slip a coin in her hand, but the woman shook her head.

"Not that," she said, in a hollow voice; "I am sent to you by one you once loved who is dying now, but who cannot die in peace without seeing you. For the love of Heaven go with me!"

Christine shuddered. That hollow, sepulchral voice seemed almost like a message from the dead.

"Who wishes to see me?" she asked, tremulously.

"I have delivered my message," replied the woman. "Will you come?"

Christine hesitated. The woman noticed her irresolution. She looked fixedly on her, and said:

"The curse of the dead, restless in the grave, will haunt you," and, without another word, she turned away.

"Stop," said Christine, "I will go."

She turned to her friends, and explained, in a few rapid words, her intention. Expostulations were of no avail, she had decided.

"Then I will accompany you," said one of the gentlemen.

"I was bid to bring only one. No harm will come to her," said the woman. Christine quietly thanked her friend for his kind offer, but said that she was not afraid to trust herself with her guide, and bidding them feel no uneasiness about her, walked rapidly away with her; she did, notwithstanding her courage, feel some misgivings, as she followed the woman through dirty and dark streets in silence. Some distance they walked, when, suddenly, they entered a dark alley-way, where the woman took Christine's hand, and led her along; a shiver of terror crept over her as she stepped carefully on. Suddenly they emerged again into light, if the flickering of the tallow-candle, at the head of a staircase, might be called so; this they ascended, and entered a small room.

A miserable pallet laid upon the floor in one corner of the room; the woman pointed to it and disappeared.

Christine approached the bed, on which laid the sick person. The moon, which had just risen, shone full upon the wan face of the invalid, as Christine bent over her. Long, fair hair fell over her wasted arms in tangled masses, and the straw, on which she was lying, had become tangled among her luxuriant tresses. Christine gently moved the hair which shaded the face of the invalid.

The sufferer turned away with a groan, then, in a hollow voice, she said:

"You do not know me. Have you forgotten your poor Annie?"

"Annie Murray!" cried Christine, much shocked, for, in those wan features, she could hardly recognize the fresh, girlish face that lived in her memory.

"Can it be possible? Poor child!" She bent over her, and kissed her brow, while hot tears fell from her eyes.

"Do not kiss me," cried Annie. "Do not weep. Your kisses and your tears scorch my very brain. I am not worthy that such as you should touch me," and she uttered a moan that was succeeded by a severe fit of coughing; she gasped for breath. Christine raised her in her arms. Annie pressed a handkerchief to her lips; when she removed it, it was stained with blood. She smiled a faint, sad smile as she looked on it, and motioned to be laid down again. After she had somewhat recovered her breath, she began:

"I know I must die. I know that I am utterly lost; and it was not for myself that I sent for you. I have suffered more than death; that last agony I could bear; but I have a child. Oh! Christine?" she cried, wildly, "I have lost my own soul—save my child's! Let me not drag her down after me. Will you promise me that you will take her—that you will watch over her—that you will save her from her mother's fate?"

She grasped Christine's hands eagerly as she spoke.

"Annie, I promise you in the sight of Heaven that I will."

"God bless you for that promise," said Annie. "Now I can die; but to think of her, in the midst of sin and shame, falling slowly, surely into the gulf of perdition that gapes before me—to lose all that is worth living for here in this world, and oh the next, Christine, the next!"

Her voice sank into a whisper.

"I can bear it myself," she said, hoarsely; "let me see my child in Heaven, and it will soothe half the torments of hell."

Christine shuddered, but she felt that these were the ravings of delirium; she endeavored to soothe the wretched woman before her—she pressed her hand gently on her fevered brow—she spoke to her of the love of Jesus—then, as she grew calmer, she said, softly,

"Sleep now, my Annie!"

Annie's eyes had been half closed; she started up at these words.

"Who called me that?" she said. "'My Annie!' *He* used to call me that."

As she said this, she burst into a fit of tears, not violent, but gentle, and Christine did not attempt to check them. Tears rushed to her own eyes, as she looked on the wreck before her, and remembered her as she had first known her. Gradually Annie's tears ceased to flow, her sobs grew fainter and fainter; she turned to Christine, and said, softly,

"I must not sleep now. When I close my eyes to sleep it will be in that slumber that knows no waking. Let me talk now, while I can. Let me tell you what has brought me here."

In a low, feeble voice, often interrupted by her emotion, Annie proceeded to tell the story of her marriage, her subsequent unhappiness, her desertion of Mr. Howard, and all that had happened during her struggles with poverty, and the relief afforded her by Harry Lansing.

Often severe fits of coughing prevented her proceeding with her tale, and, panting for breath, she would lie exhausted on her pallet; it was evident that she was exerting herself beyond her strength, but to Christine's request that she would rest now, and tell the remainder of her sad story at some future time, she only shook her head.

"My hours are numbered," she said; "the sands of life are almost run, and I must say all that rests so heavily on my soul now, or it will remain unspoken for ever."

After a short pause, she resumed:

"Harry took me to a comfortable home, and he was very kind to me, and to my Rosa. It was so new and so pleasant to me to receive unvarying kindness, and the most delicate and constant attentions, that I could not but feel grateful for them. I began to watch for his coming, and at the sight of him, as he came down the street, my heart would throb tumultuously; the hours seemed long when he was away, and when he was with me, time flew, oh, how rapidly.

"Christine, I loved him with my whole heart and soul, as I had never loved anything before but my child, and he loved me as fondly in return.

"What would I not have done or suffered for him! And when he proposed to me to become his wife, I thought it almost too great a happiness. He did not deceive me—he told me that in the eye of the law our union would not be valid, but he told me that in God's sight it would be sacred, and that he would always consider it so, and whenever the death or marriage of Mr. Howard should release me from him, that he would openly acknowledge me as his wife. He asked me if I would agree to this, and with perfect willingness I gave my consent. I trusted him implicitly, and then, I know no thought of deceiving me had crossed his mind.

"He spoke to me of the world's opinion. I only smiled. The world! What had I to do with that? He was all the world to me. He pressed me to his heart—he called me his darling, his wife—and I was too happy to speak.

"That night, in a little chapel, we were married by a minister; for though the form was nothing in law, yet I felt that it hallowed our union. I was his wife, and I repeated over and over again to myself, with a thrill of delight, the words 'till death us doth part.' And when I was mistress of the quiet, secluded home that Harry provided for us, how happy I was.

"How I tried to be as little expense to him as possible, for Harry was not rich. How hard I toiled to prepare dainty dishes for him when he came to see me—in everything I studied his pleasure, his taste.

"As I sat with my sewing in my hand, and Rosa by my side, in my own little room, how often I used to contrast my present life with my past, and the thought that I was bound to my husband, a thought that had once made me shudder, now filled me with joy.

"How I had dreaded the return home of the man who had first called me wife, and now how I counted the hours that separated me from my husband. I was very happy, and so was Harry; and when my beautiful boy was born, I felt that I had nothing more to ask for. If possible, Harry was kinder than ever—he was very fond of our baby, and very proud of him—he was with me more now, and for hours he would caress and play with our Freddie, and he would tell me, over the cradle, what he would do for and with him, when he grew to be a man. So five years of perfect happiness passed, and then our Freddie died. It nearly broke my heart. I thought it would kill me. Would to Heaven that it had—that I had laid my head down under the green grass with my boy in my arms. That was the beginning of sorrow.

"Harry tried to soothe me in my grief; he, too, was almost heart-broken at our loss; but I would not be comforted, and gradually he grew tired of my sad face. He came less frequently. He was still kind, but I felt a change. The words he uttered were the same as ever, his attentions as delicate, but the spirit that prompted them I knew, instinctively, had changed. I felt a foreboding of what was to happen, even before I would admit to myself the thought that floated through my mind.

"But for all that, when the blow came, I was unprepared for it. When he told me that he was deeply involved in debt, and that he was going to marry a rich woman, but that he should always love me, and would always provide for me, I looked at him without a word, and fell back in a swoon. When I recovered my consciousness, I was in his arms, and he was bending over me; but as soon as he saw my eyes unclosed, he laid me on a sofa and left the room, sending a servant in his place.

"Several days passed before he came again. He was very kind and tender, and I, fool that I was, hoped that he had given up his plan; but, alas! I had cherished false hopes. He spoke of his marriage as a settled thing, and thanked me for bearing it so reasonably.

"His words maddened me. 'Harry,' I cried, 'you shall not marry that woman! How dare you so perjure yourself? I am your wife.'

"His cheek flushed, but he controlled himself, and bade me listen to reason; but I only grew more violent. I threatened to expose him to the lady he was to marry; to tell her that I was his wife. Then he grew angry—he taunted me—he told me that I was guilty of a crime—that I had committed bigamy, and that I could be imprisoned—he dared me to do as I had threatened—he said bitter things, words that stung me to the very soul—words that he, of all men, should never have uttered to me. Then, when he had heaped upon me cruel, cruel epithets, till he could say no more, he threw down gold upon the table, and left the room. Never shall I forget his looks as he stood there; his dark eyes flashing, his cheeks flushed, and his tall figure drawn up to its full height. How my heart yearned for his love, and instead of that he offered me gold.

"I did not speak—I felt no anger—I was only heart-broken, and I looked at him with stony eyes and outward composure, though my very heart bled.

"I still sat there, till his footsteps died away in the distance. Then I rose—my mind was made up—I would not be a burden to him now that he no longer loved me. His cruel words rang in my ears, but even then I did not hate him. Hate him! I loved him with my whole soul—as I do still—as I always shall.

"I took my child by the hand and went out of his house—that happy, happy home. When the door closed, it was as if I were shut out of Paradise. I thought of Eve, when she left Eden behind her; but she was not alone, Adam was still hers, and she went forth hand-in-hand with him, with love and hope for companions, but I walked out of my Eden, hand-in-hand only with despair.

"I pictured to myself Harry's return to our home. I knew that several days would pass ere he would go there, and I imagined his horror on seeing it deserted, the money lying where he had left it—all unaltered, all remaining as he had last seen it—only his Annie missing.

"I knew then that he would repent the bitter taunts he had heaped upon the wife of his bosom, the mother of his dead boy.

"He did repent. I looked in the papers, and, among other pathetic appeals, I read words that I knew were penned by his hand, words of sorrow, of love, and of entreaty.

"They touched my heart. He implored me to return for little R.'s sake, and a voice in my heart urged me to comply; but as I had nearly resolved to return, I saw his marriage in the paper. The words scorched my brain.

"I thought of him amid the wedding festivities, with crowds of the gay about him, receiving their congratulations, with his bride on his arm, and the blush on her cheek, as he whispered words of endearment to her, while I, his wife, in the sight of God, was forgotten—an outcast.

"I was maddened—I was reckless. Oh, Heavens!" she murmured, burying her face in her hands, "I can say no more. From that time I was utterly lost. I never saw Harry again, and I sunk deeper and deeper, lower and lower, till here I am, a wreck of what was once Annie Murray—a vile, vile wretch, with but one spark of virtue remaining, my love for my innocent Rosa. For her sake I have endured this wretched life that I would long since, but for her, have flung away as worthless. Now I must die. I have endured what you can never know"; she shuddered as she spoke—"but the agony of the thought that I must leave my child amidst all that is vile, with no hope before her of aught save her mother's fate—that was worse than all.

"That poor creature who led you here, sinful wretch as she is, felt for me; she has been a mother, and she knew what was a mother's love. She has been very kind to me, and when I heard, as I chanced to do, that you were here, she promised to bring you to me."

A fit of coughing here interrupted Annie. Christine raised her quickly, she gasped for breath, she turned her eyes wistfully towards her sleeping child, who lay on the straw near her. Christine read her glance.

"Dear Annie," she said, "she shall be my own. I accept the sacred trust."

A gleam of joy sparkled in the mother's hollow eyes; there was a rattling in her throat.

"Oh, God!" she indistinctly articulated, and with this invocation her spirit passed to its Maker.

Christine laid her down softly on the pallet, and with streaming eyes, though no Romanist, poured forth a prayer for the repose of her poor friend's soul.

She went to the door and called for assistance; the woman who had guided her thither appeared, and with her aid the little that could be done for Annie was performed.

"Would to God that I slept with her," said the woman, in a hollow voice.

Christine's heart ached for her, and yet she involuntarily shrunk from her, but she reproached herself for the instinctive feeling of disgust. Did not our Lord speak compassionately to such as she? She thought of the touching story of the woman "who was a sinner,"[72] and with kind words and kind looks, she addressed the poor wretch before her. She consulted with her as to the funeral of her friend; she thanked her for her kindness to her during her sickness, and requested her to remain there with the mother and child, during her own necessary absence to make arrangements; then pressing her hand, she slipped into it a gold coin of considerable value, and withdrew.

The night had passed; the sun was rising as Christine left that miserable abode; her eyes were filled with tears as she went on, but she took a sad pleasure in seeing that all was done that remained for friendly hands to do.

No long funeral procession followed Annie Murray to her last resting-place; no parade of funeral pomp was there; but a group of sincere mourners stood by her grave, and as her lifeless body was entrusted to the ground, "earth to earth, ashes to ashes, dust to dust," the baptism of tears was not wanting to the consecration of that lowly mound. No mother, husband, brother or sister, stood by the grave of her, who in her springtime had been so lovely and beloved; only a little sobbing child, Christine, and the poor, guilty creature who had ministered to her, when lover and other friends had failed her, now bewailed her sad fate. Of all the troops of friends by whom she had once been surrounded, these three alone remained to pay the last tribute to her memory. A simple stone marked her resting-place, in a quiet nook in Greenwood; a plain slab, bearing as its only inscription, "ANNIE."[73]

Not many months after this interment, the death of the eminent merchant, Charles Howard, was announced, with a long notice of his life, and a long list of his many excellences; he had bequeathed large sums of money to the different missionary societies, and the remainder of his property to his dearly beloved wife, Josephine, to whom he had been united some three years. A procession of more than a mile in length followed him to his grave, and over his resting-place rose a stately marble column, bearing inscriptions testifying to his worth.

As Christine read all this in the journals, she could but contrast the fate of his wife with his own in this world; but now both had passed away from earth, both had entered that world "where many of the decisions of earthly tribunals are reversed." She could not follow the long-severed husband and wife there.

"Shall not the Judge of all the earth do right?" she asked herself, and dismissed the subject from her thoughts.

Now that she had a child to provide for, she decided that she must have a fixed and permanent home; she must devote herself as much as possible to Rosa; she had accepted her as a sacred trust, and she must not shrink from the discharge of her duties.

Ere long she was established in a small but neat house in New York, and it afforded her no small pleasure to reflect that the comforts which surrounded her were the fruits of her own industry.

Rosa, child-like, had recovered her spirits, and seemed perfectly happy in her new home. She often spoke of her mother, but she knew little of the loss she had sustained. Fortunately, grief cannot long subdue the elastic nature of a child, nor did Christine wish to make death a gloomy theme to her adopted daughter. She spoke of it to her as the entrance into a delightful world, and endeavored to rob it of its terrors.

Every day she grew more and more attached to Rosa, who had in fact one of the sweetest of dispositions; she had a most impressible nature, and was easily swayed by those she loved; always cheerful and sprightly, she was like the sunshine in the house; and her graceful, winning ways often brought her mother, as she had known her in her girlhood, to Christine's recollection. Annie had been ruined by her education, so thought Christine; and, as she saw the same traits of character in the child which had been at once the charm and the destruction of her mother, she resolved that Rosa should be so trained as to escape her mother's fate.

One other member made up Christine's family—Martha, the poor woman who had soothed Annie in her last sickness. She had not at first designed taking her into her household, but when she had urged her to leave her sinful courses and seek some respectable employment, Martha's only reply was a mournful shake of the head. "Who would employ such as me?" she said, at last. "I have tried it before now, but it was of no use, and I cannot starve."

"I will employ you," was Christine's answer. "I shall need some one who is worthy of trust in my house, to take charge of it in my frequent absences. Will you take the situation?"

With glad tears, Martha expressed her gratitude; and, great as was the confidence reposed in her, she never betrayed her trust. In fact, this very trustfulness in Christine had touched her even more than the offer of a home, and most zealously she devoted herself to the interests of her employer. As months passed on, Christine's family circle increased still more. She had often received letters from young girls, who related their trials in the way of earning their own support to her, and often asked her to advise them what to do. She exerted herself more than ever now to assist them. She trembled for their fate—innocent, unprotected, and confiding—if they came to the city in search of employment, without a home. She opened her house to them; she sought situations for them, and had the pleasure of seeing many of them engaged in lucrative employments; many, too, she placed in a position where they could learn some trade, and, while doing so, they had a home with her, and looked forward to the time when they should earn enough to repay her for the expenses incurred by her for their support; for she did not wish them to feel that they were the recipients of charity. She judged rightly that it would be far better for them to pay a small sum for their board whenever they should be able to do so.

In the evenings, she taught them what they most needed to know. They read aloud improving books, they had music, they danced, they sang, they talked freely of their plans, and to Christine they turned in all cases of difficulty. She enjoyed it all most heartily, entered into their feelings with interest and labored ever more earnestly to promote her great end; while she rejoiced in the well-being and improvement of her *protégées*, as one step towards the accomplishment of far greater designs. She had very little trouble in the regulation of her household. She was very systematic; and she arranged everything so that it went on with apparent ease. She was dignified and decided, as well as gentle; so that while all loved her, their affection was mingled with a respectful deference that made all submit readily to her requirements.

CHAPTER THIRTY-FOUR

Christine's Home

Seven years had rolled away. Ah! how much of human joy and sorrow is summed up in that brief sentence? What revolutions do the rolling years make in this world of change? What records of great deeds may moulder away in the ponderous tomes of the historian? and what lessons on the emptiness of most of the aims for which the men of the past have struggled, lived, and died does the written history of these years teach; lessons all in vain—for over and over again is the great drama of life acted—still do the multitudes press on, reaching for the apples of Sodom, which tempt them from afar with their beauty, only to crumble in pieces in their grasp, and as they turn away disappointed, thousands as eager take their places, each to learn only by his own bitter experience that all pursuit of mere earthly good can only result in vanity and vexation of spirit.

Oh, could the unwritten history of the heart, whose records lie buried in the graves of memory and experience, and which, like restless spirits, come forth from their sleep and wander through the soul, filling it with remorse and despair, be laid open, who could endure to read it?

Before the pitying eye of One alone is laid bare all these secrets of the heart, and in mercy He has shrouded it from our gaze. Seven years have passed, we say, and forgetting all that is past press forward eagerly to the future, and it is well.

Something in this channel ran Christine's thoughts, as she sat in her own private apartment, a small and neatly furnished room, where no luxuries or superfluities were to be seen. Books indeed surrounded her, but these she considered the necessaries of life.

It was a cheerful apartment, and had a very home-like appearance. On one side of the room stood Christine's writing-table, on which still laid a sheet of paper half-filled with her thoughts, and the pen stood in the inkstand as if only laid aside for a moment by her busy fingers.

Near a small centre-table, under a chandelier, sat a young girl, whose nimble fingers plied the needle, and who half-unconsciously hummed a tune. She was quite engrossed in her occupation, and not at all aware of the steady, and loving gaze of Christine, who, leaning back in a chair, by the side of a glowing coal-grate, watched every motion of her adopted daughter.

It was a pretty picture; that young girl in her quiet, feminine employment. Her slight figure, happy face, and graceful attitude, were very pleasing to Christine, and for a long time she sat silently looking at her.

Rosa had indeed grown very beautiful. Here was a singular style, and from its very novelty all the more striking; her eyes were large, deep, and intensely black, fringed by long, silken lashes, while her hair was a light brown, and her cheek so colorless that when at rest she looked like a beautiful statue. Yet this paleness was not the result of ill-health; her form was rounded and symmetrical, her step elastic, and her whole being overflowing with life and spirits, such as nothing but perfect health can give.

She was beautiful when sitting quietly as now; but when speaking, her dark, liquid eyes lighted with animation, the color coming and going as it did in her moments of excitement, in her cheek, her lips parted with frequent smiles displaying her pearly teeth, and the graceful and unconscious gestures which she made use of always in conversation, she was positively enchanting. So thought not only Christine, who rejoiced in the rare beauty of her darling, but all who saw her. Added to all this was an entire freedom from vanity, a loving heart, and a simple, confiding nature. She was devotedly attached to Christine, and influenced almost entirely by her. She had studied untiringly all that Christine had wished her to do; read books of her selection, and had received, without a question, all Christine's peculiar notions and sentiments. In her eyes, no one was so nearly perfect as Christine. She felt for her an enthusiastic affection that was almost veneration; a love entirely unmingled by fear, for though she was at times cold and stern to others, Rosa had never experienced aught but tenderness from her.

The years that had added so much to Rosa's loveliness had not detracted from Christine's personal appearance. Though never pretty in her youth, she was now a fine-looking, elegant, and dignified woman. She retained all her olden grace of manner, and still, as ever, all who were brought within the sphere of her influence acknowledged the singular fascination which she exerted over them.

Still she lectured, and for some time she had written books, which were as popular as her orations. Now no longer was her name the theme for ridicule and contempt. She was now as much praised as she had been before derided. Long since, the house which she had first taken had been too small for her increasing family, and she had moved to larger quarters, which in turn had proved too small, until she found herself at the head of what deserved the title of an Institution.

Alone, unaided, and by degrees, her system had become a gigantic one, and it required all her labors to meet the demands made upon her; her pecuniary means had all been devoted to this, and she had exerted herself to the utmost to add to the capital she found it necessary to invest. But her labors found a rich reward; she had accomplished a great work, and encomiums were showered upon her—more than this, she prized the practical ends she had gained; her protégées were universally respected, and in the search for employment, it was sufficient recommendation to any that she was one of Christine Elliot's girls.

She had the rare art of attaching them to her by a strong personal attachment, and they all loved the Home she knew how to make so pleasant. Each rejoiced in the ability to repay all that had been expended for her, as soon as circumstances enabled her to do so, and those who were preparing for active life looked forward eagerly to the time when they should do so likewise. There were among the number those engaged in every trade that was open to woman, and every year new avenues of employment were entered by them. Each on her entrance consulted with Christine as to the occupation she should take, and generally took her advice. There were students of law, theology, and medicine, and many, who had been enabled by her assistance to devote themselves to these studies, had met with no inconsiderable success.

Situated as she was in New York, ample facilities were afforded her protégées for improvement, and her hand was ever open to supply all in her power to the talented and energetic among them, who were cramped by poverty.

She had hit upon the true secret, to help those who wished to help themselves, and the good fruits of her system were every day more apparent. It became the fashion for those in want of employées to go to Christine, and thus enabled to obtain situations, she was freed from the labor at first imposed upon her, of seeking them amidst oft-repeated rebuffs.

Many were the poor and friendless girls who, by means of this Home and watchful friend, had been saved from dangers of which they little dreamed, but who, in after years, looked back in unfeigned gratitude to her as their preserver from worse than death. Many a marriage had been celebrated here in simple and unostentatious fashion, and Christine had no lack of love affairs confided to her. She endeavored to give those who were to become wives, true ideas of their duties, to render them helpmates, indeed, to their husbands; she often smiled at her match-making employment, for in all cases of estrangement her advice was asked, and she had succeeded in many cases in putting an end to lovers' quarrels. She was deeply interested in all the affairs of her children, as she fondly called them, and none of the details of life, however commonplace, were indifferent to her.

The domestic concerns of her household were equally distributed among her family; each had her task to perform, and thus what in the aggregate would have been no light thing, was made by distribution easy. Martha was housekeeper still, and felt herself second in importance to Christine alone. Yet successful as was her Home, Christine felt that this was but incidental; it was a duty that had fallen into her hands almost without her being conscious of it, and though she discharged it faithfully and willingly, still as ever was her great aim, the change of society as it existed, the acknowledgment of equal social, moral, and above all, political rights, which she deemed the corner-stone of the new edifice which she hoped to see rise from the old social system, and though she felt that, in her own day, this might fail of accomplishment, yet she looked forward to the time when it should indeed occur.

To this end all her hopes and ambition in Rosa centered; to her she would transmit this object as a sacred trust—for this she had educated her—she had bent all her energies to the one end of imbuing her child with the same grand ideas and aims that had filled her own soul, and she had the satisfaction of seeing this accomplished.

Rosa's mind was indeed a reflex of Christine's, but she had accepted all her teachings with the heart, and not the reason. She would as soon have doubted the precepts of the Bible as those of her pure and lofty teacher. Yet unconsciously, in her turn, Rosa exerted quite as powerful an influence on Christine; her straightforward simplicity and truthfulness, were qualities highly prized by her, and every year she sought her counsels more and more, and Rosa's sweetness and gentleness insensibly smoothed the rough points in Christine's character.

Rosa was very fond of all feminine employments; she was always surrounded by flowers, and liked even better than reading to work in the garden, make bouquets, sew, and even under Martha's superintendence, prepare dainty dishes for the table; then in sickness no step was so light as hers in the sickchamber, no touch so delicate, and no one so well knew just how much light to admit, or could arrange all so gently, moving cups and spoons without that jingle that strikes so painfully on the nerves of an invalid.

Every one loved Rosa, and she had a heart overflowing with love and kindness for all about her; no wonder that to Christine, who saw in her the priestess of the new temple, as well as the darling of the household, she was an idol.

Christine still sat looking at her child, sewing ever as busily, and at last interrupted her.

"Rosa, are you not tired of sewing?"

"No, dear auntie," replied the girl, for by this title she addressed Christine, "you know I could sew for hours together, I like it so much."

"It's a strange fancy," replied Christine. "For my part I have no taste for that steel implement, I like the pen better; the very feeling of it between one's fingers helps thought."

"So does the needle, auntie; there is nothing that helps me to think more than the drawing of the needle through the work."

"Well, lay it aside now, Rosa, I don't wish you to sew any more, it grows late."

Rosa at once complied, folded all carefully, laid aside all her implements in their places, and taking her little work-table set it away, then bringing a low seat to Christine's side, sat down there, and laid her head in her aunt's lap.

Christine stroked the golden, curling hair softly, and then began. "Rosa, dear, have you got the essay ready that I wished you to write?"

"Not quite, Aunt Christine," said the girl, blushingly. "What I did write didn't sound well, and I got puzzled about finishing it."

"Were you thinking of that when you were sewing?"

"No, ma'am," said Rosa, softly. "I know you will think me very childish, but I was thinking of the Christmas presents I should make this year, and of little Mollie O'Brien, when she gets her new dress on."

Christine smiled.

"Nothing pleases me more, my Rosa," she said, "than your kindness to the poor; nothing is more sad than to see a woman of intellect without heart, and, in order to do great good, she must combine both. How will your course prove," she added, musingly, "the untruth of the general opinion, that she who presses forward toward the accomplishment of our great aims, must trample under foot all the lighter, and so-called womanly duties."

Rosa blushed deeply. "Dear aunt," she said, "I can never realize all you hope of me, I fear."

Christine smiled gently. "We will not talk of that," she said. "I have no doubts; but let me tell you now of a great pleasure in store for us. I have just received a large sum of money from my publishers. That last book sold very well, and now I shall be enabled to do many things for our family that I have been obliged to leave undone for want of means. We will have a good library now, and a large one; I shall also be able to loan several of the girls sums, without the least inconvenience; I could have managed it before, but not without a good deal of trouble—now it is all arranged nicely."

"Oh, I am so glad," said Rosa, clapping her hands. "You and I will buy the books. I will see that the room leading out of the hall is in order. You will let me buy the carpet, and oversee it all, won't you, dear Aunt Christine?"

"Yes, you may do it all, if you like, only don't steal the time that belongs to your essay."

"Oh, my poor essay!" said Rosa, sighing deeply. "Dear auntie, it is very silly, so far—now that is the positive truth—but I will go to work and rewrite it. It does seem strange to me that the thoughts that come into my head should be so good, for I really think they are good till I get them on paper, and then they don't seem like the same ideas at all. It reminds me of the old fairy-books that told of changelings; some malicious elf or other, just steals my good idea and puts a weak piece of trash in its place."

"Never mind, Rosa, keep on, and your essay will come out right in time. It is 'practice that makes perfect,' you know. Now get your guitar and sing for me."

Rosa did as she was requested; she sang sweet, tender songs with great beauty of expression, and then would break out into some gleeful strain that would thrill her listener with wild delight, as if the music came fresh from the glad heart of the singer; then archly she would tune her instrument anew, and dash off in a comic song, which she would give with irresistible humor.

So passed the hours of that quiet evening, enjoyed all the more heartily by Christine that she labored so unceasingly through the day. After Rosa grew tired of singing, she talked in a low voice of her plans; no thought of hers was concealed from Christine, and with ever new delight she listened to the expressions, and looked into the depths of that fresh and pure young mind.

The love of that young girl, and the respectful affection of her large circle of protégées, had almost entirely supplied the want she had felt when estranged from her own immediate family. She was now completely weaned from them; she had felt a quiet gladness when she had heard of Bessie's marriage; but in the years that had passed since then, her old sisterly affection had been swallowed up in her increased cares; only one sentiment remained in full force: her bitter feelings towards those who long ago had treated her so unjustly; she dared not allow herself to think of this, but in the heart, the remembrance of it still rankled; but now in her happy home, sitting in her sanctum, while her darling was by her side, holding her hand fondly, and talking merrily in her sweet, clear voice, she had no thought for aught beside. Never did mother love a child more fondly, she was accustomed to say, after she had answered Rosa's inquiries as to her own mother's fate. Christine had told her all, for she considered truth a sacred virtue, and nothing could have induced her to equivocate to Rosa, painful as it was to tell her all. She had kissed away the tears that the daughter had shed, and comforted her with the assurance of her love, and again Rosa smiled as brightly as ever, for the tale was only to her like others which had brought tears to her eyes; she thought of her young mother as if she had existed only in story, for she had never known a mother's loss; the love she would have given her had been bestowed by her aunt Christine, and no mother could more scrupulously have performed all her duties than she had done.

At last Christine rose. "We must not be selfish, Rosa," she said. "Let us join the girls," and they entered the parlor.

Here were assembled a large number who had grown tired of the solitude of their own rooms, and had just entered; and others who had been together all the evening, sewing, chatting, reading, or engaged in games, as suited their humor. It was like a large family, where all were at liberty to do what they chose. Christine had a pleasant word for each as she entered, and passed round the room, and Rosa, in an instant, was surrounded by a bevy of girls.

She was in universal demand—she must sing for this one, play backgammon with another, show a new stitch to a third, and so on, but she laughingly shook her head, seated herself at the piano, and crying, "ladies, choose your partners!" dashed off inspiring tunes that set all the feet of the dancers in motion.

CHAPTER THIRTY-FIVE

Coals of Fire

"Good morning, auntie," said the clear voice of Rosa, as she stepped lightly into the study, where already Christine was at work, and, coming softly behind her, Rosa bent over and kissed her brow.

"Good morning, darling," replied Christine, looking up with a fond smile. "What have you been doing that you are so late? But I need not ask," she added, looking at the vase of flowers which Rosa held in her hand. "In the garden as usual."

"Yes," replied Rosa, "I have paid every blossom a visit, attended to all their wants, and brought a few into the house for company."

She herself was adorned with flowers; a small bouquet served her instead of a pin to fasten her collar, and a few gracefully drooping blossoms were entwined with the knot of curls, which, in her own simple, yet fantastic manner, she wore looped up behind, while here and there a golden curl escaped from its confinement to fall on her fair neck.

"Here is the very prettiest rose in the garden," said the girl; "I gathered it for you."

She placed a beautiful white rose, with a rich cream-colored tint in the centre, in a small vase on the desk before her aunt, adding:

"The rose is my flower. I love it above all others, for all roses are beautiful."

"They are, indeed," replied Christine, "and my own precious white Rose forms no exception. But now my little secretary must to business. Do you see that pile of unopened letters?" and she pointed to a large package lying on the centre-table.

In a few moments Rosa was seated by them, and rapidly glancing over their contents. Christine again wrote on in silence, and Rosa read and laid aside each letter in its turn; most of them were applications for admission into the Home, as Christine's Institution was generally called; many were words of commendation from those who sympathized in the enterprise, and still others were friendly letters from those who had left this for homes of their own. Letters too of invitation to lecture in different towns were there, and to all of these Rosa could reply without disturbing her aunt.

One letter only remained, a peculiar-looking one, directed in a plain but very old-fashioned handwriting. Rosa read it carefully, then suddenly exclaimed,

"Here is a letter from your old friend, Jotham Wiggins, dear auntie, and it brings sad news from your old home."

"Is any one dead?" exclaimed Christine, turning pale.

"Oh, no, Aunt Chris; but hear for yourself," and she proceeded to read the letter.

It contained a brief account of the embarrassment of James Cameron, and the mortgaging of the old homestead, by Farmer Elliot, to help his son-in-law; but matters had grown worse and worse. Mrs. Frothingham, to whom they had applied for assistance, had herself become involved in speculations, and could do nothing, and he concluded by saying that the mortgage was to be foreclosed on the very next week; he added that his misfortunes had broken down her father very much, and that he, and a good many more, thought that the loss of the old homestead would kill him. "You know," he concluded, "that it is hard to make old trees live when they are transplanted."

Christine listened without a word; no sadness lurked in her face—her eyes sparkled—she drew a long breath.

"I knew it," at last she said. "I felt sure that it would come. He made me homeless, and now, in his old age, he will have no shelter, and I, his discarded daughter, will offer him a home. He will be indebted to me—to me for the comforts he needs in his declining years."

Rosa looked at her in sad surprise; she saw in this offer of a home only gratified revenge. She had heard all that Christine had suffered in her youth, and had pitied her and loved her the more for it; but she had never dreamed of this; she had not thought to see so gross a taint in her idol.

Tears filled her eyes. "Poor old man," she said, burying her face in her hands, and giving way to her sorrow; sorrow even more for Christine than for her father.

"Rosa, why do you weep?" said Christine, "do you not see the hand of God in this retribution? 'Vengeance is mine, I will repay,' saith the Lord?"[74]

"Leave it to Him, dear aunt," sobbed Rosa.

"Have I not?" exclaimed Christine, "I have waited long and patiently and it has come at last—God has begun the work and has put it into my hands to finish. We are permitted to heap kindness like coals of fire on our enemy's head."

"Not in that spirit, dearest Christine," said Rosa, in the deepest sorrow. "Oh, it is most cruel to revenge oneself in that way—to gloat over the obligations our enemy is placed under. Think how dreadful would be the humiliation of that proud old man, obliged to receive even his bread as a favor from you. Could you endure to see the grey head of your father bowed before you?

Revenge is dreadful, but in that form it is horrible. It would be worse than Goneril or Regan—"[75]

"Stop, child!" exclaimed Christine, "you have spoken plainly. Do not go too far—I owe him no gratitude."

"He is your father," interrupted Rosa, softly.

"What would you have me do?" said Christine, standing before the girl; "would you have me look on in silence, and see him in poverty, perhaps in actual want, without offering him a home, from such sentimental scruples as you advance?"

"No, dearest aunt," whispered Rosa, gently; "but—" she hesitated.

"But what?" interrupted Christine.

With downcast eyes and varying color, Rosa spoke, "If that money that you have, could only pay the mortgage, then the dear old place need not be sold; and if it seemed to come from Mrs. Frothingham, he would receive it, and then you would have the satisfaction of having really done your father good, while he would not know that he was indebted to you.

"Oh, dearest aunt, that would be heaping coals of fire on his head, as our Lord meant, not with bitterness to scorch the poor, erring one."[76]

Christine was silent for a moment, and Rosa dared not lift her eyes to her face. She feared that she had deeply offended her, and almost like a culprit she sat with her head bowed down in an attitude of humility. It was but for a moment, for Christine pressed her to her heart, and kissed her again and again.

"You are my better angel," she said, softly, while hot tears fell on the fair young head hidden in her bosom. "God bless you for your true, brave words. You are right, and it shall be done as you have said, my Rosa, my blessed child. You shall write the letter immediately."

"No, dear Aunt Christine, let me sit by your side while you write," whispered Rosa, slipping from her embrace; and placing a fresh sheet of paper on the desk, she led Christine gently to it, dipped the pen in the ink and sank into a low seat by her side.

The letter was speedily written, a brief but kind epistle, as if all remembrance of the past had entirely faded from the memory of the writer, except in the delicacy which led to this indirect way of serving her father. It was a noble letter; so thought Rosa as she read it, and her glad eyes rested on Christine's face with a look of love and pride.

"Dearest, best of women," she breathed.

A look of pain passed over Christine's features; "Do not say so," she exclaimed, with a sigh; "I have sinned deeply; in contrast with the purity of your soul, my darling, I have seen clearly the blackness of my own. May God forgive me for the malice and revenge I have nursed in my breast so many weary years!"

Rosa pressed her hand over her aunt's mouth; she kissed her again and again; she would not hear her self-reproaches. In her eyes she was again all that was noble and good, and with instinctive delicacy and tact, she led Christine's thoughts skillfully away from herself to other subjects.

The letter was dispatched, containing a check sufficient, as Christine hoped, to pay the mortgage, and with a lighter heart, though this had been no small sacrifice, she consulted with Rosa on the ways and means of doing what needed to be done with the little sum remaining to them. The library was, of course, given up, but the loans must not be withheld from the girls to whom they had been promised.

"You may write and accept the invitations to lecture before those Lyceums," said Christine, "that will help me out. I had resolved not to go there, but now it will be necessary."

"I wish I could earn something," said Rosa, with a sigh; "I am the only useless idle one in the house."

"Not so," replied Christine, "all in good time your turn will come; there must be first a seed-time before a harvest. You are preparing now for the great work by and by. Before a great many years I shall be obliged to leave the stage; you will take my place. I have in your youth succored you, in my old age you will take care of me.

"You have been, as you are now and ever will be, a blessing to me, light of my eyes, delight of my heart!"

It was unusual for Christine to display so much feeling as she now did, and it gladdened Rosa's heart; now she felt that she had not offended her by her presumption, as she modestly termed her speaking to her aunt as she had done.

"All is right," she thought, joyfully, as she bent herself with new energy to the work of finishing her dreaded task, the essay. It was a pretty, childlike, and graceful effusion, and like all that Rosa did, spoke more for her heart than her head.

Christine was a little disappointed on reading it, but she would not confess it to herself. She praised all that was worthy of it, and set her child down to books of logic that she might check the exuberance of her fancy and develop her reasoning powers.

Rosa obediently read page after page, but it made little impression on her mind; even when reading of syllogisms, she was half-unconsciously dreaming bright visions in the future, or recalling fragments of poetry that floated through her mind, till, conscience-smitten at the neglect of her tasks, she would apply herself with new zeal for a short time, only to be drawn off again by her vain and wandering thoughts.

Nothing could have exceeded Mrs. Frothingham's surprise on the receipt of Christine's letter; she could hardly believe her own eyes; she read it again and again—all was a reality, and this generosity really touched Julia. She was very willing to effect a reconciliation with her niece since she had become the theme of universal admiration; she was proud of her, now that the tide of public opinion set in her favor, and she gladly availed herself of this opportunity to heal the breach between them.

She wrote a very polite note in reply, expressing, with the skill of which she was mistress, her admiration of her niece's act, without any approach to fulsome flattery, and begged to be allowed to visit her Home, in which she, in common with the rest of the world, felt a deep interest; she would not wait for an invitation, she said, unless she received an intimation that her visit would be unwelcome, but would come after carrying Christine's generous gift to her father.

Christine only smiled on reading this daintily perfumed epistle. It was so like Julia, to be changed about by the wind of popular favor; yet she could not help feeling a little elated at her triumph; she asked no more than this recognition of the excellence of her undertaking by one who had so bitterly opposed her in the beginning of her course; she felt also glad of the opportunity which this visit would afford her, of hearing all the details of home affairs.

Julia came at last, the same graceful, elegant, and beautiful being that she had been when first she had seen her niece. The arts of the toilette repaired all the ravages of years, and Rosa, fascinated by her wonderful powers of pleasing which she exerted to the utmost, could hardly believe that under that lovely exterior could lurk such unscrupulousness in the attainment of her ends, as she had proved by her past history.

She made no professions of affection for Christine, but treated her with scrupulous attention and respect.

She told her of the old homestead, of her mother's feeble health, and of her father's bowed form. She related the troubles he had experienced, and told of the relief it had been to him to know that the old farm would not pass into strange hands. The sundering of all old ties, Julia felt, would have been more than he could have borne, and though she did not dare to offend his pride by telling him to whom he owed the salvation of the dear old place, until some days after all was arranged, she had done so before leaving, and while the mother wept aloud and sobbed, "Oh John, I knew she had a good heart," he had turned away himself to hide his emotion. It had been bitter to him to accept this at the hands of her he had so harshly disowned, but the way in which she had done it, designing to keep it secret, had melted him. He sent by Julia, a message that he would be glad to see her at home, and that he accepted her loan with thanks, and would repay it as soon as possible.

At this recital, Christine could not hide her own emotion; her heart throbbed with the purest delight; her father had appreciated her motives, and accepted her gift; he would receive her too. She knew what a struggle it must have cost his proud heart to send her such messages, and again and again she invoked blessings upon the head of her brave young counsellor, who had banished her thoughts of revenge, and led her to the sacrifice which, in all kindness and forgiveness, she had made.

She resolved that she would go home. She would show her father that she did, indeed, cherish no bitterness against him, and on Julia's departure, she and Rosa went together to the beautiful village of Amity.

With feelings too deep for utterance did Christine pass over the well-known spots so familiar to her childhood, recalling, as did each haunt, emotions of joy and sorrow. Rosa was filled with delight at the ever-varying, ever-lovely character of the scenery, but she did not disturb Christine's reveries; she only gazed with quiet pleasure on all about her. But when the old farm-house was reached, and she looked on the family circle gathered to welcome the long-banished child; when, with streaming eyes, Christine fell on her knees before her father and mother, and implored their forgiveness for all that had been unfilial and undutiful in her conduct towards them, Rosa could not restrain her tears. It was a touching interview, and Christine's humility entirely overthrew the last vestiges of pride in her father's heart. He declared that he was proud of her, blamed himself most severely for his harshness, and was never happier than when listening to her account of her Home and its inmates. He said nothing of her other aims; he did not agree with her, but he respected her enthusiasm, and avoided, as did she, all topics of disagreement.

Bessie and James were living on the old place; Bessie a little careworn, but still unchanged in her cheerful, loving nature, and James, a sturdy farmer, ready to work hard to draw from the earth the wherewithal to repay the money he had been the means of losing.

Rosa, here as elsewhere, won all hearts; the two children of Bessie were never weary of hearing her stories, or joining in her merry romps and rambles over the old farm, and she, city bred as she was, enjoyed it to the full as heartily as they.

Grandma Elliot declared that she was "the prettiest little creetur that ever was," and the old farmer said that she was just what Bessie had been at her age, and having said this, he had paid her the highest compliment in his power.

Christine looked on at her evident enjoyment with delight equal to her own; she understood how the beauties of nature could attract and charm her; her rambles in the woods, her search after flowers, her restless fluttering from one beautiful spot to another, were all pleasures that she, too, in her youth had enjoyed, and she sympathized with her perfectly; but when she saw her engaged in the domestic duties of the farm-house, into which she entered with equally as great a relish, with arms bare, making some wonderful pie or pudding, or in the barnyard, milking, which she seemed, like everything else, to learn as if by instinct, she could not understand her enthusiasm.

Nevertheless, whatever Rosa did had a grace and a charm of its own that was perfect in Christine's eyes; whatever she liked to do, she would not check her in, and so Rosa worked, frolicked, or scampered over the country on horseback, at her pleasure, during the three weeks that they spent there. She had done even more than Christine to make firm the reconciliation between the father and daughter; her glad, cheerful face, her merry words and quiet attentions, had put the proud old man at his ease, and her influence, gentle and unobtrusive as it was, had softened him, whenever a touch of the old hardness had risen within him.

When she and Christine departed, the influence of her presence still lingered. Her ways, her words, and her goodness and beauty, were the frequent themes of conversation, and long that pleasant visit lived in the memories of all.

With new ardor Christine entered upon the duties and cares which she had laid aside for this short season, and again, though with no great relish for them, did Rosa bend over her heavy books, her golden curls sweeping over the pages as she read, while pictures of the country, its beautiful lakes, fields, and hills, banished all other visions from her mind.

CHAPTER THIRTY-SIX

Dr. Russell

The room was darkened, the bell was muffled, and doors were opened and shut gently, for Christine was lying very ill at her residence. For weeks Rosa had watched over her untiringly, noting every change in her symptoms, anticipating her every want, with all a daughter's devotion; she herself had grown haggard and pale from her constant attendance on the invalid, for though there had been no lack of offers from various members of the family to share her labors, and many had insisted on relieving her watch, yet she could not tear herself from that bedside, except for the little time that was absolutely necessary to enable her to take that rest which was indispensable to her own health, and ability to retain her place as nurse.

Christine had been very ill; she still was so, though she was now slowly recovering, but she was no longer delirious, no longer suffering from the extreme pain which had racked her system; even in her delirium, Rosa had been the only one able to soothe her; when her soft hand rested on the brow of the sufferer, she had been always more quiet—it was as if there were healing in her touch; and when she was not in the room, Christine had been more restless and uneasy, but now that she had recovered her consciousness, she would not allow Rosa to confine herself so closely. She insisted upon her going out into the open air, and told her, smilingly, that when she returned from her walks, she brought pure air and the fragrance of flowers with her.

Indeed, that sick-room was not like too many, a gloomy place; everything there was scrupulously tidy; the counterpane, and the cloth that covered the little table near the bed, were spotlessly white, and instead of a troop of cups, spoons, and vials, so disagreeably suggestive, a small vase of flowers stood upon it; books were there, too, from which Rosa read to Christine, and the guitar had of late taken its place in a corner.

Now that Christine could sit up for a half hour daily, she held a sort of levee of the girls, who came in if only to press her hand, and, with glad smiles, to rejoice at her recovery; by degrees, as she grew stronger, and could bear the excitement without injury, their calls became longer, and their visits to that room quite enlivened it. Christine, yet pale, but smiling her quiet, pleasant smile, and speaking in the olden, gentle voice, received new life from the buoyant spirits, merry chat, and gay laughter of her family, who, in their turn, found this room a very pleasant place. To none did it seem pleasanter than to young Dr. Russell, who, at the request of a cousin of his, a female physician, who had been in attendance upon Christine, had, when her disease was at the worst, been called to a consultation; he had approved of the course pursued by his cousin, and had made some suggestions which had proved highly beneficial, and though he had given up the case again into her hands, he called very often to see the patient, and, as she grew better, his visits, instead of becoming less and less frequent, increased greatly in number and in length. He was a young and highly intelligent man, agreeable and companionable, and his daily call very pleasantly interrupted the monotony of Christine's quiet life; for, to one who had so long been engaged every moment in some employment, this listless sitting with folded hands in her chair, was very wearisome, and she had not, as yet, strength to do anything else.

She began to wait with no inconsiderable impatience for the coming of Dr. Russell, with his frank, pleasant smile, and that cordial grasp of her hand, and cheery voice that always struck so pleasantly on the ear. He was one of those genial natures, so blessed with a superabundance of life and health that they seem to impart a share of it, unconsciously, to others; nor did Christine alone watch for his coming.

Rosa knew his ring, his footstep, and listened for both as impatiently as did her aunt, though she never expressed, as did Christine, her wonder at his delay if the usual hour slipped by without his appearance. When he did come her eyes sparkled, her color went and came, and, without saying much, she seated herself near Christine in her low seat, and bent over her sewing, listening with interest to the conversations between the Doctor and her aunt, stealing an occasional glance at the broad, white brow, and searching blue eyes of the young man, who sat in an attitude of careless grace, talking, and smiling those sweet smiles that gave at once so arch and so honest an expression to his face; he was not handsome; his figure, though muscular and well-developed, was rather below than above the medium height; his hair, though by courtesy called auburn, verged on the red, and his features were large and irregular, but there was that about him that attracted one unconsciously; he was gentlemanly in his manner, yet that was not the charm that drew one almost irresistibly towards him—it was the genial expression of the whole man—a consciousness that one felt that he was noble, kind, honest, and thoroughly good; yet he was not one of the gentle spirits; he was firm and decided; every motion declared it; his quick, emphatic manner of speaking, his firmly compressed lip, his flashing eye, all betrayed the decision of his character.

All this Rosa felt, rather than knew, from any observation of his features, for rarely did she steal a glance from under her heavily fringed eyelashes, without encountering his half-mirthful, half-serious blue eyes resting upon her, and at once she would apply herself to her work, a vivid blush would flit over her transparent cheek, and her black eyes would again fall upon the long seam she was sewing.

She looked very pretty in her brown dress, her white and rounded arm showing itself occasionally in her open sleeve, as she moved it in her work; her little foot, in its tiny slipper, peeping out from the folds of her dress, and her golden curls, half-hiding, half-revealing the delicately chiselled features, and the transparent purity of her complexion, with the occasional smiles that lurked around her rosy mouth, as she listened to the conversation between Christine and the Doctor.

It was evident that Dr. Russell thought her a very charming study, for his eyes followed her every motion; he read in her varying expression the thoughts that passed in her mind, and admired the enthusiasm that sparkled in her eye, and flushed her cheek, when the theme was of a high and noble character, and the blushing modesty which succeeded to the glow of enthusiasm as she recovered herself, and returned to the present.

Her untiring devotion to her aunt, her gentleness, her unobtrusive, but never-failing attention to the wants of the invalid, had first attracted his notice; her beauty pleased his eye, but her loveliness of character touched his heart, and, even before he would acknowledge it to himself, her face and figure would intrude itself into his thoughts, even when immersed in studies of dry and long-named bones. He had at first attempted to deceive himself into the belief that it was only the pleasure of an intellectual feast, such as the society of Christine afforded him, that led to his frequent visits; but the restlessness he had felt, and the constant watching of the door, when Rosa had not been present, as had occasionally happened, quickly proved to him that the sight of that fresh, young face had much more to do with his enjoyment of the call than he had imagined, and once certain that he loved Rosa, he began anxiously to ask himself what were his chances of being loved in return.

He began to linger longer in the hall when he went out, accompanied as he always was by Rosa, and took a long time to tell her of the little things that Christine might require; by degrees he introduced other topics, and Rosa found herself cherishing in her memory the words, and glances that said more than words, in those brief *tête-à-têtes.*

On one occasion he had asked her for a rose, in a half-sportive, half-serious way, and when she gave it to him, with averted face, and flitting blush, he could have clasped her in his arms; he had pressed her hand at parting, and that pressure Rosa felt long after her hand had fallen from his strong clasp, and in a kind of intoxication, a glow of happiness, of which she hardly knew the cause, she had seen him place the bud in his buttonhole, and listened to his footsteps as he hastened away.

Christine saw nothing of this. Rosa had already had many admirers, but she had acquiesced in her aunt's dismissal of them with perfect indifference, and the idea of her really falling in love never crossed Christine's mind.

"What a pity it is," she said, as Rosa entered the room, with light steps and dancing eyes; "that so liberal a man as Dr. Russell is in many respects, should be so opposed to our doctrines. We must convert him, my Rosa."

"Is he so much opposed to them?" asked Rosa, in a faltering voice.

"Yes, he is indeed," replied Christine, "I drew him out the other day, and he has no patience with the leaders of the movement; he only tolerates me because of this Home of ours. The poor man doesn't see that this, which he so much likes, is only the operation of that theory which is so distasteful to him."

"I am sorry," said Rosa, sighing deeply.

"And so am I," returned Christine, "but then so much the greater will be our triumph if we add him to the list of believers, and he is too much of a man, too candid and reasonable, not to listen to our arguments; in fact I think he is already interested more than he would like to confess in our views. What else would bring him here so often, and lead him to converse so long with me? There is not a doubt of it; he is becoming interested in the subject, and the direct opposition of such a man, is a more hopeful sign than indifference. Depend upon it, there is some reason, aside from my health, that brings him here so often.

"Don't you think so, Rosa?"

Rosa blushed. "I hope so," she said, then suddenly checking herself, she blushed still more deeply, and added, "I mean I don't know."

Christine laughed.

"You are answering at random, child," she said, "but I can hardly expect you to feel so deep an interest in his conversion as I do; you do not know him yet as I do, but I tell you, he is a man of more than ordinary abilities, and will exert a great influence wherever he goes. He must; the very elements that compose his character must make their mark on society and so much the more important is it that he should be on the right side."

"Yes," assented Rosa, with another sigh; for she felt as if a barrier had suddenly risen between herself and her new friend. With these views on the subject he could not feel any interest in one who had been devoted to what he so much disliked, all her life, and whose future was to be still one constant struggle for the establishment of these views.

She was unusually silent, and Christine, who observed it, decided that she was suffering now from the effects of her overexertion during her own sickness. She resolved to ask the Doctor on his next visit if such was not the case. At his next call she did so, and Rosa was directed to come and let the Doctor see her, though she declared that she was quite well. As she stood there, her color coming and going, and the hand which Dr. Russell held trembling in his grasp, while he counted her pulse, which was beating with fearful rapidity, he thought he had never seen her look so beautiful.

"She needs exercise," he said, "in the open air; riding would be very beneficial; it would do you good too, my dear madam. Will you not permit me to bring a carriage and have the pleasure of taking you and your niece out for a short drive occasionally?"

Christine willingly assented, and that very afternoon they drove out together.

What a pleasant drive it was; out on Long Island, off the tiresome noisy pavements, through the changing autumn woods, and anon past quiet farm-houses and harvest-fields, inhaling the pure, fresh air; it was like being in the country again, and Rosa's dark eyes spoke her delight. She grew merry, joined in the conversation, and her silvery laugh rang out often. Christine listened with delight equal to Rosa's own, and Dr. Russell was quite as happy as the rest of the party.

Nor was this the only drive; many more followed it, and now the Doctor came still oftener to the house; he brought books, which he sometimes read aloud, for he was a very fine reader, and which he often left for Rosa to read; then she must tell him what she thought of them, and so he would sit a whole evening by her side, drawing out her sentiments, looking at the passages which she had marked as he had requested her to do, those that she liked best, or listening to her sweet songs. She had learned many of his favorites, and she was never weary of listening to what he had to say of music or on any other theme.

Every time that Eugene Russell saw Rosa he discovered some new charm, and she, in turn, was never so happy as in his company. Unconsciously he became her oracle. Did she meet with any passage in her reading which she did not clearly understand, it was to him she went for explanation; she asked his advice on all subjects, from the care of her birds, or the nourishing of a delicate plant, to higher matters, and listened with the greatest confidence to his opinions on either subjects. She unconsciously governed herself by the expressions which she had heard from him. "Dr. Russell likes this or that, or dislikes it," was enough to influence her in her conduct. It was perfectly natural for Rosa to be guided by those she loved, and as before she had been moulded by Christine, so now she was influenced by Dr. Russell. As she had studied all that Christine had wished, so now she applied herself to drawing and German, under Eugene's direction, and as these studies happened to be suited to her tastes, she made more rapid improvement than in her former devotion to logic and rhetoric.

Dr. Russell was studiously polite to Christine; he respected her as did every one who knew her, and listened with strict attention to her views. She exerted herself to the utmost to bring him over to her doctrines; she did not weary him with long arguments, but took occasion incidentally to introduce the subject, and at times flattered herself that she was in a fair way to accomplish her object.

She was well pleased with the friendship existing between him and Rosa. "He is a valuable friend," she often thought, "and the action of his mind on hers will bring out the strongest part of her mental powers."

She had frequently spoken to him of her plans for Rosa, and while she had done full justice to the qualities of her heart, she had told him of the glorious destiny which she foresaw in the future for her child. She had dwelt with enthusiasm on the victories which Rosa would attain; the triumph over already mouldering prejudices; the planting of the standard of equal human rights on the temple of true and perfect liberty. On one such occasion Eugene had listened quietly; at her close, he only glanced at Rosa, who, sitting at a table at a little distance, was mending a pair of gloves for him; "I fear," he said, "that she will never accomplish what you design for her. Long and intimately as you have known her, I think you have mistaken her character; she is a pretty, simple-hearted girl, who is no more like you than the gentle zephyr is like the strong wind that bends all before it. You were made for a leader—she was made to be led."

"Dr. Russell," interrupted Christine, "you are mistaken. Rosa is to the full as enthusiastic as I, on the subject of human rights. Have you not seen her whole face lighted with ardor when I have spoken of life and its aims? I assure you that her whole soul is filled with the desire to obtain the high prize set before her."

"That may all be very true," answered Dr. Russell, "but it only proves my former assertion. She is only echoing your sentiments; you have led her into this way, and she follows your footsteps. She loves you most sincerely, and whatever you say she accepts as truth."

Christine shook her head.

"You do not understand her," she said. "Men never can understand such characters as hers. You always associate weakness with gentleness. You cannot understand how all the sweet womanly virtues, and feminine graces can so entwine about a fixed purpose that it is hidden from sight—yet it is there; the basis on which all rests, and which underlies the whole character. So it is with Rosa. I have not led her arbitrarily into a field, and bid her work there; I have only taken her by the hand and placed her upon a summit, from which she could see all that was to be done, and with full purpose she has resolved to enter the vineyard, and to work while God gives her strength to do so."

Her eyes flashed as she spoke.

"Oh, Dr. Russell," she said, "all my hopes are centered in that young girl; not only do I love her for all her sweetness of disposition, her thousand home virtues that one must live with her to discover, but for her enthusiasm, her self-devotion to a cause in which she has nothing selfish to gain, and perhaps much to lose; for this I feel a pitying tenderness towards her, and as I look on that fair young head, with its wealth of sunny curls, I grow sick at heart sometimes, fearing that the martyr's crown may encircle it. But no, no; it is the laurel wreath that she shall wear. The worst of the conflict is over—she shall enter into its gains."

Her eyes rested on Rosa, as she spoke, with a glance of the purest affection, not unmingled with pride, as she saw her in imagination crowned with the laurel wreath, and heard in the distance, the acclamations that would swell at her triumphant coronation as the benefactress of her sex.

Nothing could have been greater than the contrast between the two women at that moment. Christine with kindling eye and lofty expression, looking like some inspired prophetess wrapt in visions of the future, and Rosa, quiet, placid, and calm, sitting at her work with downcast eyes and unruffled face, as if wholly absorbed in her trivial employment.

With a feeling half of triumph, half of pity for Christine, Eugene looked on Rosa.

"Yes," he said, with a comic smile, "She looks like a second Joan of Arc—a fit leader for an army, ready to do or die."

"Pshaw!" replied Christine, impatiently, "she might not, I admit, choose to don the armor like that heroine. She might perhaps shrink from leading an army, but she has that within her that might make her a second Godiva,[77] ready to do and suffer all for the good of those about her; she is naturally retiring, and extremely sensitive, but she is aware that these are faults, and tries to overcome them; in truth they are more faults of her physical than of her mental organization. She has shrunk from public speaking, and I have not wished her to commence her public life too early, but now she is about to make her début; she is to deliver an address next week, and I doubt not, will be eminently successful."

Dr. Russell bit his lip; at this moment Rosa approached, saying, "Your gloves are all in order now," and at the same time she extended them to him; he took them coldly, thanked her almost without glancing at her, for he felt really angry. Yet what right had he to feel so? He had known all the time that Rosa was destined for a lecturer; why should he feel surprised or offended that she was to begin her course?

Rosa felt his coldness, though she did not know its cause; she turned pale, and without a word took a seat near Christine.

"I have just been telling the Doctor," said her aunt, "that you are going to lecture next week."

Rosa was silent, and Christine continued, "It would give us both great pleasure to see you there. Will you go?"

"No!" exclaimed Eugene, shortly, and in a voice of suppressed passion.

Tears rushed to Rosa's eyes; she drew back in the shadow of her aunt's chair, and by a strong effort subdued her emotion.

Christine only broke into a merry peal of laughter.

"Then you won't lend your countenance to any such heinous proceeding," she said; "you will have neither part nor lot in the matter. But you will think better of it, my dear Doctor; I'll venture to say that we shall see you in the front seat that very evening, for curiosity is not exclusively a feminine trait, though it has been generally conceded that woman has the lion's share of it; besides, you will want to see how Rosa succeeds."

"It would be no gratification to me, to see Miss Rosa standing before a mob of people, even if cheered and applauded by them," returned Eugene, coldly.

Christine looked hurt.

"I had given you credit for more friendship than such a remark would seem to indicate," she said. "I had supposed that you would have felt some interest in Rosa's success, in the career for which she has been destined, and which she is about to enter, even if you did not agree fully with her in the sentiments which she is to spend her life in establishing. I had thought, too, that of late your views on that subject had undergone considerable modification—that you were beginning to see that there was some truth in our theory, that we were not wholly in error."

"I am very sorry," returned Dr. Russell, "if I have misled you with regard to my sentiments; if I have done so, it has been entirely unintentional. You have treated me very kindly; I have enjoyed my visits here very much, but if I have been admitted under the false supposition that I was a convert to your doctrine, or at all likely to be, it is due to myself as well as to you to acknowledge that such is not nor will be the case, and after such an open and candid avowal, which I would have made sooner, had I supposed that you misunderstood me, should my calls hereafter prove unwelcome, I will no longer repeat them."

He rose, bowed gracefully to Christine, and was about to retire; she waved her hand toward a chair.

"Take your seat again, my dear Hotspur," she said.[78] "What under the sun has led you on to such a rhodomontade, I haven't the slightest idea, nor am I aware that any remark of mine could have been construed into the notion that your visits were agreeable only because I hoped to make a convert of you.[79] I am sure that you do not need the assurance that neither Rosa nor I could be so narrow-minded or illiberal, as to wish for no friends who do not agree with us in all points.

"Just be calm now. Own that you misunderstood me—give me your hand, and let us be good friends again."

Eugene had in fact grown cooler, and saw that in his anger at the announcement of Rosa's forthcoming lecture, he had really allowed his passion to get the better of his judgment.

What earthly reason had he for feeling as he did, at the bare idea of her beginning the life-task, for which, as Christine said, she had been educated. Unconsciously he had made far different plans for her, and now that they were to be thwarted, he could not at once wish her success in a cause which he felt would ruin all his hopes of future happiness. But he was only making himself ridiculous, he felt, by displaying his disappointment and chagrin, and therefore he took the seat which Christine offered, and endeavored to control himself.

"Let us understand each other fully, now," he said. "Let me tell you just what are my views on the subject."

"Never mind it," said Christine. "Say no more. Let us agree to disagree."

"No, Christine, it is better that you know just what my opinions are. I do not wish to sail under false colors. I want to be a fair and open enemy."

Christine laughed.

"Well, then, open your batteries, and pour in a broadside if you will. We never run from a fair challenge."

"Nor is this a challenge," replied Eugene. "It is rather a declaration of my sentiments."[80]

"Very well, I am ready for that; it is my motto, as well as our country's, 'We offer peace, ready for war.' But now for the declaration."

Rosa sat with folded hands in a bay-window, whither she had withdrawn, and as she sat half-hidden by the rose-colored curtains, she listened with breathless interest to what Eugene had said, and waited to hear what more he had to say.

"I declare, then," said Eugene, "that I do agree with you in your ideas about the better compensation of poor laboring women; I believe that they should have more avenues of employment open to them, as is gradually taking place now. I believe there are laws which are unjust, and I hope and believe that they will be altered so that woman may be secured in many rights which are such in reality, that they may not be rendered liable to have their earnings taken from them by drunken and miserable husbands, and a few other and kindred rights that are not yet given them.

"I admire the idea of your Home; and its practical workings are no less admirable. I honor you for your devotion to it. Further, I like the idea of female physicians; I think they are needed, and whenever I see a woman who is studying, I will assist her as far as is in my power, and will willingly testify to her skill and intelligence if I can honestly do so; so far I agree with you. But I have an utter abhorrence to a woman's stepping out of her sphere. I think that the wish to vote, the claim to universal suffrage, is based on sophistical arguments, and if granted would destroy all the most beautiful part of woman's nature. I have a horror of seeing women flushed with political frenzy, of seeing them engaged in a scramble for office, electioneering, making stump-speeches, and all that sort of thing. Faugh! It is disgusting. No delicate woman could wish to enter on all this did she know what she asked."

"My dear Doctor," interrupted Christine, "all that last part of your speech is mere sentimental nonsense. If politics are what you describe them to be, then is there all the more need of the pure and delicate influence of woman, to raise them up to something like their true level."

"In truth, so there is," replied Dr. Russell, "but not as you propose doing it. She can do nothing by stepping down into the mire but sully her white garments, but let her be educated, and be elevated so that her influence may be felt in the next generation. Let her remain in her true sphere, home, and do you say that is a narrow one? What can she ask more than to mould the character, to stamp the destiny of a whole age?

"Oh, Christine, who can tell the influence of a noble mother? Silent but powerful, constant, though imperceptible it goes on, till finally the results, great and glorious, of the labors of the pure and true woman, are made manifest. The greatest men that the earth has ever known, have had noble mothers, to whom they are indebted, not only for life, but for all the higher and purer parts of their nature. The women of Sparta are as renowned in history as her sons, and in our own time what do we not owe to the mother of Washington? What true woman would not rather have done her work, quiet and unostentatious as it was, than to have enjoyed the glory of an Elizabeth; the life of one was simple and retired; that of the other brilliant, indeed, but one died, and her influence was, and is, felt by a great nation, even to this day; the other died also, and all her glory died with her, her sceptre passed into the weak hands of the imbecile son of a weak mother, and the march of progress was at least arrested. The aims of one were selfish, of the other unselfish. One was the true mother, the other, the great monarch;—as women, as patriots, who would hesitate as to which was the greater?"

He paused, and Christine said, softly, "This, too, is one of our aims, to make woman what she should be, to rouse her to a sense of her high destiny; all this we would do, and not leave the other undone. For this high calling have I spent my time, my talents, thus far, and, God helping me, so will I do till I die, and with the same spirit has my Rosa entered upon a like duty, not expecting to find her path all flowers, but undaunted by the thorns on which she must tread, she has resolved to press forward. God bless her for her self-sacrifice. Will you not, with me, bid her God speed on her way?"

Dr. Russell's eyes flashed. "No," he said. "Not so do I look upon it, and seeing it as I do, feeling that I would sooner see a wife or sister of mine laid in her coffin, with her hands folded on her breast, than entering on such a career, I could not utter words of encouragement to one in whom I feel so deep an interest."

Rosa pressed her hands tightly over her heart, and grew even paler, but said nothing. Christine, too, was silent, and Dr. Russell continued:

"Do not construe my words into disrespect to you, Christine. You have proved yourself a true woman; misguided as I may think you in some respects, I honor your sincerity, your loftiness of purpose, and the work that you have done will live after you. Your name will be handed down to posterity, not by your struggles for political rights for your sex, but by your successful efforts to save the poor and homeless, to open doors for their livelihood, and to make them true women like yourself. I respect and admire you, not as a talented Woman's Rights lecturer, but in spite of it; and now," he said, as Christine still remained silent, taking her hand, and raising it to his lips, "after this candid expression of my views, can we still remain friends?"

"And why not?" asked she, cheerfully. "Perhaps some day we may be nearer alike than now in our views. I respect honesty of conviction, and freedom of opinion in others as I claim both for myself."

"Good-night then, Christine," he said, rising. I thank you for your continued friendship. Good-night, Miss Rosa," he continued, approaching her, and taking her hand, but letting it fall immediately, without that warm pressure with which he usually held it. She raised her eyes to his face, it was cold and stern, and with a heavy heart she saw him turn away.

Christine was unusually silent after Dr. Russell's departure, and Rosa was secretly rejoiced at her taciturnity, for she felt in no mood for conversation. As they parted for the night, Christine folded her in her arms, and pressed her to her heart in the fondest manner.

"God bless you, my sweetest flower, my precious darling," she said, as she released her at last, and retired.

That night Rosa's pillow was wet with tears. She felt that all was over between Eugene and herself—the beautiful dream had faded, the consciousness that she was beloved, that had made earth so bright to her, had died out, and she was left to grope in the darkness. She was very unhappy. She shrank from the course which, not many months ago, she had looked upon with enthusiasm; she felt that she was unfit for the destiny to which she had been devoted; she had a vague, terrible foreboding that, when she stood before that audience, her lips would unclose, and no sound would issue from them; she pictured herself thus, her own humiliation and Christine's disappointment and sorrow. She could not sleep; she paced the floor till she grew weary, then she crouched in a large easy-chair, and waited for the morning. She thought of Eugene, of his cold look, his careless grasp of her hand, and her heart ached as she felt that he no longer loved her. Had she not deceived herself all the time in imagining that he did care for her? She reviewed the past, his many little kind acts, and glances that had spoken more than acts. How happy she had been—and now—she groaned aloud.

She thought of her future life, when Christine would be taken from her, and she would be left in this great world alone. Alone! She shuddered as the realization of her desolation came over her. "And I am so young," she murmured, "I must live so many weary years."

She chid herself for her weakness, but she could not overcome it. She sank back in her chair, pressed her hands over her eyes, and wept softly and quietly. Hers was not a stormy nature to be shaken violently by the passions, but with a weary melancholy that was almost despair, she gave herself up to her sorrows.

It was her first real grief—her life had hitherto been so calm and bright that she had known sorrow only in books, and had felt only a pleasing sadness at its recital—now she was unprepared for it. Christine had so shielded her from every evil that she was the more overcome by this blow.

Eugene, too, was restless and miserable. Was this the end of it all? he bitterly thought. Yet, what else could he expect from the pupil of Christine Elliot? Had she not been more than mother to her, and had she not, from the very first moment after she came under her care, instilled into her mind the principles which she herself held sacred, and taught her to look forward to no other future than that of a champion of these all-important claims? He chid himself for his own folly; had he not known all this from the first. What madness had it been to allow himself to fall so deeply in love with her. How could he hope to undo the teachings of years?

By turns, he was angry with her, with himself, and with Christine; then he would resolve to forget her. He would never marry a Woman's Rights lecturer, even would she be willing to become his, which he hardly dared hope; he tried to think of her as a bold, unblushing woman, and so steel his heart against her; but that slight, shrinking figure, that sweet young face, so quickly covered with blushes at every emotion, that beautiful eye, soft, yet bright that sunk before his ardent gaze, rose before him, and he knew that she was as modest and retiring as she was lovely.

That sad, anxious glance of hers, as he had bid her a cold good-night, haunted him, sometimes thrilling him with joy, as he hoped that he was not indifferent to her, and again making him more angry with her than ever that she should, after all that he had said, still persist in her chosen career. He resolved that he would not visit her again, and for some days he kept his resolution.

Rosa waited, hoping that he would come; she listened, in a fever of excitement, to every ring at the door-bell, only to be disappointed again and again. She watched at the window, to see if he did not pass by the house, at least, but he did not make his appearance, and, with a sigh, she would turn away.

Christine perceived Rosa's unhappiness, for she was not skillful in hiding her feelings, and to her aunt's watchful eye every change in her countenance was familiar; but if she suspected the cause of her low spirits, she did not appear conscious of it—she was more than usually affectionate, she cheered her as to the success of her lecture, she told her of her own feelings at the time she first addressed an audience, she set her to tasks which occupied her so completely that she had little time for reflection, but all her efforts were in vain to bring back the bright smiles to her darling's face. She longed to take her to her heart and lead her to speak of her troubles, but she respected her feelings too much to try to pry into them, though she could have done so, and she waited with no little anxiety for Rosa's confidence. For the first time, she had a secret which she withheld from her more than mother.

CHAPTER THIRTY-SEVEN

All's Well That Ends Well

It was evening—all day long had Eugene Russell felt an irresistible impulse to visit the Home, to see Rosa once more.[81] "We can be friends," he said to himself, "if nothing more; and the sudden cessation of my visits might, perhaps, betray my secret"; so endeavoring to excuse himself, in this way, for the call he was about to make, he threw aside the *London Lancet*,[82] which he had held in his hand for some time, but in which he had read but little, and hastily exchanging his dressing-gown and slippers for a more suitable street costume, he was speedily on his way.

It was a pleasant, but cold October evening; the stars were shining brightly, and the streets through which he passed were a blaze of light; crowds of people were thronging to the different places of amusement, and if, here and there, a pallid face and haggard look was to be seen in that crowd of smiling and gaily dressed people, if a hand was extended for alms to those who were spending so much on their own gratification, as they swept by, it was only as if a dark shadow had, for an instant, fallen on the path, and was speedily forgotten.

Eugene heeded them as little as the rest of the crowd through which he passed; he was wrapped in his own reflections, imagining Rosa all smiles, brilliancy, and animation, at the result of her début in public life, for she had delivered her first lecture, and had been eminently successful; her youth, her extreme beauty, and the grace with which she had delivered her address, even more than the essay itself, had charmed her audience, and Christine read the comments of the press with more anxiety, and listened to the praises and congratulations of friends with more delight than she had ever felt for herself. Rosa, too, had seemed more like herself; she could not but feel gratified that she had passed through the ordeal so successfully; but amid all the kind words that fell on her ear, one voice was wanting; one word of commendation from Eugene would have been of more value to her than all the praises lavished upon her, and that word she would never hear; she had incurred his displeasure, she had forfeited his friendship, she had lost his love. In the midst of all her success her heart ached. Oh, what was the value of this hollow triumph? she asked herself. What did she care for fame, if underneath it all she must always bear this unsatisfied, restless heart? She felt at times, too, self-reproach for what she deemed her hypocrisy, for, alas! her heart was not in her work; she was not sustained, as was Christine, by the ardor and enthusiasm with which she entered into the cause—unlike her aunt, her whole soul was not enlisted in it. She was very unhappy, though she did not wish to distress Christine by her sadness, and tried to overcome it, or at least to hide it from her aunt.

On this evening she was alone—Christine had left home that morning, to go some distance to deliver a lecture before a lyceum; she would be absent for two or three days, and during that time Rosa was to commence a second lecture.

Literary labor was rather distasteful to her; had it not been for her great affection for Christine, and her desire to do all in her power to gratify her, she would long since have given it up, but she devoted herself faithfully to her task now as heretofore; she had toiled all day, till weary and dispirited as evening approached, she laid aside pen and paper, carefully arranged all that was disorderly in the room, and having had the fire replenished, threw herself, exhausted in body and mind, on a sofa. She was very lonely without Christine, and very sad; at last she could no longer restrain her emotion; she wept softly and quietly, till, somewhat relieved by her tears, she fell asleep. She was still lying there when Dr. Russell was ushered in by the servant, who knew him well, and knew that he was one of the privileged few admitted to Christine's private sitting-room, so merely informing him that he would find Miss Rosa within, she opened the door and turned away.

Dr. Russell at first thought the room was empty; as he glanced around, his eye rested on the sofa where Rosa was lying; the gas was low, and the fire-light fell on the figure of the girl, lighting it up with its red glow; he walked softly towards her, and gazed in breathless silence on the beautiful picture. Her attitude of perfect unconsciousness was graceful in the extreme; one little foot peeped from out the drapery of her dress, and one hand fell at her side, while a book which she had evidently been reading had slipped from her grasp to the floor; her head was partly supported by her other hand, while her sleeve, which had fallen back from its position, displayed her bare arm, white, rounded, and polished, gleaming through her golden curls, which, escaping from their confinement, fell in graceful clusters on the sofa-pillow which supported her head; her expression was sad, a tear gemmed her dark and long eye-lashes, which swept her transparent cheek, and a deep-drawn breath, that was almost a sigh, parted her lips at intervals; she looked like a child who had sobbed itself to sleep, and who even in its dreams has not quite forgotten its sorrow. A faded rose-bud drooped on her breast, and as he looked at her, he sighed; she too looked like a fading flower, yet never had Eugene seen her looking so lovely; her expression touched his heart; he longed to have the right to take her in his arms, to waken her with a kiss, but not for worlds would he have done so; her innocent beauty filled him with a feeling that was almost akin to awe; he resolved at first to steal out of the room softly, that she might not feel embarrassed on her waking, but he reflected that the servant had probably told Christine of his arrival, and that she would be in presently, so that his abrupt departure would strike her as singular, and he therefore seated himself in an easy-chair, taking the book which had dropped from Rosa's fingers, to read until Christine appeared. It was the Bible, a small and well-worn copy, and here and there passages were marked in pencil; he looked upon it with reverence, for he felt as if he had a glimpse into that pure young girl's heart.

He sat there lost in a revery, not reading, but resting his head upon his hand, thinking seriously and profoundly. Christine did not of course come in, and buried in his own reflections, he had almost forgotten that he expected her, when Rosa suddenly opened her eyes; she started as her eye rested on the young man opposite, who, with bowed head and downcast looks, did not appear conscious of her presence; she had been dreaming of Eugene, and now she could hardly persuade herself that his actual presence there was not a part of the illusion. She looked again; it was certainly he, how long had he been there? She blushed painfully, hesitated for a moment, then rose and approached him.

He looked up, saw her confusion, and hastily informed her that he had just come in, a few moments since, that he had expected Christine every instant, and apologized for his intrusion.

Rosa blushed still deeper, but replied, "My aunt is out of town for a few days; she has gone to deliver a lecture." She stopped short, the mention of a lecture recalled her own, and with crimsoned cheeks, neck, and brow, she sat down in the chair which Eugene offered her.

He was silent, for he knew not what to say, and she felt that he too was thinking of the subject that occupied her; his silence fell heavily on her heart, she could bear it no longer. With a great effort she, with a forced smile and faint attempt at gayety, said,

"I too have lectured, as you doubtless know, have you come to offer your congratulations on my success?"

He looked at her with a reproachful glance.

"Rosa," he said, in a voice of mingled sorrow and tenderness.

That glance, that tone was more than she could endure; her lip quivered, her chest heaved, and she burst into tears.

At the sight of her sorrow all Eugene's resolutions vanished, all his stoicism melted; in an instant he was at her side, holding her hand, telling her of his love, soothing her gently, speaking fond words of endearment, while she still wept, and said nothing, but allowed her hand to rest in his clasp. Gradually her sobs ceased, as she listened, with downcast eyes and beating heart, to the tender words he spoke.

"Rosa, speak to me," he said; "dearest, loveliest tell me that I may hope for a return of the affection I feel for you."

Rosa lifted her eyes, liquid and tender, to his face with a smile that thrilled to his very soul, like the sun "clear shining after rain," and in a moment she was pressed to his heart while he called her his bride, his wife.[83]

She gently withdrew from his embrace, and seated herself on a sofa.

"It seems like a dream," she said, softly; "I am afraid every moment that I shall wake and find it one."

Eugene's eyes sparkled with delight at these words; he threw himself on an ottoman near her, and looked at her with his whole soul in his eyes. He watched her every motion, admired her every charm, and the thought that she was *his* made her loveliness doubly delightful in his eyes.

"Rosa, darling," he said, "if I were a severe creditor I should exact heavy payment now from you, for you have made me very wretched for a few days past; as it is, I must be paid, let me tell you how," and he drew her closer to him.

She smiled and blushed, but withdrew her hand from his.

"I too have been unhappy," she said, softly; "I owe you nothing. Ah, you were cruel to treat me so—to torture me so with the thought that I had lost your friendship, just on account of that unlucky lecture."

At these words Eugene's countenance changed. He rose, and standing before the girl, said:

"Rosa, I have told you that I love you, as I do, better than my own soul, but let us understand each other; dearly as I love you, and hard as it will be to tear myself from you, yet never can I consent to your pursuing the course, as *my wife*, for which you have been destined by your aunt.

"Rosa, my wife must live for me—her heart must be wholly mine. I could not endure it, to see her sacred name bandied about in the journals, to hear it sneered at by brutal men, to have her loveliness the bait to attract crowds to see her and hear her speak."

He ground his teeth as he spoke.

"Rosa, all these visions of fame, all this fever of ambition, all these enthusiastic dreamings of future revolutions in society to be brought about by you must be given up, if you become my wife. You must be content to remain in the narrow sphere of home, to preside over the common household affairs, to discharge those duties which every woman, who assumes the position of head of a family, should be proud to attend to, and oh, Rosa, never has a wife been respected, cherished, or loved as you shall be. In place of a world's admiration, I offer you a husband's true and devoted love. In place of a life-long struggle for a niche in the temple of fame, which cannot bring happiness even should you gain it, I offer you the shelter of a quiet home—a home which, though humble, it shall be my study to make a happy one. Can you be content with this?"

He paused, and Rosa began in a faltering voice,

"I love you very, very dearly, Eugene; to gratify your wishes I would do much, but—"

He interrupted her,

"I know what you would say," he exclaimed, almost fiercely; "I ought to have expected it. What else could I look for in Christine Elliot's pupil! Fool that I was to imagine that so paltry a thing as a manly and devoted heart could compensate for the thwarting of an ambitious woman's plans!

"You love me, but not as well as notoriety; you would gratify my wishes, but not at the expense of your own inclinations; you would, perhaps, consent to become my wife, if at the same time you might still devote yourself to the public; you have tasted the honeyed cup of flattery, and it is too sweet to put aside for the wholesome but sometimes unpalatable counsel of a true friend.

"When did an ambitious woman ever hesitate to trample love under her feet if, by so doing, she could ascend higher? What does she care that a bleeding heart lies beneath her if, by making it a stepping-stone, she gains a higher foothold in her rugged path.

"How could I expect you to descend into the hum-drum reality of common life after having entered the whirl and excitement of a public career?

"The sacrifice is too great; you will not admit, even to yourself, the true reasons for your disinclination to sink into a quiet home; you will declare that you are a victim to your duty; you will stop all self-reproaches with the idea that you are a second Iphigenia,[84] ready to be immolated; you will assert that you are called to a wider field—that there are aims and aspirations which you have no right to check.

"I know it all. Spare me the enumeration of it from your lips. You are standing now where two paths diverge; ambition and love are before you, and you have chosen—one must be sacrificed, and you have made your selection.

"Rosa, farewell; you have not only destroyed my own but your future happiness also. Believe me, ambition is a siren that charms only to destroy. But why do I waste words? It is all in vain."

He turned away as if to go, but Rosa sprang forward and laid her hand upon his arm. That touch subdued him. Many times during his rapid speech she had essayed to interrupt him, but he would not hear her, and now she began in a tone of the deepest earnestness, and with eyes filled with tears,

"Eugene, how entirely you have misunderstood me. You talk of my sacrifices; how little you know my heart. Eugene, to be your wife, to be the sharer of your home, however humble, to toil for and with you, to be all in all to you, do you call this a sacrifice? It would be to me perfect happiness. I confess it. I could ask nothing more for myself.

"I shrink from public life. I was not made to lead the way in a great cause, however much I may believe in its truth. I have long felt my incapacity. I have long seen that I was unfit for the place for which I was destined. I have hoped and prayed that I might not be obliged to assume it, and how gladly, did I only consult my own feelings, would I embrace the fate you offer me, the beautiful lot, too bright and tempting for me to hope it may be mine. Not for myself do I hesitate; not even, as you supposed, for the lofty aim of being a benefactress to my sex; not from ambition, for I have no higher one than to share your fate, be it glad or sorrowful, but for my more than mother, Christine."

Her every word bore the stamp of sincerity, her eyes spoke volumes of trusting love, as she went on,

Christine

"She has been everything to me. She took me when a child, from the midst of sin and sorrow, and with untiring care, and never-failing love, she has cherished me in her heart. She has made my life very happy; she has devoted herself to me; in me she loves not only the child she has reared, but in me, also, all her hopes centre.

"She is a noble, a glorious woman. When I look upon her sometimes, as her face is eloquent with enthusiasm, I feel as if she were something higher and holier than a mere mortal. She is a second Miriam, and, like her, fit for the great task of leading on a people, careless and indifferent to their own good, into the promised land. She hopes that I shall take her place. Ah me, I, poor, weak little being, to take her place! I should faint by the way; I feel it, but I cannot tell her so. Should I fail her it would break her heart. Should I not be ungrateful, after she has spent so many years on me, nurtured me, educated me, loved me, did I desert her, and the place which she has all her life struggled to enable me to reach? Eugene, I love her scarcely less than I do you; the struggle is not between love and ambition, but between my love for my mother and for you. Alas! my heart pleads for you, but gratitude, no less than love, draws me in the opposite direction. What shall I do? What ought I to do? I cannot trust myself to decide."

"Forgive me for my injustice," said Eugene, pressing her to his heart. "I understand you now, and I honor you for your tender regard for Christine's feelings, but because she has shielded you during your past life, she has no right to make you miserable for the future. She can have no higher claim on you than I. Does not your own precious Bible tell you that, you "shall leave father and mother and cleave unto your husband?"[85] It is your duty to become my wife. Be mine, best, loveliest; with her consent if she will give it, but if not, without it."

"Oh, Eugene," cried Rosa, in a tone of the deepest sadness. "Can it be that you counsel me to such a course? What but unhappiness could result from a union such as you propose, without the consent of my more than mother? And could I so easily shake off the duty I owe her, what security would you have for the discharge of my duties as wife? What respect could you feel for me, did I let my wishes so far lead me astray? No, Eugene, never will I be your wife without her consent."

"Rosa, suppose she should never grant it?" exclaimed Eugene. "Suppose she should forbid you even to see me?"

"It is my duty to obey her, Eugene; but she would not be so unjust. She is kind—she is reasonable—she loves me. I can trust my fate in her hands. When she returns, you can write her or see her, and I, too, will tell her all. Leave me now, dear Eugene, and do not come again till she returns. It would not be right for me to receive you under the circumstances, without her consent; you do not think it would be, yourself, do you, dear Eugene?" she asked, gently.

"Now you ask too much, my Rosa," he replied, playfully. "Do you expect me to pronounce sentence on myself—to banish myself from her I love best? but do you say what you like, and I am bound, like a true knight, to obey you; but take care, don't be too severe. It will be my turn one of these days to retaliate."

"You invest me with absolute power then, do you?" she returned, with a bright smile. "Very well then, I will issue my commands in true queenly style. Retire now from our royal presence, and do not presume to return until summoned by royal mandate."

He bowed gracefully.

"As a mark of favor," she resumed, "Sir Knight, you may kiss my hand," and she extended it to him.

"Oh, but that's too much, my princess," he said, pressing it warmly. "I obey all the rest, but the hand savors of tyranny." He pressed her to his heart again and again, and as he bade her good-night, he said:

"I shall wait with the greatest impatience for Christine's return. I never knew before how great a loss her society would be to me. Good-night, my own Rosa," and he was gone.

With a happy smile she sat on the sofa, long after Eugene had departed. She lived over again the scenes of the last few hours; she contrasted her happiness with the sadness she had felt, when she fell asleep; it was as if she had fallen asleep in a dreary place, and had been transported into fairy-land.

One thought alone checked her joy. What would Christine say? She would not allow herself to think that her decision would be unfavorable. She treasured up every word she had ever heard her utter in his favor, and resolutely banished all forebodings of evil from her mind.

CHAPTER THIRTY-EIGHT

Life-Plans Thwarted

Very pleasant dreams haunted Rosa's pillow that night, and when she awoke in the morning it was with the blissful consciousness that her dreams were only shadows of a still pleasanter reality. With a light heart she set about the tasks which the day before had been so distasteful to her, and she carolled scraps of merry songs as she flitted about the house and garden. She longed for, yet dreaded, her aunt's return, but not even the fear of Christine's displeasure could over-cloud the sunshine of gladness that filled her heart.

The day passed, and the next was nearly spent, and Christine had not yet arrived. Eugene had not disobeyed Rosa's request; he had not called, but he had written her several playful, tender notes, telling her that she had not forbidden his pen to talk to her, even if he could not see her.

Rosa was poring over these missives for the twentieth time, sitting on a low seat, and reading them by the fire-light, when she heard a carriage stop at the door; in an instant she had thrust the crumpled notes in her pocket, ran to the door, and in another moment was folded in Christine's arms.

"Oh, how glad I am to see you!" she cried, as she led her aunt to the cheerful sitting-room, and took off her outer garments.

"And I am as glad to see home and my Blossom again," returned Christine. "This travelling by railroad is such weary business. I long to get out of this dusty travelling-dress, and into something clean."

She rose as she spoke and entered her chamber, and Rosa left her there to make her toilet. When she again entered the study the fire was bright, the curtains drawn, the gas lighted, and on a small table was spread a substantial supper. Rosa was just setting a chair in readiness for her aunt.

"I knew," she said, "that your supper would taste better here than in that great, lonely dining-room, and I knew that you must be hungry after your long journey. Sit down now, dear auntie, and taste of the toast. Isn't it good? I made it myself, and even Martha owned that it was excellent."

"Everything is as nice as possible, Rosa, from the snowy tablecloth and bright silver, down to the toast and tea, to say nothing of this broiled chicken. You do credit to Martha's teaching, my dear. You deserve a diploma as housekeeper."

Rosa blushed and smiled, and began to ask something about Christine's tour.

It had been a very pleasant one; she had been kindly received, treated with every attention, and had been listened to by a crowded audience. "But, Rosa," she concluded, "everybody was more interested in the Home, and its progress and success, than in my theory and doctrines. But it is always so, the majority of mankind cannot see the truth or importance of a theory, which, when reduced to practice, they applaud. I have put a little in practice, and they all express their delight; you shall do far greater things, and receive a far greater meet of applause, as well as a far greater amount of self approval, which is worth all the rest. Yet I have labored with my might, in all singleness of purpose, and why should I reproach myself, if I may not see the results for which I had hoped. It is a human weakness to wish to see the harvest in the field, where we have wearily toiled to sow the seed, but if God wills that I should labor, and others enter into my labors, I must submit, and I can do so the more readily since he has raised up so efficient a laborer in one so dear to me; since he has granted to me to see who shall carry on the work I have begun. No, Rosa, I do not regret all the weary toil that I have undergone, since it is to lighten your task."

Rosa listened to all this in silence. How could she speak the words that would so quickly put to flight all those happy thoughts? How could she tell her what a bitter disappointment to all her cherished plans her idolized daughter had prepared for her? Yet, was she not playing the hypocrite in listening to these plans without a word? Was it not wrong to allow her to continue another moment in her delusion?

She felt that she must speak, and was upon the point of doing so, when a rap was heard at the door, and a bevy of the girls came to pay their respects to Christine.

"Let us go to the parlor," she said, "I wish to see all my children"; and Rosa followed her there, where, in the universal festivity and excitement that Christine's return occasioned, she had no opportunity to say anything of a private nature. She dispatched a note to Eugene, informing him of her aunt's return, and resolved on the morrow to acquaint her with all that had transpired during her absence.

It was with rather a faint heart that Rosa entered the study the next morning, with no settled plan as to how she would introduce the subject, though she had been revolving a thousand different methods, all of which she had as summarily dismissed as unsuitable; she was spared the trouble of further scheming by Christine, who held up a letter as she entered, and smilingly said,

"Another is added to the list of your victims, Rosa; and who do you think? I could never have imagined. No less a person than Dr. Eugene Russell avows his love for you in, to do him justice, a very well expressed and sensible love letter, as love letters go, and asks my permission to address you. Who would have thought it?" she continued, gaily; "that he, of all men, who is so strenuous an advocate for keeping woman in her much-talked of sphere, should so far forget himself and his prejudices as to ask a Woman's Rights lecturer to become his wife! Ah, well, 'to this complexion must we come at last.'[86] Love is a universal leveller, as you can testify. High and low, rich and poor, believers and unbelievers, radicals and conservatives, all bow before it and my Rosa. But it is all in vain. Sighs and tears, vows and protestations, all fall unheeded on your ear. Who would think, my dear, that, under this exterior," and she laid her hand playfully on Rosa's shoulder, "was hidden such an obdurate heart. Here is the letter," and she extended it to her child.

Rosa took it and turned away, as if to read it, but, though she looked at it for many minutes, and it was written in a plain, bold hand that the veriest child might have read, she knew no more of its contents from its perusal than if she had been studying the Egyptian lore of hieroglyphics. At last she folded it and returned it to her aunt.

"Shall I reply to it, or will you, Rosa?"

"You, if you please, dear aunt, as it is addressed to you."

"Very well," said Christine, turning to her writing-table, and with her hand resting on the paper, while she held the pen in her hand, she said,

"Shall I reply in the old stereotyped form, or, considering the circumstances, which render this proposal rather different from its predecessors, shall I vary a little from the usual acknowledgments of the honor, etc., which soften the way to the bitter words of rejection?"

Rosa was standing behind her, and with downcast eyes, but firm voice, she said: "You say truly that this proposal requires a different answer from any other which I have received; for, Aunt Christine, I love Eugene Russell with my whole heart, and should you give your consent to our union, nothing would be wanting to my perfect happiness."

The pen dropped from Christine's fingers in her astonishment at these words. She turned around and fixed her deep-searching eyes on the face of the trembling, blushing girl who stood there.

"Rosa, my child," she exclaimed, "is it possible that I have heard you aright? You would accept him! I must have misunderstood you."

"No, dearest aunt," replied Rosa, in a voice scarcely audible.

"It cannot be," persisted Christine, "that after devoting yourself to the noble work upon which you have just entered, after rejecting again and again the offers of gentlemen whose wealth and talents might have, indirectly, at least, aided the cause you have professed to love, that you might the better discharge your duties unfettered by selfish and private considerations, that you would now deliberately give up all that you hold most sacred, and become the wife of a man who has never disguised his hostility to the cause with which you have identified yourself so recently.

"He is fascinating, I admit. He has made an impression upon your fancy, but it is only a momentary infatuation, my Rosa, that has for the time led you astray."

"No, dearest aunt, it is no more fancy, no foolish and momentary infatuation. I love him with my whole heart—better than I do aught else on earth—better than I do my own soul—"

"Better than you do your duty, your God?" interrupted Christine, sternly. "Alas! rash and misguided girl, you are not the first one who has been led from the straight and narrow path of the right by the siren voice of love, only to find too late that its promises of happiness were delusive, that out of the path of duty there is no peace or joy. But I am your mother, Rosa—I cannot see you plunge recklessly into the wrong—I must hold you back—and though you may think and call me cruel now, yet, hereafter, you will thank me; but even should you not do so, I shall have the assurance that I have done my duty towards you."

"No, dearest aunt, my more than mother, never shall I think you cruel—never shall I doubt your love," said Rosa flinging her arms round Christine's neck. "Whatever you may decide, you will need no compulsion. I would never marry without your consent. Believe me, I am not ungrateful for your care all these years, or for your tenderness that has so guarded me that I have never felt the want of a mother's love. I would do nothing willfully to offend you. Should you require it, I will promise not to see Eugene, but I cannot promise not to love him, for that would be out of my power. Oh, dearest aunt, did you never feel for some one a love that was almost a species of idolatry, a love that was all in all to you, so that with him you loved, you felt that nothing earthly could mar your happiness, and without him all earth's joys were as nothing, and worse than nothing? Oh, Christine, so do I love Eugene. Yet, dearly as I love him, I will abide by your decision, but before you pronounce sentence upon me, hear me."

Christine did not speak—she buried her face in her hands— Rosa's words had brought back to her, in all their freshness, the sorrows of her youth; the old, long-buried love that slumbered in her heart sprang up, and again she felt, in all its bitterness, what had been her loss. Rosa hardly observed her emotion; she threw herself on the floor by her side, and taking her aunt's passive hand, she went on:

"Long ago, before I ever saw Eugene, I had become painfully aware of my unfitness for the position for which you destined me. I knew that my place was not in public. I knew that I could never be what you hoped I might become. I am not, nor can I ever be, like you. You are as far above me as the heavens are above the earth. You can enter with enthusiasm and with power, on the great work of revolutionizing society, and you can accomplish great deeds; but I, though your ardor may carry me for a moment out of myself, when left alone can do nothing.

"I love all domestic duties—all that you deem drudgery. I am fit only for home duties, for a humble private life. God has given us different gifts, and when, disgusted with our own, we reach after those of others, the result is only miserable failure. You can write words that breathe, and utter them so as to move all hearts; and I, how poor and pitiful are my efforts, even when you, with your strong intellect, assist me. I am a little star that shines only in the light reflected from you.

"I repeat it; I am not fit to enter into the task set before me. I do not wish to—I would gladly withdraw from it.

"All this I felt long ago, but when I saw Eugene, when I loved him as I do, how empty seemed such a life as I must lead, even if I could do all that you pointed out to me as in my power. It is selfish and weak, I know, but the love of Eugene is worth more to me than the gratitude and praise of a whole people.

"You cannot with your great heart understand this—you do not know what it is to be so selfishly engrossed in the love of one."

"Rosa!" exclaimed Christine, "you know not what you are saying. I, too, have loved as devotedly as you—I, too, have suffered when my idol was taken from me; yet I entered the path into which God had led me, and in it I have found, if not happiness, at least peace."

"Ah me," sighed Rosa, "you could do this, but I am too weak. I could not like you, do, I could only endure. But I will say no more. I have told you all—you know my disinclination to the work you have set before me, and my love for Eugene. My fate is in your hands. I am your child. Do with me as you will."

Christine groaned aloud.

"Is this the end of all?" she said, sadly; "have all my life-long struggles accomplished only this? What can I hope that I have effected by my teachings, when the child of my love, on whose infant and ductile mind I have instilled all my principles; to whom I have looked as a proud example of what education could do; and not only that, but to whom I was to transmit the task of carrying on the yet scarcely begun work of destroying old prejudices and the establishment of our glorious doctrines, of instituting a new era in society and in the history of woman, deserts me? What can I expect from others when she fails me, throws aside as worthless all I have endeavored to teach her to hold sacred, and cares nothing for the great principles the advocacy of which I have all her life long led her to look forward to as her mission.

"I have struggled—I have toiled on, unheeding all opposition, through scoffs, jeers, and the vilest abuse—and for what? What have I gained? What good have I accomplished! My life has been a miserable failure!"

"Oh, dearest aunt, do not say so!" cried Rosa. "Is not this very Home, within whose walls we now are, a lasting monument of your good works? How many have you saved from death and worse than death! Where is not your name the synonym for all that is good, pure, and self-sacrificing? Where are you not honored and respected, even by those who were once your bitterest enemies? And what do I not owe you? All a mother's love, all the watchful care that has shielded me from every sorrow—and I am not ungrateful. No, dearest mother, I will not fail you! I will go on in the course for which you have destined me. It is the least I can do to repay you, for all I owe you. You may write to Eugene"; she burst into tears.

"Forgive me," she said, looking up with streaming eyes; "that I cannot help weeping. It is not that I am unwilling to do what you would wish, but I am weak—I cannot control myself now.

Let me shed these tears, for, though I am ready to do my duty, I cannot help it, indeed I cannot. You will forgive me that I had forgotten what I owed to you, will you not, and you will still love your Rosa, dearest aunt."

Christine's answer was to clasp the girl to her heart, "And could you think that I would accept the sacrifice of your young life? Could you think that I would immolate you on the shrine of my idol? Oh, Rosa, how little you understood me. Not from love or gratitude to me would I accept what was denied to your love of the cause. Not for worlds would I have you obey my voice when no echo to its biddings was found in your own heart. I would not have you take upon yourself so great a work unless your whole heart was in it. Rosa, how could you so doubt my love for you, as to think I could take advantage of the holiest part of your nature to make you a slave to my will? Oh, Rosa, it is a fearful thing to hold in your hands the destiny of another, and that other one so dear to me as you have been, as you still are and ever will be. It was your happiness and well-being alone that I sought. I thought to do it in my own way. You have convinced me that I was wrong. I had well-nigh in my blindness wrecked your happiness. Forgive me, Rosa. May you be happy with Eugene since you love each other, and may God bless you, my darling. May you find in the man of your choice, not one who will love you better than I have done, for that is impossible, but one who will guide you better than I have been able to do."

She would have unwound the clasp of Rosa's arms around her neck, but the girl still clung to her.

"Oh, mother!" she cried. "Do not leave me. Do not banish me from your heart. Never speak again as you have done of your errors in my education. Never was there a more devoted mother, never one dearer to her child, nor have you failed, sweetest mother, in your teachings. You have made me what I should never have been without you. The influence of your pure, unselfish life will never die out of my heart. God helping me, it shall never die out of my life. There is a private, a secret, unobtrusive influence which all may exert in behalf of the wretched and the erring, against all that is wrong and unjust in society, and though God has not given me the power or the will to do what you have done, yet in my own narrower sphere all I can do shall not be left undone. Your life has not been in vain! Oh, how can you think so when you look at your children of this Home, and on your Rosa? God grant that my life may be as rich in good works as yours!"

Christine pressed Rosa closer to her heart, and a tear fell on her golden locks.

"You do not think me ungrateful, sweet mother," said the girl, looking up into her face.

"No, my Blossom," was the reply. "You have never been wanting in love or obedience to me. You have ever been a dutiful child. You have not failed me, but our cause, and since you could not devote yourself to it with heart and soul, perhaps it is better to have discovered it before it was too late. Now, my dear, let us say no more about it. I will write immediately to Dr. Russell."

But Rosa still clung to her.

"Do you really love me as well as ever?" she whispered.

"Oh, my Blossom! My foolish child, is there any need to ask that?"

She kissed the girl tenderly, and gently withdrew from her embrace.

"Then I am very happy," murmured Rosa, softly, as she seated herself near her aunt, and watched the rapid movement of her pen as she wrote. It was a brief letter and soon dispatched.

Eugene read it again and again; it contained merely an appointment for an interview at the Home that evening, and study it as he might, he could find nothing which he could construe as either favorable or unfavorable to his suit.

CHAPTER THIRTY-NINE

The Wedding

It seemed as if the evening would never come, but come at last it did, and at the appointed time Eugene was seated alone with Christine in the study.

"I have received your letter," began Christine, in a firm voice, "and though I tell you frankly that you are not the one I should have chosen for my child, had I wished her to marry, yet," she paused; the well-worded and dignified speech which she had prepared remained for ever unspoken; her voice trembled. "Dr. Russell," she said, "it is a sacred trust that I repose in you. Oh, be kind to my Rosa!"

He seized her hand, pressed it warmly, and replied:

"Your trust shall never be betrayed. She shall be as the very apple of my eye. How can I thank you enough for your confidence?"

Christine made no reply. She turned away, and touched a little bell, spoke a few words to the servant who appeared, and in a few moments, Rosa, all blushes and smiles, entered the room.

As she came in, and laid her hand softly in Eugene's, he could have clasped her to his heart, but Christine's presence prevented his obeying his first impulse, and he contented himself with a warm pressure of the hand he held, and a few whispered words that made her eyes sparkle more brightly, and her blushes more vivid, as she took a seat near him.

Christine, on the opposite side of the room, sat with a book in her hand, apparently quite engrossed in its contents, and her presence was soon almost forgotten by both Rosa and Eugene, as they talked in a low voice together. Christine was not reading, or at least, if she read, it was a page in her own heart's history. How vividly did this scene recall to her, those delightful evenings with Philip, when Julia had withdrawn from the group, as she was now doing, and had been, like her, forgotten.

Where was Philip? Where had he been all these weary years? In her turn now she had forgotten the presence of others; in spirit she was far away, and Rosa and Eugene still talked on in their subdued tones.

Rosa had just concluded giving a brief account of her interview with her aunt.

"I did not give you credit for so much courage, my Rosa," replied Eugene. "You dared to beard the lioness in her den, and more wonderful still, you came off not only unscathed but victorious. I had no idea that she would give her consent so readily; after all her air-castles for you that she would look on and see them all demolished."

"You do not know her as I do, Eugene. She is the most unselfish of mortals. It was, indeed, a severe blow to her—how severe you can hardly realize, unless you remember that with all her soul she has devoted herself to a cause which she holds sacred, and she has depended on me to do all that she has left undone, and must leave incomplete."

"She would have sacrificed you to her Moloch," interrupted Eugene.[87]

"Do not say so," replied Rosa. "She looked upon it as a consecration to the highest and purest life; when she found that to me it was a sacrifice, she gave up all her cherished plans for the sake of securing my happiness, though I know it was a bitter disappointment to her. I placed my fate in her hands, and my confidence in her unselfish love was not misplaced. Never say again that no woman can sacrifice ambition to love. Has not Christine done it?"

"I will say no more," answered Eugene, "for it is one of Woman's Rights to have the last word on any subject, and heretic as I am, on some points, I believe fully in respecting that."

"But," urged Rosa, "I want you to understand, and love her as I do."

"I honor and admire her now, and, I dare say, when I know her better I shall love her—will not that content you? At present I am too much engrossed in one fair lady to have much interest in others."

"Selfish man!" said Rosa, playfully.

"You, at least, since you are the cause of my fault, should not reproach me for it," rejoined Eugene, and then in a more serious tone, he went on to speak to Rosa of the future, while she listened, and neither thought of the flight of time.

Weeks passed, and though Christine could not so readily forget her severe disappointment, yet she tenderly loved Rosa, and the sight of her happiness did much to dispel her own sadness.

Preparations, too, for the wedding were going on, and in the excitement and bustle that attend upon such occasions, Christine had but little time for reflection.

The appointed evening came at last. The house was brightly illuminated, and crowds of people were assembled there, for not only were the members of the family, of themselves no small party, present, but many of those who had formerly been there, and who had always felt a deep interest in all the occurrences at the Home, on such an occasion as the marriage of Rosa, could not fail to be there.

Rosa looked very beautiful in her simple white dress, as she received the congratulations of her friends, and Eugene gazed at her with mingled pride and affection, as he saw her graceful ease, and listened to her playful words and silvery laugh.

It was an occasion of mingled sadness and joy to Christine; she could but feel sad as she gave her darling to another, even had she cherished no other designs for her, but she knew that Eugene was a good and noble man, and the bitterness of her own disappointment had somewhat passed away. She could but feel happy, too, when she looked around her, and saw not only her protégées, but her father, her mother, Bessie and Mrs. Frothingham, as well as Helen and Mrs. Warner, all chatting together pleasantly under her roof. Had she not, after all, much to be grateful for? She had regained the love of those, who, for a time, had been estranged from her; she had been enabled to triumph over all the wrong done her—even to turn the evil into good, and as she looked on the happy faces about her, and at Rosa's bright smile, she felt that she had not lived entirely in vain, though she had not attained what she had once hoped to see, the results of her labors, her theory in successful operation.

Will Linton approached her as she stood lost in thought, and began to talk to her. He looked careworn, as if life had been a toilsome thing, and, in fact, so he had found it. He had struggled long, and though he had both genius and talent, he had not been fully appreciated. Poverty had been his constant companion, and had it not been for the elastic temperament of his wife, he would long since have yielded to despair—but she was as cheerful as ever, though Christine drew from her the facts that they were poor, and that Will had not been able as yet to paint the historical picture which he had so long hoped to transfer from his brain to the canvas. They had removed to New York, hoping for better times. Mr. Harper had long since died, but his fortune had been lost; he had engaged in speculations which

were to treble his wealth, but they had failed, and in his old age
he was left destitute, and his proud wife had been obliged to
owe her support to her son-in-law, the artist; but worse than
narrow circumstances had been the loss of two beautiful children, the pride of Helen's heart; tears which no penury could
draw from her eyes, fell at the mention of the names of her lost
ones; but she wiped them away as Will's step was heard, and met
him with the olden, loving smile and merry words that cheered
him more than volumes of encouragement or advice to hope
for better things could have done; while Helen was happy, he
could not be sad; they had never been in actual want, but the
thought that Helen should be obliged to toil as well as himself was very painful to him. He cared not for himself but for
her; but she would not suffer him to be sad, she was so gay, so
light-hearted, that he could not be long with her, without sympathizing in her cheerful spirits.

Mrs. Warner was the same as ever, gentle and dignified, enthusiastic and true. For her, Christine felt a deep affection, unlike that she bore towards any other of her friends; they understood each other perfectly, and to her, Christine could breathe
all the most secret thoughts of her heart.

The wedding was a very pleasant one, not only to the happy
bride and groom, but to all present, but when all was over, the
bridal party had departed, and other friends had gone, then
did Christine realize that she was alone. She missed Rosa everywhere; she missed her light step, her ready hand, and the
sight of her pleasant face, the consciousness of her presence
which had been a source of so much satisfaction to her. Dearly
as she had loved her, Christine had not realized how closely she
was connected with the comforts of the Home. All went on in
its usual course, but the charm of it all was lost. She felt sometimes as if there had been a death in the house, and though
Rosa, living near by, came very often and took her old place by
her side, it only made her sense of the loss she had sustained

more painful when she left her again. But her child was very happy in her new home, and she would not distress her by allowing her to see how very much she missed her. She plunged again into all her pursuits with new zeal, wrote, read, and applied herself more closely than ever.

CHAPTER FORTY

 Shadow and Sunshine

It was late in the afternoon; Christine was sitting absorbed in her studies when she was interrupted by the entrance of a servant, who handed her a folded paper.

She glanced at the address; it was in a handwriting entirely unknown to her, but as her eyes rested on the feeble and uncertain characters within the sheet, she trembled and turned pale; it needed not the signature to assure her from whom it came, and tears rushed in her eyes as she read the words,

"Christine, I am dying. By the memory of our old love, I conjure you to come to your own

"Philip."

The hand that had penned those lines had evidently been feeble. The letters were half-formed and almost illegible; it looked little like the bold and firm handwriting that she had known so well, yet it was strangely familiar to her.

"Where is he?" she cried, turning to the messenger.

"If the lady will go," replied the man, with a low bow, "I have a carriage at the door."

"I will be ready instantly," said Christine, and in a few moments she was on her way.

She sat in the carriage, feeling, rapid as was the progress, that she could hardly wait to arrive at her destination; her heart beat violently, her eyes swam with tears; all the past was forgotten, she had but one thought; Philip still loved her, and he was dying!

Suddenly the carriage stopped. She followed her guide up the wide staircase—the door opened into a darkened room, whose silence was only broken by the heavy breathing of the sufferer; by the bedside sat a man, evidently a physician, who watched with close attention every change in his patient's symptoms. Softly as the door had opened he had observed it.

"Did she come? Is she here?" he cried, and as Christine approached and took his hand, he fixed his eyes upon her, with a look of the tenderest affection.

"Oh Christine!" he gasped, and could say no more.

The physician raised him, and administered a cordial which seemed to refresh him. He motioned to all to leave the room, and as the door closed, and they were alone, he said, softly:

"I knew we should meet again—Christine, I could not die in peace without seeing you once more."

"Oh, my Philip!" cried she, while her tears fell fast on the pallid hand she held, "to meet thus after so many weary years! To find you—" she choked, and could not speak.

"Dying," said Philip, with a strange calmness; "yes, dearest, it is even so, but do not weep—I am very happy, for you are by my side. Christine, do you love me still?"

"Love you! oh Philip, with my whole heart I love you, I have never ceased to do so."

A faint smile flitted over the sick man's features. "God, I thank thee!" he murmured.

He paused a moment. "Christine," he gasped, "I have been very unworthy of your love; can you forgive me?"

Her only reply was to press her lips on his pallid brow.

"I have but a few hours on earth," he went on, "will you grant my dying request? Promise me that you will!"

"I promise, dearest Philip," she answered.

"Be my wife," he said, "that my wife's hand may smooth my pillow, my wife's kiss rest on my pale lips, and her hand close my failing eyes! Do you consent, my Christine? You have promised," and he gazed at her with a look of entreaty.

She could not speak; she only bowed her head in token of assent. He pointed to a bell on the table, she touched it, and in a moment several persons entered, a clergyman and several witnesses.

It was a solemn sight, that marriage in the death chamber; the pale and ghastly countenance of the bridegroom, hardly more pale than that of the bride, as the man of God pronounced those solemn words that made them one; with a trembling hand Philip placed a ring, which slipped from his attenuated finger, on Christine's, and gasped, "Kiss me, my wife!" as the ceremony ended.

She bent over him fondly; she kissed him with tearful eyes, and wiped the damp from his brow.

Philip was exhausted, but he roused himself.

"Is Mr. Murdoch here?" he asked, and as he approached, he said, "Is all ready?"

Mr. Murdoch bowed.

"Proceed then!" he said, "my time is short."

With a dry cough the man of law began to read.

"I give and bequeath to my wife, Christine Armstrong, my entire fortune, consisting of—" and here he enumerated, as rapidly as possible, all that followed—at its close, he put a pen into Philip's fingers, and he feebly signed his name, the witnesses added their signatures, while Christine looked on half stupefied.

At last all was done, and all left the apartment save the new made wife and the physician. With a strong effort Christine restrained the tears that seemed to distress her husband, and bent over him, applying restoratives, and doing everything in her power to contribute to his comfort, while she whispered fond words that seemed to thrill to his very soul.

The physician gave some directions and left the room; Christine glided after him.

"Is there no hope?" she gasped, as she stood with him in the hall.

The Doctor shook his head doubtfully. "There is not a chance in a thousand," he said. "It is the crisis in his fever, he is weak and—"

"Then there is a chance," cried Christine, joyfully.

"So faint a one that I dare not bid you hope," replied the Doctor, evidently touched by her anguish.

"While there is life there is hope," she returned; "oh Doctor, let nothing be spared; save him and I will bless you for ever. Do not leave him!"

"I will return shortly," said the physician, and again Christine was at that bedside.

Philip would have spoken to her, but she would not allow it; she laid her finger on his lip, she bent over and kissed him repeatedly, and he could only look at her with the fondest expression.

Ere long he began to wander; incoherent expressions fell from his lips—he seemed to be in great suffering, and with anxious face the Doctor stood by his bedside and administered a potion. As he did so, he said, softly, "I have done all in my power, I have exerted myself to the utmost, and the result is in God's hands—a few hours will decide all."

Philip was still delirious, he tossed wildly, but still clung convulsively to Christine's hand. Oh the agony of those few hours, as the wife sat by the bedside of her dying husband. With what fervor did she pray to God to grant her the life of him who was all the world to her, though her lips moved not and no words were spoken.

Gradually the sick man's struggles grew less violent, he seemed to sink into a death-like stupor; Christine looked at the physician, there was no hope in his face, and with a deep sigh she sank half fainting on her knees by the bedside. She buried her face on the pillow, she could not see him die! Her hand still was held in the death grasp—when that pressure relaxed she knew that all would be over. She did not look up, she was conscious of nothing about her, till a voice whispered in her ear, "The crisis is past, he sleeps. If that sleep is unbroken he may recover."

The revulsion from despair to hope was too great; she fainted, and would have fallen to the floor had not the friendly arms of the physician caught her. When she recovered her consciousness, she was lying in another room.

"Let me go to him!" she gasped. "I cannot remain here."

Her earnestness was so great that she was permitted to return, and, lying on a lounge, she listened to the regular breathing of the sick man with a thrill of joy that could find no expression, save the outgoing of her heart to Heaven in thankfulness for the granting of her prayer.

No sound broke the silence on which depended the life of the sufferer. But Christine's eyes did not close that night; she lay there in perfect silence; she hardly dared to breathe lest he should waken, and when, as morning dawned, Philip languidly opened his eyes, she was at his side in an instant, and though he could not speak, he seemed content only when she held his hand in hers.

Again he sank into a gentle slumber, and the physician addressed her—

"Mrs. Armstrong, your husband will now, I hope, recover. Care and attention will soon restore him again to health."

"God bless you!" said Christine, fervently. "Under God I owe his life to your skill."

He bowed silently, and withdrew. She was alone with her husband. Her husband! The words had a strange charm, and her new name, Mrs. Armstrong, kept sounding in her ears. Philip's wife! Her heart beat rapturously at the thought, and with tender glances she gazed at the sleeper.

There were the same features that had been so indelibly impressed on her memory—that broad, white brow, those long eye lashes, that beautiful mouth, those waving, brown locks—all was unchanged, save the pallid and hollow cheek, and the threads of grey here and there mixed with the soft, brown hair; but never in all the pride of his manly vigor had she loved him so tenderly as now. All was forgotten save her great love for him; and for the days that followed she was wholly absorbed in the most delicate and sedulous attentions to his wants. He was very feeble, and the slightest noise seemed to disturb him. Christine alone could do everything in just the way he liked; she alone could arrange his pillows comfortably; she alone could lift him into an easy position; her step alone did not jar everything, and only she could drape the curtains so as to make a pleasant light; in fact she was indispensable to his comfort, and he was uneasy if she was out of the room even for a few moments.

It was impossible for her to go to the Home; her first duty was to her husband, and dispatching a note to Martha, she informed her that she was engaged in nursing a sick friend, and left to her, as she had often done before, the cares of the household.

Slowly, as weeks passed, did Philip regain his strength; he could sit up for a short time, but this did not lessen Christine's confinement. She must sit by his side, and read to him, talk to him, or sing to him, as suited his fancy; and to all his caprices she yielded as patiently as she would have done to a sick child.

It was a pleasure to her to feel that she was so necessary to his comfort and happiness, and his constant dependence upon her for everything seemed to attach her to him, if possible, even more strongly than ever. No matter how wearied she was, she was ever ready to attend to his slightest wants, even to anticipate his wishes, and his fond looks amply repaid her for all her fatiguing cares. Never had she been happier than now, when, with utter self forgetfulness, she devoted herself entirely to Philip.

But there came a change. Slight indeed, but not the less acutely felt by one of Christine's peculiarly sensitive temperament and quick perceptions. As Philip gradually regained his health and strength he depended less on her; he would sit for hours silently, and she would find his eyes resting upon her with an expression she could not interpret; he would sigh deeply, and his brow would contract as if in pain—he seemed restless and unhappy.

She saw it all. The chain that bound him to her was galling. As a nurse she had been valuable to him, her presence had been delightful, but as a wife it was unwelcome. When prostrated by sickness, and, as he supposed, on his death-bed, his old love had revived, but now that life lay before him, he revolted at the idea of calling Christine Elliot—known worldwide as the leader and champion of Woman's Rights—his wife.

As she thought of all this, she understood his fitful moods, his alternations of kindness and coldness; she read in it the struggle between love and pride; her heart ached, but she was not one to sit idly and brood over her sorrow; there was a remedy—she would not burden him with her unwelcome presence.

How she rejoiced in the forethought that had prevented her declaring her marriage to her friends, leaving Philip himself to do so when he recovered. It need not be made public now. She would never claim the title which Philip would blush to own. She did not feel angry or resentful, her love was too unselfish for that; he was not to be blamed if he had mistaken the nature of his feelings towards her. She would not show by her

manner that she felt the change; so she resolved, but unconsciously there was a difference.

She no longer addressed him by the tender epithets she had
at first bestowed upon him. She feared to disgust him by any
familiarities, and no longer laid her hand on his pallid brow,
or twined his curling hair around her fingers. She determined
to remain with him until he needed her no longer, until he was
quite recovered, and then she would free him from her presence for ever; but while this tumult was going on within, outwardly she was as calm as ever. Yet this second separation was
by far more painful than the first had been. Now she was his
wife. She had in these few weeks known what happiness was
in the sacred tie that united them. She had felt that to be his
beloved wife was all that she could ask to fill up her cup of joy
to the full, and now to have it dashed away just as it was put to
her lips, was hard indeed. To be an unloved wife was more than
she could bear; to be to the world one in name, yet divided in
heart, she felt, was a hollow hypocrisy she could not assume.
No, she was every day more firmly resolved that, miserable as
a separation would make her, it would be more endurable than
a mere outward form of union, which irritated while it bound
them together.

She had been reading to him, one day, for a long time until he had fallen asleep, lulled by the sweetness and softness
of her voice, for he was still weak and easily fatigued; he lay
half reclining in an easy-chair, his thin hands folded, his eyes
closed, and his long eye-lashes sweeping his cheek, to which
the faint color was just returning.

Christine looked at him with the purest affection. She felt
drawn by an irresistible impulse toward him. In a day or two,
they must be parted forever. Once more she must press her lips
on his brow. He was sleeping, her caress would not annoy him,
she was his wife, and she must give him one parting kiss. She
stole softly to his side, and bent over him gently—her breath

floated over his cheek as she touched her lips to his marble brow, then glided again to her seat, laid her head on the table, and sighing half audibly, "Oh, Philip! Philip!" she allowed her tears, which in the agony of parting she could not check, to flow unrestrained.

She had been weeping softly and quietly for some moments when she felt a hand laid on her shoulder, and looking up she saw Philip standing by her side. He was deathly pale, and the hand which rested on the table, as if to support him, trembled.

Christine was frightened by his excessive agitation; gently but firmly she led him to a seat, bathed his brow in cold water and offered him a glass of the same pure liquid.

He took it without a word, then began: "Christine—" his voice trembled.

"Do not talk now, Philip," she said, "you are not equal to the exertion—you are not so well to-day, I fear. Are you not suffering? Can I do nothing for you?"

Philip groaned.

"I must speak," he said, with an effort; "I have felt for some time that it must come, and the sooner it is over the better for us both."

"Oh, Philip!" cried Christine, while she grew deathly pale; "I know what you would say," and she pressed her hands tightly over her heart; "say it," she added, "I can bear it all!"

"Christine," he said, hardly heeding her words; "you have been very kind to me—you have borne with all my caprices, and they have not been few, with my selfishness, great as it has been. You have been all, and more than all that I could ask. Believe me, I have not seen your noble self-devotion unmoved. It has not been lost on me—I am not ungrateful for all I owe to you, but—"

Christine wrung her hands in anguish. She could bear it no longer. A choking sob escaped her, "Oh, Philip," she gasped,

"I know it all, but spare me—I cannot hear those words fall from your lips."

"Always kind, always self-forgetful," replied Philip, faintly; "but selfish as I am, I am not the wretch you take me for. I have seen it all, and there is no other alternative—we must part."

Christine's only reply was a flood of bitter tears.

"Do not think that I have not seen your sadness, my wife. Have I not seen your tears, when you thought them unnoticed? Have I not seen, day by day, the struggle to look cheerful, when I knew that your heart was bleeding?"

"Christine, I am very unworthy—I have always been unworthy of your love; yet I have loved you, darling, as few men can love; but through it all I have been selfish and exacting. I feel it—I know it.

"Long ago, when we were parted, I tried to hate you. I went to foreign lands, I plunged into dissipation, I was reckless, careless, and was resolved to forget you—but it was impossible. Everywhere your face, your words, followed me. Your hand seemed ever to restrain me. It was my destiny to love you!

"Everywhere I saw beautiful women, who vied with each other to attract the rich young American—but from all I turned away, and my heart cried out always, Christine! Christine!

"I read in the papers of your public life. Step by step I watched your progress. All your words I read, and gradually your influence, silent but strong, gained complete ascendency over me.

"All the pleasures of earth, as I had called them, palled upon my taste. I lived a secluded life in the midst of gayety. In my own humble way, I sought to do what would please you did you see my works.

"I never hoped to regain your love—but at last I could bear so great a separation from you no longer. It had been, at first, enough for me to read of your glorious work, of your Home, to hear of its progress, to see your name coupled with all that was holy, noble, and true; but I longed now to see you—unseen by you to watch your face, to see your smile. I came to my native land—at last I was in the same city with you.

"But I fell sick—I was dying (so the physicians said), and the old longing to see you rose up in my soul—it would not be kept down.

"I felt that to the dying man you would come once more, and I did not over-estimate your forgiving spirit. You came—you granted my request—you became my wife.

"Christine, love was stronger than death, and I recovered. You never failed in all the duties of a fond wife—God bless you for it—and I, fool that I was, lived on for a time, satisfied with the present, with no thought of the future, in my selfishness thinking only of my own happiness, forgetting that it was too bright a dream to last.

"Thank God, I woke to what I was doing before it was too late. I would not have you sacrifice yourself in your noble self-devotion to me.

"I felt that you had granted to the prayer of the dying what would have been denied to the living man. I watched you narrowly. I felt a change. I saw that you were unhappy under the chains I, in my selfishness, had imposed upon you, and I resolved that you should not be my slave.

"You are free—but I solemnly avow to you that, selfish as has been my act, I would not have been guilty of it—of working on your noblest feeling to chain you thus—had I known what would have happened.

"I believed I should die, Christine, and I felt that you would not shrink from performing those last offices which were all that I should require, and that you would not think it too much to bear my name after I was gone. I wished, too, to enable you to receive without scruple all the wealth that has lain idle in my hands, for I felt that you would do great good with it, and it was very pleasant to me to think that even though I was dead,

I could yet in some sense be associated with you in your glorious work.

"But it was a selfish wish, and like all such wishes and acts, has brought with it its own punishment.

"Now I do all in my power to retrieve my error. You are free. The law binds us—would that I could free you from that, but I cannot."

His voice faltered.

"Christine," he added, "can you forgive me for the wrong I have done you?"

In an instant her arms were round his neck, her head resting on his shoulder, and her voice cried out, joyfully,

"Oh, my Philip! my husband! thank God that the law still binds us.

"I am your wife, as I swore, 'till death us doth part'; with my whole heart I promised it—with my whole heart I prayed for your recovery, and God granted my prayer.

"Philip, dearest, I love you! I am only happy when with you. It is the greatest joy that I have that we are irrevocably united. Will you send me from you now?"

Philip pressed her closer to his heart, in a transport of joy, but suddenly releasing her, he said,

"Christine, do not deceive yourself, or me. Do not prepare for us both a whole life-time of misery. Do not let your unselfish pity for me lead you to mistake sympathy for love. You have been unhappy—I have seen it—it has not been without a cause."

"Dearest husband," rejoined Christine, "how can I convince you of my love? It would make me miserable to part from you. I have been unhappy, but it was because I thought you no longer loved me. I felt that you regretted our union, that you shrank from owning the Woman's Rights lecturer as your wife. Beauty was never mine; I felt that I had lost the only charm I ever possessed, youth, and that you were chafing under the tie which, in your sickness and perhaps delirium, you had fastened on yourself. I had resolved to leave you, to free you from the heavy chain, though the effort nearly broke my heart, but I loved you and sought your happiness—yet, when you began to speak to me, I felt that to hear you say you no longer loved me would kill me.

"When you went on to tell me all, joy kept me silent—I could not speak. But now we understand each other. Now away with all doubts.

"We love each other, and let us feel henceforth perfect confidence in each other's affection.

"I am your wife—oh, blessed title, and thrice blessed thought that nothing but death can separate us."

Philip held her in his close embrace. "My own dear wife!" he murmured.

She looked up with a happy smile. "This is our second, our true bridal, my Philip."

"It is, indeed," he said, and, rising, he drew a black ribbon from his neck, to which was attached a ring.

"This ring," he said, "has always been worn next my heart; it is the one I put on your finger long ago, as a token of our betrothal; you gave it back to me when we were parted. Now I replace it on your finger, as the sign and seal of our second, our true marriage."

He suited the action to the word, and pressed a kiss on her lips, saying, "God bless you, my darling wife, my beautiful Christine!"

"Beautiful!" repeated his wife, with a smile and a sigh. "I wish I were for your sake."

"You are," he answered, "I would not have a feature altered," and he gazed on her with proud affection.

Indeed, if she was not regularly beautiful, she was lovely; the beauty of her soul lighted up her face, and breathed in her every movement. His eyes followed her as she moved about the room, and he admired the quiet elegance of her every gesture, and his heart repeated, "beautiful in life, in heart, and in soul!"

Not many months had elapsed, and Christine and her husband were established in the Home. Their marriage had been made public; they had received letters and visits of congratulation, and had paid visits to the old homestead, and to Mrs. Warner and Mrs. Frothingham.

Now both were absorbed in the enlarging of the Home, for into all her plans for the establishment of this Institution, her husband entered with zeal equal to her own. His hand was ever open; his judgment matured, and she found herself depending on him, as she would hardly have believed herself capable of doing. In fact, she bid fair, as Rosa said, smilingly to her husband, to become a model wife, with hardly a will of her own. She quoted Philip's opinions on all subjects, and he was, in turn, ever ready to defer to her.

He had already given an order to Will Linton for the historical painting, which was to adorn the library of the new Home, and Helen and Will were as happy as possible; nor was Elder Wiggins forgotten; settled in an humble, though comfortable home which Christine and Philip had provided for him, he yet occasionally preached, or drove the plough, as best suited him, for he was still active and vigorous in his old age, and could not enjoy a life of indolent repose, though surrounded by all the comforts his declining years demanded.

Every day Christine saw something more admirable in her husband; every day they were more and more closely united; one in heart, one in soul, united in their aims and aspirations, their lives passed on smoothly and pleasantly. Nor was theirs a mere selfish happiness; they lived, not for their own present gratification, but in living for others, in doing all the good in their power, they found their exceeding great reward.

They were sitting one morning in their study. Christine had been leaning on the back of her husband's chair, looking at the plan of the building, which was shortly to be erected, listening to his suggestions, and making her own, but now both were silent.

Christine's eyes were full of tears, but they were blissful ones. She was thinking of the past, and of the way in which God had led her along.

Philip looked at her fondly.

"Are you building air-castles?" he asked, drawing her gently towards him.

"No, Philip," she replied, "I could build none pleasanter than the reality—I am very happy.

"Over rough ways God hath led me
To the path of perfect peace."

Notes

1. The references are all to popular romantic or gothic novels: *Julia de Roubigne* (1777) by Henry Mackenzie (1745–1831); *Thaddeus of Warsaw* (1803) by Jane Porter (1776–1850); *Mysteries of Udolpho* (1794) by Anne Radcliffe (1764–1823). This is the first of many references comparing Christie to Miguel de Cervantes's hero in *Don Quixote* (1605).

2. Ps. 17:15.

3. *Pizarro* is a tragic melodrama by Richard Brinsley Sheridan (1751–1816).

4. Town in Aroostook County, Maine.

5. The quotation is commonly attributed to Charles Maurice de Talleyrand (1754–1838), a French statesman known for his witticisms.

6. Cars: train cars.

7. In the *Arabian Nights*, Sinbad is carried from a shipwreck to safety by a roc, a giant mythological bird.

8. Founded in the mid-1840s, Woodland Vale was a fashionable suburb of Newton, Massachusetts, near Boston.

9. Stomacher: a vestlike lady's garment worn over the chest and stomach.

10. In Alfred Tennyson's poem "Mariana" (1830), the young maiden is "a-weary" and wishes for death as she waits for her lover, who has forsaken her. The Pre-Raphaelite artist John Everett Millais painted "Mariana in the Moated Grange" in 1851.

11. In Greek mythology, Argus was a monster with one hundred eyes ordered by Hera to guard the maiden Io from Zeus.

12. Charles-Paul de Kock (1793–1871), a French writer whose popular novels

of Parisian life were generally considered inappropriate reading for young women of the period.

13. Isa. 42:3; Matt. 12:20.

14. Matt. 6:34.

15. A berthe is a collar, usually of lace, attached to the top of a low-necked dress, and running all round the shoulders.

16. Jer. 6:13–14.

17. From parables in Matt. 5:15, Mark 4:21, and Luke 11:33.

18. Eccles. 1:2.

19. In Greek mythology, Eris, the goddess of discord, threw a golden apple on the wedding table of Peleus and Thetis, stating that the apple belonged to whomever was the fairest. Zeus asked Paris to name the fairest, and Paris selected Aphrodite, who had bribed him with the promise of the most beautiful woman alive, Helen, wife of the king of Sparta. Paris took Helen from Sparta, sparking the Trojan War.

20. Luke 15:7.

21. John 8:1–11; Isa. 65:5.

22. Luke 7:19–22.

23. Ps. 121:1.

24. Job 19:25.

25. The nineteenth-century movement that argued for greater rights for women was known as "woman's rights." Woman's rights advocates usually argued for women's education, careers, suffrage, and an end to sexual double standards.

26. Matt. 5:11.

27. Matt. 13:38.

28. In the Old Testament, Miriam is a prophetess, the sister of Moses and Aaron, who helped to lead the Israelites from Egypt into the Promised Land.

29. Naiads are water nymphs in Greek mythology.

30. In the Old Testament, Uzzah was struck dead when he reached out to steady the Ark of the Covenant and in doing so touched the Ark, in violation of God's law.

31. *Essays of Elia* (1823), written by Charles Lamb under the pseudonym Elia, covered a range of serious and humorous topics.

32. 1 Sam. 3:18.

33. Greek mathematician.

34. A reference to the last line of John Milton's sonnet "On His Blindness."

35. Matt. 1:3.

36. Oliver Goldsmith (1730–1774), "The Deserted Village" (1770).

37. Matt. 10:37.

38. In biblical tradition, Anak had three sons who were the descendants of a race of giants.

39. Matt. 10:19; Luke 12:11–12; Ps. 81:10.

40. Gen. 3:16.

41. 1 Tim. 2:12; 1 Cor. 14:34–35.

42. Prov. 31:10–31.

43. Gal. 3:28.

44. 1 Cor. 11:5–6.

45. Acts 8:23.

46. Prov. 19:1.

47. Jenny Lind (1820–1887), known as the "Swedish Nightingale," was an internationally famous soprano.

48. Fanny Kemble (1809–1893) was a famous British actress and an abolitionist.

49. Henriette Sontag (1806–1854) was a famous German opera and concert soprano.

50. Sappho, seventh-century Greek lyric poet and teacher; Demosthenes, fourth-century Greek orator; Alexander the Great, fourth-century king of Macedonia who conquered Persia.

51. Luke 9:62.

52. In the book of Esther, the king's traitorous counselor, Haman, is incensed when he sees Mordecai standing at the gate, refusing to pay him homage. Mordecai, who was Jewish, refused to bow to anyone but God.

53. Embezzlement.

54. Phil. 4:7.

55. Matt. 6:2,5,16.

56. Elizabeth Barrett Browning (1806–1861).

57. Alexander Pope (1688–1744), *Imitations of Horace*.

58. Matt. 13:32.

59. Lord Byron (1788–1824), *Childe Harold's Pilgrimage*.

60. Thomas Hood (1799–1845), "Song of the Shirt."

61. Job 38:11.

62. The Melodeon was a theater in Boston from 1839 to 1878.

63. Shakespeare, *Othello*, act 3, scene 3.

64. Prov. 13:12.

65. Henry Wadsworth Longfellow, "A Psalm of Life" (1838).

66. Matt. 10:16.

67. Rom. 3:8.

68. Luke 19:22.

69. The Milesians were ancestors of the inhabitants of Ireland.

70. Luke 20:25.

71. Rom. 13:1.

72. Luke 37–39.

73. Greenwood Cemetery in Brooklyn, New York, was known for its beauty and was a tourist destination.

74. Rom. 12:19.

75. In Shakespeare's tragedy *King Lear*, Lear is forsaken by his power-hungry eldest daughters, Goneril and Regan.

76. Rom. 12:20.

77. According to legend, Lady Godiva begged her husband to remove the heavy taxes from the residents of Coventry, and he replied that he would if she rode naked through the town. Godiva let down her hair to cover herself and rode through the streets, and her surprised husband lifted the taxes.

78. Henry "Hotspur" Percy (1364–1403) was killed in rebellion against Henry IV and is also a character in Shakespeare's play *Henry IV*; a "hotspur" is a rash, impetuous person.

79. "Rhodomontade" or "rodomontade" is talk that is boastful, vain, or inflated, an overly excited declamation.

80. Ironic reference to the "Declaration of Sentiments," which was drafted by Elizabeth Cady Stanton and presented at Seneca Falls, New York, in 1848 at the first major woman's rights convention. The declaration calls for women's equal political and social rights.

81. The title of this chapter is a play by William Shakespeare.

82. Respected medical journal founded in 1823.

83. 2 Sam. 23:4.

84. Iphigenia, eldest daughter of Clytemnestra and Agamemnon, was sacrificed by her father so his fleet could continue its voyage to Troy during the Trojan War.

85. Gen. 2:24, Eph. 5:31, and Matt. 19:5 state that "a man" will "leave his father and mother" and cleave to "his wife" and the two will become "one flesh."

86. David Garrick (1717–1779), "Epitaph on Quinn."

87. In the Old Testament, Moloch was a deity worshipped by the Canaanites, who were said to sacrifice their children to him.

In the Legacies of Nineteenth-Century
American Women Writers series

The Hermaphrodite
By Julia Ward Howe
Edited and with an introduction by Gary Williams

In the "Stranger People's" Country
By Mary Noailles Murfree
Edited and with an introduction by Marjorie Pryse

Two Men
By Elizabeth Stoddard
Edited and with an introduction by Jennifer Putzi

Emily Hamilton and Other Writings
By Sukey Vickery
Edited and with an introduction by Scott Slawinski

Nature's Aristocracy: A Plea for the Oppressed
By Jennie Collins
Edited and with an introduction by Judith A. Ranta

*Selected Writings of Victoria Woodhull:
Suffrage, Free Love, and Eugenics*
By Victoria C. Woodhull
Edited and with an introduction by Cari Carpenter

*Christine:
Or Woman's Trials and Triumphs*
By Laura Curtis Bullard
Edited and with an introduction by Denise M. Kohn

To order or obtain more information
on these or other University of Nebraska Press titles,
visit www.nebraskapress.unl.edu.

www.ingramcontent.com/pod-product-compliance
Lightning Source LLC
Chambersburg PA
CBHW020453120925
32494CB00002B/6

* 9 7 8 0 8 0 3 2 1 3 6 0 9 *